PENGUIN METRO READS
PRADYUMNA

Usha Narayanan is a gold medallist with a master's degree in English literature. She has had an eventful career in advertising, media and the corporate world, as creative director, features writer, web editor and communications manager. Her debut novel, *The Madras Mangler*, a suspense thriller, was received positively by readers and the media. Her next book is a romcom, *Love, Lies and Layoffs*. To know more about her, visit www.ushanarayanan.com or email her at author @ushanarayanan.com. Find her also at www.facebook.com/writerusha or tweet @writerusha.

W0246915

PRADYUMNA

SON OF KRISHNA

USHA NARAYANAN

Penguin
metro reads

An imprint of Penguin Random House

PENGUIN METRO READS

USA | Canada | UK | Ireland | Australia
New Zealand | India | South Africa | China | Singapore

Penguin Metro Reads is part of the Penguin Random House group of companies
whose addresses can be found at global.penguinrandomhouse.com

Published by Penguin Random House India Pvt. Ltd
4th Floor, Capital Tower 1, MG Road,
Gurugram 122 002, Haryana, India

Penguin
Random House
India

First published in Penguin Metro Reads by Penguin Books India 2015

ISBN 9780143424161

Typeset in Requiem by Manipal Digital Systems, Manipal
Printed at Manipal Technologies Limited, India

www.penguin.co.in

MIX
Paper | Supporting
responsible forestry
FSC® C043100

To my grandmother Janamma,
a rare and lovely soul.

Om namo bhagavate tubhyam Vasudevaya dhimahi
Pradyumnaya Aniruddhaya nama Sankarshanaya ca

Let us chant the glories of Vasudeva and his forms of
Pradyumna, Aniruddha and Sankarshana.

I

The Peacock Boat

'No, my prince, no . . . !' The girl's clear voice rose in the air above the still waters of the lake fringing the palace of the asura emperor Kaalasura. There was a loud gasp and then soft moans and murmurs, the sounds of young love.

Huge brass lamps filled the room with a warm glow. On the low bed, a young girl lay with her head in the lap of a handsome bare-chested warrior. His shoulders were powerful and his arms rippled with muscles that flexed with his every movement. His face was chiselled in clear lines and his hair tumbled like dark rain clouds. A bright yellow dhoti was tied around his waist. A rope of lustrous pearls round his neck vied with the sparkle in his eyes as he lowered his lips to hers.

'Do you really want me to stop?' asked Vama. 'Don't you love me?'

'Every girl in the kingdom loves you. But whom do you love?' The girl pouted. 'Krithika says she hasn't slept a wink since she met you. Vikruti forgets her dance steps. Rajini threatens to scratch my eyes out if I dare look at you.'

'Don't you know I love you more than anyone else?' he asked as he pressed soft kisses on her face and her lush, curving lips. His hand caressed her slender neck and ran down to her tiny waist.

But Tara was not to be distracted. 'Then there's your mother, the queen,' she said, a frown darkening her heart-shaped face. 'She turns into a monster whenever she sees you with a girl.'

Tara was very young—barely seventeen, the same age as Vama. She had recently been appointed as an attendant to Mayavati, Kaalasura's wife, and was terrified of incurring the queen's wrath. She had seen what the queen did when she caught her son with Roopmala, the lead dancer in the court. Her screams had brought her attendants and guards rushing to the prince's chambers. They had stood watching as the queen dragged the girl from her son's bed by her long braid, raining blows on her body so hard it made the onlookers cringe.

'You are my slave, my servant. You eat my food. You wear the silks and jewels I throw at you. And you dare covet my precious Vama?' The queen screeched like a flesh-eating pishacha. 'I'll gouge out your eyes! I'll kill your family and torch your whole filthy village! Then I'll hang you above the fortress gates as a warning to all harlots!'

Mayavati snatched Roopmala's earrings, tearing the girl's earlobes, ripped the pearl armlets from her arms and pulled off her girdle bearing Kaalasura's emblem of two intertwined serpents. Next, she tugged at the girl's garments to strip her naked.

Roopmala threw herself at the queen's feet, weeping. Mayavati kicked her away and gestured to the guards to drag her out of the palace. The queen's eyes were wild as she flung vases and jugs at the girl's receding back. She shouted at the other maids, threatening to burn them alive if they ever made eyes at Vama.

Tara knew that Vama could not stand up to his mother, and toyed with the girls only when he was sure that the queen was not around. He always chose the easy path and preferred to enjoy the luxuries of the court rather than toughen his body on the battlefield. Though Tara was madly in love with him, she could not risk losing the comforts of the court and being forced to return to the grinding poverty of her village.

Until recently, her world had been limited to the hovel that her large family occupied, eking out a precarious living. Then she had caught the eye of the courtiers who had been looking for pretty young girls to wait on the queen. Her parents had been elated at the stroke of good fortune and now looked to her to rescue them from their life of deprivation. She could not sacrifice their interests because of her feelings for the prince.

Tara was enraptured by the beauty of the new world she inhabited. She loved the soft beds, the scented baths and the magical palaces and gardens. She liked performing delicate tasks for the queen—rubbing sandalwood paste on her body or singing her to sleep. And when her son was not involved, Mayavati was a generous mistress, giving her maids gifts of gold and money that they could send to their families.

Tara looked up at Vama's face as a new thought struck her. 'Do you know that Roopmala was thrown out of the city gates and not even allowed to bid her family goodbye?' she asked him.

He shook his head. *So that was why he had never seen her again!* He had been afraid to ask his mother, and the other girls had been too terrified to speak.

Tara was still talking. 'Why does your mother behave like a jealous lover? Doesn't she know that girls will naturally flock to you?'

She stopped as she saw his despondent face. Why was she wasting her precious time with him by quarrelling? 'Play me a song on your flute, my love,' she said, her eyelids fluttering. 'A song just for me.'

His face cleared as he raised the flute to his lips. The music transported him to another time and place where he wore a crown and danced in the midst of a bevy of girls. He twirled the girls around and felt their glossy braids flicking his cheeks. Their soft arms clung and caressed. His blood pounded to the rhythm set by their anklets.

He looked down at Tara and saw that her eyes were half-closed in desire. Her breasts were heaving under her gauzy silk robe. She was so entrancing, with skin that smelled of roses and sandalwood paste, and bee-stung lips that teased and tantalized. He felt a deep tenderness and swore to himself that he would keep her safe.

The cuckoos in the trees stopped singing as the music burst through the air. The trees bent their boughs to listen, and the deer forgot to graze.

But the idyll was not destined to last long.

Someone was approaching.

Someone whose rage sent the deer scampering away.

2

Trapped

Queen Mayavati had been prowling around the gardens for an hour now, looking for the prince. She had told Vama to practise archery with his guru. But when Sandilya told her that the prince was not with him, she knew at once that the stupid boy was with some wench, making love to her. When would the fool realize that it was an honour to be accepted as a student by Sandilya?

Sandilya was the finest pupil of Bhargavarama, a warrior sage who was an incarnation of Vishnu. Shiva had blessed Bhargava with his mighty axe or parasu and given him the name 'Parasurama'.

Guru Sandilya had learned both the astras and the shastras from Bhargava. He thus knew the secrets of supernatural weapons as well as the wisdom enshrined in the holy texts. Sandilya had once single-handedly razed a platoon of soldiers and there was no doubt that any student of his would prove invincible as well.

Mayavati had neared the lake and could hear the squawking of parrots as they gorged on ripe mangoes hanging from the surrounding trees. A pair of swans glided regally past brilliant lotuses and lilies floating on the waters. Jasmine and jacaranda flowers released their fragrance into the warm air.

The lake was a magical one created by the divine architect Mayaa, famous for constructing the palace of illusions for the Pandava princes, which made their enemies, the Kurus, burn up with envy. Mayaa had also fashioned three fortress cities— of gold, silver and iron—for the three sons of the demon king Tarakasura. Brahma had said that these asura cities would be indestructible unless pierced by a single arrow and Mayaa had planned the cities accordingly. 'These asura domains will be ever-moving, one on a disc on earth, one in the sky and one in the heavens,' he said. 'They will be aligned in a single line for only a few seconds in a thousand years, when the star Pushya is in conjunction with the moon. There will be little chance that anyone can destroy them.'

Stunned by the ingenuity of the design, Kaalasura had ordered his men to bring Mayaa to him. 'Build me a palace that will be the envy of Indra, the lord of the heavens, and rival the magnificence of Vishnu's abode, Vaikunta. Gird it with golden walls and soaring turrets. Surround it with enchanted lakes and forests. Ensure that day and night answer to our will and birds sing through the year. Make the girls beauteous and seductive, and let wine flow from crystal fountains. And above all—never let death or disease enter our regions.'

'So shall it be,' said Mayaa, bowing before the emperor who had acquired the occult powers of rakshasas and pishachas. Kaalasura could change his form at will, become invisible or fly to the ends of the earth.

After conquering earth and sky, the asura king had invaded the kingdom of the nagas, the snakes whose home was seventy thousand yojanas below the earth. Their seven realms were ruled by the monstrous Kuhaka, Kaliya and Sushena. Half human and half snake, they lived in palaces with diamond pillars and ruby thrones. Kaalasura waged a gory battle with them for a thousand years, finally defeating them and seizing their treasures.

'Spare our lives, and we will be your slaves,' begged the nagas. But Kaalasura disregarded their pleas and cut a bloody swathe through their ranks. He then dragged the terrified naga queens to his harem.

As he looked around restlessly for new thrills, a courtier brought him news of the beautiful princess Mayavati of the neighbouring kingdom. 'She too will be mine,' he growled. 'Who will be fool enough to stand in my way?'

He turned invisible and stormed into Mayavati's palace. One look at her enchanting face and voluptuous form, and his body blazed with passion.

I will be the envy of the devas if I should possess her, he thought. He materialized before her in all his finery and overwhelmed her with his passion and his fabulous gifts.

'No apsara from the heavens can match your charms,' he raved.

'Marry me and share my bed or I'll smash your bones,' he bellowed.

'Come to me, my empress and I'll make you the envy of every woman born,' he thundered.

She bowed her head under his onslaught and married him in a grand ceremony attended by the gods.

Years passed and even as their son grew to manhood, the queen's beauty continued to shine bright. The other asura queens watched and wondered. 'What sorcery does she use to retain her glowing looks?' they whispered amongst themselves. 'Even Time seems to be spellbound by her charms and leaves her untouched. No wonder our king's desire for her remains unquenched and grows stronger by the day. What use are we all when he always prefers Mayavati's bed?'

'Our king is besotted,' muttered the asura ministers. 'He does not realize that Mayavati lusts for her son and not for her husband.'

Indeed, the queen was obsessed with Vama and tracked his every movement.

Here she was, hurtling through the pavilions in a desperate search for him, her jewelled skirt and odhni swirling angrily around her magnificent body with every stride. Her attendants hurried to keep pace with her, darting fearful looks at her grim face.

And then the queen heard it—the sound of Vama's flute coming from the direction of the lake. She turned towards the sound, her face a mask of fury. She raised her hand to stop her attendants and raced down the crystal stairs to the edge of the water. Where was he? She couldn't see him. He must be inside one of the houseboats. *Curse him!*

The boats were in the shape of peacocks, swans, elephants, and one was like the mighty eagle Garuda, Vishnu's vaahana. Amethysts and aquamarine glinted on the sides of the boats and fragrant creepers shed their blossoms on the decks.

The notes of the flute were coming from the peacock boat. She ran up the steps to the deck, the folds of her skirt muffling the sound of her anklets.

She stepped into the inner chamber and gnashed her teeth when she saw the two bodies entwined on the bed, unaware of her entry. Vama had set down the flute and taken up a peacock feather to caress the girl's face. Mayavati saw that it was Tara, the youngest and loveliest of her attendants. The girl's lips were parted and her breath was coming in quick gasps. Her skirt had ridden up her shapely thighs, and her odhni was untied. Vama moved the feather down to her breasts. She quivered and moaned. He raised his other hand to push aside the silk garment—

'Vama!' Mayavati shouted, unable to bear it any more. She charged forward. Her skirt swirled over the golden salver placed by the bed and it fell with a clang, startling the lovers. The girl sprang to her feet, clutching her garments to her body, and backed into a corner.

'Mother?' Vama's voice was shaking.

'I can't bear to look at you!' Mayavati railed. 'Drunken fool! Lecher! You shame us all with your behaviour. Romping in bed with a slave instead of training with the bravest warrior in the kingdom . . .'

Tara slipped out of the room on stealthy feet, fearing for her life.

'Please, mother . . .'

'Don't call me mother! How many times must I tell you?'

She dragged him up from the bed and raised her arm.

A bloodcurdling cry split the air.

'Tara?' he screamed.

Trembling.

Panic-stricken.

3

City of the Blue God

The silver chariot emerged from a cloud bank and glided smoothly towards the shimmering city of Dwaraka, its towering gates and walls glinting with rare gems. In it was seated Yudhistira, the eldest of the Pandava brothers, sons of King Pandu. The dark giant by his side was his nephew Ghatotkacha, so named because his head (utkacha) was shaped like a ghata, a clay pot. Behind their carriage flew twenty more chariots, bearing Yudhistira's brothers Arjuna, Bhima, Nakula and Sahadeva, as well as their retinue.

All the chariots, along with their horses, had soared to the skies, impelled by the breathtaking occult powers of the young giant.

Ghatotkacha was entranced by his first glimpse of the city, with its vast moat encircling the walls of gold. Wild ducks and snow-white swans swam in the waters amidst the deep red lilies. The River Gomati Ganga flowed around the city in worship. The Mandakini and the Mahanadi entered the city through fifty silvery streams to caress the feet of the lotus-eyed Lord Krishna. The glorious Raivataka Hill loomed large in the background. The city spread out over a length of 864 yojanas and a width of 512 yojanas. Some 8000 war chariots bristling with weapons stood guard over its citizens, proud members of the Yadu clan.

'See how the city glitters like it has just fallen from the heavens!' said Yudhistira to his nephew. 'This is the home of our living god Krishna, who is Vishnu himself . . . Dwaraka is revered as one of the seven gateways to moksha. The council hall here outshines heaven's crystal hall Sudharma, which was built with the help of your grandfather Vayu, the wind god. The god of riches, Kubera, lives in Dwaraka and ensures that no one in the city is ever hungry or poor.'

Yudhistira and his brothers, sons of Krishna's aunt Kunti, had been invited to Dwaraka to participate in the happiest celebration in its history. This was to mark the birth of two sons to Krishna's queens—Rukmini, the daughter of the king of Vidharba, and Jambavati, the daughter of the bear king Jambavan.

Yudhistira was happy to have the company of his beloved nephew, the son of his brother Bhima and the rakshasi Hidimbi. The young Ghatotkacha, blessed with magical powers, had grown into manhood in just a few days following his birth. The Pandavas had watched in wonder as he grew in spurts, from baby to toddler to boy to man. The giant had just as quickly equipped himself with all the skills that his father and uncles could teach him. He had learned wrestling from his father Bhima and archery from Arjuna, whose skill was unequalled in the three worlds. Ghatotkacha then studied the Vedas and shastras from Yudhistira.

When the Pandavas had prepared to leave the forest after completing their period of exile, the giant had been heartbroken. He knew he could not go with them, nor could he leave his mother whose home was the forest.

'Why do you wish to return to the cruel world of men?' he had asked Yudhistira. 'Stay with us and we will make sure that you lack for nothing. How will I survive without your wisdom and love?'

'You are young in years but very wise,' Yudhistira had said, clasping the giant's arm fondly with his two hands. 'You know that as the eldest of the Pandava sons you must help us carry on with our duties and not stand in our way.'

Ghatotkacha saw the tears in his uncle's eyes and the gloom on the faces of the other Pandavas. He pulled himself together and did not weaken again. It was the Pandavas who turned back to look at him sadly when they made their way out of the forest.

'Do not worry, uncle,' he had said to Yudhistira in parting. 'Call me whenever you set out on your travels, and I will fly to you so we can be together again. And when you need me at any time, just think of me and I will appear before you.'

So it was that Ghatotkacha was now riding with Yudhistira in his airborne chariot, plying him with questions on Dwaraka.

'The city was designed by Visvakarma, the architect of the gods, to rival Indra's city, Amaravati,' said Yudhistira. 'Krishna chose this location and asked Visvakarma to build him a breathtaking capital. The architect sought more land which was, however, not available as the area was bounded by sea and mountain.'

'An impossible request, then,' said Ghatotkacha.

Yudhistira raised his hands above his head in worship. 'Can even the seas stand in the way of Vishnu, the lord of Vaikunta? Of course not. Krishna invoked the sea god Varuna, and urged him to retreat by eight hundred yojanas. Varuna was delighted to obey. Subsequently, Visvakarma laid the foundations of a giant city of nine lakh mansions, which he then built with crystal and silver, and studded with emeralds.'

'Truly, a city blessed by the gods,' smiled his young ward. He gestured with his hand and the chariots settled gently down outside the city's walls, to continue the journey on land.

The glossy white horses drawing the lead chariot clattered over the city's wide roads and quadrangles, past magnificent temples and rows of palaces.

'These palaces are for Krishna's eight queens and 16,000 wives,' said Yudhistira.

'Sixteen thousand wives!' exclaimed Ghatotkacha, with a barely concealed grin that earned a sharp look from his uncle. This was an exciting story that had to be shared with his friends!

'Don't let your imagination run riot, young man,' said Yudhistira. 'As I have told you earlier, you must always look for the truth that underlies events. Only people with evil minds try to drag others down to their own level.'

'So tell me then, what is this truth?' The youngster's eyes sparkled as he considered and discarded several bizarre explanations.

'Krishna married these women not out of lust, but out of compassion. The vile Narakasura had imprisoned them as it had been predicted that a woman would kill him. So the asura seized all the women in his kingdom, hoping to escape death. But Krishna succeeded in killing him with the help of his queen Satyabhama.'

'Then why did he not set them free?'

'He did. He sent them home in palanquins, along with gifts of gold, elephants and horses. But the women returned to him in tears, saying that their people had refused to take them back. They had taunted them as fallen women who had shared the asura's bed. How could Krishna allow them to suffer for the asura's crimes? He restored their respect and happiness by marrying them himself.'

Ghatotkacha was silent for once. After some time he said, 'Uncle, perhaps there are other women in need of rescuing? Because I . . .'

'Enough, boy!' The sharpness in Yudhistira's tone did not reach his eyes. *Boys will be boys, even if they are giants possessed of magical powers,* he thought. 'That is a question for Krishna himself. You should ask him when you are in his presence. In fact, he probably has a response ready for you already!' Yudhistira bowed in respect to the Blue God, so called because of his dark skin. 'Krishna is the avatar of the supreme Vishnu who dwells in the eternal waters. He is both time and timeless, the lord of endless galaxies and the soul of every living thing. It should not surprise you then that he is the husband of 16,000 women in one small part of the universe.'

'Well, if the women are all taken, I will look forward to the sumptuous feasts,' said the irrepressible giant. 'I hear the people of Dwaraka have laid up mountains of rice, lakes of butter and milk, and chambers piled high with every kind of sweet confection. And to wash all this down, they have golden jars filled to the brim with the most delicious wines. If the food is as delightful as promised, I may well stay back in Dwaraka.'

'Do not jest about wine and women when you talk to Balarama, who is easy to anger, and is never far from his brother Krishna,' said Yudhistira. 'Balarama is an avatar of Adisesha, the thousand-headed snake on whom Vishnu reposes. He came to earth as Lakshmana when Vishnu took birth as Rama, while Vishnu's chakra and conch were born as Bharata and Shatrugna. The three are the lord's greatest devotees and cannot bear to be separated from him.'

The chariot hurtled forward, soon reaching the gardens surrounding the residence of Rukmini, Krishna's principal queen. Peacocks danced on the lawns and called to them as they entered the palace. Strings of pearls dangled from canopies above and ornate seats were laid out in the spacious halls. Richly robed servants washed their feet and brought them madhuparka—offerings of honey, butter and sugar, curd and water.

The visitors entered an immense hall where two exquisite gold cradles had been set up for the newborn sons. They saw the gopalas and gopis of the Yadu clan, cowherds and their wives, in their multicoloured finery. The saptarishis or seven sages were there too, as was Devarishi Narada, messenger of the gods. They had all blessed the infants at the naming ceremony that morning and offered their respects to Krishna, who had then left to attend to his duties as the chief of the Yadus.

The chieftains of other clans were present too. The king of Vidharba and the bear king Jambavan had arrived to bless their grandsons. A hundred cooks were busy in the royal kitchens, preparing a lavish feast for the visitors.

Necklaces, crowns, diamond-studded girdles, priceless incense and other treasures from the four corners of the world lay in glittering heaps. Prize steeds from Arabia, brought as gifts for the newborn, pawed the ground in the courtyard, lifting their heads to snort at the sky.

The Pandavas bowed their heads in salutation to Narada, who began to narrate the story of the divine birth of the two infants.

The hall fell silent, as no one wanted to miss a single word.

The heavens were silent too, as gods and goddesses, the guardian spirits of the eight directions and the divinities of the seven realms gathered to listen. The celestial gathering knew that the tiny ripple that had originated in Dwaraka could one day inundate the world . . .

The forces of karma were gathering. And all of humankind was under threat.

4

Danger

Vama ran out on to the deck of the boat. The sky had darkened and he could not see clearly through the murkiness. The air was still and a brooding silence made him hold his breath in fear.

Where is Tara? Was it not her voice that I heard? he wondered. Jagged streaks of lightning illuminated the sky and a sudden thunderbolt shattered the silence. Another spine-chilling scream drew his eyes to the far end of the boat's deck and to the horror being staged there.

Vama saw a giant with a wolf face and a grotesque body throwing the screaming girl in the air.

Ketumalee. One of Kaalasura's dreaded commanders. The demon tortured and scalped his prey with his cloven hoof, terrorized sages and desecrated their sacrificial offerings. He roamed the kingdom as a tiger, lion, vulture or shark, striking down his victims on land, sea and sky.

A huge figure with charred black skin snatched Tara from mid-air as if she was a toy. Vama's heart pounded in panic as he recognized the other demon terrorizing Tara—Netraasura,

named after the third eye on top of his head, with which he
paralysed his prey. Vama could smell the terrible stench of
rotten flesh that swirled around the demon, for he lived in
cremation grounds and ate the bodies he snatched from the
pyres.

O Shiva, not these two!

Both demons enjoyed taunting Vama, tearing off his
ornaments or pelting him with bones. They invited him to
share their bed so they could teach him how to please men.
When he tried to run away, they cursed him as being a disgrace
to the asuras and threatened to kill him. Vama wished he had
learned the art of becoming invisible from his mother. Then he
could have sprinted past them without their knowledge. But
now he was trapped.

The demons were tossing Tara back and forth, not caring
if she lived or died. Why would they care when they could
destroy whole villages on a whim? Some months ago, Vama
had been travelling with Roopmala in his chariot when they
came across a village that had been reduced to smouldering
ruins by Netraasura and Ketumalee. Black smoke shrouded the
dwellings and burned bodies lay everywhere, splayed in horrific
poses. Roopmala had screamed when she saw the corpses
oozing brain matter and spilling out gory ropes of intestines.

A woman had jumped into their path, almost falling under
the hooves of the horses. Her head was bloody and her eyes
were swollen from crying. 'They took my child, my young,
innocent daughter,' she screamed. 'Save her, please . . . please.'

An old man had pushed her out of the way; his eyes were
crazed, and blood gushed from a severed arm. He stuck his face
close to Vama's and hissed, 'The devils pierced my wife's skull
and drank her blood. Save us, prince!'

But Vama had spurred the horses and cannoned past,
determined to stay away from the demons.

He could not, however, stand by now and watch them abuse Tara, who had come here only to see him. She was innocent, undeserving of this assault. He had to intervene.

He forced himself forward, his teeth chattering. 'Let go of her, you monsters,' he shouted. 'I command you as your prince.'

They turned to look at him, their jaws slavering. 'The little boy is eager to rescue his playmate!' heckled Netraasura. 'Isn't she a tasty little morsel?' He pinched Tara's cheek with a clawed hand, leaving bloody streaks.

'You command us? You want us to obey you?' Ketumalee roared.

'Let her go now or . . . or . . .' Vama stuttered. Where was the sword he had discarded?

'Or what?' laughed Ketumalee. 'You'll kill us with your flute?' He snatched Vama up in one huge arm and shook him like a crocodile shaking its prey. He opened his slobbering mouth, revealing yellowed fangs. As Vama pulled back with a scream, the demon's head morphed into that of a snake, hissing at him through row after row of serrated shark teeth.

'What are these baubles you wear?' asked the snake, yanking at the pearls around Vama's neck. The string broke and the pearls scattered. Blood rushed to Vama's head. He felt faint. Ketumalee changed into his demon form again and began to toss Vama to the skies, laughing uproariously. Any moment now, Vama could crash to the ground and lose consciousness.

'Why don't we pull off your clothes and see if you are really a man?' asked the asura, grabbing Vama's dhoti that had begun to unravel. Vama whimpered, his frenzied mind casting about for a way to kill himself before he was disgraced any further.

Netraasura closed in, egging the other demon on with his yowls.

And then the voice rang out. 'Set him down and step away. Now!'

Ketumalee whirled around, a shadow of doubt crossing his face when he saw the challenger. It was that hussy Mayavati, the emperor's favourite queen. Where had she come from? She had caught him teasing Vama once before and had warned him to keep away.

The queen turned on the other demon. Tara dangled upside-down from his huge paw limply for she had swooned in fright. 'Set the girl down, cur, or face my wrath,' she called out.

Netraasura was made of stronger stuff. He turned a challenging gaze on her, and opened his mouth to taunt her. But the words died on his lips as he stared at her body and face. *How can anyone on earth resist this woman's beauty?* he thought. *What is it about her that weakens my sinews and attacks my heart?*

He shook his head like a war elephant shaking off the enemy's arrows, and lunged at Mayavati.

'Oh, my beautiful queen,' he growled. 'Would you like to join me and the girl in bed?'

Mayavati's knees trembled. She was not sure that she would survive a direct battle against the combined strengths of the two demons. She had not had occasion to use her occult powers for a long time, and her callow son would be of no help. He was not skilled in either warfare or magic. She would have to use her wits if she wanted to survive.

She straightened her shoulders and raised her voice. 'How dare you speak to me in that tone? I am Mayavati, the beloved of the emperor of emperors, the conqueror of Indra. My guards await my orders to chop you into pieces and cast them into the depths of the sea, where vicious nagas will shred your flesh.'

She flexed her fingers and a glittering noose appeared in her hand, pulsing with occult power. The demons glared at her with blood-red eyes and prepared to attack.

'I am no mortal woman to be so easily frightened, demons,' she said. 'Watch and tremble as I unleash my mahamaya.' As she spoke she enlarged herself, matching the monsters in girth and height. Then, as they stared at her with bulging eyes, she grew taller still, so that she towered over them. 'Leave at once or face Kaalasura's anger when I summon him,' she thundered.

'Before you can do that, I will stun you with my third eye and smash you to a pulp!' Netraasura howled and took a step forward.

Ketumalee held back. He was wary of Mayavati's powers and even more fearful of attracting the emperor's wrath. Just the previous day Kaalasura had flayed a servant with a whip that had a hundred thousand cutting edges. The man had screamed until he collapsed in a bloody heap. The guards had thrown his broken body off the ramparts of the fort for the vultures to pick on. All because the king had not liked the way the servant had looked at him . . .

Maybe it would be wiser for them to retreat.

He pulled at Netraasura's arm, making him drop the girl. Tara crashed to the ground and came to her senses with a moan. Ketumalee shot a warning glance at his companion and bowed to the queen. 'Forgive us,' he said. 'We were merely teasing the prince. Permit us to leave.'

The queen concealed her relief. She must escape with her son at once.

'Run, you fool,' she hissed, looking at Tara, who stumbled off the boat and darted into the woods surrounding the lake.

When the queen turned back, she saw that Netraasura still stood in her way, unwilling to bow to a woman.

'Why run from her as if we are gutless?' he asked his partner. 'Can't we find the emperor a more beautiful whore?'

Mayavati raised her occult noose over her head in a threatening gesture and began to recite a dark, arcane spell.

Ketumalee backed away, dragging Netraasura with him.

Her voice followed them. 'This is your last warning. The next time you come near Vama will be your last day on earth.'

The demons vanished in a puff of smoke. Mayavati turned to Vama who stood with his face burning, knees knocking together. He had narrowly escaped being stripped and flayed, but only because his mother had intervened. What humiliation could be greater? He kept his eyes trained on the ground and waited.

Mayavati's voice lashed at him like a whip. 'Once again you have shown yourself to be a coward. Dangling in the air, screeching for help. A toy soldier armed with a flute. What do you know of weapons? You have no skill with the bow or the mace or in the magical arts. All you can do is plead for mercy.'

'Forgive me, mother,' said Vama, shrinking before her contempt. 'I swear that I will train day and night with my guru until I prove worthy.'

'What use are the repeated promises you make when all you care for is pleasure? You dress up in silks and strut around like a peacock. You do not value your guru, who can make the very elements bend to his wishes. You do not respect my skill in mahamaya, which can bring you manifold powers. Oh, why do I waste my breath when you never listen?'

'I will obey you this time,' said Vama. 'I will start now, at once. Teach me how to use the occult skills.'

'Do you think it is so easy?' she asked. 'You cannot rise from a bed of passion and declare yourself ready to learn the sacred arts. You must conquer your body with prayers to Durga, the supreme goddess and the slayer of Mahishasura. Prepare yourself so that you will be worthy of divine knowledge. Eat a godly diet, refrain from meat and wine, and perform tapas.'

'Let me begin by worshipping you as my first guru,' said Vama, bending forward to touch her feet.

She recoiled from him as if from a cobra.

'Don't fall at my feet,' she shouted. 'I've told you this before. Throw yourself on the mercy of Durga, the goddess of vidya and avidya. Pray for her divine light to shine upon you.' She turned and strode away.

The demons she chased away today will be waiting for me tomorrow, Vama thought. *I must ask my father to send his men to protect me.*

5

The Fiery Eye

That night, Vama had a vision so vivid that he felt he was in heaven, watching a divine drama unfold.

Lord Brahma was seated on his swan in Brahmaloka, the highest of the seven worlds. Vama watched as the Creator gave life to the brilliant sun, the moon, the earth and the ten prajapatis—deities who would assist him in the creation of all living things. Then Brahma created Kama, the god of love and the most handsome man in the world.

'Go and ignite passion in the hearts of my creations,' said Brahma to Kama. 'Ensure that all the species multiply and populate the corners of the earth.'

He gave Kama a mystic bow strung with five kinds of flowers—the blue lotus, the jasmine, the white lotus, the mango flower and the flower of the Ashoka tree.

Then came Brahma's most breathtaking creation—a woman who would partner man in procreation. 'I name you Shatarupa,' Brahma said to her, 'for your face and form are as brilliant as a hundred full moons.' She was indeed beautiful, with cherry-red lips, lush breasts, a tiny waist and curving hips.

Kama, eager to test the powers of his bow, shot his first arrow . . . At Brahma himself.

The skies shuddered, the mountains heaved and the rivers flowed backwards. For the arrow inflamed Brahma's heart and filled it with a sinful passion for his own daughter.

Brahma devoured Shatarupa's lovely form with his eyes and began to woo her. 'You are enchanting. Come to my arms,' he pleaded.

'You are my creator, and hence my father. Banish these sinful thoughts from your mind!' she replied, eyes widening in horror.

'Yes, I am the Creator, and the whole world bends to my will. Come to me, my love,' he said, his mind in disarray.

'It is against heaven's laws and will offend the gods,' she cried out and scurried to hide in the west. Brahma sprouted a head that faced west and began to track her every move. She ran to the south, and to the north, but before long he had four heads and four pairs of eyes to follow her. His lust blazed higher the more it was denied.

'I will fly to the skies,' she said and flew above his head. A fifth head appeared atop the other four so he could gaze upwards. There was nothing Shatarupa could do now except surrender at the feet of Shiva, who is Rudra, the fierce one.

An incensed Shiva appeared before Brahma and flayed him with words. 'How can you, the Supreme Creator, lust after your own daughter?' he thundered. But Brahma was not prepared to listen, for Kama's arrow had overpowered his reason.

'I must punish you so that men realize that even the gods will pay for their sinful behaviour,' said Shiva.

He hurled his flaming trishul at Brahma. Volcanoes spewed molten death and thunderbolts split the sky. Mother Earth trembled as the trident slashed off the Creator's fifth head and reduced it to ashes.

The severing of his head in this shocking manner brought Brahma tumbling from his throne.

Shiva still seethed with rage. 'Your despicable act has made you impure and rendered you unfit for worship,' he said. 'I decree that henceforth no temples will be built in your honour.'

Brahma's shame stoked his anger. He turned a wrathful face to Shiva. 'Do you imagine that you are above passion?' he challenged. 'A time will come when you too will succumb to Kama's arrows. You too will be overcome by lust. Be warned that you will flounder that day, just as I did today.'

The Creator turned his fury on Kama next. 'You dared to shoot your arrow at the one who gave you life. You will pay for this sacrilege and be reduced to ashes one day.'

Prince Vama shook like a leaf as he watched the fierce battle between the gods and heard Brahma's dire curse. He struggled to emerge from his vision, but his struggles merely transported him to another unfamiliar world.

There he saw Kama, still alive and glorious, lying on the grass by a sparkling stream. Around him was the fervour of springtime, the season of love. Peacocks danced on glistening rocks. Golden fish and turtles swam in the crystal-clear waters. Honeybees buzzed around mango blossoms, lured by the nectar. A cuckoo warbled a sweet welcome. A fawn peered from behind a tree.

By Kama's side lay an enchantress swathed in silken garments who was more beautiful than even the apsaras. Vama knew that this was Rati, Kama's beloved. She was the goddess who quenched all desire with her beguiling charm, but kept the flames of desire burning forever. Her beauty was ethereal yet sensual, earthly yet divine. Her skin was fair and glowing, her eyelids curved and half-closed. Yellow sapphires garlanded her neck, and jasmine strands were threaded through her lustrous black hair.

Rati turned her radiant face to Kama and rose from the grassy bed, pulling him up with her. She led him under the shade of the mango trees and seated him on a swing made of creepers. She nestled on his lap and drew him close. Their garlands dropped unheeded to the ground. The bells on her girdle tinkled as it fell free. Their eyes, blazing with desire, locked together in a dance of passion.

Vama watched spellbound as Kama spread sandal paste on Rati's golden limbs. She in turn anointed his arms and chest with musk.

The animals and birds hushed as they listened to her shringara rasa, the melodies of love. Kama's flute joined her in the divine music.

'Manmatha . . .' she whispered, for his arrows inflamed hearts with love.

'Shubhangi,' he called her, for she was most beautiful.

She clung to him, closing her eyes in surrender. His lips descended on hers, filling her with ecstasy.

'Will we always be together, my love?' she asked, a sudden fear shooting through her soul and making her tremble.

He pulled her closer still. 'No one can separate us—god or man, time or fate. Our love will outlast the sun and the stars.'

'Do you swear that you will never leave me?' she persisted, her eyes tear-filled, her heart pounding.

'You are my soul, my very breath. Your love will keep me alive, even when I am not with you,' he said. 'I give you this jewel to wear as a mark of my devotion.'

He fastened on her wrist his bracelet, bearing the image of the makara, a sea dragon.

He beguiles her with sweet words but does not promise to stay with her, thought Vama as he watched from above.

Rati could not resist Kama's caresses as the fire blazed higher in her blood. He carried her to the dewy grass and made frenzied love to her, as if he too shared her fears. *Why does it seem as if this will be our last time together,* he wondered.

Kama pulled away from her, brushing the dishevelled hair from her face and kissing her forehead, her lips and her cheeks.

'I must go now, my love,' he said.

'No, no,' she moaned. 'Stay with me.' Her eyes were shadowed with a grim foreboding.

'Do not look at me like that,' he said. 'You know I must obey Indra's commands. But I will be back.'

'How can you be sure? I have a deep fear in my heart, my lord,' she pleaded.

He turned his face away and rose from the grassy bed. He soared over the forest and she followed, unwilling to let him go. She flew to his side to take his hand in hers. Tears ran down her cheeks and her body trembled. Her eyes looked at him in mute appeal.

Kama's face was resolute. There was nothing more to be said. On his back were his bow and jewelled quiver of arrows. He careered higher up the slopes of a mountain, past forests shrouded in snow until he reached the dark, silent cave that was his destination.

'No, my lord,' whispered Rati. 'Do not enter.' *Why would he not listen?*

'I have no choice,' he said. 'I will do my duty, come what may. Indra tells me that I am the sole hope of heaven and earth, and that my arrow is the only weapon that can save the world from the evil Tarakasura. The demon oppresses the devas, carries off their queens and scorches the earth. And none can stop him, for Brahma has decreed that only Shiva's son can kill him.'

'But how can Shiva sire a son when he is lost in tapas in a cave?' she protested.

'That is why my role is so vital,' he replied. 'I must awaken passion in Shiva's heart for Parvati, so that their union may bring forth a son to save us all.'

'No!' she wailed. 'Why must you pay the price for Brahma's boon? Why should you die for the world? I will not let you go. No, not even if the ocean rises to the skies, or the earth sears me with fire from its volcanoes.'

Kama's face was adamant. He focused on his inner voice and thrust Rati from him with a firm hand. He would not flee like a coward from the wrath of Shiva. He would sacrifice himself if need be, so that dharma could prevail.

She shivered and sobbed. 'Listen to me,' she said. 'I have seen many dark omens. A fiery comet plunged into the sea . . . the clouds rained blood . . . and a sparrow killed a falcon. Something terrible is about to happen. I entreat you, my heart. Let us try to escape our dreadful fate.'

Prince Vama gasped as he saw a dark mist with a smouldering centre hovering over the heads of the lovers. 'Run away,' he whispered to them, but of course they could not hear him.

'I have a vision of the future that frightens me,' sobbed Rati. 'I see your smiling face behind this cataract, this passing cloud. I chase after you but never catch up. I hear your voice in the fragrant breeze and the sound of your steps on these grassy beds. Your parrot chirps to me of eternal love, but I never hold you in my arms again.' She clung to him in desperation.

Kama hardened his heart and shook her off. He strode into the cave, head held high.

Deep in the shadows, he saw a figure suffused in a dazzling white light. Lord Shiva, clad in a tiger skin, his eyes closed in vairaagya—renunciation of the world. Shiva's hair was long and matted. He was seated on the glittering coils of the thousand-headed naga king Vasuki, holding the snake's tail as a sign of his domination over the underworld. Smaller snakes slithered around his body, their hoods raised, mouths spitting fire, ready to attack. Their task was to protect their dreaded god in the same way their ancestor Vritra had guarded the cosmos before creation.

A fierce heat and a petrifying cold at once assaulted Kama. His legs froze, his eyes dilated in terror. The awful radiance mesmerized him. His mind knew what the gods had ordered him to do, but his soul trembled at the enormity of the offence he was about to commit.

Was this the place where Brahma's curse would destroy him? Was he to die at the hands of the three-eyed Shiva, the ultimate destroyer? Did he still have time to turn and flee to the depths of the ocean?

Rati had followed him into the cave, though her limbs quaked. She read the terror in his face and continued to plead. 'Let us flee to the most desolate corner of the earth, my love,' she said. 'We will shut ourselves away from gods and men alike, in leafy forests and rippling bays. We will make love on snowy hills and crystal lakes. As long as we have each other, what more do we need?'

Kama's heart begged him to heed her request, but Indra's injunction held sway over his mind.

'Is there nothing I can do to stop you, my heart?' she wailed.

He shook his head and took one last look at the face of the woman he loved. Her sobs pierced his very soul.

Then he strung his bow with a flowered arrow.

Darts of fire splintered the sky. A thunderous wind roared into the cave. Jackals howled and carrion birds cawed like the spirits of the dead. He composed his mind, took aim and loosed off the arrow.

A fiery pillar of flames sprang up before him and a blazing eye seared him. 'Flee, you fool, or I will burn you to ashes!' A terrible voice shook the cave.

The voice juddered in Vama's ear. It was he and not Kama who was running . . . faster and faster, to escape the flames. Soft hands pulled him forward, but the eye was too close behind. It engulfed him with its blistering heat, sucking him into the heart of the blaze. His every breath was now a gasp of agony.

Her voice still pleaded. 'Do not die. Do not leave me. How can I live without you?'

What was happening to him? Had he entered Kama's body? Why couldn't he wake up from this ghastly vision?

He focused on her voice, clung to it, knowing that she was his last hope. She would do anything to save him. *Hold me tight, my love . . .*

'O father of the universe, Brahma, protect your son,' she pleaded. 'O Vishnu, you who lie on the divine serpent, save him. Shiva, O three-eyed Supreme, do not allow him to die . . . not when he is merely carrying out his duty.' There was despair in her voice, a wild terror . . . and deep, deep love.

He could no longer see anything. His senses were fading. He was plummeting into a dark abyss.

'The gods be cursed,' she was now screaming. 'Without Kama, there will be no happiness on earth. The bull will desert the cow, the horse will leave the mare, and the bees will forsake the flowers. Men and women will abandon love and the earth will bear no more children. Life itself will cease to exist.'

Vama whirled deeper into darkness, his mind echoing with questions. Who was he? Why was this happening? Why did he have to die? Who was this woman who was fighting for him? Would he look into her face again?

Then a voice swooped down from the heavens to silence every cell of his being. 'You have forgotten!' it clamoured. 'You have spurned the task for which you were born.'

Vama had no voice, no body.

The voice thundered again. 'Do you fancy yourself born on earth merely to seduce women? Is this the way you worship the lord of Vaikunta?'

'Who are you? Who am I?' Vama shouted in his mind. 'Reveal yourself!'

'I am Bhargavarama, the Slayer of Kshatriyas,' the voice boomed. 'You have not proven yourself worthy to see me or to lay claim to your destiny. Wither away, fool—with your wine, women and wantonness.'

The voice faded. And only nothingness remained.

6

Sons of God

The gathering in Rukmini's palace settled around Narada to hear him speak of the mysteries of the gods.

'These infants were born through the grace of Shiva himself,' said the devarishi. 'When Rukmini and Jambavati yearned to have children, Krishna flew on Garuda to Shiva's abode in Kailasa to pray for a boon. On the way he stopped at the ashram in Badari, the most sacred place on earth.'

'Please pardon my boldness, Devarishi,' said Ghatotkacha. 'Can you tell us more about Badari so that I too may aspire to make my way there?'

'The secret of wisdom is to have a questing mind,' said Narada. 'I am happy to share my knowledge with you and the others here. Badari, located on the banks of the Ganga, is the place where Rama, an avatar of Vishnu, atoned for the sin of killing the demon Ravana. Badari is therefore so sacred that even thinking about it can help you attain moksha.'

'Badari is also venerated as the place where Vishnu performed severe penances for a thousand years, in the age after Rama's,' said Yudhistira.

'Yes,' nodded Narada. 'The world was hurtling towards Kali Yuga, the darkest age, and Vishnu knew that mankind would need his help to survive the evil Kali demon. He therefore carried out this penance and divided his soul into two parts. These two parts were Nara and Narayana, and they descended to earth as Krishna and Arjuna.'

'I love these stories of the gods and the devas!' exclaimed Ghatotkacha.

'Now allow me to continue the story of the birth of the two infants, my child,' said Narada. 'After praying in Badari, Krishna soared to Kailasa, the mountain that gleams like a giant pearl from heaven. Shiva welcomed him joyfully and blessed him with the boon he sought. However, he said something that bears great significance for the future.' He paused, his eyes looking bleak.

'What is it, Devarishi?'

'He said that each child would exhibit the precise characteristics that their mothers had prayed for.'

The sages looked worried. *What had Rukmini and Jambavati prayed for,* they wondered. *How will it affect the future?*

Rukmini's son was named Pradyumna, the Mighty One. Jambavati's son was named Samba—attended by Amba, or mother. And indeed, the future would reveal Jambavati's excessive influence on Samba.

Arjuna, the Pandava stalwart, moved to stand by Pradyumna's cradle, placed side by side with Samba's in the great hall of the palace. He gazed with fond eyes at the child.

'I shall be Pradyumna's guru in the arts of warfare,' he declared.

'I shall be his spiritual guru,' said Yudhistira.

Not to be left behind, Ghatotkacha said, 'But I, and only I, will teach the infant the secrets of the magical arts.'

A loud crash made them whirl around. Jambavati, who was seated by her son's cradle, had dropped a golden platter of fruits. Their eyes flew to her face, which was livid with rage. It was obvious that she had dropped the tray on purpose to divert their attention from Pradyumna.

The noise startled the two infants and they began to wail. Jambavati's attendant picked Samba up while Rukmini picked up her son and rocked him in her arms to calm him.

Yudhistira moved forward to placate Jambavati. 'Permit us to bless your son Samba, O queen,' he said.

'After you blessed her son first?' she spat at him. 'Why do you always choose her over me? How is my son inferior to hers?'

The assembled crowd turned to watch the unseemly conflict. Jambavan placed a gentle hand on his daughter's arm, but she shook him off and continued in a louder voice, making sure that everyone could hear her. 'Why is Rukmini given preference in everything? Is she more important than I am? If she is a princess, then so am I. If Krishna loves her, he loves me more! And now her son seeks to overshadow mine. Arjuna says he will teach him the astras and Yudhistira the shastras. Even this savage Ghatotkacha prefers Rukmini's child to mine,' she said.

Rukmini placed her infant back in his cradle and moved towards Jambavati. 'Why do you feel this way, sister?' she asked in her soft voice. 'Your son is more precious to me than my own, and I would give my life to protect him. So would everyone in our kingdom.'

'Stop your pretence! If you are so noble, promise me that you and your son will step aside and crown my son after Krishna!'

'*After Krishna?*' Rukmini staggered in shock.

'How can we think of a life without our Blue God?' muttered the angry crowd. The cowherds moved forward to confront the woman who had voiced the unthinkable.

Narada intervened. 'Your anger causes you to utter hasty words, Jambavati. I beg you to calm down.'

'How dare you instruct me?' Jambavati turned on him. 'You, a wandering minstrel with no home or family to call your own? It is no wonder they call you Kalahapriya, because you create trouble wherever you go. Why do you think I will listen to you?'

The crowd gasped as everyone knew that Narada was venerated by devas and asuras, kings and commoners.

'I seek pardon on my sister's behalf,' said Rukmini to the sage, placing herself between the two. 'Please disregard what she said in the heat of the moment.'

'Who are you to apologize for me? Are you going to decide what I should say and when? These men may favour you and encourage you in your conceit, but no one can stop me from speaking up for my son. I will protect him even if no one else will!'

Rukmini looked at her rigid face and turned to Narada. 'Please come with me, Devarishi,' she said, leading him away from the angry queen. She offered him a goblet of wine and cooled him with a jewelled fan.

When he had returned to his usual calm, she asked him to enlighten them with one of his tales.

'I will tell you a story of envy that led to downfall,' said Narada. The guests settled down at his feet to listen, while Jambavati turned her back on them. She well knew that Narada's story was directed at her.

'Once, Queen Satyabhama wanted to show that she loved Krishna more than Rukmini. So she took a pledge to give him away in charity.'

'Give the lord away? That's sacrilege!' Ghatotkacha exclaimed.

'Listen to the whole story,' said Narada. 'She bequeathed the lord to me, saying that she would reclaim him by giving me his weight in gold. In this way, she hoped to dazzle him with the magnitude of her love.'

'What happened then?'

'I warned her that if her gold was not sufficient to outweigh him, he would remain my slave forever. "Do you want to take this huge risk?" I asked.'

'Did she listen?'

'She did not, for she was puffed up with pride.' He paused. Everyone was listening, engrossed. Ghatotkacha moved closer.

'She made Krishna sit on one pan of the balance and placed her jewels and gold on the other. The scales did not move. She had her slaves bring her all the ornaments from her palace, but these too did not suffice. Then she pulled off the ornaments that she wore and piled them on top of the jewels that were already on the pan. This failed too. She turned in desperation to the other consorts and asked them to part with their gold. Still, Krishna's weight was greater than that of the jewels, showing that some mystic force was in play. Satyabhama's eyes filled with tears as she finally realized that she might forfeit her lord forever. What could she do now?'

'So does this mean that Krishna is still your slave?' burst out Ghatotkacha. 'Will he do exactly what you say?'

'Be patient and listen,' said Narada. 'Satyabhama realized she had one last resort—to fall at the feet of her rival. She turned to Rukmini who was sitting in meditation and pleaded with her. "Please add your jewels to the scales and save our lord," she said.'

'What did you do then, O queen?' Ghatotkacha asked Rukmini. 'I hope you cursed her and refused to help.'

Rukmini smiled indulgently at him. 'I said a prayer to Krishna and placed a single tulsi leaf on the pan.'

'The tulsi,' murmured Ghatotkacha. 'The offering that Vishnu favours above all.'

'At once the scale moved!' said Narada. 'Rukmini showed the world that the lord does not desire riches, rituals or a grand temple. All he seeks is true devotion or bhakti that will set you free from maaya—the delusions of the world. I made his message clear to everyone by removing all the jewels from the pan. Even then, the single leaf outweighed the lord!'

'All praise to Krishna,' murmured the gopalas.

Everyone's eyes turned to Jambavati to assess the effect of the story on her. Would she realize that pride and envy would only come between her lord and her?

However, that was not to be. Jambavati could not accept criticism or advice from anyone. She turned with renewed rage towards Narada, prepared to attack him again and drive him away. But she stopped in her tracks when she saw that the sage's face was blanched white, and that he was gasping for breath. He staggered to his feet, though he seemed to be on the verge of collapse. Ghatotkacha, who had been seated at his feet, stretched out an arm to steady him. He then placed him gently in his seat again. Rukmini kneeled at his feet and looked up at Narada's face with concern.

'What is it, Devarishi?' she asked. 'What troubles you so?'

'I see disaster. I see doom,' Narada said in a hollow voice. 'A new curse has befallen the Yadus . . .'

7

Tortured

The ministers and high priests of Kaalasura's court lined up to greet him when he drove down from his palace. Prince Vama waited with them, his nerves twisted in knots, reliving the horrors of the previous day.

First, Ketumalee and Netraasura had humiliated him, making him feel like killing himself. Then, the awful nightmare with Kama in Shiva's cave had pummelled him awake and left him distraught.

Why had fate suddenly become so unkind? He was happy living the life of a cosseted prince; he did not want to don the mantle of a warrior, or take on the responsibility of living up to his mother's expectations. Now, a spectral voice had joined her in condemning him as a wastrel who was unfit for his mission.

He would not let a nightmare affect his life. His mind had probably conjured up visions from his memories of old tales in order to help him escape from reality. But he knew a better way to forget his troubles—by seeking solace in Tara's arms.

Why was everyone pushing him to put his body through gruelling training sessions? His mother had made him promise to learn the martial and magical arts. His bosom friend Hasmukha, so named for his sweet smile, wanted Vama to join him in combat exercises. 'Once you hone your skills, I will ride behind you carrying your banner,' he had said.

Hasmukha headed a legion of the emperor's army and was the son of Kaalasura's venerable minister, Sunaka.

'My body is made for the soft limbs of girls, not the harsh terrain of a battlefield,' Vama had laughed. 'I like wearing fine silks, not the heavy armour of a soldier. So please don't torment me with this advice.'

Hasmukha's face lost its smile. 'You may not want to fight, but you still need to protect yourself,' he said. 'The demons taunt and assault you on your way to your guru's ashram. They will continue attacking you for they envy your good looks and your position as the heir to the throne. Forgive me, but do you not wish to retaliate when they call you a coward?'

Vama had turned his back on his friend and heard him leave quietly. Hasmukha would be happy now if he knew that Vama had decided to take action. That was why he was waiting for an audience with his father, the emperor. Things had come to a breaking point; he needed protection from Netraasura and Ketumalee. But that did not mean that *he* must take up arms himself! It was his father's duty to provide a phalanx of guards to protect his son and heir. Vama would insist on this today.

He peered down the broad avenue leading to the court, hoping to catch sight of the emperor's chariot coming from his palace. The trees had laid down a fragrant carpet of buttery yellow laburnum, milk-white magnolia and brilliant coral flowers on the road for the royal entourage.

Suddenly, the chant of 'Kaalasuraya Namaha' rose from a thousand throats, as sharper eyes than Vama's spotted the emperor's cavalcade.

'I am the only god,' Kaalasura had declared. 'Henceforth you will chant my name instead of that of the devas!'

Sixty thousand priests rode at the head of the procession, chanting in worship. Behind them apsaras danced and the gandharvas or heavenly musicians sang songs in praise of the emperor. Kaalasura's chariot was huge, drawn by ten black horses. Fierce serpents hung from the sides, and kinkaras, the attendants of Yama, guarded him.

As the golden chariot passed by, people on either side of the road fell prostrate on the ground in obeisance. Vama too offered his respects and then rose to follow in the wake of the chariot. It halted some distance away in front of the high steps leading to the court hall.

The emperor swaggered up the steps and then proceeded down the length of the carpeted hall to his immense ruby throne with its diamond canopy. A giant of a man, he wore a coat of gold chain mail and several necklaces. Diamonds the size of pigeons' eggs studded his girdle. A glittering emerald snake with a raised hood surmounted his crown.

Dancers wearing diaphanous silks showered him with rose petals. His courtiers dazzled in velvet robes and sparkling ornaments. Trumpets blared, proclaiming his supremacy over the three worlds.

Behind him came his queen Mayavati, clad in a red silk sari sewn with precious stones, and wearing jewels that covered her from head to toe. Her lustrous tresses were adorned by circular discs of rubies and pearls representing the sun and the moon. Around her neck hung several strings of coral. Her armlets, girdles and even her toe-rings were set with gems. She moved gracefully to take her place on a smaller throne beside the emperor.

The high priests began their hymns of reverence. They offered aartis to their god Kaalasura, with golden lamps lit by a thousand wicks soaked in ghee. They distributed prasad to his devotees—laddus rich with raisins, almonds and ghee. They sprinkled them with holy water, fragrant with tulsi leaves, which they had used to bathe his feet.

When the rituals were complete, two enormous guards wearing only loincloths and carrying heavy wooden clubs dragged in an emaciated priest who was too weak to walk.

'He must have refused to accept Kaalasura as god,' whispered an old man, one of the spectators, to his cousin who had come from his village. 'They are thrown into dank, dark dungeons infested with snakes, and tortured until they repent. If he remains stubborn, the soldiers will behead him in front of Kaalasura's idol in the courtyard.' The cousin's eyes grew wide in fear.

'The demons have killed many priests and their families,' said a man standing by their side. 'They plunder the ashrams and drive out the inmates to beg on the streets. But those who agree to worship the king are rewarded with rich gifts.'

Kaalasura pounded his royal staff on the ground and the crowd fell silent.

'Have you repented?' he roared at the priest in chains. 'Are you ready to accept me as the god of gods, the overlord of Rudra and Vishnu? Chant my praise and I will spare your life.'

The priest pulled himself up and spoke in a quavering voice. 'I offer you the respect due to a king, Kaalasura,' he said. 'But I will pray only to Vishnu, the Supreme Protector who lives in Vaikunta with the goddess Lakshmi.'

'Arrogant fool!' growled Kaalasura, bounding from his throne in rage and striding forward towards the gathering. The crowd gasped and backed away, afraid that he would kill them all. 'How dare you defy me? I will cut off your head and fling it from the ramparts. I will pierce you with my spear and boil you in oil. I will flay your skin and make you howl like a pishacha.'

His men looked at his face, waiting for a sign that they could begin the slaughter of the priest.

Kaalasura stopped in front of the gaunt prisoner and lifted him up by one arm so he was level with his eyes. 'I don't need a weapon to kill you. Just one twist with my fingers and your head will roll,' he growled, and dumped him back on the ground.

The holy man shook his head in a daze and drew on the last vestiges of his strength. He staggered back to his feet and looked at the emperor who loomed over him like a grisly mountain.

'I know your men will slice me into slivers at the mere lift of your eyebrow. The smallest child in your kingdom knows how you torture anyone who defies you.'

'Then why resist, puny priest? Fall at my feet and seek forgiveness.'

The priest's voice dropped. 'The very thought of pain and torture fills me with dread, for I am a man of the mind, not of the body.'

The crowd watched spellbound. Would he surrender? Would he fall to the ground and clasp Kaalasura's feet? What choice did a starved ascetic have when confronting a beast?

'Still talking?' Kaalasura roared, and the very walls of the court shook. The citizens crowded closer, not wishing to miss the slightest nuance.

The emperor was cunning and liked to sport with his victims. Once he made the man grovel, he could still order his men to kill the priest.

A bright ray of sunlight fell on the face of the holy man. Was the sun god Surya asking his devotee not to give up on the old gods? Or was he asking him to yield to the inevitable?

'Look at the light on his face,' whispered a courtier. 'It is a sign of impending death. The emperor will kill him the moment he falls at his feet.'

'The price of defiance is a ghastly death,' said the holy man. 'But the price of surrender is far greater. You can kill me only once, but I will suffer a thousand deaths each time I chant your name.'

The crowd gasped as the meaning of his words sunk in. The emperor reeled in shock.

The priest's voice rang out in the sudden silence. 'Do what you will. I will chant only the name of Vishnu: Om namo bhagavate Vasudevaya!'

The mantra from the Bhagavata Purana, Sage Vyasa's divine text, reverberated in the vast hall. The commoners who had gathered joined in to recite the mantra that liberated souls from their sins.

Kaalasura heard the chant and howled like a monster from hell. His voice brought the soldiers out of their stupor, and they rushed at the priest with weapons drawn. They slashed at his frail body and dragged him away by his long tuft of hair. The priest continued to chant with his last tortured breaths. The gathering stood transfixed by his courage.

The emperor roared once more and whirled his sword at the attendant nearest to him, killing him in a trice. The crowd began to run pell-mell before he could turn his wrath on them.

Before long, only Kaalasura, the queen, a few senior ministers and Vama himself remained in the hall.

Vama stood silent, weighing his course of action. Maybe he should flee too and wait for a more favourable time to speak to the emperor. However, he knew he would never get another such opportunity when Kaalasura was alone. He could not bear even one more day of being at the mercy of Ketumalee and Netraasura. He was revolted by their foul behaviour and the memory of the noxious stench of death that billowed around them. His anger surged as he recalled their insolence and his mother's contempt.

He decided to take his chances and took a step forward. Mayavati shook her head at him as if to warn him off. But he was not willing to wait.

'I bow to you, wise father, lord of the three worlds,' he said to Kaalasura, and waited for permission to speak.

Kaalasura turned glaring red eyes on him. 'What is it?' he snarled.

Vama paused, wondering if he should back away.

'What is it you want?' The emperor's voice rose impatiently. Vama had no choice but to speak.

'I must bring to your notice, my father, the crimes of your commanders Ketumalee and Netraasura,' he said. 'Their arrogance and depravity have crossed all bounds. They attacked a young dancer of your court before my eyes and abused me when I ordered them to stop. Pray command them to honour me as your heir and their future king.'

He calmed himself with a deep breath and looked up at his father. Behind the emperor, he saw his mother's face, bleached white in terror.

The emperor was silent—too silent. Something was amiss. What was his father thinking? Would he charge at him with a naked sword? Vama's throat went dry.

Kaalasura's face twitched. His voice shattered the uneasy calm. He began to howl and shriek, as his body convulsed and tears ran down his cheeks.

He was laughing. The ministers watched with their mouths agape. Then they took their cue from him and began to laugh too, though no one knew what had brought on this mirth. Those who had rushed out of the hall came running in again, eager to discover what was happening.

Vama's heart froze and started again at a gallop. He took a hasty step backwards. Mayavati clasped Kaalasura's arm and whispered soft words in his ear.

Kaalasura shook her off and began to speak. Vama felt as if the ground beneath his feet had fallen away.

8

The Destroyer

A brooding silence had fallen over the gathering in Dwaraka. Those who had come to rejoice in the birth of the Yadu infants were taken aback by the ugly turn of events. First, there had been Jambavati's spiteful attack on Rukmini. Now Narada was speaking of a new curse.

Mutters and murmurs spread through the crowd. They began to fidget uneasily.

'How can the lord's clan be cursed when he is the Supreme?' Ghatotkacha asked his uncle.

Yudhistira drew him to a quiet corner of the hall. 'He may be god, but in this life he has been born as a human and must follow earthly rules. He too is subject to karma or fate, which is determined by our actions now and in previous lives.'

'Fate is inescapable, is it not?'

'Yes, that is true. However, we create our own fate by how we choose to live. Good deeds result in good fortune, whereas evil brings ruin, sometimes to several generations. This is what happened to Krishna's clan, which takes its name from its ancestor Yadu. Yadu's father King Yayati cursed Yadu and his kinsmen, saying that they would never sit on the throne.'

'Why would a father deprive his own son of his right?'

'Yayati's lust was the cause of all the ills that befell the clan. He was unfaithful to his wife Devayani, the daughter of Sage Shukracharya. The sage found out about this and cursed the king, turning him into a decrepit old man. Yayati broke down at this and pleaded for forgiveness. The sage told him that he could get rid of his weakness if someone else agreed to give up his youth for him. Yayati asked his son Yadu to make the sacrifice.'

'A tall demand, merely to indulge his own lust . . .'

'That was precisely what Yadu said when he refused to help his father. Yayati turned on him and cursed him and his clan. He rewarded another son Puru who obliged him, by bestowing the throne on him and his children.'

'But Krishna's uncle Kamsa was king, and Kamsa's father Ugrasena before him. How could this be possible?'

'Kamsa and his father called themselves kings, but were not anointed through the requisite rituals. They both paid the price for offending their ancestor. Ugrasena was thrown into prison by his son. Kamsa lived every moment in fear as it was prophesied that his sister Devaki's son would kill him. Eventually, Devaki's son Krishna killed Kamsa.'

'And now, a new curse on the clan . . .' said Ghatotkacha.

'It looks like Narada has been revived. Let us return to our places and find out what he has to say,' Yudhistira said, leading the way.

'Speak to us, Devarishi,' Rukmini was saying. 'Help us prepare for what is to come.'

Then Narada spoke. And she wished he had not.

The devarishi's voice was low and shaky. His eyes were pools of pain. His violent grip on his veena made its strings snap with a discordant twang. 'I see a dark future that makes me quake,' he said. 'One of these newborns will ravage the world and raze the entire Yadu clan. And worse still—he will erase the name of Krishna from the face of the earth.'

Agitated whispers broke out, mixed with a few curses. 'No. No. An infant setting off an apocalypse? That cannot be!' the cowherds murmured.

Ghatotkacha looked at his uncle with anguished eyes. 'We cannot doubt Narada, the trikaala jnani who knows past, present and future. How will we survive Kali Yuga without the help of Krishna?'

The women wept as they gazed at the dewy faces of the infants. The men grasped their swords and milled around, helpless to face an enemy that lay hidden in the future.

'We do not know which of them is the destroyer,' shouted a soldier. 'Let us kill them both.'

His commander turned on him and ordered his men to drag him out and throw him in prison. Tempers were frayed and it seemed likely that a melee would break out.

'How can we kill innocent children?' shouted a cowherd. 'We are not child-slayers like Kamsa, who ordered that all infants be killed since he did not know which of them would turn out to be his killer.'

An uneasy calm descended, like a dark sea under whose surface monstrous forms twisted and turned.

Into this silence entered Krishna, who instantly sensed the mood of the hall. A murmur rippled through the assembled guests. His queens and the sages, kings and cowherds alike rushed towards him with heart-rending cries.

'Save us, lord,' they wept.

Krishna looked over their heads at Narada, and they communed without words. The lord felt two soft hands clasping his feet. Hot tears anointed them. He lifted up the prostrate Rukmini and wiped her tears.

'O lord, how can this be? Is this what fate has in store for our sons?' she asked, fresh tears coursing down her face. 'Narada tells us we should prepare for annihilation. That these infants will be responsible . . . Tell us that it is all a lie.'

'What Narada says can never be untrue,' said the Blue God. 'There is no doubt that what he says shall come to pass.'

'But how can we accept that? Look at their pure faces, their innocent smiles. How can you tell us that these infants will bring about such evil? How can our prayers to Shiva prove false? This cannot be their fate. You must not allow this, Krishna.' Her voice rose as despair turned into anger.

He ran gentle fingers over her head as he tried to calm her. 'I cannot overturn fate, but I can offer you some comfort, my queen,' he said. 'Though one child shall bring about disaster, it will be within the powers of the other to save us. But it will be a long and fearsome struggle, one that he may not be able to win.'

Even as Rukmini struggled to decipher Krishna's meaning, a furious Jambavati pushed her aside and flung herself into his arms in a frenzy of threats and tears.

'My son cannot die, my lord,' she said. 'Not my son. He is not the destroyer. He cannot be.' She glared at Rukmini. 'I will not let you favour Rukmini again. Let us kill her son so that mine may live.'

Her words slashed the air round the tender child in the cradle like a sword.

The listeners gasped. Rukmini swooned. Ghatotkacha gathered her up in his strong arms and placed her gently on her throne. Her maids patted her cheeks, trying to revive her, while her father, the revered king Bhishmaka, bristled with anger, his hand flying to his sword.

'This woman will stop at nothing. She will sacrifice everyone for her son,' shouted a gopala. 'How easily she pronounces death on the little one.' He moved forward with his men to attack the queen.

Krishna saw their fury and stepped between them and Jambavati. 'Calm yourself, my queen,' he said. 'Your words are not becoming of you.' He turned to the angry crowd and told them that they could discuss the matter in the assembly the next day.

The cowherds obeyed their lord and turned away, still muttering. They bowed to Rukmini who was now sitting up in a daze, and began to trickle out of the hall.

Ghatotkacha bowed too and followed the Pandavas out of the room, his heart breaking. He cast an angry glance at Jambavati as he passed her. *I can kill you in a trice, if only my uncle would let me,* he thought.

Jambavati glared back at him. She was the queen and need not concern herself with the opinions of peasants or asuras. She turned her back on the crowd with a toss of her head and frowned at Krishna for rebuking her in public.

'Come here, you fools!' she screamed at her servants. 'Let us carry my son away from this cursed place and these evil eyes. *I* must safeguard Samba for even his father seems to be against him.' She flounced away without a word to Rukmini or Krishna, and her maids followed her, carrying baby Samba and his cradle.

As the chamber emptied out, Rukmini's attendants bowed and left the godly couple alone for the night.

'Why does Jambavati nurture such hatred towards me and our son, my lord?' asked Rukmini. 'I do not care about her anger towards me. But now she uses harsh words against you, the lord of the universe. Why do you not stop her, Krishna, and force her to obey you?'

'My words and actions are aimed at guiding people on to the right path, but their destiny remains in their own hands. They choose their path according to their own nature and understanding. I have provided Jambavati with many opportunities to free herself from sin, but her redemption lies within herself.'

Rukmini bowed her head to his wisdom and soon fell into an exhausted sleep on a couch placed near Pradyumna's cradle.

Krishna came to stand by the crib, fondling the child's soft cheeks and smoothing the tendrils of hair on his head. A shadow crossed his face.

'Everything plays out according to destiny, my son,' he whispered. 'I cannot save you now . . .'

The dark figure lurking in the shadows waited for him to leave the room.

9

Disowned

Prince Vama's insides twisted as he watched his father's huge form shake with laughter. Why was Kaalasura laughing when he had merely sought protection from his enemies? Didn't his father owe it to the son who would succeed him to the throne?

'*You?* My heir and future king?' Kaalasura laughed louder still, pounding his thigh with his fist. 'Who told you that? Did you really think that a pale weakling like you could sit on my throne? Just look at me, and then at yourself.'

'But . . . but . . . I am your son.'

'Who said you are my son?' bellowed the emperor. 'Listen to me, you craven mouse! You are an orphan with no name or family. Mayavati yearned for a child of her own kind, and I brought you here so she could amuse herself with you. How can you be my heir when I have so many strong asura sons?'

Pandemonium broke out among the listeners as they discussed what Kaalasura had said.

'Didn't we suspect something like this ourselves?' they muttered. 'How else could the prince look so different from us?'

'I thought the queen had a secret human lover,' said another. 'But I was too scared to say it aloud.'

Vama saw the avid, hostile faces closing around him like a snarling horde . . . The most fearsome was the demon he had regarded as his father.

He could hardly absorb the implications. His father was not his father. His mother was not his mother. He was a poor orphan. The kingdom he had regarded as his birthright was no longer his.

The jeers of the ministers echoed in his ears. He looked past the emperor's cruel face at the woman responsible for his humiliation. She was the one who had kept him in the dark all these years, using him as a plaything.

Mayavati was looking at him with tears in her eyes, her hand stretched towards him.

How could you do this to me? Vama wanted to shout at her.

Kaalasura struck his staff on the ground. The hall grew silent. 'I have grown tired of your whining face, you fool. I would like nothing better than to toss you to the wolves so they can shred your pasty flesh with their ravenous jaws. Or I could chop your head off and mount it on my palace walls.'

He began to advance towards Vama.

'Run, Vama,' screamed Mayavati, clinging to Kaalasura's giant feet in an attempt to hold him back.

Kaalasura roared again, delighted by the sport. He shook Mayavati off and howled at Vama. The courtiers, the dancers, the soldiers and the commoners laughed as the disowned son ran for his life.

Mayavati staggered to her feet and ran behind Vama, catching up with him at the gates. He flung her away, seething with rage. 'Don't touch me! You are the reason for my disgrace. You let me believe I was the prince when I am a nobody. You set me up for this humiliation. How could you?' he screamed.

'Listen to me, my prince . . . my darling. Come to my arms so I can comfort you.'

'Don't call me that,' he shot back. 'I am not a prince and you are not my mother. You are not fit even to be a foster mother. Which mother kisses and cuddles her grown son like a lover? You are a whore . . . well suited to be the wife of the asura. Tell me . . . did you cast a spell on him so he would disown me and you could carry me to your bed?'

Mayavati staggered back, blinded by tears.

'Don't come after me. I will never forgive you!' shouted Vama as he hurried away.

She stood watching, afraid that she had lost his love forever.

Vama was distraught, overcome with agony and despair. Earlier that morning, he had come upon the dancer Krithika plucking flowers in the gardens. She had clung to him, asking him to come with her to her bedchamber. But now, when he had stood squirming before the emperor, she had turned away from him in disdain. There would be few takers for his company henceforth, as he could no longer dispense favours and jewels as their prince. Those who stayed loyal to him would be ostracized by the emperor.

Hasmukha came to him when he heard the news and told him that he would stand by him even if it would make him Kaalasura's enemy. 'We'll decimate Kaalasura's army and take over the kingdom,' he said, trying to bolster Vama's spirits. 'My legion of soldiers is loyal to me and will follow wherever I lead. My father Sunaka will advise you as your minister, for he loves you even more than he loves me.'

'How long will your soldiers fight by your side when faced with demons belching fire and hurling mountains? Who will fight for a pretend prince who is untested in battle, and whose limbs are weak? Leave me now, my friend, so I can think upon my next course of action.'

Vama retreated to a secluded grove with a babbling stream where he normally romped with his playmates. Here peacocks ambled around with fans unfurled, and deer roamed free. He threw himself down on a carpet of green grass, his eyes blind to the beauty around him.

Who are my parents, he wondered. *Did the asura soldiers kill them and snatch me from them?* He was alone in the world, at the mercy of his enemies. He had no hope of surviving their attack, as he had learned little from his guru when he had had the chance. Sandilya would not be interested now in teaching someone who was a nobody.

He understood at last the reason for the chasm separating him from the emperor whom he had considered his father. Kaalasura had never shown any fondness for him and had often held up his loutish sons as models for Vama to follow. Vama too had hated the demon king's habitual cruelty.

It had all been an elaborate charade staged for Mayavati's amusement. His mother—no, the queen, he thought scornfully—she too would turn on him now that he had called her a harlot and spurned her love.

He wished he had learned the arts of magic and warfare instead of wasting his life in dissipation. He was a knave and a fool who deserved the mockery of the one who called himself the Slayer of Kshatriyas. He was a cursed soul torn apart by dark dreams in which he faced the wrath of Shiva.

What talents could he call his own? Just his good looks and his music. What did these things matter when he had been stripped of power and wealth? He was a false prince with no kingdom, one who had no skills to advance in the world.

No more velvet beds, no coy glances, no dancing under the stars. He was truly alone . . .

'Vama, Vama, are you there? Please answer me.' Hasmukha's frantic voice cut through his melancholy.

I do not want to talk to him now, thought Vama, looking around for somewhere to hide. But before he could move, the warrior had stormed into the clearing and seen him. His face was clouded, a sight so rare that Vama knew at once that something was amiss.

'I thought I would find you here. Didn't you hear me calling?' asked Hasmukha, his voice rising. 'Tara is in terrible danger. She came out of hiding to look for you when she heard what happened in court. Kaalasura's son Chitrasena spotted her and carried her off into the jungle. We must hurry if we want to save her from his clutches.'

Vama sprang to his feet in alarm. He took up the sword and mace he had brought along to defend himself in case of attack. 'I know where his forest mansion is located,' he said. 'I will go there while you gather our friends and bring them.'

Hasmukha held him back. 'Chitrasena's brothers would have joined him in the hunt by now. Wouldn't it be better if I came with you?' He looked like he wanted to say more, but was not sure if he should.

Vama was not listening, his mind fraught with images of Tara being stripped and molested by the barbarians. 'Go now. Do as I say,' he ordered, and ran towards his horse.

The gleaming white stallion had gorged on the sweet grass and drunk its fill from the clear stream. It now flew on swift feet through the winding paths of the forest, taking Vama closer to the girl who had courted danger in order to see him.

The mansion was nestled deep in the woods, on the bank of a placid blue lake overgrown with pink lotuses. The entrance to the mansion was hidden and known only to a few.

Inside were luxuries of every kind—soft beds, choice foods, fine wines and even musicians to entertain the pleasure-seekers. This was where Chitrasena and his brothers brought their women.

Vama dismounted from his horse and charged into the mansion with his sword drawn.

'Oh, look who's here!' mocked a coarse voice. He saw Visvaksena and Srutasena barring his way with their huge, fleshy arms bearing bludgeons.

'Let me pass,' demanded Vama in a fever of impatience, listening for Tara's cries from the inner chambers.

'Why should we, fool?' asked Visvaksena, his eyes flashing.

'Why don't you see if you can get past us?' challenged Srutasena, the youngest of the brothers.

'I can and I will,' said Vama, slashing at him with his sword. The asura moved backwards while his brother attacked from the side. Vama stepped aside to avoid the blow and lunged forward again, slicing Srutasena's chest with his sword. The asura howled in pain, and his brother sprang at Vama. His bludgeon descended with a force that would have smashed Vama's head to pulp if it had connected. The light-footed Vama sidestepped the blow, which glanced off his shoulder instead, almost dislocating it.

The pain was blinding, but Vama could not stop now. He bounded forward and hacked at Visvaksena's throat. Blood gushed out and the asura crashed to the ground.

Vama rushed into the inner chamber and saw Atisena laughing while Tara struggled on the bed beneath Chitrasena. The asura was holding her immobile with his huge bulk and plundering her lips with his mouth. Her panic-stricken eyes spotted Vama and she screamed to him for help.

Atisena looked up on hearing Vama's name and moved to intercept him. 'Carry on, brother, while I dispatch this fly with a single blow,' he said.

He staggered towards Vama like a mountain, his eyes red and his gait unsteady. Vama's left shoulder was throbbing unbearably; he had to move fast before he fainted. He vaulted forward, his sword flashing in an arc to slash Atisena's arm and move up to his face. Blood flowed down the asura's face, blinding him. Vama pressed home the advantage to smash him with his mace.

So focused was Vama on this battle that he did not notice Chitrasena creeping up behind him, spiked bludgeon in hand. The sudden *whoosh* of air as the weapon descended on him alerted him to the attack. He danced forward at the last second, but the blow thudded on his back, almost breaking it. He crashed to the floor, unconscious.

Srutasena stepped cautiously into the room, blood still spurting from his wounds. He saw his enemy on the floor and charged at him with his raised club.

Chitrasena stopped him with a cry. 'Do you want to set our father off on one of his murderous bouts, brother? You know he strikes like a crazed beast when we act without his permission. Let us bundle up this fool and take him to court. When he hears what happened here today, our father will no doubt order us to kill him.'

They trussed Vama up, threw him on the back of a horse and hauled him before Kaalasura. They gave the emperor a heated report of the fight and the injuries that Vama had inflicted on them.

Kaalasura was livid and unleashed his occult powers. His eyeballs turned white and deadly like a serpent's. His body and hair shot scarlet flames. His fangs grew ten yojanas long.

Hissing snakes reared their heads around him, opening their jaws wide as a prelude to attack.

'Kill the upstart. Kill him now,' he trumpeted like a maddened bull elephant. 'He must not live to see the sun rise another day.'

IO

The Lost Child

The dark figure lurking in the shadows of Rukmini's palace waited for Krishna to leave the room and then stepped in softly and took his place by the cradle. The mother slept on, exhausted by the day's events. There was no one to challenge the intruder.

He stared at the angelic child lying on a bed of soft velvet. He could snap the infant's neck in an instant and leave the body for the father to find. Or he could make Krishna suffer every day of his life, wondering where his son was and whether he still lived.

A loathsome laugh rumbled from the intruder's throat. He hated the cowherd and the way he was worshipped as a god on earth. He decided what he would do. He bent and snatched the child up in his massive arms, casting a spell to render both of them invisible.

Jolted rudely from his warm cocoon, Pradyumna wailed in protest. Rukmini woke up with a start and jumped up to attend to her child.

The cradle was empty.

Her shriek shattered the silence. Her attendants hurtled into the room, followed by bodyguards with their swords unsheathed.

'My child is gone! O my child,' gasped the queen. 'How could this happen? Why did I sleep and let you be taken?' She collapsed in a storm of tears.

The guards ran from room to room, but found no sign of either the child or the intruder. Others sprinted to the gardens and the broad avenue that ran past the palace. How had the enemy entered when they had been standing guard? They had heard nothing—neither running feet nor galloping hooves. How had he escaped without a trace?

Lamps sprang to life across the city as people were jolted awake by the horrific news. Crowds gathered outside the palace.

'This must be the beginning of the disaster that Narada prophesied,' they whispered to one another.

Krishna's chariot swept through the agitated crowds and halted at the palace doors. He hastened to his queen. Rukmini threw herself into his arms, making inarticulate sounds like an animal in pain.

'He is gone, he is gone! I closed my eyes for a moment and . . . How could I have slept when I knew there was evil in the air? I am to blame.' Her piteous cries brought tears to Krishna's eyes. 'Who could have taken him from us, and for what purpose? Only a wicked mind would snatch a newborn from his mother . . . and now my son is in the hands of this monster—' She was unable to continue as huge sobs racked her body.

Krishna spoke to her in a soft voice, offering her comfort. Rukmini's body stilled and her eyes flew to his face. 'Is it Jambavati? Could she have kidnapped him in order to kill him? Was that not what she threatened to do? Sooner or later, she always achieves what she wants.' She tore herself free from his arms. 'I must run to her and seek her mercy.'

He held her back with a gentle arm and looked into her eyes. 'No, no. That cannot be. Jambavati is not so heartless. She was merely expressing her rage.'

'Then who is our enemy? How is it that *you* do not know, my lord?' Her voice grew shrill as a new suspicion came to her mind. 'How could this happen to the son of Sahasraaksha, the one with a thousand eyes? Why did you not protect the son who was born to us after years of prayers to Shiva?' She pounded on his chest with her fists.

Suddenly, her hands dropped. 'You knew this would happen, but did nothing to stop it. That was why you told me about karma and its consequences.' Krishna said nothing, merely looking at his distraught queen with compassion.

'Do you mean to say that our innocent child is laden with such a burden of karma that he had to be kidnapped, maybe even killed? I will not accept this. I cannot. Nor will I sacrifice my son to destiny. Not my little one . . . Bring him back to me. Even if he has reached Yamaloka, the abode of the dead . . .'

Her legs buckled at the thought and her eyes clouded. She dropped to the ground. 'Is he . . . is he dead? Have Yama's messengers snared him with their noose? Are desert sands and hell fires roasting his tender feet? Is he wandering hungry and thirsty on the banks of the Vaitarani river that flows with blood . . . helpless, friendless, without shelter?'

An unearthly cry tore its way out from deep within her. The birds froze in the sky. The rivers rose from their beds, anguished by the travails of the goddess born on earth to save humankind.

Krishna's murmurs of comfort were futile. Rukmini's thoughts skittered down dire pathways. 'He cannot be in the hell of naraka, for he is without sin. He must be in swarga, being welcomed by sages and celestial dancers.' She paused. 'But still . . . all the treasures of heaven cannot equal a mother's love. They cannot cherish him the way only I can.' Her voice dropped into stillness, the silence of death.

Krishna could not bear to watch her in such pain. 'He is where he is meant to be, my love,' he said. 'He is in the hands of destiny.'

She staggered to her feet as she saw a glimmer of light in his words. 'So does that mean you know where he is, my lord? How can you not, when you are all-powerful?' She shook him with frenzied hands. 'Bring him back to me. Do not let an evil foe tear him from us when he is so young. Do your duty as his father before you protect the world.'

Narada, who had arrived to offer solace, stepped forward now, as he could no longer stand to watch her agony.

'Do not lose your soul to grief, my queen,' he said. 'Do not forget the eternal law: Whoever is protected by Vishnu cannot be killed, and whoever is to be killed by him cannot be saved. This is his divine leela.'

Rukmini turned on Narada, her grief making her strident. 'You call this leela, Devarishi? How can the loss of a child be sport to a mother whose sole instinct is to protect him? How can I take comfort in empty phrases when I am struggling to bear my loss?'

Narada could not take offence at words that sprang from a wounded heart. 'You can overcome sorrow only when you understand that it is inevitable, my queen,' he said in a gentle voice. 'You can appreciate happiness only when you have experienced pain. Life spins around constantly like the chakra on Vishnu's finger. Joy and sorrow unfurl like the spiral of his conch.'

'More platitudes,' she snapped. 'What other words can you utter when you are but an ascetic? You have nothing to forfeit— wife or child, kith or kin. How can you fathom a mother's heart? How can you understand the anguish that tears me apart?'

Narada realized he needed to be patient. Rukmini had forgotten that she was the divine consort of the lord of Vaikunta, who governed all creation. She was a mortal now, destined to suffer the sorrows of humankind.

He tried again. 'Evil and goodness have existed side by side from the time of creation,' he said. 'Brahma himself created rajas and tamas, passion and darkness, after he gave life to the goodness of sattva. He created the rakshasas and the yakshas, the serpents and the flesh-eating pishachas. The righteousness of dharma was followed by adharma, which let loose falsehood and wrath, disease and death.'

He paused. She was listening to him now, and her face was calmer. It was time to remind her of who she really was. 'Remember that you are the divine Lakshmi, born from the ocean of milk. And that your birth was followed by that of your evil sister, Alakshmi, the embodiment of strife. Good will triumph in the end, but not without a struggle.'

Rukmini fell silent, trying to still her agitation and focus her mind on the Blue God who was her ultimate refuge.

Narada bowed to the celestial couple and went his way. He had a tougher task ahead—to counsel a soul whose thoughts hovered on a lower plane. How could he enlighten someone who had wished death on another's child in order to preserve her own? This was a thought too evil to comprehend, even among mortals. How could it be tolerated in Krishna's wife?

Narada entered Jambavati's palace and found her seated on her throne, cradling her son, protected by a ring of maids and bodyguards.

'My son is the blessed one. He is safe while *her* son is lost!' she gloated. 'So what if the Pandavas favour her? She flounders in sorrow now while I look forward to the time when my son will rule Dwaraka, and I will reign as Queen Mother.'

Her smile grew wider when she saw Narada. This was her chance to get back at the sage who had lectured her in front of her guests.

'Come, Devarishi, celebrate the beginning of my son's rise. Share our joy in the extinction of the pretender.'

'Why do you speak as if you are ignorant of truth and dharma, my queen?' asked Narada. 'The evil that you exhibit will return to haunt you in life after life.'

She waved a rude hand of dismissal and bent over her son, calling him the future king.

Narada saw that she was determined to rush headlong towards her doom, and would force her son to follow her down the same path.

Would Samba choose to be arrogant and thoughtless like his mother? Or would he imbibe the wisdom of his father? The future stood waiting for him to choose.

II

Secrets Revealed

'Don't kill Vama, my king,' sobbed Mayavati as she threw herself at Kaalasura's feet, braving the flames and hissing serpents. 'Have pity on him. I have raised him like a son and cannot bear to see him slain. Punish me if you will, but do not take his life. I swear that I will keep him away from you and your sons. Please, please, have mercy.'

Vama sagged in the arms of the guards, his body battered and bloody. He listened to Mayavati begging for his life, feeling the humiliation in every pore of his body. It would be better to die now than to die every moment as a prisoner.

Kaalasura looked down at Mayavati's agonized face, her lovely eyes awash in tears. Her puny son was no threat to him, and he would win her abiding gratitude by sparing his life.

'I revoke the death sentence for the sake of my queen,' he declared. Mayavati stumbled to her feet, overcome with relief. 'Remove him from my sight at once,' he told her. 'And be warned that the next time he angers me will be his last.'

The queen's attendants helped her carry Vama to her palace, where Sandilya supervised the cleaning and binding of his wounds. Vama lay silent, broken in body and spirit. He did not deserve their tenderness after the way he had scorned their advice and insulted them.

He could not blame fate for the turn of events, for life had given him many opportunities, but he had allowed himself to be led astray by the tinkle of anklets and the lure of kohl-lined eyes. Now he stood exposed for what he was—a wastrel who was unable to save himself or his girl—

Oh God! What happened to Tara after I collapsed in a heap at Chitrasena's feet?

'Tara? How is she? Is she alive or dead?' he cried out.

Mayavati's eyes flashed. The girl seemed to be his only concern, even though he had almost died because of her.

'I came to the forest mansion with Hasmukha when he told me you were in danger,' she said. 'But I was too late to save you. Chitrasena had already left for the court, dragging your unconscious body.'

'I asked Hasmukha to bring my friends to help me,' said Vama. 'Why did the fool call you?'

Mayavati rose and began to pace up and down, her face set in anger. 'You seem to have forgotten that this *fool* is the only friend you have now,' she said. 'And he has paid a heavy price for it. The emperor banished him and his legion to the outer bounds of the kingdom for having helped you. And your other *friends* will never venture anywhere near you.'

Vama lowered his head. He had forgotten that he was no longer a prince who could rely on the support of his followers.

His shamefaced expression fuelled her anger. 'Did you stop to think even for a moment before setting off to rescue the girl? No, you imagined yourself to be an Arjuna who could defeat all his enemies on his own. You trusted others and ignored the one person who cares for you. You did not remember the woman who saved your life by debasing herself in front of the whole court'.

This is what I have been reduced to now, thought Vama, wallowing in self-pity. *This woman saves me again and again only so that she can chastise me. She wants me to be a slave who depends on her for his life. Must I live in this way?*

Wait. She has not told me what happened to Tara. He asked his question again.

'Lust always comes first with you,' she jeered. 'But don't worry. Your little whore is safe. I found her hiding in the woods, and whisked her to safety with my mahamaya.' *She will never come near you again if I can help it.*

She hated the girl who had tempted Vama with her lissom body and coy glances and endangered his life, not once but twice. She would destroy anyone who came between her and Vama.

Vama's guru stepped forward to steer his pupil's thoughts in the right direction. 'You must forget the girl now, Vama,' he said. 'Devote yourself to your saadhana—self-discipline and training. Before you can train your body, you must focus your mind, opening it to the rhythm of the universe. Reach beyond your bodily desires to yoke the core energy within you. To achieve this, you will need to practise rigorous physical postures, tap into your chakras—your body's energy centres— and control your prana, your invisible life energy.'

Vama's mind drifted away, unwilling to wrestle with these lofty concepts.

Mayavati pulled him upright and hissed in his ear, 'Focus, Vama. Concentrate on the stillness within you. Chant the mantras we have taught you. Exercise restraint and renunciation.'

'And you must pray to Durga, the slayer of demons, who wields weapons in her eighteen arms,' said Sandilya. 'She is the wildest of the wild and the gentlest of the gentle. She is the goddess of war; without her blessing you can achieve nothing. Chant her hundred and eight names and free your mind of every other thought. Then wait in total humility for her to bless you.'

They left him alone to toss and turn until he finally fell into a restless sleep.

Early the next morning, they came to initiate him in his saadhana—purifying his body, controlling his mind and preparing his soul.

'Your success as a warrior will hinge upon your mastery of the bow,' said Sandilya. 'You must practise day and night until you learn to unleash sixty arrows in the time it takes your enemy to shoot one. Then we will move on to the art of wielding the mace, sword, lance and axe—weapons that will be the key to winning a war. But before everything else, you must first work on honing your body, putting it through a tough regimen to bring it to peak fitness.'

'Look at me, guruji,' said Vama, with a confident grin. 'I am young and virile, and capable of defeating any soldier in our army in speed and agility. I am ready to measure my strength against yours too, if you wish.'

'Vama!' exclaimed Mayavati, shocked at his insolence. But the guru calmed her with a raised hand.

'Let us do that,' he said, leading him to the courtyard, where a giant rock lay buried in the soil. 'Why don't you exhibit your prowess by lifting this rock off the ground?'

Vama was taken aback as he eyed the huge boulder; it looked as if it had lain there from the beginning of time. But he could not retreat now.

He bent down, grasped the rock with both hands and tugged. His fingers slipped and the soft skin on his hands sheared off. He took a shuddering breath and closed his eyes. Then he knelt, encircled the rock with his arms and heaved again. He gasped and strained; sweat poured down his face, but the boulder would not budge. He staggered to his feet, his whole body wracked by pain.

'You are young and strong. I'm sure you can do it,' he heard his guru say.

Was Sandilya taunting him? Vama bent again to the rock, determined to pull it out, even if he broke his back doing so. He grunted, putting all his strength into the task. His eyes bulged, blood rushed to his head and he heard a roaring in his ears. He collapsed next to the boulder.

Sandilya said not a word, merely dragged Vama a few feet away with a careless air. Then he returned to the boulder, centred his consciousness and bent to grasp the rock in his arms. His muscles corded, his teeth clenched and he heaved with his whole body. And the boulder moved, rising slowly but steadily from the hardened earth.

The guru held it up in his arms for what seemed to be an endless moment, then let it fall to the ground with a resounding crash.

Vama sat abashed, gazing at the immense size of the rock, while confronting the truth about himself. He would not be so quick to boast in future.

Mayavati moved away silently, leaving teacher and pupil together.

Now, the real learning began. There were exercises to hone every part of his body, organ by organ. Several days were needed just to sharpen his visual reflexes, so he would be able to react quickly to threats and discern the right moment to inflict a killing blow. He learned how to be constantly aware of his environment so that his enemy would not catch him unprepared.

He worked to increase his speed, to enhance the flexibility of his arms and wrists, his neck and torso, and to control his heart rate. Any and every object became a tool to be used to sculpt his shoulders and back. The boulder he had been unable to move became the gauge to measure his strength. He celebrated the day he was first able to lift it off the ground, and slowly progressed till he could run uphill and down again, carrying it in his arms.

Vama mastered a hundred holds and locks, and grew adept at delivering blows at stunning speed. He learned that even his head could be used as a powerful battering ram to injure his opponent.

Countless such excruciating sessions later, Vama finally felt confident that his body was ready for battle. He was bruised and scarred, and every bone and muscle felt tortured, but he was no longer afraid of pain, nor did he flinch from the toughest challenge.

But Sandilya had merely begun the process. 'You have reached the threshold of what you can achieve. You need to push your body further with the power of your mind,' he said.

By now, Vama had begun to enjoy the pursuit of perfection and he gave himself over to his guru, following his every instruction until he could bend his body to his will.

Sandilya offered some rare words of praise. 'I always knew that you were meant for great things,' he said. 'But until now you were lacking in sudarshan—the clarity of vision to distinguish right from wrong.'

'Life had to take everything from me before I realized that I could rely only on myself,' Vama replied.

'You are now ready for the next step. You must elevate your soul to become worthy of the divine astras and the mantras that control them.'

While Sandilya forced him to confront the truth about his body and mind, Mayavati transported him to another world, to a higher consciousness. Here, nothing was as it seemed and the unreal became real.

'I will teach you the secrets of mahamaya, whose benign power can vanquish the malevolent forces of the asuras,' she said. 'Otherwise, the demons will torture you with dreadful hallucinations and melt your strongest weapons with just a glance. They will raze your army without even using weapons and hypnotize fierce animals into fighting for them.'

'I will learn this mystic art with your guidance,' said Vama, wiser now after his earlier humiliation.

'The asuras' physical strength is far greater than yours and can only be countered with sorcery,' she said. She chanted a quick spell and conjured up a bevy of luminous apsaras who paralysed his senses with song and dance. He fell into a trance, dropped his weapons and began to follow them, totally in thrall to their charms.

She snapped her fingers and he came out of the spell, shocked at how easily he had been ensnared.

'You can terrorize your enemies or mesmerize them,' she said. 'Both work equally well. You must learn to employ their own fears against them.'

Vama nodded. At once, his head fell off his shoulders and rolled on the ground. He cried out in fear and wondered how he was still able to see what was happening. Mayavati was standing over his severed head, brandishing a sword. And, horror of horrors, his headless torso was still standing in front of her. A chill raced through his bones.

Then his body began to topple to the ground, even as his arms flailed, trying to join his severed body with his head.

He woke from the nightmare with a scream and stood trembling as Mayavati put a comforting hand on his shoulder. 'These spells are worth learning, don't you think?' she asked.

Vama drew in deep breaths to slow his racing heartbeat and gulped down some water. Then he stood silently before her, waiting for her to commence the lessons.

Days sped by as he strained to follow her instructions but failed every time. The occult arts were not as easy to master as the martial arts he had learned from his guru. He began to panic. Each attempt seemed worse than the previous one. Her impatience mounted even as his confidence dwindled.

'You seem to be curiously clumsy now, when you were so adept at your earlier pastimes,' she remarked. 'Flirting, dancing, playing the flute, hiding from your guru . . .'

'If I could take back those giddy years, I would,' he said, his voice subdued. 'I curse myself for every moment I wasted when I should have focused on what really mattered. Please be patient with me a little longer.'

Pacified by his sincerity, Mayavati tried to break through the barrier that was holding him back. There was little time to spare, as the asuras would soon chase him down and kill him. He had no chance of survival in his current state.

Vama laboured to understand the fear that gripped his mind and blocked his progress. He resolved to speak out, hoping that she would be able to help him.

'My nights are tormented by dark dreams of Shiva's third eye burning me to cinders,' he said. 'A dire voice mocks me every time I close my eyes. I fear that I am cursed in some way.'

She gasped and opened her mouth to reply. He raised an arm to stop her and continued. 'I suspect that this dark secret is the reason I am unable to advance. I must understand what it is, or I am surely doomed.'

How much can I tell him? she wondered. *Is he ready for the answers?*

He looked at her troubled face, and something within impelled him to reach out to her. He clasped her hand in his and united their energies. He closed his eyes and delved into the deepest recesses of his mind.

His mouth began to chant without conscious thought. It was a hymn to Kamakshi—she in whose eyes Kama resides.

'O Shakti! Wife of Shiva! The one who holds Kama's sugar cane bow, his flower arrows and his parrot. Help me, mother goddess,' he prayed.

A dazzling light entered his body and flooded the dark corners of his soul. He saw himself for who he truly was—Kama, the god of love. And before him was not the Mayavati he had known, but the ethereal Rati herself, revealing herself to him in her eternal form. She was pure, peerless, perfect—the pinnacle of youth and beauty.

'Tell me everything, my queen,' he pleaded.

She nodded, her face lighting up with the radiance of love. 'Yes, it is time. Who else can reveal the secret of your life better than the one who stood by you through your ordeal?'

'I know now that it was your voice that spoke to me as I burned,' he said, his eyes aglow. 'It was you who tried to hold me back from my fate and then sobbed as I died.'

'Yes,' she replied, her lips trembling as she relived the horror of that time. 'I've been waiting for a long time to tell you the story of our love, and the tragedy that tore us apart. And of the hope born through the blessings of the Trimurti—Shiva, Vishnu and Brahma.'

They sat together with clasped hands as Mayavati took him back through the labyrinth of time. 'You are indeed my Kama, reborn on earth after being destroyed by Shiva's third eye,' she said.

'What was my crime that I deserved to be immolated?' he asked, like a child trying to understand his father's anger.

'Shiva had immersed himself in tapasya, removing himself to a remote cave. Soon afterwards, the terrible asura king Tarakasura began to oppress the world in his quest for boundless power. The heavens too could not withstand him as the asura had secured a boon that he could be killed only by Shiva's son. The devas prayed to the three-eyed god to give up his asceticism, but were unable to arouse him from his trance. They were left with only one weapon, which could very well rebound on them and lead to a fiery conflagration.'

'And what was this weapon?'

'It was your potent arrow of love that could rouse passion even in the heart of the god with the matted locks. Indra ordered you to use your arrow to bring together Shiva and Parvati, the daughter of Mount Himavan, so that the son born to them would save the world. You carried out his command and awakened desire in Shiva. The union of the divine couple was followed by the birth of Karthikeya, who vanquished Tarakasura with his golden lance.'

'So what was my crime—that I saved earth and the heavens?'

'You not only saved the world, but did so knowing that your action would lead to your death, for you knew that you were the last hope of the world.'

'And the all-knowing Shiva still opened his fiery eye?'

'Shiva cut off Brahma's head at the beginning of creation for succumbing to his lust for his own daughter,' said Mayavati. 'Shiva was furious that he too had fallen victim to your arrow, just as Brahma had prophesied at the time of his own fall. Moreover, Shiva's tapasya had been broken by your intervention, and he took out his rage on you.'

Vama sat in silence, drowning in memories of another place and time.

Mayavati's trembling voice broke his reverie. 'Don't you recognize me as your wife Rati, my lord?'

His inner eye was now fully open and he saw himself with her, cavorting in streams and soaring with her across the skies. He saw again the dreaded cave and felt the terrible fire singe his body. He smelled the smoke and heard Rati's cries as she watched him burn. He heard her plead and threaten the Trimurti, asking them to bring him back to life.

'I could not envision life without you, my lord,' she said. 'I plunged into a penance lasting many yugas, seeking your return. I gave up food and water and controlled my very breath. Trees and shrubs grew over my body and shrouded me from the world, yet Shiva refused to relent . . . I had nothing left to offer except my life. I decided I would kill myself, becoming one with you in the fire that had taken you from me. I invoked the fire god Agni, and the flames sprang up before me.'

Vama looked at her with streaming eyes, feeling her agony in his very marrow.

She continued with her story. 'Agni told me to be patient a little longer and not to give up my life. But I could not bear my pain any more. I stepped towards the fire, joining my hands in prayer as I chanted Shiva's names. Kailasapati, Sadasiva, Nilakantha, Somanatha, Kedara, Tryambaka, Nirguna, Saguna. And then . . .'

Her voice dropped to a whisper and her eyes took on a faraway look as she relived that ineffable moment. 'Shiva and Parvati appeared before me in a blaze of light. Parvati took the form of Kamakshi and promised me that I would be one with you again. You would be born in another form and I was to await you in the court of Kaalasura.'

She sighed. 'And so I waited, until I recognized my Kama in the infant that the asura brought to me. And since that day, I have spent every moment yearning to take my place by your side.'

His heart thudded as he felt the pangs of an ancient love that transcended the laws of time and space. This noble goddess had tried to hold him back from danger and then wept over his scorched body. She had pleaded with the gods and staked her life to save him.

Mayavati moved towards him, her arms open to embrace him once again. He swayed towards her, drawn by her lush body, her parted lips and her tender eyes. He remembered their fierce lovemaking on grassy beds, hilltops and sandy beaches. Was it a memory, a vision or merely the promptings of a lustful body? Anxiety stabbed his belly and seared his mind.

He recoiled from her, his face paling. 'How can I accept you as my wife when I know you as my mother?' he asked. 'It would be just as grievous a sin as Brahma's desire for his daughter. Moreover, it is against dharma to covet another's wife.'

Mayavati staggered back. 'I swear by the sun, the moon and the stars that I am as chaste as Arundhati, the wife of Sage Vasishta,' she said. 'I have never been Kaalasura's wife, in body or spirit.'

'Do not lie. Remember that I have seen you myself—serving him, fondling him.' His lip curled in disgust.

'I made the world believe that it was me. But in reality it was a shadow I created to perform the duties of Kaalasura's wife in court and in bed. I will prove it to you if you accompany me to the asura's antapura.'

He nodded in agreement. They turned invisible and flew to Kaalasura's many-roomed mansion, passing through twelve immense gates, each guarded by a fierce asura, until they entered the emperor's private chamber.

Vama saw with his own eyes the shadow Mayavati who was anointing the demon's chest with sandal paste and saffron. The false wife cooled him with her soft caresses and burned him with deep kisses, inflaming him and making him oblivious to the deception.

He realized that Mayavati had spoken the truth. They returned once again to her palace, where they sat together while she recounted the rest of her story.

'You can see how I kept him happy, winning his favour so that I could protect you until you grew into manhood. I have been waiting a long time to see you destroy the despot.'

She gazed deep into his eyes as if to read his mind. 'Are you ready to kill Kaalasura so that we can be together again, my lord? Will you be my Manmatha once more and accept me as your Kamapriya?'

He sat silent, struggling to absorb all that she had revealed.

She took the final step to bare her soul and place herself at his mercy. 'I was born for you, my love. And I will die for you,' she whispered.

Her body trembled. Her heart was filled with yearning. She had done everything she could and must now await his answer.

Still he hesitated . . .

12

The Kalahapriya

The day began on an ominous note for Kaalasura. He awoke from a drunken sleep to the sound of many feet running helter-skelter around his chamber. He summoned his bodyguards with a roar and ordered them to find and kill the fools who had dared to disturb him. The commander returned soon to say that they were unable to find any intruders. Kaalasura ran him through with his sword in anger. Unable to sleep after all the commotion, he rose from his bed and made his way to the court.

One of his spies entered on trembling feet, prostrated himself before him and awaited permission to speak. Kaalasura saw his agitated face and gestured with his club.

'I have dreadful news, my lord,' said the spy, casting a frightened look at Mayavati who was seated at the feet of the emperor.

'Talk, imbecile,' roared Kaalasura.

'I followed the queen as per your orders and heard her speaking to her son Vama,' he stuttered. He paused, looking again at the queen.

Kaalasura laid a huge hand on Mayavati's shoulder to hold her captive and urged him on. 'Speak, or lose your head.'

'The queen said that the woman who attends you in bed and in court is an illusion she created with her mahamaya. She told Vama that she loved him as her husband and asked him to kill you in battle.'

Kaalasura sprang to his feet, shouting like a mad man. He pounded his chest with such force that his gold armour sheared off and fell to the ground. His son Vikrasena pounced on the spy and clubbed him down for being the bearer of bad news. Soldiers removed the still-twitching body from the court and threw it to the vultures. Enraged, Kaalasura lifted the illusory Mayavati by her hair, baring her throat to his sword's edge. 'I will kill you now, impostor,' he thundered, frothing at the mouth.

'Hold your blow, lord,' called out a minister in a loud voice that cut through his rage. Kaalasura paused, glaring at the man with bloodshot eyes. 'It would be wiser to imprison the shadow so you can hold Mayavati's powers captive.'

Kaalasura's cunning brain pondered this. He whispered instructions to a slave and sent him forth. He then chanted an arcane spell to conjure up an iron cage before him. A snap of his fingers and the shadow Mayavati flew backwards into the cage and collapsed in a heap. The cage magically sealed itself so that neither door nor lock was visible.

'Now the whore can no longer help her weakling son and I will capture them both,' gloated Kaalasura.

'Why capture them, glorious father?' asked Vikrasena. 'Just raise your finger and I will dice their bodies and scatter the pieces to the wind.'

'What joy will I gain by granting them a swift death, when I can make them suffer and scream and beg? Once I have had my fill, I will throw their bloodied bodies on the ramparts for the vultures to shred.'

His voice rose. 'A whore and her cowardly son . . . How did they think they could defeat me, the Trilokadipati, ruler of the three worlds? Indra hides from me in the netherworld. The ashta dikpalakas, the guardians of the eight directions, have fled their posts in terror. The sun stops at my will and the world trembles at my whims.'

His voice dropped, as though he was speaking to himself. 'I always wondered if she burned for me the way I did for her. She served me in bed, but who knew what was in her heart? I fulfilled her every desire and gave her control over my dominion. I showered her with rare gifts from the deepest seas and the farthest heavens. Still, she seemed remote and unhappy. I thought this was because she was barren, so I brought her a child with features like her own. And now, the woman wants to take that son to bed? I'll kill them both.'

In the skies above, the heavenly messenger stood listening, realizing that it was time to set destiny in motion. For it was Narada's role to guide the universe through the kalpa, the time taken for it to go through a complete cycle of creation and destruction.

'I will answer your question, Kaalasura,' the devarishi said, as he materialized before the king.

Chitrasena barred his way with a giant arm. 'Ah, the Kalahapriya,' he said. 'Flee from our kingdom at once. Do not try to foment conflict as is your practice.'

Minister Sunaka frowned at him and welcomed Narada with folded hands. 'Greetings, Devarishi,' he said. 'The wise know that you bring tidings known only to the gods. They also realize that your intervention leads to the victory of good over evil.'

Narada bowed to him and moved forward to greet Kaalasura. 'I bring you news from the heavens, though it is probably not what you would like to hear. Nevertheless, it is my duty to warn you,' he said.

'What can a beggar like you say to frighten the lord of the universe?' laughed Kaalasura.

'How easily you forget that you are mortal! Pay heed now, O king, for your days are numbered. You abused your powers to desecrate the gods and oppress the people. Death now knocks on your gates.'

Kaalasura snarled like a rabid beast. 'The god of death has fled his throne in fear of my legions. I command life and death now. I could toss you to the whirlwind or crush you under the wheels of Surya's chariot. So be careful what you say with your irreverent tongue.'

'My reverence is to Vishnu, not to asuras blinded by power. Silence me if you can, but remember that you cannot overthrow your karma.'

'I scoff at karma and the other lies propagated by gods to control men. No one, human or god, can bring about my death.'

'Karma governs men, gods, cities and even demons. You have invited doom with your vile deeds. You lead a sinful life, governed by lust and greed. You attack the devas, ravish their queens and defile the apsaras and gandharvas. You disrupt sacrifices to the gods and throw priests into dungeons. The time has come for you to face the warrior who will dispense justice.'

'Who is this warrior who dares confront me? Is he the god of war?'

'He is the child you snatched from his cradle in Dwaraka, the one your queen nurtured as her own. He is now a full-grown man, eager to dispatch you to another world.'

Kaalasura raised his head to the skies and howled with laughter. His courtiers shuddered and, outside, the horses yoked to his golden chariot panicked. The emperor's eyes glittered, bright and sharp like daggers.

'Are you saying that it is Vama who is ordained to kill me? A weakling whose mother had to save him from my anger? I could have killed him the day I snatched him from Krishna's palace, or any day since. I can snap his neck now with just a flick of my fingers. Why, even the weakest of my soldiers could kill him with ease, if he has not already fled to a distant corner of the earth.'

'Your arrogance clouds your mind, Kaalasura. I am here to offer you a final chance to redeem your soul. Return the devas' powers to them, make devout offerings and . . .'

Kaalasura bellowed with rage. 'Stop now or lose your tongue, ascetic! You will soon see how I destroy Vama and my adulterous queen.'

Narada looked at him with a mocking smile. 'You do not know who they really are, do you? Vama is Kama reborn on earth due to Rati's prayers and Shiva's blessings. Mayavati is Rati herself, here to help her lord attain the skills needed to destroy you.'

So my queen was using me as a pawn all along, thought Kaalasura, trying but failing to control his anger. He lashed out with his razor claws at the soldier pressing his feet. The man fell back, bleeding, and another took his place, fearing for his life.

'The gods have sent a remarkable warrior to oppose me. The god of love, who shoots flower arrows, fights with a flute and dallies with women.' He thumped his chest with his fists and thrust out his chin. 'I will crush him with my very breath. I will make him and the harlot wish they had never been born!'

'Do not trouble yourself, father,' said Vikrasena, flourishing his sword. 'I will bring you the false prince and his wench, so you can decide how they will die.'

Kaalasura roared his consent, pawing the ground like a ferocious boar.

The asura had made his choice.

There is nothing more I can do here, thought Narada as he vanished from the court.

13

The Other Son

Samba, the son of Jambavati and Krishna, basked in the attention lavished on him in the absence of the child who had gone missing many years ago. He now rivalled his father with his noble face and splendid body. His easy charm and smile won over the courtiers. The young queens of Krishna, the warriors defending Dwaraka and even the commoners sang his praises.

The young prince was a maharathi, an expert warrior who could fight 60,000 bowmen at once without being vanquished. A powerful wrestler, he could kill a thousand enemies with his bare hands. When he cast his javelin, he resembled Indra hurling his vajra, the invincible thunderbolt. When he set out to battle wearing his armour of gold, his radiance was blinding.

No one had heard anything about Pradyumna since the night he had disappeared and he was now just a dim memory. However, Rukmini, who had been blessed with nine other sons, still pined for her firstborn and prayed for his safety. Krishna's parents, Vasudeva and Devaki, gave her courage, saying that her son would soon return to her.

Jambavati was proud to have finally eclipsed the other queen and doted on Samba, the first of her many sons. Samba revelled in her adoration and grew up accustomed to having everyone fall in with his wishes. When thwarted, his temper became unstable and he acted in a mean and vengeful manner.

Once, he brutally spurred his horse in order to win a race against his friends until it collapsed and died.

'He was a noble animal who carried you faithfully for many leagues, master,' his old groom, who had taught him to ride, had said to him later. 'You should not have pushed him so.'

Samba, seething at the rebuke, had knocked down the man and ordered his minions to throw him out.

'If this is how he treats a faithful servant who carried him on his shoulders as a child, what will he do to us if we displease him?' worried his other servants. They ensured that they never stood in the way of his whims.

His royal mien won the hearts of the loveliest maidens in the kingdom. He swore undying love to them and lavished them with jewels and silks. But all his promises were forgotten when he set eyes on a pretty newcomer. The girls he abandoned went into a decline. In desperation, one of them sought Jambavati's intervention.

'You wish to marry my son?' Jambavati screamed. 'Princesses from the most powerful kingdoms wait for my son to throw them a single glance. And you, a lowly servant, think that you can sit on the throne by his side! You will pay for your lust, harlot.'

She summoned her men with a toss of her head. The girl was never seen again; it was rumoured that she been sold as a slave.

'You are a god, my son,' said Jambavati, 'the saviour of our clan. Do not waste your time with such worthless people.

Instead, prepare for the day when you succeed your father as the chief of the Yadus.'

Samba's arrogance grew by the day, and he began to act as if the crown was already on his head. 'I will be a better king than my father, and Dwaraka will be more powerful under my rule,' he declared.

Jambavati's fierce championing of her son prevented the ministers from offering him their counsel. The powerful mother–son duo terrorized anyone who challenged them.

Samba continued to indulge his appetites without check. His fondness for wine, his amorous flings and his insolence towards his elders finally brought him to Krishna's notice.

The father summoned Samba and advised him to be modest and respectful. 'An ideal ruler must be benevolent,' he said. 'Avoid passion and arrogance which bring down even the mightiest. Remember the downfall of Ravana, king of Lanka, scholar of the Vedas and staunch devotee of Shiva. He lost everything, including his life, due to his lust for Rama's wife Sita. Model your behaviour on that of Rama, the Maryada Purushottama, the ideal man.'

Samba bristled with anger at this unaccustomed rebuke. He glared at the courtiers, whom he suspected of laughing at him, and hurried to his mother to complain.

Narada was speaking with Jambavati when Samba broke in unceremoniously to heap curses upon his father.

'Who does he think he is?' he ranted. 'Toothless lions should not curb young cubs who snatch what they want from life. He compares me to a rakshasa and advises me to emulate Rama's Ekapatnivrata—a vow to have only one wife. And this stricture comes from a man who frolicked with countless gopis in Vrindavan when he was just a boy.'

Before Jambavati could say anything, Narada began to speak. 'It is sacrilege to speak of the lord in this way, Samba.

Especially when it was Krishna himself who was incarnated as Rama in the Treta Yuga. The sages whom Rama met during his exile in the forest knew him to be the Supreme and desired to become one with him. Rama told them that their desire would be fulfilled when they were born as gopis during his next avatar. It was due to this boon that Krishna danced with the gopis in the raasa leela, the dance of total surrender.'

Narada closed his eyes and joined his hands over his head in reverence. 'This dance symbolizes the union of all living things with the lord—of prakriti, the female, with purusha, the male. How can you denigrate this as lust?'

Samba grimaced. 'How the old fool raves,' he said. 'I do not believe tales told by liars.' He turned to his mother for help.

Jambavati hastened to placate him with her caresses and reassurance. Samba returned to the royal court to meet his mates, confident that Krishna would have left to attend to his duties. Narada followed him there, hoping to reason with him again when he was away from his mother.

The courtiers and Krishna's sons rose and bowed in respect to the rishi. However, Samba, seated in the midst of his idle gang, merely laughed at him.

'Why do you laugh, Samba?' asked Narada, frowning.

Samba disregarded him and spoke to his friends. 'You may be fooled by Narada's present demeanour, but he is not as humble as he pretends to be,' he said. 'He has had to pay a heavy price for his arrogance in the past.'

'Tell us more,' his friends egged him on.

'What are you saying, Samba?' asked an angry Narada.

'I merely repeat a story our father told us,' said Samba, his eyes gleaming. Turning to his friends, he said, 'Narada once performed a penance so severe that Indra's throne began to shake. He grew afraid that the sage would take his place and sent his apsaras to lure him from his tapas. Narada continued with his penance and forced Indra to accept defeat. This success went to the ascetic's head and he travelled to the different lokas boasting about his prowess. Vishnu decided to curb his pride and sent him a vision of a beautiful princess, Visvamohini.'

'Stop now,' pleaded Narada, raising a hand towards Samba, but the prince was enjoying himself too much to stop.

'Narada was captivated by the princess and desired to marry her. He went to Vishnu and asked him for "a face like Hari's" to ensure that the maiden chose him during her swayamvara. Vishnu granted his wish. But things did not go as expected. The princess recoiled when she saw Narada's face. And even as he froze in shock, she garlanded Vishnu who had entered the hall just then.'

'But why did she recoil when he had Hari's face?' asked one of Samba's brothers. 'And why did Vishnu come to the swayamvara when he knew Narada wanted to marry her?'

'Narada was just as confused. Then two shivaganas, Shiva's attendants, advised him to look at his face in a pool of water. Narada saw his reflection and was dismayed, for he had been given the face of a monkey. The ganas laughed at his expression, and he cursed them to be born as demons.'

'Narada must have been angry with Vishnu for this deceit.'

'He certainly was,' said Samba. 'He cursed Vishnu to be born as a human and to be separated from his beloved, just as Narada had been separated from Visvamohini. He also said that Vishnu would need the help of a monkey to guide him in his search for his queen.'

'So that was why Rama was separated from Sita and needed Hanuman's help to trace her,' murmured the courtiers.

'You have still not answered my question about the monkey face,' said Samba's brother.

'Narada asked Vishnu the same thing,' Samba replied. 'Vishnu told him that the whole swayamvara was an illusion he had created to deflate Narada's pride. The princess was Lakshmi in human form, and she would naturally choose Vishnu as her husband. He explained that Narada had been fooled as he had forgotten that "Hari" also means "monkey" in Sanskrit.'

The gathering erupted in laughter. 'You make the same mistakes repeatedly, Samba,' said Narada. 'You mocked Sage Durvasa's gaunt face and form earlier, and he cursed you, saying that you would lose your good looks one day. But you have still not learned to respect your elders.' So saying, Narada stormed out, unable to bear it any more. He determined in his anger to teach the young cub a much-needed lesson.

The devarishi got his opportunity one evening when Krishna's younger wives were cavorting in a lake and drinking wine freely. Samba, who was a mirror image of his father, joined them in the waters, making them believe he was Krishna. Narada saw him caress their faces, splash them with water, wrap his arms around their waists and whisper lustful words in their ears.

The sage was shocked by this behaviour and the way the queens reciprocated Samba's attentions. He invoked Krishna in his thoughts and the lord appeared. The Blue God stood in the shadows with Narada and watched as his younger queens frolicked with Samba, anointing him with musk and caressing his shoulders.

Krishna's eyes darted fire.

Narada grew afraid. *What have I done? Can I still stop this?*

'They are young and need your guidance, Krishna,' he said softly.

'Things have gone too far for that,' replied the lord. 'Yatha raja tatha praja. As the ruler, so the ruled. If I allow my son to flout dharma today, my people will follow his example tomorrow. He must be stopped, and I must do whatever is needed to achieve that.'

He strode out of the shadow of the trees. 'Cease your revels now!' he roared.

The young wives who were clinging to Samba's bare chest froze. Their mouths opened in shock to see their lord on the shore. Samba stood motionless, his hands smeared with sandal paste that he had been applying on their bodies.

'Your behaviour is an offence to the sanctity of marriage,' Krishna said to his wives. 'You will pay for your lust by falling prey to our enemies as soon as I shed my earthly form.'

The queens wailed and ran out of the waters, clutching their disarranged garments.

Krishna turned to Samba. 'You covet my queens when you should give them the respect due to a mother,' he said. 'You have exploited the similarity in our appearance and abused my trust. You will pay heavily for this sin.'

Samba trembled and stayed silent, knowing that he had breached the code of righteous behaviour.

'I curse you to be struck with a foul disease that will disfigure you and put an end to your pride. No longer will anyone mistake you for me, and the scars of leprosy will remind you constantly of your offence.'

So saying, Krishna left the place, unable to look any longer upon Samba's face.

Immediately, Samba's face and body erupted with ugly lesions. He collapsed in pain and was unable to stand up again. His servants carried him in a litter to his mother's palace, their faces betraying their revulsion.

Samba looked at his mother and wailed in desperation. Jambavati was shocked to see the misshapen body of her son and fell into hysterics.

'Your face and body so deformed! I cannot bear to look upon your pain. Who did this to you? I will kill the monster who did this!' she shrieked.

The servants haltingly explained what had happened. She flailed at them with her fists and her curses.

'Why did you knaves not protect him? How could Krishna inflict this pain on Samba when his wives are to blame? Harlots! Every single one of them. Throwing themselves at my young son because their husband is old.'

The servants cowered, closing their eyes and ears against her blasphemy.

She caressed her son's mottled face and wailed to the heavens. 'Who will save my darling when his own father is against him? He is jealous of you, my beloved son. He knows you surpass him in strength and fame. So he inflicts this ugliness upon you.' Her breath came in gasps and her eyes spewed fire. 'I curse Krishna and his wanton wives! I curse Rukmini and her jealous eye which have caused this misfortune!'

Jambavati then turned on her attendants and screamed at them, asking them to bring her husband at once. Krishna arrived to find his queen lying on the floor, her loud wails the only sound in the eerie silence that shrouded her palace. Her hair, usually pinned in artful styles and decked with flowers, fell to her waist in a tangled mess. Her garments were faded and old, unworthy of a queen.

'How could you do this to my son?' she shouted when she saw him, flinging her ornaments at his face. 'You have marred his beauty with a hideous and painful disease. How dare you punish him when your shameless wives are the ones to blame?'

Does she not understand that her son is equally guilty, he wondered. *Does she not see that her blind support has made him what he is?*

'Why are you silent?' she cried, springing to her feet and raking him with her nails. 'Did you really think I would not

realize that this is Rukmini's doing? She is jealous that my
son is alive while hers is dead. And you—you encourage her
by favouring her. Why, my lord? Why do you hate Samba so
much? Do you doubt that he is your son?'

Her maids gasped and looked fearfully at his face, but
Jambavati was still ranting. 'If you think I have been unfaithful,
tell me so and I will accept it. But I cannot let you torture Samba.'

'Your sick mind conjures up its own hell, Jambavati,'
Krishna said, holding her hands to stop her tearing at him. 'You
are poisoned by pride and an endless desire that can never be
satisfied.'

'You torture my son and then attack me?' She hissed like
a cobra about to strike. 'I will tell the world the truth that you
are trying to hide. You are jealous of Samba because he is virile
while you have grown feeble. You are afraid your queens will
flock to his bed.'

Krishna saw that she hovered on the edge of madness. He
tried again to calm her.

'Your envy addles your mind and leads you deeper into sin.
Your rash actions and words harm not only yourself but your
son as well.'

'I will never listen to you. You must listen to me.' Her shrill
sobs drowned his voice.

He took a step away from her.

Samba deserves my sympathy, he thought, looking at his son with
a new compassion. *How can I blame him when this woman controls his
thinking? I must help him redeem himself.*

He put a hand in blessing on Samba's head. 'I cannot take
back the curse, my son, for you brought it upon yourself with
your actions,' he said. 'However, I can show you the path to
redemption. Go to the banks of the sacred Chandrabagha river
and pray to Surya, the source of healing and good fortune. He
has the power to restore you to your old self.'

Samba's eyes flashed with hatred, but he turned his face to hide his expression from his father.

My mother is right, he thought. *You mask your jealousy by claiming that you acted in accordance with dharma. You torture me and then pretend to show pity. I too will pretend until I return to my old form. And then I will expose you to the world.*

He reined in his roiling thoughts and faced his father. 'I am grateful for your mercy and will follow your advice,' he said.

His attendants carried him in a palanquin to the shores of the Chandrabagha. He chose a serene spot on the bank, close to where the river flowed into the sea. He bathed in the mystic waters and offered obeisance to Surya.

As he prayed, his men watched and wondered, *Will the sun god take pity on him and make him whole again?*

14

The Seduction

Vama and Mayavati sat side by side on two ornate thrones in her royal chambers. Her questions to him echoed in the air: 'Are you ready to destroy Kaalasura so we can be together again? Are you ready to accept me as your Rati?'

She waited for his answer, gazing at him with painful intensity. The gods had ordained that Kaalasura would die at Vama's hands. What if he was not ready to battle the asura? She could flee this kingdom with Vama, for she was not strong enough to kill the demon on her own. No. She had never fled from battle. She would send Vama away to safety and fight alone if need be.

However, before she died, she needed to hear his answer to her second question. Did he recognize the depth of her love? Would he accept her as his long-lost queen?

The silence grew heavier. Her soul shrivelled as she realized he was going to reject her.

Vama looked into her tearful eyes. She looked again like the Rati of old, having discarded her earthly disguise. Her

face was pure and flawless, her mien divine. He knew that
he had to repay her for her faith in him through the ages. He
knew she had been his wife before the flames had burned
him. However, more recent memories tortured his mind. He
remembered her face as she had rocked his cradle and sung
him to sleep. He heard her voice lashing at him after she
rescued him from the demons. How could he forget all this
and take her to his bed?

It was easier to accept his mission to kill Kaalasura. The
asura had sinned against the gods and mankind for long, and
deserved to die. Vama could not be a coward and refuse to fight.
His face hardened. 'I will fight the demon and return dharma
to this kingdom, or die in the attempt,' he swore.

Mayavati's eyes welled with tears as she saw youth cross into
manhood. She realized too that Vama was unwilling to accept
her as his wife. It was time she gave up hope. She would help
him win against the asura, and then retire to a mountaintop to
end her life in prayer.

She bowed to him and left before the tears could flow down
her cheeks.

After she left, Vama focused his mind on the task ahead. He
would seek Sandilya's help to harden his body and spirit further
so that he could face the asura in single combat. If there was
a duel, he would not need a huge army to fight against the
demons. But he could not be sure that Kaalasura would accept
a challenge from someone he held in such contempt.

The soft tinkling of anklets disrupted his thoughts. Who
had the audacity to disturb him without permission? Or had
his fall from grace rendered him weak? He whirled to face the
door.

He was astonished to find that his visitor was Tara, whom he had thought he would never meet again. The girl ran into the room and threw herself into his arms. Vama crushed her to his chest, and hence did not see her eyes turn glassy and opaque.

'I thought Mayavati had whisked you far away with her magic,' he whispered joyously.

Tara blinked once and her eyes returned to normal. She pulled back to arm's length and gazed adoringly at him.

'Your mother banished me from the kingdom in order to keep me from you,' she said. 'But I made my way back in secret. How could I stay away from the hero who risked his life for me?' She pressed hot kisses on his face.

'You seem even more beautiful than I remember and much bolder,' he murmured. 'I can hardly believe I have you in my arms again. Why did you come back, risking death and worse? Don't you realize that the danger is greater now that I have been disowned?'

'I cannot live without you, my heart,' she whispered, running her hands over his shoulders and his body, inciting him to make love to her.

Vama's heart pounded and his body turned weak with desire. He wanted to lose himself in her lush body and forget the terrible plight he was in. He drank in the adoration in her luminous eyes, her glowing face and her tender lips. He moulded her body closer still and ran his fingers through the lustrous hair that tumbled down her back.

She pulled back from him and quickly loosened her garments, then leaned into him again and touched his lips with hers, setting off a fierce surge of desire. He was fast losing control.

'Let us make love, my prince,' she said in his ear, her body moving sinuously against his. 'No one will be able to separate us then, not even the arrogant Mayavati.' She spat out the name with hatred.

Mayavati. The mention of her name had a sobering effect on the prince. He struggled to emerge from the sensual haze. He removed Tara's arms from around him and stepped back. Guilt flooded his mind. How could he forget the woman who had challenged Shiva himself to win him back? She had been prepared to immolate herself in order to bring him to life. And now . . . Could he use the same body to betray her?

His passion ebbed, leaving him clear-eyed. He put some distance between Tara and himself, ignoring her frantic protests. 'Too much has happened since we dallied on the boat,' he said firmly and turned away. 'My life as a prince is over and I must devote myself to my mission. Though I am moved by your love, I must ask you to leave and not seek me out again. My loyalty lies now with Mayavati. My future too is with her.'

Moments later he heard a terrible hiss and swung back in time to see Tara metamorphosing into a loathsome nagakanya. Her upper body was that of a woman while below the waist she was a snake with slimy green scales. Instead of a human head, she had five serpent heads with glowing eyes and flames shooting from their jaws. As he watched in horror, she grew in size until she was double his height. Writhing snakes tumbled from her hair. Her long forked tongue flicked in and out of her mouth as she glared at him with three bulbous eyes. He felt his strength draining from him and struggled to recall what Mayavati had taught him about tackling nagas, bhootas and other demons.

'A nagakanya can take on any shape to trap your soul,' Mayavati had said. 'If you succumb to her lures and mate with her, she will bite you and draw out your lifeblood. All that will remain of you will be a broken shell, racked by pain as you wait for death.'

'What weapon should I use against her?' he had asked.

'Recite the mantra I taught you and lop off the serpent heads. Remember that if she is unable to seduce you, she will paralyse you with her venom. The poison is so virulent that one blast of her breath will make you collapse.'

Vama backed away from the nagakanya, knowing that he must stay beyond her reach. He began to chant the mantra to Garuda, the implacable foe of snakes. As his chant grew louder, the kanya began to shrink in size until she equalled him in height. Her hisses grew louder and she slithered towards him with her mouth agape.

Vama raised his sword and dodged away, trying to keep away from her paralysing breath. Everything hinged now on his being able to deliver the fatal blow before she could attack him with her poison.

But it was already too late. The serpent loosened the coils of her neck to close the distance and rammed her fangs into his neck. As the poison raced through his body, his limbs turned rigid, every breath became a struggle. He wrestled against the effects of the venom and willed his body to move.

'I will shred your body,' she hissed. 'I will crunch your bones and drink your blood. Your life is over, mortal.'

Vama felt his senses fading, but his mind warred with his body, asking him if this was how he wanted to die, seduced by a nagakanya. No, not this way. He could not allow that. He focused his mind on Sarparati, the enemy of serpents. His lips trembled and he heard his feeble voice chanting, 'Om Garudaya Namaha.' His voice grew louder as the divine name suffused his veins. Gradually his limbs emerged from their torpor.

The nagakanya let out a blood-curdling shriek and reared up to strike the final blow.

'Om Garudaya Namaha,' Vama shouted as he raised his sword and struck off her five heads at once. Her dying clamour was deafening. Black ooze spurted from her open neck and she crumbled slowly into a putrid pile of dust.

Mayavati came running into the chamber, just as the kanya disintegrated. 'My lord, you are safe. You are safe!' she exclaimed and clasped him to her heart. 'My maid informed me that Kaalasura had sent an occult slave in the form of Tara to kill you. I was afraid you would fall under her spell and I would be too late. How did you manage to escape, my lord?'

'I could not betray your devotion to me, my queen,' he said. 'I could not dishonour your pain and sacrifice.'

She gasped, her eyes lighting up with a wild hope. Did this mean that her magnificent Kama was hers again? She waited in agony for his next words.

'I pray that I have not forfeited your faith in me,' he said. He reached out to clasp her hands in his own, his eyes overflowing with the intensity of his feelings.

'I was born for you, my love,' he said. 'And I will die for you.'

As she heard him repeat the words she had said to him earlier, tears poured down Mayavati's face. She had a sense of finally coming home. She brought out the makara bracelet, the symbol of his love that she had cherished through the ages. Vama fastened it on her wrist again and the years of pain and separation vanished as if they had never existed. All that was real was this moment, this place, this life. When he held her, she became someone else, someone she had always been. She was his Kamapatni, the wife of Kama, and Ragalata, the vine of love.

Their bodies melted together and their mouths met in an explosion of passion. Heaven descended to earth as they renewed the love from which all life originated. There was no night or day, nothing except their skin, their touch, their lips and their heated breath.

The bright rays of the sun finally broke through their haze of passion. They forced themselves apart in order to perform their ablutions and prepare for the day ahead.

She offered flowers and the bilva or bael leaf to the shivaling, the symbol of Shiva. 'My prayer to Shiva and Parvati has brought us together again,' she said. 'Their blessing will help us overcome all obstacles.'

'Our battle with Kaalasura looms over us,' he said. 'I wonder what chance I have against the conqueror of heaven.'

'I bring you a gift, my love, to celebrate our union . . . a secret that is bigger than any you have heard before.'

'Do not make me wait. Tell me what you mean.'

'Kaalasura did not speak the truth when he called you a *nobody*. You are the heir to a chieftain, and the hope of a great clan. You are the son of the demon-slayer, the one whose banner is the noble Garuda.'

Vama collapsed into his seat, trying to make sense of her words. He had been a prince, then a pauper, and now he was a chieftain's son. He was unable to absorb it all.

She caressed his face and answered the question in his eyes. 'Your father is Krishna, the lord of Dwaraka. He is an avatar of Vishnu—Purushottama, the greatest of all beings. He is Prabhava, the one in whom all things are born.'

'And my mother?' Vama whispered.

'She is the gracious Rukmini, Goddess Lakshmi born on earth. She is the destroyer of sin and sorrow, who blesses us with grace and good fortune.'

Mayavati sat beside him and began to tell him the story of his birth. 'The name your parents gave you is Pradyumna, the Mighty One,' she said.

'Pradyumna,' he repeated the unfamiliar name. Questions tripped off his tongue. 'Why did my parents not rescue me from the asura when it would have been so easy for them? Did they not care?'

'Your mother was distraught when you went missing. But your father left you here to fulfil your mission.'

'If that was his wish, then I will carry out his command, or die in the attempt. I will seek him out only if I succeed and prove myself worthy.'

'You must win this battle, my lord, and then prepare yourself for an even bigger war,' said Mayavati.

'A bigger war? With whom?'

'You were born at the same time as Samba, the son of Jambavati, another of Krishna's queens,' she said. 'Narada prophesied that one of you would destroy your clan and all of mankind.'

Pradyumna felt his euphoria change to despair. Would his travails never end?

'Does this mean that if I manage to defeat Kaalasura and return to my people, I will only bring them death?'

'No, my lord. You could never be the destroyer.' Mayavati soothed him with her gentle touch. 'Krishna in his infinite wisdom said that the second son could well save mankind.'

'Samba and I seem to be a singular pair. Where does this brother of mine live?'

'In Dwaraka.'

'So he grew up in Krishna's care while I was fostered by asuras. How then do you expect me to be the one who saves my clan?' His shoulders slumped. 'Vama or Pradyumna. I am always the ill-fated one.'

'Remember, you can shape your karma by your actions and the choices you make,' said Mayavati. 'As can your brother.'

He sank back in his seat. 'A saviour or a destroyer,' he whispered. 'Which one am I?'

15

The Demon Horde

Chitrasena was instructing his soldiers in the grounds surrounding his palace when his father came to see him, accompanied by his commanders.

'Our spies tell us that Mayavati's son is preparing for war,' Kaalasura said, then grimaced and corrected himself, 'not her son, her husband. He has taken my harlot wife as his own, saying that she is his wife Rati. And she has donned a more youthful form to suit her claim.'

'It is the same lie that Narada told us,' said Chitrasena. 'A mother and son in bed together is an offence to the gods they worship. But I forget—these two claim to be gods themselves. I warned you many times that they were conspiring against us. Now you see that their bond is unnatural, one based on lust.'

'They will pay for their crimes, son,' bellowed Kaalasura. 'I have imprisoned her shadow so she cannot help Vama. The fool seems to believe that he is really Krishna's son, born to kill me. He has taken to calling himself Pradyumna.'

'The commoners flock to him in huge numbers, father. Sunaka has deserted us, along with his son Hasmukha and his legion. They have declared themselves the forces of light fighting the forces of darkness.'

'I will grind them into the dirt where they belong.'

'Do not grow agitated, father. You have me and your other sons. Just the sight of us lined up against him in battle will send this upstart into convulsions of fear. Even if he is the son of the man-god, he cannot withstand the might of our combined armies.'

'My anxiety springs from Narada's prophesy, which foretells my death at Vama's hands. The weakling surprised me by killing the nagakanya I had sent to seduce him. I am also disturbed by several dark omens. Lakes spewing blood and thunder crashing down from a clear sky. Headless monsters with a hundred arms and legs dancing over our land. I hear jackals howling through the day while a vulture circles my head. Death itself appears in my dreams as a black-skinned woman singing a dirge, with a bloody mouth and red eyes.'

'Your brain is addled by fear,' said Chitrasena. 'Your thoughts are unworthy of the conqueror who made battlefields run thick with gore. You have hewn thousands with your sword and filled hell with the cries of the dying. Where has your valour gone that you now fear ghosts? Are you afraid of a mere mortal, a toy you brought for your faithless wife?'

Kaalasura's spirit surged at these strident words. Chitrasena continued to exhort him. 'I will put an end to this folly, father. Go back to your palace and your dancers and wait for the day I bring you Pradyumna's head.'

Chitrasena's warriors erupted in deafening war cries. Drums set up a frenzied beat and trumpets proclaimed the victory that was to come. Kaalasura's other sons poured into the field on their massive chariots. Behind them came their armies of rakshasas riding on the backs of panthers and wolves, pishachas mounted on boars and lions, and the bhootas on flying rodents and hyenas. Some of these monsters had one huge eye, some had two and some had none at all though they were still able to see. The asuras following them had three or more heads and rode on elephants and horses. The dreaded Ketumalee and Netraasura led their thundering army, uprooting trees and mountains to be used as weapons. The nagas slithered to the battleground in their thousands to avenge the death of the nagakanya.

Hasmukha sat beside his friend, whom he still called Vama, telling him about the vast army that was arrayed against them. 'It will be difficult, perhaps impossible to win against them,' he said. 'We have merely one legion fighting with us while their phalanx extends to the horizon and beyond. The commoners love us, but they have neither the arms nor the training to fight the asuras.'

Mayavati was with them too in their tent, wondering if she had made a mistake. The more she looked at the enemy legions, the more she feared the consequences of taking them on. What chance did Pradyumna have against the demon horde when this was his first battle? Her love for the young warrior made her vulnerable to fear and undermined her courage.

'The odds are stacked against us. I blame myself for forcing you to fight him,' she said miserably. 'I was so happy that my prayers had brought you to me, but little did I know that the gods were laughing at us. They knew we were not destined to live together. My karma is so dark that death waits to strike you down again. Perhaps Yama wishes me to give up my life as I had promised before. I am ready to make the sacrifice, my lord, if this will ensure your victory.'

Sandilya too was anxious. Their army had pledged their loyalty to Pradyumna and would fight to the death. Pradyumna showed excellent promise, but the guru was not certain that he was ready to take on the might of the asuras with his new powers. Instead of protecting the young man, had he pushed him beyond his capabilities? Had his own ambition clouded his thinking, leading them to the edge of disaster? How would he face Mayavati if the worst were to happen?

Pradyumna looked at their downcast faces and rose from his seat. The others looked up at him in silence. He stood erect, his face glowing like the rising sun on top of the eastern mountains. His muscled forearms bore deep wounds from the gruelling training sessions that had taken over his days and nights. His stance was assured. He showed every sign of transforming himself into the son of the lord of all living beings.

'This is not the time to lose heart,' said Pradyumna, refusing to give in to his own doubts. They had inspired him with their strength and now he must do the same for them. 'I agree with you that our foe is mighty. But we cannot draw back from the battle like cowards. Do not forget that we are led by Guru Sandilya, the finest student of Bhargavarama. Our commander is Hasmukha, who laughs as he effortlessly denudes the battlefield of enemies. We have the support of the virtuous Sunakha and the unmatched mahamaya wielded by Mayavati. Why then should we allow our fears to defeat us even before the battle has begun?'

The council sat together with renewed hope to plan their strategy and determine how they could use wile and speed to succeed against the superior numbers of the asuras.

Once they had worked out the warcraft, Pradyumna rose to carry out his other duties, leaving them with a message of inspiration.

'Guruji, you told us that the battle against evil is never easily won,' he said. 'You goaded us with tales of battles that Lord Vishnu has fought against the asuras through the ages. Honour, you said, is the only thing that is permanent in an impermanent world. At last we have the honour to fight in the name of Vishnu, in the name of dharma. Let us fight then and rid the earth of the evil that chokes her. Let us fight until victory is ours.'

Bugles, drums and other instruments of the asuras boomed and rumbled, issuing a challenge to the upstart.

Pradyumna left the conclave to meet his men. The commoners had followed him readily into battle, for they were eager to end their suffering under Kaalasura. The demon killed them on a whim and snatched the fruits of their hard labour. They longed for peace under a benevolent ruler and the freedom to worship their gods. When they learned that their prince was the son of Krishna, their god on earth, come to deliver them from the asura, they rejoiced in the vindication of their faith. His abduction, his upbringing as an asura prince, his being cast out by Kaalasura and his resurgence to claim the throne—these became part of a heroic tale that was told and retold. People crowded the rooftops, waiting for the first glimpse of their deliverer, and joined him with fervour in their hearts and crude tools as their weapons.

When Pradyumna appeared before them in his armour, his men cheered him as the true heir of their Blue God. 'Look at the splendour of his body and face. How could anyone mistake him for an asura?' said one soldier. 'If I were Kaalasura, I would be too scared to step out of my palace,' said another.

However, there were many sceptics too, who expressed their doubts freely. 'Kaalasura's demons are brutal and powerful and have killed thousands, whereas this youth has spent his life in dalliance and dance. Even if he is the son of god, his body is that of a mortal. How will he overcome the demonic hordes?' they said.

Pradyumna climbed up to a raised platform to address them all. 'Today you have every reason to be proud,' he said. 'You are beginning a war to take back your land and honour from a tyrant who causes agony and death wherever he goes. We must gird ourselves to fight to the death to claim what is ours. We will fight in the name of Krishna!'

Pradyumna's men cheered and hollered, sounding their drums and trumpets and waving banners with the emblem of the makara. They set off to their battle stations on the wide plateau outside the city. The earth shuddered as the asuras took up positions against them—the eleven sons of Kaalasura along with their mobs, arrayed like an insurmountable mountain wall. Weapons glinted in the sunlight and flags fluttered proudly. Horses and elephants shifted restlessly as they waited for the action to begin. Conches signalled the commencement of battle.

Across the field flew a silver chariot yoked with snow-white horses bearing a heroic figure clad in white silk, rising like the full moon on a dark night. It was Pradyumna, the fair son of the Dark One, come to lead his men into the battle for dharma. His warriors raised conches to their lips to declare their challenge and brandished their weapons. Their war cry reverberated across the field.

The sons of Kaalasura felt a new fear strike their hearts when they saw Pradyumna's splendid form and courage. Had they underestimated the powers of the enemy?

Chitrasena shook off his unease and charged forward. 'We spared your life once, pretender. We showed you clearly that you were a changeling in our midst. Why then do you court death again by challenging us?'

'This is not a quest for a throne, but a quest for dharma,' Pradyumna replied. 'Move out of my way or it will be you who faces death.'

'So speaks the weakling who hides behind his harlot. Do you think Mayavati's powers will save you in this battle too, fool?'

'No, I will fight you myself. My wife will stay out of the battle unless I invoke her.'

Mayavati heard his oath and worried that he was increasing the odds against himself.

'Pray to your gods then,' said Chitrasena, sounding the call to attack. His army charged towards the enemy like a hurricane smashing into a tidal wave. The asuras rushed forward with lusty cries, overwhelming Pradyumna's troops with javelins, discs, cudgels, spears and battleaxes. Heads rolled off, bodies were bludgeoned and limbs strewn to the eight directions.

Death cut a wide swathe through the ranks of Pradyumna's men. The commoners fighting with makeshift weapons were the first to fall before the demons who surged ahead like the Pralaya, the end of the world. The screams of the dying men struck terror in the hearts of their mates who began to flee. The asuras chased them down and gouged out pieces of their flesh that they swallowed whole. The beasts that served as their mounts lashed out with hoof, claw and fang to shred the fleeing foot soldiers.

Pradyumna and Hasmukha fought as if each were a phalanx of soldiers himself, shooting a hundred arrows in the time it took the enemy to shoot one. They whirled and battered their foes with sword and mace, sending the asuras howling in fear. Their weapons flew faster than thought, imbued with the flame of righteousness. They hewed off craggy heads, scaly backs, and mountainous thighs and chests, fighting back to back, screaming challenges to the enemy.

But when they killed ten of their foe, a hundred surged in
to fill the breach. Their valour could only delay the rout of their
forces, not prevent it. The demons ripped out the entrails of
the fallen and kicked their heads around in macabre play. They
used sorcery on the men, sending them into convulsions and
making them vomit pieces of their own flesh. They shrieked
fiercely as they stomped on the enemy and pounded them into
the ground.

As gore flooded the battlefield, Mayavati stood watching,
unable to help, bound by her lord's oath. Pradyumna's valour
was equal to that of his father. But a war is not won merely
by ambition and passion; success depends on superior strength,
strategy and above all, the karma of the leader.

Was Pradyumna fated to win?

16

The Revenge

The growing death toll gnawed at Pradyumna's resolve. Had he plunged into battle without sufficient thought? Had his thirst for revenge blinded him? Would it be wiser to retreat now and fight later when the odds were in his favour? He drew his guru aside during a pause in the battle and disclosed his fears.

'I am to blame for our terrible plight,' he said. 'I brought death upon these innocents only to stare now at a humiliating defeat. How could I have hoped to win when our numbers are so few?'

'I will repeat what you said yourself,' said Sandilya. 'This is not the time to doubt yourself. The power of evil is such that it deceives you into thinking that it has won. This victory, however, is short-lived. In the end, it is virtue that shall triumph. So blaze your way back into battle, my prince!'

Pradyumna set off with a new resolve, cutting down the enemy like Yama himself with his staff of death. He cast his javelin on a demon wolf that clutched a soldier in its slavering jaw, slicing its head off in a crimson burst. He flayed limbs, shattered bodies and slaughtered countless asuras. His silver chariot seemed to be everywhere at once, appearing in a puff of smoke wherever the battle was at its fiercest.

The dead asuras and their beasts piled up on the battleground. Hyenas and wolves slunk in to feast on the corpses while vultures screeched overhead.

Pradyumna's men fought with new hope. For the first time, Sandilya began to wonder if the tide had turned. He charged to the side of his young student to combine his strength with Pradyumna's.

The gods, who had been watching with doubt, were finally convinced that they were witnessing the birth of a new hero. 'Pradyumna has proved his valour against an asura who defeated us all and snatched my throne,' said Indra, who yearned to regain his place as the king of the heavens. 'But even the son of Vishnu cannot outlast a battalion on his own. And if he were to fail now, we will all have to cower in terror again.'

'His courage in battle has made him worthy of our help,' said Agni. 'Pradyumna is our only hope in the face of the humiliation Kaalasura heaps on us every day.'

Indra cast a spell over the battlefield so that time stood still and the combatants froze in mid-stride. He flew down on his elephant Airavataa and blessed Pradyumna with his vajra. He gave him his own chariot, with the divine Matali as charioteer. Agni gave him the use of his invincible astras, and Varuna blessed him with his noose of water, which could choke hundreds of foes in a moment.

Pradyumna prostrated himself before the deities in gratitude.

Indra restored the ebb and flow of time and the battle resumed. A sudden flurry of action in the asura army heralded the arrival of a new warrior; Kaalasura's commander Ketumalee had entered the fray and advanced rapidly towards Pradyumna.

'Prepare to die, coward!' roared Ketumalee. 'Feast your eyes on my form, for it will be the last thing you see before you die.'

Pradyumna's blood chilled as he saw the old enemy who had humiliated him time and again. This time his queen could not intervene to stave off his death.

'Courage, my lord,' Mayavati's voice whispered in his ear. 'Avenge your dishonour at his hands. Send him flying to where Yama, with his thirty-two arms and fanged mouth, waits for him.'

Pradyumna's fear passed. 'I remember every humiliation I suffered at your hands, demon,' he growled. 'I swear that I will wash my shame in your blood today and make you pay for your crimes.'

Ketumalee hurled a disc towards Pradyumna, burning with blue fires that set the air ablaze. Pradyumna blocked it with Indra's vajra and the disc crumbled into dust. The demon roared and let loose a torrential flood that nearly swept Pradyumna's chariot away, but the son of god sent up a prayer to Agni and discharged the Agneyaastra, the weapon of flames, which vaporized the waters. The demon split himself into several animal forms that converged on Pradyumna with cloven hoofs, fangs and horns. The warrior unleashed a flurry of arrows that severed their heads. Ketumalee resumed his usual form and returned to his chariot, only to face Pradyumna's raging volley of arrows that took off the heads of his charioteer and his horses. Five more arrows blasted the wheels and axle of the demon's chariot. Before Ketumalee could recoup, Pradyumna struck with his mace and smashed his head to pulp.

The deafening cheers that followed Ketumalee's demise brought Netraasura flying to this corner of the field.

'Take me on if you dare, coward,' cried Netraasura as he galloped forward on the back of a hideous dragon. 'I have sworn to kill you and take your harlot to bed.'

'I will tear out the tongue that speaks ill of my queen,' Pradyumna roared. 'You are foolish to think that you can kill

me. Did you not see what happened to Ketumalee? The blood
of the young girls you ravished is calling for your death. The
priests you tortured rejoice now that your end is near. Run
away and see if you can escape the dreaded arm of justice.'

Netraasura flew at him in a hot rage, hurling axes and
spiked maces tipped with poison. Pradyumna shot a luminous
cloud of arrows to protect himself and his chariot, killing a host
of asuras. The soldiers slipped and stumbled in the now knee-
deep gore on the field. The beasts ridden by the asuras deserted
their masters to feast on the corpses and drink the flowing
blood.

'I dare you to fight with me, one on one,' screamed
Netraasura. 'Do you have the guts, weakling?'

Pradyumna descended from his chariot in reply, though his
charioteer Matali whispered a warning. The two foes charged
at each other like wild elephants, their maces crashing together
with the sound of thunder. Blood gushed from their wounds,
but they continued to fight. Their men formed a circle to cheer
them on. Netraasura struck with his bludgeon. Pradyumna
stepped aside, but the blow glanced off his thigh. His eyes
clouded with unimaginable pain. He directed his mind away
from the pain and rushed towards Netraasura.

'Don't look at his third eye or you will be paralysed,'
Mayavati's voice warned him.

The image of Arjuna shooting at his target while looking
at its reflection in a pool of water flashed through his mind.
He lifted his shield and looking at the demon's reflection in it,
heaved his mace at him. Netraasura crashed to the earth like a
colossal tree, crushing many of his army under him.

The devas showered flowers on the brave Pradyumna, but
the battle was far from over.

The Mighty One now had to destroy Kaalasura's ruthless
sons. His hope was that the asura princes would be caught

unprepared, secure in the belief that their huge numbers meant assured victory.

Chitrasena called out to the youth he had always hated. 'Surrender to us, boy. Do not force us to soil our swords with the blood of a baseborn fool. Look at our troops whose numbers rival the waves in the sea. Run away if you want to save yourself.'

'Wicked spawn, my birth is far superior to yours,' replied Pradyumna. 'You and your brothers advance like fools, blind to the abyss that yawns at your feet. Our forces may be small, but we have dharma on our side. You will be destroyed in the tidal wave that now sweeps over the earth.'

On came the asuras, brandishing swords, tossing trees and sending forth occult weapons. They wrenched off heads, vaulted over bodies and jeered as they shrugged off axes and arrows hurled at them.

'You will lose the battle within the hour when faced with their numberless troops,' Matali warned Pradyumna. 'Pray to Indra for his Aindraastra that will bring a thunderstorm of arrows crashing from the sky.'

The warrior invoked Indra who gave him his fierce weapon, which inundated the enemy with a fusillade of arrows. Pradyumna, Hasmukha and Sandilya hurtled forward to finish the enemy off. They wiped out ten of Kaalasura's sons, who were accustomed to hiding behind the threat of their demonic armies.

Srutasena, the only son who survived the onslaught, goaded his horse with a cruel spur and escaped to their citadel. He ran inside in a panic and broke the news to his father.

'We are lost, we are defeated!' he wailed. 'Pradyumna fights like ten Indras and has killed all ten of my brothers. Their bodies lie untended, food for the ravenous beasts. I am the only survivor, but perhaps not for long.' His hysterical lament struck fear in the hearts of the assembly.

Kaalasura's eyes rolled like a madman's. His sons killed by the viper he had nursed in their nest, now in league with his favourite queen . . . This could not be true! His evil karma held him firmly in its grip. He concluded that this was all a hallucination sent by the gods to torment him.

'Why do you lie, fool?' he roared.

'It is the truth, my father. No one can stop the warrior that Vama has become. The gods help him with their boons and their weapons, calling him the long-lost son of Krishna.'

'Cease this foolishness! If this story were true, why did they not come to his rescue all these years? The boy is nothing but the son of a cowardly cowherd.'

Srutasena grew frenzied as his father refused to listen. He moaned in fear and screamed, 'We must escape at once or we too will lose our heads!'

'I know what this is,' said Kaalasura. 'You are a phantom sent to frighten me.' He sprang from his throne and ran his sword through Srutasena's heart. 'Come to me, my son,' he ordered. 'I have freed you from the demon that possessed you.'

His courtiers gawked at the mangled body that lay motionless on the ground.

Kaalasura watched and waited. Then, as the truth dawned on him, he let out an anguished wail, a ghastly cry that echoed to the skies.

'Did I kill my son? The youngest, my most precious, the last of my sons? I am a fool, I am a cursed father,' he mourned, beating his breast.

But his arrogance soon rose to cloud his mind again. 'The great Kaalasura does not run away,' he proclaimed. 'I am the Trilokadipati who defeated Indra, Agni, Yama and Varuna. I swear now upon the body of my son that I will bind Vama with my sorcery and slay him.'

17

Adi Shakti

Kaalasura's war chariot, glorious, golden, was drawn by a thousand roaring bears yoked with hissing serpents. It was as tall as a small mountain and armed with an inexhaustible store of golden spears, bows and arrows. Tiger skins decked the body of the chariot and the skulls of the many beasts and men the demon had slain dangled from the frame. Four formidable war ministers, eight thousand cavalry, a million infantry soldiers, two hundred war chariots and countless serpents escorted him on to the battlefield.

Pradyumna's men looked at the massive force in despair. They had already battled scores of demons, Netraasura, Ketumalee and Kaalasura's ten sons. Their own army was severely depleted and the survivors bore terrible wounds. Yet here came another retinue, armed with macabre weapons and led by the asura who made the three worlds tremble.

Mayavati saw the asuras thundering forward, turning cartwheels with the joy of battle, and felt a deep foreboding. As the emperor's wife, she had watched Kaalasura emerge unscathed after battling the devas and their celestial weapons. He was an expert in sorcery and strategy, and respected none of the rules of dharmic war. Pradyumna had to break through the asura's defences somehow, but what if he couldn't? It was too terrible a thought for her to contemplate.

Soon, the two forces stood face-to-face. Conches were sounded to signal the start of war. Kaalasura roared out a taunt. 'I thought you would have run away to graze your father's cattle. Instead, you stand quivering before the king of kings.'

'Do you know who you are speaking to?' asked Pradyumna. 'Did you not hear Narada's prophecy that I was born to kill you? You are the one who must tremble and beg forgiveness. And maybe, I will spare your life.'

'Empty threats from a weakling! Have you said your farewells to your conniving wife? Tell her you will not be separated from her for long, for I will dispatch her to naraka soon after I claim your head. Come on, pretender! Look upon the face of your death.'

The skies were blanketed by the storm of arrows that the two foes shot at each other. Pradyumna knew that he had to make a swift end to the battle before his army collapsed. He unleashed an astra that enveloped Kaalasura's army in darkness. Taking advantage of the confusion caused in the enemy ranks, he and his lieutenants ploughed in to slaughter them. Kaalasura countered with an incandescent astra that lit up the battlefield like the fire at the end of time. His men hurled huge boulders on Pradyumna's soldiers, which the warrior repelled with gusts of fierce wind.

A master of sorcery, Kaalasura employed his mystic powers to rain phantom lions and elephants on his foe. Realizing that these were mere illusion, the prince reassured his soldiers and dispelled them with his mahamaya. The asura then showered them with real beasts that hacked and clawed them to death. He transformed into a gigantic lion and sprang at Pradyumna's chariot, knocking Matali off and slashing at the horses so they ran amuck. Swiftly the prince flung Varuna's noose around the lion's neck and began to choke it. Its huge tongue lolled out and its eyeballs began to bulge. Scrambling to save himself, Kaalasura reverted to his own form, climbed into his chariot and fled to the outer regions of the battlefield.

'This youth fights like no god I know,' he said. 'I should have killed him when he was a child. Now all my powers seem insufficient.'

'Yes, my king,' agreed his commander. 'He grows stronger each day with the blessings of the Trimurti. The only way to kill him is to use Durga's mace that you won through your harsh penance.'

Kaalasura's eyes gleamed and pride surged to his head again. 'The mace that no god or demon can survive . . . it will rid me of this upstart forever. I will use it to send him headfirst into naraka.'

'But think carefully before you act, my lord. Did the goddess not impose conditions on how you could use it?'

'I can employ it only once, and that too when my life is at stake. What better time than now, when I stand alone, bereft of my brave sons?'

Indra, who had spread his protection around Pradyumna, descended to his tent to warn him of the danger. 'The asura's next assault will mean your end, for he plans to use a weapon against which even my vajra is powerless,' he said. 'He plans to invoke Durga's mace, imbued with the powers with which she killed the asuras Sumba and Nisumba.'

'Does this mean that the war is over? Have my people and I lost? How terrible to have come so far and lost so many, only to face defeat . . .'

'There is one hope still, that the goddess herself will protect you like she did once before. But to achieve this, you must convince her that your purpose is noble and that your cause righteous.'

So saying, Indra blessed him and returned to devaloka.

'I will not give up now,' declared Pradyumna, beginning a fierce invocation to the goddess. He chanted her praises as the destroyer of evil, the slayer of demons, the bestower of moksha and the abode of strength. He addressed her by her countless names. But the destroyer of asuras, Sarvasuravinasha, did not grant him the boon he sought.

Instead, she inflicted upon him alternating blasts of incendiary heat and chilling cold, making him burn and shiver, tremble and shriek. But still he persisted in prayer. Then she sent down a torrent of the most loathsome creatures who dug into his flesh, gouging out his eyes and eating away at his organs.

'Kill me if you so desire, my fierce mother,' he cried out. 'I submit myself to your will.'

And then, when his senses began to fade into oblivion, the goddess appeared in a beam of light that enveloped him and healed his tortured body.

'May your divine mace show mercy on me,' he sobbed, his forehead touching the ground at her feet. 'Bless your child, Adi Shakti.'

'Tathastu—so be it, my son,' she said, bathing him with her grace.

Pradyumna raised his eyes to worship the radiant goddess seated on a rampant lion, holding aloft her bow and arrows, her spear and thunderbolt.

The next morning, Kaalasura's battle cry roused the opposite camp as his chariot tore up the ground and came to a stop before Pradyumna.

'Today is the last day of your life, pretender,' he taunted. 'Your men will watch while I burn you in the flame of my anger. They will weep as they see me avenge the killing of my sons. The world will understand the fate that awaits braggarts who defy their emperor.'

'You are the pretender, Kaalasura, not I. You tremble in fear after seeing how I squashed your commanders and your sons. Flee now if you wish to live a little longer. But be warned that I will hunt you down wherever you may hide.'

'You talk boldly, wretch, but it'll be your men who flee the field. For I will turn my wrath on them the moment you fall.'

Kaalasura raised his massive arm and displayed a mace that glittered with an unearthly fire. 'Look upon the weapon of Durga that will bring your worthless life to an end,' he roared. 'Soon you will be dead and I will dance upon your shattered bones.'

He hurled the mace at Pradyumna's chest with a force strong enough to break a massive mountain in two. The divine mace flew towards the challenger, searing the air with its cosmic power. Time froze. The skies burned red. And the seas filled with blood.

Pradyumna stood still, eyes closed, staunch in his faith, hands joined in worship of the goddess. As the mace drew nearer, his soldiers wailed, and Kaalasura shouted that victory was imminent.

And then—the miracle happened. The mace morphed into a garland that fell around Pradyumna's neck. A luminous light enveloped him. His army shouted, 'Jai Durga Mata!' and raised their weapons over their heads.

The asura blinked. Pradyumna stood unscathed, adorned with a garland of blue lilies. What had happened? A deep foreboding filled Kaalasura's heart. What was he to do now? He had nothing left to fight with; his body seemed drained of every drop of blood. He would have to hide if he hoped to live. He fled from the field to his tent.

An awful voice interrupted his dismal thoughts. 'Do not fear, Kaalasura. I am here to help you.'

Kaalasura looked up to see a ten-headed serpent, his mouths gaping to reveal his hideous fangs. Festooned on his body were thousands of hissing snakes.

'You help me? Do you know who I am? Do you realize I am the king of the nagas and you are my slave like the others?'

'I know who you are, Trilokadipati. But you do not know that I am the invincible Nagapasha, created by Brahma to destroy Nagasura.'

'A giant-killer! Where were you hiding when I was killing the nagas?'

'The deceitful Vishnu was the cause of my absence. He grew jealous of my dominion over the three worlds and laid a cunning trap for me. He said, "Stay away from the islands ruled over by my eagle Garuda. His huge body fills the skies, his wings shake the earth, and the world mistakes him for Agni because of his lustre. Snakes are his mortal enemies, and he will tear you to pieces if you confront him."

'"You think I am afraid of a mere bird?" I hissed, my pride cut to the quick. "I will challenge this Garuda in his own domain." Alas, I was no match for the winged monster who reduced me almost to death, forcing me to seek refuge at Shiva's feet. I have been waiting since then for an opportunity such as this, to avenge myself on Vishnu and his vile bird.'

'But why would you help me, when I torched the mansions in nagaloka and took your queens prisoner?'

'An enemy's enemy is a friend. I hate no one as much as I hate Vishnu who forced me to spend years cowering in fear. Use me as your arrow and I will devour his son with my venom.'

This foolish snake could very well serve my purpose, thought Kaalasura as he rode back into the battlefield, accompanied by Nagapasha. He headed straight towards Pradyumna, who shone like the morning sun in Indra's chariot.

Kaalasura gave no warning as he crept up behind his enemy and let loose his serpent arrow. Nagapasha flew through the air, releasing thousands of snakes that fell on to Pradyumna's army, spitting poison and striking terror. Pradyumna had no time to turn and defend himself before Nagapasha cannoned into him, suffocating him with his coils and stretching his many mouths to sting him with a thousand fangs.

The grisly poison burned through Pradyumna's veins. His body turned blue, his eyes glazed over and his senses deserted him. An ominous silence descended on the battlefield and darkness fell even though the sun had just risen.

'Recite the Garuda mantra and save yourself,' Mayavati's voice whispered in his ears. But every cell in his body was numb and every breath he drew was agonizing. His limbs slowed their desperate flailing.

'I will break my lord's command and go to his help,' Mayavati cried out. 'I cannot watch him die.' She summoned the forces of mahamaya to help her.

But her efforts were met by a yawning emptiness. Instead of a surge of divine energy, she heard the echo of Kaalasura's demonic laughter.

'Treacherous woman, did you think you would get away with your deceit? Your powers are now in my control, trapped in my occult hold. You can do nothing but witness his agony.'

Mayavati's mind flashed to the cage that imprisoned her shadow. She struggled to tear down the bars and free herself, but her arms were feeble, bending like the slender rushes that grow by the side of the river.

'No, no,' she screamed as she watched the warrior grow still.

'The upstart is dead!' bellowed Kaalasura. 'I have killed the man-god's son. Let the revelry begin.'

Drums pounded out a frenzied beat as the drunken asuras followed the victorious king back to his citadel.

Pradyumna felt himself being swept away to the shores of the Vaitarani, the river of death. Mayavati railed at the Trimurti for taking her lord from her again. Hasmukha and his soldiers stood frozen, unable to accept this terrible end to the battle. Their eyes flooded as they gazed at the countless bodies rotting in the sun, broadcasting their defeat. There was nothing left for them to do except cremate their dead and mourn their cause.

'Alas, dharma has been vanquished today,' said Sandilya. 'We must flee to the jungles if we want to escape Kaalasura's ire. Or plunge into the fire and immolate ourselves.'

Mayavati had already escaped to a different plane, immersing herself in her memories of happier times. She was flying over ethereal lands, hand in hand with her beloved. She was on his lap, his eyes gazing into hers. He was calling to her to join him in a world from which there was no return . . .

She had in her hand a vial that would unite them in death if not in life.

18

Arjuna of the Thousand Hands

The wails of those who mourned the fall of Pradyumna and his army had tapered to a muted moan. The eyes of the survivors had run dry and their hearts had lost hope; now they looked for ways to end their own lives.

Then a great wind arose, breaking the masts from which the banners flew. Brilliant flashes of lightning lit up the sky. Thunderclaps shook the mountaintops. Giant trees were ripped from their roots.

A deep fear took hold of Nagapasha.

He loosened the coils with which he had bound Pradyumna and raised his hood to survey the surroundings. The smaller serpents skittered into holes or hid under the dead beasts on the field.

Hasmukha and his army looked up as a breathtaking light filled the heavens. They saw the mighty Garuda soaring towards them, his golden wings blotting out the sun. His massive body was emerald in colour and his eyes were piercing. He vaulted to the ground like an incandescent thunderbolt, his loud shrieks shaking the earth.

'Vishnu's winged comrade is here,' said Sandilya. 'Obeisance to the warrior who has come to save the lord's son but alas, you are too late.'

Nagapasha released Pradyumna from his grasp and tried to escape before the giant bird spotted him. But Garuda was swifter than thought. He lifted the evil snake in his huge beak and ripped him to pieces with his gigantic claws. His screeches echoed across the battlefield as if to announce that his long-time foe was dead.

Garuda then bent over the dying prince, flapping his wings to set off a refreshing breeze, and murmured softly to the battered warrior. Pradyumna heaved, drawing in one tortured breath and then another. His strength was returning, bit by bit. He opened his eyes to the radiance of Garuda and folded his hands in worship.

Garuda spoke to him in his majestic voice. 'Vir Pradyumna!' he said. 'I come to pay tribute to a friendship that extends across the yugas. Arise from your swoon, brave warrior, and lay claim to success.'

The prince's strength multiplied a hundred fold. He rose to his feet in one swift movement and bowed to the celestial visitor.

'You must seek the help of Bhargavarama, for Kaalasura can be killed only by his divine axe,' said Garuda. His task completed, he let out a magnificent cry, unfolded his colossal wings and soared into the heavens to return to Vaikunta.

Pradyumna's troops exulted in his miraculous revival. They beat their gongs and drums, blew their conches and danced with joy.

The warrior looked for the woman he loved, for the queen he had thought of in his dying moments.

'Where is Mayavati?' he asked. 'Where is she?'

'In your tent,' said Sandilya. A look of horror crossed his face. 'She did not wish to live after you died. I tried to turn her mind . . .'

Pradyumna flew like the wind, praying to all the gods to save her. He rushed into the tent and saw Mayavati sitting with her eyes closed, removed from the world in mind and spirit, the poison ready in her hands.

'No, no!' he screamed, knocking the vial from her hand. 'I am here. I am not dead. Return to me, my love.'

Mayavati opened her eyes and looked at him with wonder. 'You came back to me. You are alive,' she whispered, taking him in her arms.

They devoured each other with their bodies and souls, still afraid to believe that they had won a reprieve. They would make the best use of what might still be their last day on earth, for the next day was sure to bring Kaalasura back into the fray.

Finally, they left their tent in order to convene a war council with Sandilya, Sunaka and Hasmukha, to discuss their strategy for the final war.

'Kaalasura has returned to his fortress in the belief that I am dead and they have won,' said Pradyumna. 'But his spies will soon discover the truth and he will return with all his might.'

'Do not lose hope,' said Sandilya. 'The lord of the sky, Gaganeshwara, has told you how you can kill Kaalasura. You must invoke Bhargavarama and secure his axe.'

'How? Tell me everything about him, so that I may discern the path forward. I know he is fierce—so fierce that he beheaded his own mother Renuka on the orders of his father Sage Jamadagni. What kind of son would do this? Isn't killing one's mother a more heinous crime than disobeying one's father?' asked Pradyumna.

Sandilya nodded. 'Bhargava knew that well. His soul was in torment. It was his sworn duty to obey his father who was also his guru. At the same time, he did not want to kill his mother and his brothers.'

'Then?'

'He knew that Jamadagni would kill them himself if Bhargava refused. He had to find a way out of his dilemma, and that too at once. He decided to obey his father and severed the heads of his loved ones, one by one. And then, as he had expected, his father granted him a boon as his reward. Bhargava requested that Jamadagni restore his family to life.'

'A wise strategy, indeed . . .'

'Bhargava is one of Vishnu's avatars; he took birth on earth in order to re-establish dharma. The earth and even the heavens were being threatened by the lawless and arrogant Kshatriyas. Bhargava killed their king Kartaviryarjuna and decimated the entire clan. Then he performed an Aswamedha or horse sacrifice and gave away all the conquered lands to priests as he did not crave wealth.'

'A warrior whose mind was focused on a higher plane . . .' *No wonder he taunted me in my dreams on my dissipated life.*

'Yes. Bhargava retreated to Mount Gandhamadana to worship Lord Dattatreya, who is the embodiment of the Trimurti. Dattatreya blessed him with the treatise *Tripura Rahasya*, the mystery beyond the Trinity, which is the secret to freeing mankind from the cycle of life.'

'My obeisance to the Chiranjeevi who will live forever.'

'Life can never be eternal. When we say he is a Chiranjeevi, it means that Bhargava will live until the end of this kalpa. He will spend all his days performing penances for the slaying of the Kshatriyas.'

'But why perform penances when he was born to kill them and save the world?'

'Killing is a sin, and even a god must pay for it. That is the law of dharma.'

'So if he is still atoning for his sins from long ago, why would he add to his burden by helping me kill Kaalasura? I fear that this is not likely to happen.'

'You forget that his axe is the axe of dharma. Surrender to him and seek his blessings. He is sure to help you.'

Sandilya taught Pradyumna the rituals of purification. He taught him how to focus his mind on Jamadagni's son and begin his tapas. This quest would be tougher than any he had undertaken before, but he could not afford to fail.

Mayavati, Sandilya and the entire army joined Pradyumna in prayer, seeking the grace of the warrior saint. They knew that time was not in their favour. Bhargava would have to answer their prayers before Kaalasura attacked again or all would be lost.

Pradyumna trembled, for he was alone, though he was in the midst of his people. A foreboding of disaster oppressed his mind.

It seemed as if several yugas passed by while they waited. The soldiers began to prepare for their death. Others continued to pray and hope.

A blast shook the earth. Horses and elephants stampeded. The wind gusted and blew the armour off the backs of the soldiers. Mayavati chanted louder. Pradyumna opened his eyes only to close them against the flame-like radiance that threatened to sear his vision. Dare he hope that Bhargava had come to bless him?

Sandilya had said that Bhargava's lustre was such that only those who were pure at heart could look upon his face. Pradyumna lowered his eyes, prostrated himself before the austere visitor, and submitted his soul to him.

'Look at me,' said a resonant voice. Pradyumna narrowed his eyes and looked up at a giant of a man clad in deerskin, with matted locks and a glowing face. Bhargava was not carrying Shiva's axe but he did have the kamandal or vessel in which a rishi carries sacred water.

'We have met before, don't you remember?' asked Bhargava. 'You were an arrogant and reckless fool. You killed the pious, and brought death to generations of Kshatriyas. I snatched your life to put an end to your depredations. And now, you have the audacity to invoke me and seek my help?'

As his voice rose, the earth opened up at Pradyumna's feet with a deafening boom. He looked right into the bowels of hell. 'This is the world where you belong,' said Bhargava. 'See how the sinners are beaten by rods and clubs. They cry for salvation where there is none. They are parched by thirst and tormented by hunger. And eaten alive by snakes and vultures.'

Pradyumna's marrow froze with a terrible fear. This voice from his nightmare had come to usher him to his death. But what was this crime of which he was being accused?

He saw the sage raise his kamandal and sprinkle some holy water on his head. The world splintered around him and he hurtled into his past life.

Kartaviryarjuna, great king of the Haiheyas, blessed by Dattatreya with a thousand hands and a golden chariot that could roam the skies at will. Intoxicated by power, he ravaged the earth and the heavens, defeating and imprisoning even the mightiest of kings, Ravana.

Then his karma took him to the ashram of Bhargavarama's father, Sage Jamadagni.

The rishi welcomed the king and his army respectfully and offered them food and shelter. The spread was so lavish that the king was consumed by envy.

'This feast is grander than any served in my court,' he said. 'How can an ascetic like you commandeer such riches?'

'These are the blessings of Kamadhenu, my fabulous cow, who is dearer to me than my life,' said Jamadagni. 'She is a gift of the cosmic ocean, and the gods reside in her. She has the power to grant me anything I desire.'

The king was eager to possess this miraculous cow. 'You should not hide a treasure like this in your ashram,' he said. 'Give me your Kamadhenu and I will shower you with riches beyond imagination.'

'I tell you she is my mother and my goddess, and you ask me to sell her to you?' roared Jamadagni. 'Abandon your greed and go your way, Kartavirya.'

The king's fury clouded his mind. He would not be thwarted. He commanded his soldiers to carry the cow and her calf away to his capital.

Kamadhenu and her calf shed pitiful tears as the soldiers dragged them from their home. Jamadagni and his disciples tried to stop them, but they were no match for the king's army.

When Bhargava, who had been away in the forest gathering materials for a yagna, returned to the ashram, he was shocked to see the injured ascetics and the disarray caused by Kartavirya's army. Jamadagni was more agitated than Bhargava had ever seen him, his eyes red and his hair loose as he mourned the loss of his divine mother.

'I swear upon the gods that I will punish Kartavirya and recover Kamadhenu and her calf,' declared Bhargava. He flew after the enemy soldiers with his astral powers, catching up with them just outside their citadel.

The king deployed seventeen formidable platoons of elephants, chariots, horses and infantry to fight the lone enemy. But Jamadagni's warrior son ran through them like a fierce lion taking on a group of hyenas.

Kartavirya himself emerged from his fortress, stringing arrows on five hundred bows with his thousand arms. No one had ever survived a battle with this fearsome warrior. Bhargava calmly shot down all the enemy's arrows with those from his bow.

'Confess your mistake and return the treasure you stole,' he called out to Kartavirya, offering him one last chance to repent. The king replied by uprooting trees and hurling them at him.

Bhargava chanted Shiva's name and raised the axe of dharma. The axe whirled around the enemy like a typhoon and severed his thousand arms, as if they were the hoods of a serpent. Then it flew at Kartavirya's neck and, in one swift move, separated his head from his body.

The triumphant warrior brought Kamadhenu and her calf back to the hermitage. Jamadagni's eyes filled with tears on seeing them again. After lauding his valour, the sage asked Bhargava to retreat to the hills to perform penances for the sin of killing Kartavirya and his soldiers.

However, the battle was not yet over. The angry Kshatriyas decided to avenge their king's death. They stormed into the ashram and attacked the sage and his disciples while they were deep in meditation. Drunk with blood, they beheaded the sages and kicked the heads about, and desecrated the bodies by placing heads on the wrong torsos. Finally, they carried away Jamadagni's head so that his son would not be able to perform the last rites.

Bhargava's intuition warned him of a calamity, and he interrupted his tapasya to return to the ashram. He was stupefied when he saw the carnage. His heart twisted in anguish when he saw his mother wailing beside her husband's headless torso. She beat her breast twenty-one times in grief as she described the desecration that had taken place.

Bhargava's rage rose like a red cloud and blinded him. 'I will avenge this dishonour,' he vowed. 'I will travel the earth twenty-one times to avenge the godless Kshatriyas who killed my father and defiled his body. They will pay for the sin of slaughtering unarmed ascetics.'

He set forth, armed with his axe, bow and arrows, and a murderous heart. He severed their heads, just as they had done to the rishis, and filled five lakes near Kurukshetra with their blood.

Pradyumna quaked.

Slaughter. Decimation. A clan destroyed. All caused by his own excesses as Kartavirya. His evil karma was following him in life after life. It was time to end it.

He lowered his head and bared his neck for Bhargava's blow.

19

The Axe of Dharma

The killing blow did not descend. The silence remained unbroken. Pradyumna raised his head.

Bhargava and he were stranded on an unearthly landscape where time had no meaning. The sage was bathed in a white radiance that was terrible to behold, while Pradyumna was shrouded in the darkness of a soul in naraka.

His tormented soul erupted in words. 'Forgive me, wise one. I shudder as I see the avalanche of death I set off by coveting what was not mine. A world submerged in blood, generations destroyed . . . I wish I could go back in time and remedy my blunder. Alas, I know it is not possible. How foolish of me to think that I should kill again, and that too with your mighty axe! I realize I must retire to the hills in order to perform penances for my sins, in the same way that you did.'

'Did I flee when I had to put down the evil Kartavirya? Did I go back on my vow to rid the world of the sinful Kshatriyas? You speak like the weak prince you are, devoted to the pleasures of the bed. You choose to run away at the first sign of

adversity. You abandon the wife who restored you to life with
her tapasya. You desert your guru, your companions and the
people who risked their lives to support you. All that matters to
you is that you save yourself, leaving the others behind to pay a
horrible price.'

Pradyumna trembled as each word lashed at his soul.
Bhargava's voice rose in scorn. 'A true warrior does not avoid
his duty when it becomes difficult. He does not turn his back
on valour, for it is his only path to heaven. Is this how you
honour Indra, Agni and Varuna who came to your aid? Is this
how you venerate Durga who turned her mace into a garland
of lilies? Remember Sarparati, the enemy of serpents, who
flew down from his lofty perch in Vaikunta to save you from
Nagapasha. Shake off your base thoughts. Rise and lay waste to
your enemies.'

The young warrior was too agitated to listen. 'I have spilled
too much blood already,' he said. 'How can I spill more? How
can I fight this asura when I know my karma is darker than his?
I will be sending my sweet Hasmukha, his father, my guru and
my beloved queen to their deaths. I will be sacrificing many
thousands who trusted me with their lives, little knowing what
I really am.'

'Your words betray your ignorance, stripling. It is the
nature of this world that whatever is born must die. When
the dead are consigned to the fire, their body is burned to
ashes. But their souls are eternal and inhabit other bodies, as
if casting off worn-out garments and wearing new ones. You
do not decide when you or anyone else dies, just as you do not
control the time of birth. You cannot be responsible if these
people choose to follow you into battle for a cause they believe
in. So shed your fear of death and decide how you should live
instead. Remember, if you retreat now you will be condemning
the world to darkness and evil.'

Pradyumna was still struggling with his inner fears. 'Even if I fight and win this war, how will it help redeem my soul?' he asked. 'It was his lust for conquest that led to Kartavirya's misdeeds. The arrogance of power incited wickedness in Kaalasura and his sons. My heart is paralysed by sorrow and confusion. How can I fight? It would be best if I were to die unresisting at the hands of the asura, in recompense for my earlier sins.' He buried his face in his hands and wept.

Bhargava realized that he was fighting a battle far more difficult than any he had fought before. It was a fight for Pradyumna's spirit. If he failed now, the world would pay a heavy price.

He began to speak in a gentler voice. 'You cannot give up your duty just to avoid adding to your karma. Men must act even if their purpose is only to survive. The wise man acts righteously, without being attached to the fruits of his actions. It is the craving for rewards that leads to lust, greed and anger—the three gates to hell. As Kartavirya, your actions were motivated by greed and arrogance. But now you fight for righteousness, and to fulfil the purpose for which you were born.'

The light of Bhargava's wisdom attacked the darkness of Pradyumna's soul and flooded it with peace. 'Your words unveil the truths hidden from mankind,' he said, 'and show me what I must do.'

'These truths have been spoken earlier—to the sages, to Surya and to Manu, from whom all men were born. And they will be spoken again in the future, whenever man needs god's guidance.'

The panic drained from Pradyumna's soul. Time began to march again. Horses whinnied and pawed the ground. Drums marshalled the soldiers to their positions.

A new fire coursed through Pradyumna's veins. He prostrated himself at Bhargava's feet. 'Your discourse has destroyed my weakness, Bhargava,' he said. 'I surrender to

Vishnu and vow to complete my mission or perish in the attempt. I beg you: have mercy on me.'

Bhargava placed his hand on the prince's head. 'You have shown yourself to be heroic, my son,' he said. 'I would gladly give you my parasu, but I no longer carry it since I became an ascetic. I had to leave it with someone worthy of it, a task that proved almost impossible. No deva or human was able to wield it, as it carried a terrible burden of blood—that of my mother, my brothers and countless Kshatriyas.'

'Which great god now holds your weapon?'

'Not a god, but a goddess. I laid my parasu at the feet of Varahi Devi, the slayer of demons. She is the one with the face of a boar, who is the shakti of Vishnu's varaha avatar. Cast yourself on her mercy and she will bless you with the weapon.' With these words, the noble Bhargava disappeared.

Pradyumna worshipped Varahi with hymns of praise. 'I bow to you, O consort of Sri Vishnu, fifth among the seven goddesses—Brahmi, Maheshwari, Kaumari, Vaishnavi, Varahi, Indrani and Chamundi. I worship you, O source of valour, vigour and victory. I adore you, incomparable goddess, who devours demons and protects her devotees. Let victory ride on my shoulder in this war. I seek refuge in you, boar-faced destroyer of evil.'

She did not appear. Pradyumna continued his prayers, forsaking every thought and the very consciousness of time. His hands formed the sacred mudras, his mouth chanted the Varahi mantra. He raised the living consciousness of the goddess to his heart, then up his spine to his crown so he could tap into his divine purpose. His body thrilled to the sublime, and he became one with the pure force of the Devi.

She appeared before him then, clad in red garments and riding a fierce lion, bearing weapons in each arm—trident, spear, chakra, mace, bow, arrows, thunder, shield and axe. She was infinite, invincible and inimitable. With her came countless yoginis, tantric spirits and demons like brahma rakshasas and yakshas. Her fierce energy blinded Pradyumna and his legs gave way. He paid obeisance, touching his forehead to the ground.

The goddess blessed him with divine vision so he could gaze upon her. 'What is the boon you crave, my son?' she asked.

'Hail to thee, Varahi. Bless me with Bhargava's parasu and the strength to destroy the demon Kaalasura!' he said.

Varahi raised her hand in benediction. 'I bless you, Pradyumna. Return in triumph to Dwaraka where your mother Rukmini awaits, eager to clasp you to her bosom.'

The parasu flew from her hand to his in a brilliant flash. The surge of its power jolted through his whole body. He chanted her names again in ecstasy as she vanished from sight with her spectral brigade.

'Victory to Pradyumna,' proclaimed the devas from the skies.

'Victory to our king,' echoed the soldiers on land.

Many yojanas away, Kaalasura woke from his sleep, his heart pounding with terror, fearful that his end had come. He hurried to his court without his usual pomp and panoply, his senses in disarray. There he found his spies waiting for him.

'Nagapasha is dead, torn to pieces by Pakshiraj, the lord of the birds,' said one of them, too agitated to wait for Kaalasura's permission to speak. 'Garuda has revived Pradyumna, and he is at our gates with a resurgent army.'

Kaalasura reeled, his senses fogging over.

'The people worship Pradyumna as the deliverer, and whisper about strange sights and divine manifestations,' the spy continued. 'The man-god's son sends you a message, my lord.' He stopped, afraid to go on.

Kaalasura snarled and raised a giant arm, ordering him to speak.

'He demands that you come out and face your death, instead of hiding behind your walls like a lowly coward.' The spy stood shivering, waiting for his end.

But it seemed as if the emperor was paralysed. His arrogance and swagger were gone. He huddled on his throne and moaned. To whom could he pray when he had declared himself god?

20

Sambaditya

Days had rolled by, months and then years. Samba, Krishna and Jambavati's son, had shut out the foulness of his disease from his mind and focused instead on the power of healing, immersing himself in chanting the Gayatri mantra to Surya.

Om bhur bhuva svah tat savitur varenyam
Bhargo devasya dhimahi dhiyo yo nah prachodayat

I worship thee, the supreme creator of life, the remover of sin and sorrow, the bestower of light and happiness. Guide my intellect in the right direction.

The seasons changed once more as Samba continued to pray for deliverance. His penances grew in intensity, but Surya did not appear before him. Losing all hope, Samba decided that it would be better to die than to live with the disease coursing through his veins. But before he could take the final step, Surya relented. He appeared in his dazzling chariot drawn by seven white horses that represent the days of the week and the colours of the rainbow. As the chariot wheels turned, they caused day and night, and the changing of the seasons. Guiding his chariot was Aruna, whose body was the red sky that appears at dawn. Aruna was Garuda's elder brother and the father of Jatayu, the vulture king who had fought valiantly to rescue Rama's wife Sita when Ravana abducted her.

Samba opened his bleary eyes with great difficulty when he finally felt Surya's radiance upon him. He wept like a child when he realized that the sun god had answered his plea. He prostrated his deformed body before him, shaking with fear and anxiety.

'I am pleased with your tapasya,' said Surya, his voice booming like thunder. 'Ask now for a boon.'

'You know my suffering, you know my pain. Liberate me, O Surya, from the disease that tortures my body. Give me back the youthful vigour I enjoyed before sin blinded my eyes.'

'So be it,' said Surya. 'Bathe once more in the sacred river and you will return to your former glory. Now, ask for another boon that I offer as reward for your humility.'

'Grant me the honour of building you a temple that will be unsurpassed in glory. Bless the sinners who shall pray there so they too may enjoy your grace.'

'I grant you this boon as well. Let your temple rise to the skies as a warning against the dangers of wealth and pride.'

Samba watched spellbound as the glorious cavalcade rose into the heavens. Then he hurried to the river and plunged into the sacred waters. His lesions melted away. His face and body became even more resplendent than before. As the healing waters flowed over his limbs, he saw a radiant image floating towards him. He lifted it in his arms with reverence.

A voice addressed him from the skies. 'This vigraha of Surya is a gift from Visvakarma, the architect of the gods. He made it from the kalpavriksha, the heavenly tree that fulfils all desires. Install this image on this sacred ground, where sages once had an ashram to worship the sun. The temple you build will be renowned for all time as Konark, the abode of Arka, the Sun.'

Samba ordered his men to bring together the greatest artisans, sculptors and architects in the land to build this temple. Visvakarma came too and used his magical powers to quicken the pace so that the temple would soon take shape, majestic and proud. Its form was inspired by Surya's chariot drawn by seven horses, with twelve pairs of intricately decorated wheels forming the base. The entrance was guarded by a sculpture of two giant lions crushing a war elephant. The elephant in turn was trampling a man.

'The lions and the elephant represent pride and wealth— both of which cause the downfall of man,' said Visvakarma.

Sculptors carved thousands of exquisite images of warriors and deities, dancers and lovers, birds and mythical creatures on the temple walls.

Learned priests installed the image of Surya after performing the prescribed rituals. Seers and kings from every corner of the world came to attend the consecration.

'We have visited many kingdoms and seen many temples, but none equal your tribute to the sun god,' they said to Samba. His mother too praised him and said that his fame now surpassed that of even the devas.

Samba swelled with pride, immediately forgetting the lessons of the past. He began to indulge feverishly in his old pursuits, as if to make up for the deprivations of the past few years.

Narada watched his decline with sorrow and counselled him when he caught him alone without his boorish companions.

'You have forgotten the humility and piety that earned you Surya's blessings, prince,' he said. 'As your pride soars, so will your sins. You will be born again and again in an endless cycle of life and death. You will never rise to the lord, but flounder in a state of sin.'

'Stand aside, Narada, before I raise my hand against you,' said Samba. 'I have not forgotten that you were the reason I was cursed in the first place.'

'Don't you realize that you brought it upon yourself with your actions? You laughed at Durvasa and me, and lusted for your father's wives.'

'But look at me now. I am young and handsome again while you are still ugly. And my pain has resulted in a magnificent temple that the whole world venerates.'

'You forget that you are merely the instrument of the lord—nimitta maatram bhava,' said Narada. 'The gods favour those who are humble, for humility is the mark of greatness. Let me tell you a story of something that happened a long time ago. The Pandya, Chola, Kalinga and Pandava kings had come to visit the grand new city of Dwaraka. I told them I had seen a colossal crocodile and praised him as the most wonderful of creations.

'The crocodile replied that the Ganga was greater than he was as she was home to many creatures like him. I accepted the truth in his words and paid obeisance to Ganga. She said that the sea god was greater than she was as he provided sanctuary to many rivers like her. The sea in turn sang praises to the earth that supported him. The earth paid tribute to the greatness of the mountains that protected her. The mountains hailed Brahma as the supreme power. Brahma praised the four Vedas. The Vedas said they owed their power to the sacred yagnas. Finally, the yagnas said they worshipped Vishnu for he was the Supreme Being.'

Narada took a breath and looked expectantly at Samba. But the young man's face merely revealed his impatience. The sage continued: 'I went to Vaikunta and praised Vishnu as the greatest power in the universe. And do you know what he said? He said that the devotees who prayed to him with pure hearts were greater than he was. When the greatest of the gods is so humble, how can you be so proud? Shake off your conceit if you wish to transform your destiny, prince.'

'My destiny is safe as the saviour of my clan and the world. Go away, rishi, and spout your nonsense elsewhere.'

He strode away to give directions to the men making the final arrangements for the consecration of the temple.

The happy day soon arrived. Trumpets and conches blared. Cymbals and chants followed. The ceremony got underway. Samba watched the rituals from a lofty perch on the back of a caparisoned elephant. He received the first honours, disregarding the venerable seers and kings who had assembled.

'I declare that henceforth this place will be known as Sambapura,' he said. 'The god here will be called Sambaditya, so the world will remember that Samba built the temple to Aditya.'

The old ministers murmured. 'Rethink your decision, king,' they said. 'This name indicates that you are lost to pride, the very quality that Surya asked you to avoid.'

'I listen to no one,' he replied. 'The name shall remain.'

21

Asura Samhaara

The sun had risen on the fateful day when the winner would be decided. Only one of the opponents would survive. Would it be Kaalasura, the invincible warrior of a thousand battles? Or Pradyumna, the mortal son of a distant god?

The mood was sombre in Kaalasura's palace. The king's fear grew as his wives wept and begged him not to set out that day. 'We have seen terrible signs, lord,' they said. 'Our clothes reek of death. Flesh rains from the sky and cold terror grips our hearts.'

A dark fire flashed around the demon king's head, betraying his disturbed mind. Kaalasura threatened to cast his wives into the dungeons if they persisted in weakening his resolve. He ordered the citadel doors be thrown open and sallied out, commanding his forces to follow him. The beasts howled as they poured out on their loathsome vaahanas, armed with their fearsome weapons.

Ready for the onslaught, Pradyumna's men stood beside their valiant leader, who was armed with divine astras and aided by Sandilya, Hasmukha and his commanders.

'Make a quick end of the asura,' Sandilya advised. 'It is time
to relieve Mother Earth of this enormous burden of sin.'

However, this was easier said than done. The demons let fly
a storm of arrows and maces that obscured the sun and flayed
the enemy. Their weapons of sorcery shimmered, shattering
the mortal forces with their dark energy. The battlefield was
once again choked with blood and the screams of dying men.

Hasmukha fought like Lakshmana by the side of Rama,
shooting a glittering stream of arrows to protect his men.
Sandilya employed the Twastarastra that enveloped the
asura army in delusions, causing them to attack one another;
thousands of demons died before Kaalasura could counter
with his own sorcery. He invoked the Parvataastra that made
mountains rise from the earth and rain down on the enemies,
crushing them like ants under an elephant's foot.

Pradyumna sprang to the defence of his men with a fusillade
of arrows that shattered the mountains into pieces that fell
harmlessly to the ground. The soldiers cheered lustily at their
prince's mettle.

Howling like a beast of prey, Kaalasura released his
Sammohanaastra. The soldiers succumbed to its lure and
believed that they were in Indra's court, watching the apsaras
dance. As they dropped their weapons and stood motionless,
the asuras descended on them and hacked them to death.
Sandilya came to their rescue, invoking the Suryaastra, which
dispelled the illusions with its indomitable power.

The other demons wreaked havoc on the soldiers, feasting
on shattered bodies and limbs and lapping up crimson pools
of blood. The occult warriors sliced and diced with their
swords, playing macabre games with their victims. They
created thousands of rampaging lions that caused Pradyumna's
forces to flee in terror. Kaalasura himself assumed a giant form
that reached the skies and advanced on the enemy, crushing

hundreds with every step. He picked up horses and foot soldiers with one sweep of his giant hand, tossed them into his mouth and chewed on them.

Pradyumna streaked like lightning on his chariot and obstructed Kaalasura's path. He aimed the fiery Agneyaastra that was designed to burn through armour and pierce the opponent's heart. Kaalasura thrust his commander in front of him to protect himself. He then wielded his own astra to kill Pradyumna's horses, bringing him crashing to the ground. The asura advanced with a roar to finish him off before he could recover.

Sandilya saw that the prince was in grave danger and shouted to Hasmukha. 'To Pradyumna,' he screamed. 'Fly like the wind. Save him at any cost.'

Hasmukha raced his chariot towards his leader. He reached out an arm to lift him into his own vehicle. Sandilya kept the asura and his demons at bay with a fiery stream of arrows that were swifter than the eye could follow.

The fight grew more desperate as Pradyumna and Kaalasura continued their face-off. Kaalasura's body was riddled with arrows and he bled from a hundred wounds. Pradyumna fought more with his will than his body. The two intercepted each other's astras and deflected them back, killing thousands with each exchange.

Their maces clashed like two comets colliding in the skies. Their swords clanged together, the fiery sparks blinding the spectators. Morning slipped into noon and then the sun began its descent. The fight raged on, with no clear winner.

'It's time to end it!' screamed Sandilya. Pradyumna realized that he would have to take the initiative rather than merely defend himself.

Even as he planned his move, the demon snatched Hasmukha off his chariot and raised him above his head, ready to smash him to the ground.

It was now or never. Pradyumna invoked the divine parasu. It flew into his hand, its head glinting like a ferocious planet, its radiance swamping the occult forces. The young warrior let the axe fly towards the asura.

It hurtled through the sky with the thunder of the Pralaya, flying like the Sudarshana chakra, Vishnu's divine discus. It severed Kaalasura's neck with a tremendous flash and explosion, accompanied by the stench of sulphur. Kaalasura's head rolled to the ground amidst a crimson flood.

Pradyumna flew to snatch Hasmukha in mid-air as he fell from the asura's lifeless hand.

Kaalasura's colossal body fell to the ground, setting off earthquakes that fractured the mountains. A dreadful cry rose from a hundred thousand asuras. In his palace, Kaalasura's wives tore at their flesh in agony. Unholy screams echoed through the realms as the fiends realized that their reign had ended. They would now pay for their sins with their blood and sinew.

The devas and apsaras rejoiced. Rishis, kinnaras and gandharvas chanted: 'Pradyumna, Jaya Jaya!'

'All hail the mighty son of Krishna,' said Sandilya. 'Your samhaara of Kaalasura will inspire all future generations.'

Its task completed, the parasu disappeared in a beam of light. Kaalasura's death released Mayavati's shadow from his spell and the queen flew to her true lord, resplendent in all her beauty and power.

'You have done it, my lord. You have proven yourself a worthy son of the living god,' she exclaimed.

Hasmukha blew a long blast on his conch to announce the victory. The soldiers jumped from earth to heaven and broke out casks of wine.

Pradyumna entered the citadel at the head of a joyous procession. The demons that still lived were put to the sword, but the commoners were spared, for they too had been victims of the asura.

'You have accomplished a mission that even the gods could not,' said Mayavati to her lord when they were finally alone, as she sought to soothe his wounded limbs and his troubled heart.

'My first war has ended in victory and my mind should be at peace. My tortured body aches for the comfort of sleep, yet, even as my eyes close, I startle awake, tormented by the faces of all the men who have died for us. Each of them was born to a woman who loved him, and had a wife and family who await his return with a hope that dwindles by the day. I have come to realize that death and pain are universal, and that a war leaves us with nothing to celebrate.'

His voice faded as he fell into a restless sleep born of exhaustion. Mayavati sat by his side, comforting him with soft murmurs and touches as he battled his demons all night long.

The next day, after performing purificatory rites, Hasmukha was crowned king of the realm, and his father Sunaka was appointed his adviser. Sandilya decided to stay with them to instruct the new king on his royal duties as prescribed by the scriptures.

'It's time for you to return to Dwaraka so you can take your place as Rukmini's son,' said Mayavati. 'She has waited long years, wondering if you were alive or dead. Imagine her joy when you return in a blaze of glory!'

'We will go to Dwaraka together,' he said.

'You have paid your debt to me by accepting me as your wife, my lord. I am at peace. I will not hold you back.'

'Do you think I will leave you now? Don't you remember what I said?' He clasped her to his chest.

'I was born for you, my love. And I will die for you,' she whispered.

His real home, his godly parents . . . Pradyumna was impatient to see them, but he was also diffident. How would they receive him? Would they accept him readily or treat him as an unwelcome stranger? His mind conjured up several versions of his homecoming, and he grew increasingly nervous.

Eventually Mayavati and he arrived at the gates of Dwaraka. He bowed his head in reverence to the city that sparkled like a celestial jewel on earth. They hurried to Rukmini's palace and sought permission to enter. The guards escorted them inside, impressed by Pradyumna's startling resemblance to Krishna. Rukmini, who was conversing with Narada, turned to look at them. Her heart pulsed with an unaccountable affection when she saw the warrior's face. *He is as old as my son would have been if he were still with us,* she thought. *Where are you my son? Do you know your mother is pining for you?*

Narada, who had been waiting for this day, rose to his feet with unbridled joy to welcome the visitors. 'This is none other than your son, Rukmini,' he said, 'the little one stolen from you as an infant. He has slain Kaalasura, the demon who had abducted him, and has returned to your bosom, drawn by your love.'

As the devarishi spoke, Pradyumna gazed eagerly at Rukmini, the mother who had waited for him all this while. He took in her benevolent eyes and her aura of grace. Rukmini wept tears of joy as she beheld her son. She could hardly believe what Narada had said to her, though she knew in her heart that it was true.

'I have imagined this scene so many times in my dreams, my son,' she said. 'I have watched you in my mind's eye growing from a child to a youth to the warrior that you are now. But I was never sure that my dream would be realized.' She lifted her arms in welcome. 'Come to me so I may hold you and convince myself that you are not a creation of my mind.'

He strode forward, touched her feet and sought her blessings. Her tears fell on his head as she raised him and embraced him. 'I bless you with long life and happiness,' she murmured, her voice trembling.

'Your son is Kama who was reincarnated in your womb by Shiva's boon,' said Narada. 'The woman by his side is Mayavati, Rati incarnate, who helped him kill Kaalasura. She has waited and prayed through the ages for her husband to return from the ashes of Shiva's anger.'

Mayavati bent forward to touch her feet. Rukmini embraced her and kissed her forehead. She sat them down beside her and inundated them with questions about their life in the asura court, trying to bridge the gap of many years.

All of a sudden, a harsh voice broke into the idyll, like a drop of poison in a jar of nectar.

'I heard that the destroyer of our race is back in our midst,' said Jambavati, whose spies had told her of the arrival of the lost son. 'And with him his harlot, who was earlier the asura's wife.'

Rukmini's eyes darkened with pain as she heard the voice of her tormentor. The young couple reeled in shock and looked at the intruder in distress.

Narada intervened, seeing that Rukmini was unable to speak. 'You are mistaken, Jambavati,' he said. 'Mayavati was never Kaalasura's wife. She had created a replica of herself to attend to him. In fact, she is Rati, who brought Kama back to life with her tapas.'

Jambavati ignored him, targeting her attack on the newcomer, hoping to drive him away with her ferocity.

'Didn't Narada tell you about his prediction that you would destroy our race?' she asked. 'Why have you come now? Is it to die at the hands of my son Samba before you can unleash death with your asura whore?'

Rukmini covered her ears, unable to bear the rants of a disturbed mind. Pradyumna was struck with a mind-numbing horror. Dark fears swirled around him again. The queen's strident words seemed an augury for the future.

He had not shaken off his karmic burden after all. He had brought it with him into his new life.

22

The Homecoming

The silence was harrowing. The shock inflicted by Narada's revelation at the cradling ceremony was still raw. Was the sudden return of Pradyumna a sign that their days of peace and privilege were coming to an end?

The tense atmosphere was broken by the entry of Krishna, his parents, Vasudeva and Devaki, and his elder brother, Balarama. They had heard of the return of the lost son and hastened to greet him. Tears poured down the cheeks of the old couple who had given up hope of ever seeing their grandson. Pradyumna sought their blessings.

Krishna's eyes welled with tears as he saw the son whom the asura had stolen in order to torment the father. There was a lot that he wanted to say to Pradyumna but could not, in the presence of so many others. He feasted his eyes on his son's magnificence and waited for a more propitious time to share his emotions.

Jambavati's spite flared when she watched the grandparents shower their affection on the prince. She darted away when talk began of holding a grand feast to celebrate his return.

Messengers were dispatched to neighbouring kingdoms to inform the rulers of the homecoming. The news spread through the city and the people rushed to see their long-lost prince, bearing gifts of love. The girls in the court cast wistful glances at his splendid form and face, and envied Mayavati for having claimed him before they had seen him.

Rukmini could not get enough of the son from whom she had been cruelly separated all these years. She clung to him and looked for ways to pamper him. She prepared choice sweets with her own hands and fed them to him. She spent every waking moment listening to him and Mayavati talk about their life at the asura court. She suffered through every moment of his battle with Kaalasura and agonized at her son's trials. Her affection was displayed in her frequent embraces, her tears and her every action.

After some days had passed, she stopped worrying that fate would snatch her son away again and began to plan his future. One thought took precedence in her mind over all others. She wanted to arrange Pradyumna's marriage to a girl of her choice, someone who would strengthen the ties with her family. It was the accepted practice for princes and kings of the time to marry several times, and she voiced her desire to Krishna.

'Shall we send word to the kings of the world that we seek proposals for our son?' asked Krishna with a smile, knowing well that this was not what she wanted.

Rukmini hurriedly explained what she had in mind. 'I want Pradyumna to marry my brother Rukmi's daughter Rukmavati, my lord,' she said. 'I have long dreamed of this, though it seemed impossible for such an alliance to ever happen. The rift caused by my wedding can only be healed by another wedding.'

Rukmi had never fully recovered from his humiliation when Krishna had snatched Rukmini from under his nose and married her. He had vowed not to return to his capital Kundinapura until he killed Krishna and rescued his sister. However, he had failed in this and was forced to build a new capital for himself. His sole ambition in life was to defeat Krishna, and he prayed incessantly to Shiva, finally securing a boon—a bow that made him invincible. He had also aligned with the kings Jarasandha and Sishupala who were hostile to the Dark One.

Krishna knew all this, but did not want to oppose his queen who loved her brother and wanted to reconcile with him. He agreed, therefore, to her proposal and sent a letter to Rukmi, suggesting the alliance.

Rukmi did not want to foster ties with his enemy and returned a missive stating that his daughter would choose her own husband through a swayamvara. His hope was that she would not favour any son of Krishna's. However, he could not forbid Pradyumna from participating in the swayamvara, as doing so would be tantamount to declaring war.

News of Rukmini's message and of the swayamvara reached Jambavati and her son, who were upset by the grand welcome given to Pradyumna. Samba had expressed his resentment openly to his mother and his coterie.

'Does this nobody, an asura by upbringing, hope to take my place?' he ranted. 'How can he surpass the fame I have earned by building the matchless Sambaditya temple?'

'He cannot aspire for a place even at your feet, son,' said Jambavati. 'You must use this swayamvara to show him how insignificant he is. Once the princess Rukmavati lays eyes on you and hears of your exploits, she will choose none but you.'

Unaware of their plans, Rukmini approached Pradyumna and urged him to take part in the swayamvara. Pradyumna stayed silent, not wishing to take another wife and hurt Mayavati, who had been unswerving in her devotion. His mother pleaded with him, telling him how she longed to make up with her brother.

Mayavati took matters into her own hands and spoke to Pradyumna when they were alone.

'Your mother is eager that you attend Rukmavati's swayamvara, my lord,' she said.

'I assure you I will not marry another woman when you are everything that man or god may desire,' he promised, trying to comfort her. 'I will not dishonour my queen who brought me back from Yamaloka.'

'I am truly blessed,' she said. 'But I will not stand in the way of your marrying again, for I know that I am the love of your life.'

'But the rage you displayed when I was with Tara and the other dancers . . .?'

'When we were in Kaalasura's kingdom, I was doubtful of ever winning your love, and hated every woman who cast her eyes on you. But I have won your heart since, and I am certain of our love. Besides, I know that it is a common practice for royals to unite kingdoms through marriage.'

Pradyumna looked into her eyes, still in doubt.

'I know that you are Kama incarnate, my love,' she said. 'Women will flock to you like bees to a fragrant flower. Make your mother happy by telling her you will do as she wishes.'

Pradyumna took her in his arms and proved his love for her, using not words but the finesse of the Rupastra, one whose beauty is his weapon. He showed her again his expertise in Kama Shastra, the many ways to achieve bliss—by arousing, attracting, intoxicating, burning, thrilling and killing with love.

Rukmi's capital Bhojakata came alive with preparations for his beloved daughter's swayamvara. A vast field had been chosen as the venue for the grand event, and magnificent mansions were set up for the visiting kings and their retinues. The domes of the pavilions glittered with jewels and shone like the turrets of Indra's Amaravati. King Rukmi had organized eight days of revelry that included sporting matches and banquets.

On the day of the swayamvara, festive flags were hoisted and drums pounded a joyful beat. The entire city gathered to watch the proceedings from behind barriers. Jugglers, musicians and magicians entertained the crowds, and fresh flowers released their fragrance in the breeze.

The suitors made their stately entry, wearing silken robes and opulent crowns, and carrying jewelled swords. Each of them looked like a deva on earth, struck by Kama's arrows, eager to win the hand of the exquisite Rukmavati. Each king or prince was a nonpareil in power, physique and vigour, and with him came his courtiers who fluttered about like planets revolving around the sun.

The contenders glared at one another before bowing to the cheering throng. The people watched and assessed the merits of the suitors.

Their favourite was Samba, luminous in his princely garb, his tremendous arms attesting to his valour. 'Behold the son of Krishna!' the people cheered, feasting their eyes on the prince who closely resembled his godly father.

'The princess will choose him,' they said. 'He is unmatched in battle and blessed by the sun god, whom he honoured with a glorious temple.'

Samba was intoxicated by the adulation and grew more certain that he would win the day, though his rivals did not regard him as their equal.

A flurry of drums announced the arrival of the princess. Clad in bridal finery, Rukmavati descended from her chariot with her attendants around her. Her beauty cast a spell on the crowds and the suitors. Her face was serene, glowing with an inner purity that could not be matched by any artifice. Her body was graceful, every movement smooth and charming. The mightiest of her suitors felt helpless in the clutches of desire and yearned to take her to his kingdom as his queen.

Pradyumna, who had made a quiet entry on to the field, felt his heart leap at the sight of Rukmavati's radiant, shy face. He saw she carried in her hand the bridal garland studded with rubies and emeralds. *Who is going to be the lucky one,* he wondered.

The royal trumpets sounded. Silence fell as Rukmi led his daughter forward and announced the commencement of the contest. 'I welcome all you mighty rulers to the swayamvara of the princess of Vidharba. May the gods bless her and guide her hand!'

Rukmi walked with his daughter past the kings and princes seated on their thrones, telling her about each of them—their name, lineage and claim to fame. The suitors focused their eyes on her glowing face and petitioned the gods to be chosen. And even after she had passed by, each suitor hoped she would return to him after she made a full circle.

Rukmavati moved slowly ahead, looking upon each face as her father spoke of their achievements. No one seemed to catch her fancy. When she came to Samba, the young prince turned his adoring eyes on her.

'Samba, the son of Krishna, ruler of Dwaraka,' said Rukmi. 'Valiant warrior of a thousand battles. The builder of the splendid Sambaditya temple in Konark.'

Rukmavati paused for the first time, her hand on her father's arm, and gazed at Samba's face for an intense moment. Samba's heart beat faster as he waited for her to garland him.

Who else can match me in birth, grandeur, youth or wealth?

Still, the princess looked and pondered.

What is holding her back?

Samba felt a fever of impatience and wished he could reach out and grab her hand. He forced himself to be patient. How did a few moments matter when he was going to spend a lifetime with her?

Suddenly, her expression changed. She shook her head slightly, turned her back on Samba and moved away.

Samba could not believe his eyes. She had rejected him! How could she? He was shattered. This was not what he had come for. The invincible warrior could not return empty-handed and lose face before his people. What should he do? Should he snatch her by force and fight off her father and the other kings? Would he be able to defeat all of them and their legions?

A hush descended on the spectators. Even the birds in the sky seemed to have fallen silent. Everyone had been certain when Rukmavati paused before Samba that he was her choice. What had gone wrong?

The princess stood before the next suitor. 'Pradyumna, the Mighty,' said Rukmi. 'Kama reincarnated. Son of Krishna. Slayer of Kaalasura, the demon who vanquished the devas.'

So this is my sister's son, he thought. *A glorious scion of a noble mother. Maybe I should have given more thought to Rukmini's offer of an alliance.*

Rukmavati stared at the resplendent prince. Her breath caught in her throat and she lowered her gaze in blushing confusion. Her heart told her at once that he was the man she had seen in her dreams, the one the gods had chosen for her.

Her eyes flew to Pradyumna's face again and she saw him looking ardently at her, his gaze searing her body and her soul. The field, the crowds, the other kings, her father beside her—everything melted away.

Her hands lifted of their own volition and placed the garland around his neck.

There was a stunned silence.

Then the crowds erupted in loud cheers that echoed to the skies. They were happy that their princess had chosen wisely. Pradyumna too was the son of the living god. Reports of his heroic battle against Kaalasura had reached their ears.

They raised banners of celebration. The reverberation of their dancing feet shook the earth. Priests in their hundreds began to chant hymns of blessing.

Rukmi felt a pang that his ruse of holding a swayamvara had not prevented this alliance. The rejected suitors, including Samba, shouted their displeasure. Some of them rose from their seats, muttering threats.

'How can she choose someone who is not of royal blood? Pradyumna, like his brother Samba, comes from a cursed tribe and can never sit on the throne. He can become at most a chieftain after Krishna, that too if his brothers allow him. We cannot allow him to take away the princess.'

'At least I am a true son of Krishna,' said Samba. 'Who knows who Pradyumna is and where he came from?'

'I will seize her by force,' said a demon king, his eyes darting wildly. 'Rukmi has insulted us by inviting us and giving us false hope. He stands by while she chooses the killer of my brother Kaalasura.'

'A cowherd chosen above all of us?' screamed another. 'We will kill him first and then the treacherous Rukmi and his daughter.'

The spurned suitors advanced with crazed eyes and raised swords, ready to hack them to pieces. Their soldiers followed, their eyes filled with bloodlust.

Pradyumna stepped forward, putting his frightened bride behind him, and pulled out his sword.

'The princess has spoken,' he said. 'Those who wish to challenge her decision will have to fight me.'

His bold stance and majestic form silenced his opponents. But Samba drew his sword from its scabbard and prepared to attack. Sage Kashyapa, who had accompanied the princes to Bhojakata, held him back.

'Do not disgrace your clan by fighting your brother, prince,' he said. 'Do not allow enemies to exploit your differences. Accept your defeat and stand by his side.'

Pradyumna dispatched the princess and Rukmi to safety behind their guards. Then he raced to his chariot and took up his bow. A few kings decided to take him on and picked up their weapons. They converged upon Pradyumna, attacking from different sides, like jackals around a lion. The prince was unfazed, and used the skills he had learned in his war with Kaalasura to rout them. The other kings fled before he could turn to them.

When order was finally restored, Rukmi formally announced the wedding and sent messengers to invite his sister and his kin. Krishna and his queens travelled to Vidharba with their retinue. Rukmini was ecstatic to be able to renew ties with the people she had left behind years ago.

The wedding was solemnized with all the holy rites. Sages and elders blessed the couple and wished them a prosperous life. The bride and groom left for Dwaraka soon after in chariots laden with jewels and brocaded garments, spices and fragrances, gold and gems, with horses, elephants and an army of attendants following them.

They arrived to an enthusiastic welcome in Dwaraka to begin their life together. Mayavati embraced the new bride and invited her into her home with a generous heart. The entire city rejoiced, except for the two whose schemes had failed, leaving them angrier and more resentful than before.

23

Samba in Chains

'Finally, we are punishing this wretch for taunting Pradyumna all the time!' The shrill voice of the young lad broke the stillness of the night.

'Ssh!' said the huge figure beside him, his bald head shining in the glow of the lamps as he led the way into the bedchamber. The guards surrounding the palace and the antapura had all fallen mysteriously asleep. But the giant would rather not have the intended victim wake up and thwart his plan.

'He is snoring,' whispered the young lad, looking at the figure on the bed.

Ghatotkacha leaned forward and lifted up the bed along with its sleeping occupant in one huge hand. His partner in mischief, the young Abhimanyu, hopped on to the foot of the bed. The giant flew through the immense doors and out of the palace, effortlessly carrying the bed bearing the two men.

He flew to the outskirts of the city and descended on to the deserted burial ground that was shrouded in a thick pall of smoke. A few pyres still flickered, lighting up the surroundings with an eerie glow. Abhimanyu jumped off the bed and ran to hide behind a giant tree.

Ghatotkacha tilted the bed suddenly, and the sleeping Samba tumbled on to the rough ground and awoke with a start. He looked up at a ring of dead spirits howling at him, towering over him, attacking him with their noxious, half-burned limbs. He began to scream and struggled to his feet, dodging their blows and kicking feet. He tried to run, only to be hauled up by a skeleton who threw him into the hands of the waiting spirits. One twisted off Samba's head in one quick move and threw it high in the air. The prince's eyes stared wildly out of his severed head and he howled as the spirit tossed his head straight into the flames of a pyre. He felt the fire singe him, and he screamed and pleaded for mercy. His headless torso ran berserk, trying to escape the blows that were being rained on him from every direction.

Finally, Ghatotkacha took pity on him and sent his head whizzing back to settle on his torso. The spirits disappeared as suddenly as they had appeared, and Samba ran for his life, not stopping until he reached his palace again. The giant and his young companion laughed until tears ran down their cheeks.

This was too much fun to stop with just one expedition. A few nights later, the two made their way into Samba's antapura again. Abhimanyu hid behind the pillars while Ghatotkacha took the form of Samba's favourite wife and awoke the sleeping man with his caresses.

Samba was delighted that his wife was so eager for his lovemaking and embraced her in a surge of desire. Then he fell back in shock as his wife clawed his back in a frenzy, tearing his flesh into tatters. He watched aghast as the demure face of the maiden transformed into an ugly face with bloodshot eyes, and her lush body became that of a hairy, knobbly dwarf sitting on his chest, reaching out with his claws to throttle him. He struggled and tried to scream, thrashing on the bed. But the dwarf's hold was too strong and Samba soon lost consciousness.

'Let him go!' shouted Abhimanyu, afraid that Samba would die.

The two left as silently as they had come, waiting until they were some distance away from the palace before roaring with laughter.

Pradyumna found them a short while later, having been warned by his inner senses that the two were up to mischief. Abhimanyu chortled loudly when he saw Pradyumna. 'You will never guess what we did to Samba. I won't be surprised if he never lets his wives enter his bedroom again!'

'What did you do?' Pradyumna asked Ghatotkacha sternly, knowing at once that the giant was behind the scheme.

'Why did you have to tell him?' Ghatotkacha glared at his young follower. 'My pious brother will put an end to all the fun we have been having. Anyway, I think Samba will be afraid to close his eyes hereafter, don't you? He's not going to forget his experiences very soon!'

'Tell me what you did,' Pradyumna asked again, trying not to laugh. He did not want to encourage the pair, though he knew that whatever they did was out of loyalty to him.

As the two took turns regaling him with the torment they had inflicted on Samba, he began to laugh too, his mind conjuring up the ridiculous spectacle of Samba struggling with spirits and a murderous dwarf. But, in the end, he warned the two not to continue with their tricks.

Ghatotkacha turned on Abhimanyu for spoiling their capers. He had thought of many more ordeals that he could put Samba through. 'You are still so callow,' he said. 'You need to grow up and learn to judge the right time to say or do anything, if you ever want to fight alongside us adults. Until then, you can play with the other children in Dwaraka. Maybe you would like to twirl my moustache before you go, seeing how you don't have one of your own. And work on that shrill voice of yours, which betrays how young you really are.'

'I am just as brave a soldier as any in the kingdom,' Abhimanyu retorted. 'Remember how I subdued you when you stopped my mother and me from passing through your forest. I learned archery from my noble father after all.'

'I did not know then that you were my uncle Arjuna's son,' said Ghatotkacha. 'But I returned the favour by abducting Vatsala for you, didn't I? Weren't you crying because Balarama had decided to get her married to Duryodhana's son Lakshmana?'

'Don't forget the fun you had at Lakshmana's expense,' Pradyumna intervened.

'Yes, brother. I pretended to be Vatsala and squeezed Lakshmana's hand so hard that he fainted,' laughed the rakshasa. 'Then I appeared to him as a monster with three hideous heads, so that he ran away, shrieking that he would never get married!'

Abhimanyu was still rankling under the giant's insult and squared up to him. 'Not just archery, I also learned battle arts, including the secret of the chakravyuha, when I was still in my mother's womb,' he said.

'You may know how to enter that battle formation, but you do not know the way out. What use is this knowledge to you then?' Ghatotkacha shot back.

'My father has promised to teach me soon. And Pradyumna has taught me to fight with the mace and sword,' said Abhimanyu. 'He says I am now as skilled as he is.'

Pradyumna smiled as he listened to their bickering, his heart filled with love for his two cousins. His life was blissful. His young wife Rukmavati adored him, and Mayavati was unfailing in her support. He was happier than he had ever been before.

Back in his palace, Samba was still brooding over his failure to win Rukmavati's hand.

'What does he have that I don't?' he snarled to his mother. 'He can never be my equal in looks or fame.' He smashed his fist into the palm of the other hand. 'I was certain she was going to choose me when she stood gazing into my eyes. Then what went wrong?'

'That devil Rukmini and her brother Rukmi are to blame,' said Jambavati. 'They pretended to hate each other while plotting the whole thing. Rukmavati clearly chose you, but her father pulled her away towards Pradyumna.'

'That must be what happened.' Samba nodded, clutching at this explanation which allowed him to preserve his dignity.

Narada had made a quiet entrance as they were speaking and addressed him with gentle words. 'You are letting envy distort your vision and distract you from your responsibilities, Samba,' he said. 'This will only lead you towards sin.'

'Aha, the kapi-vaktra, the monkey-faced,' jeered Samba. 'Always jumping in where you are not welcome. Your own father Brahma cursed you to wander without a home, because you refused to marry and have children, yet you presume to be qualified to advise our family.'

'The mischief-maker is busy as usual,' Jambavati chimed in. 'An ascetic with an unseemly attachment to Rukmini. That must be why he accuses us of being envious of her and her son.'

'Your intemperate words expose your envy, Jambavati,' said Narada. 'You enjoy every comfort, yet you cannot bear their happiness. You plot against them, forgetting the pain they have endured over the years. Samba, don't you realize that it is

Pradyumna who should envy you? Your parents have cosseted you every day of your life whereas he did not even know who they were. He had to wage a horrific battle with demons in order to find them. After all that, he has never once shown you disrespect or retaliated when you sneered at him.'

'Ignore the fool and listen to me, son,' said Jambavati. 'The only way you can avenge your shame is to win the hand of a grander princess. I know just the right one for our purpose— Lakshmani, Duryodhana's daughter, who was promised to you. A battle is brewing between Duryodhana and the Pandavas who seek a share in the Kuru kingdom. If you marry Lakshmani, you will fight alongside Duryodhana against the Pandavas who have always favoured Rukmini and her son.'

'An unwise choice, queen,' said Narada. 'Duryodhana is consumed by envy and disregards even Krishna's counsel. He is not to be trusted, as you know yourself. He went back on his promise to give his daughter to Samba in marriage and has arranged a swayamvara for her instead.'

'It does not matter. My son will win her hand when he attends the swayamvara,' said Jambavati, gesturing to the devarishi to leave.

'And if she spurns me, I will seize her by force, like Arjuna abducted Subhadra,' said Samba, his eyes glinting.

'The auguries are bad. Nothing good can come of this,' said Narada. But the spiteful mother and son would not listen.

Samba's plans to attend the swayamvara were foiled by Duryodhana, who chose not to invite any of the Yadu princes.

Balarama was offended and sent Duryodhana a stern message. 'How dare you insult us by reneging on your promise and then excluding our whole clan ?' he asked.

'I am doing exactly what you did,' Duryodhana shot back.
'You promised your sister Subhadra to me. Then Krishna
helped Arjuna abduct her. You pledged your daughter Vatsala
to my son Lakshmana. Again, Ghatotkacha kidnapped her. Not
only that, he disguised himself as the bride in order to terrify
my son. How dare you question me now?'

Samba reacted like a petulant child when he heard of
this exchange. 'My father is to blame for all this. He helped
Arjuna and Abhimanyu marry the women they desired, thereby
ruining my chances of marrying Lakshmani. Ghatotkacha uses
his skills to help Abhimanyu, but does not help me.' He strode
up and down, cracking his whip against the walls. 'I do not need
anyone's help. I will storm the swayamvara, snatch Lakshmani
from the Kuru court and prove that I'm as brave as Arjuna.'

For the next few days he made secret preparations to go to
Hastinapura, the Kuru capital. On the appointed day, when he
entered the swayamvara hall, Duryodhana's men barred his way
and told him he had not been invited.

'Stop me if you dare!' snarled Samba, pulling his sword
from the scabbard.

The Kuru elders whispered to Duryodhana, telling him
that he should not allow a fight to mar the auspicious occasion.

'Let the fool pass,' Duryodhana said to his soldiers. 'He will
soon realize that my daughter has no wish to marry him.'

Samba sheathed his sword and strode past them, head held
high. Of course, the princess would choose him and no one else.

Alas, this was not to be. Lakshmani swept past him without
a pause, leaving him infuriated.

His anger boiled over. 'How dare you ignore me?' he shouted.
'I am going to make you my bride even if I die in the attempt.'

He seized her by the hand and began to drag her to his
chariot. She screamed and dug in her heels. The Kuru scions
charged at them to rescue her and avenge the insult.

'This fool and his clan must be taught a lesson,' they vowed. Six maharathis—Karna, Shalva, Bhurisrava, Yajnaketu and Duryodhana, along with their commander Bhishma—each capable of taking on 60,000 warriors at a time, rushed to challenge Samba.

Samba was a maharathi too, but was outnumbered six to one. *Better I leave with my bride than take on so many of them,* he decided.

'Come with me,' he shouted at Lakshmani, and pulled her into his chariot. As he took up the reins, Karna raced forward in his chariot to bar their way with a mighty shout.

'Scoundrel!' exclaimed Karna. 'Trying to run away like a thief? Stop and fight if you dare!'

Duryodhana's chariot came flying to join that of his commander. 'So, the valiant Yadu flees from his enemies, like all his clan. Face us like a warrior or die with our arrows in your back.'

'The invincible Samba does not run,' replied Krishna's son. 'Get ready to face my fury!'

Samba took up his arms and shot a flurry of arrows that covered the sky like a canopy and devastated the Kuru soldiers. But the maharathis fought back, surrounding him and beating him down with their concerted attack. Samba managed to keep them at bay for a long time, but was finally overwhelmed by their sheer numbers. As he slowed down, the enemy closed in on him like a pack of jackals. Karna shot down his horses, while Shalva destroyed the spokes of his chariot wheels. Duryodhana cut the string of his bow so he could not fight. The Kuru soldiers swarmed on to the chariot to bind him and carry him off to the dungeons. Duryodhana revived Lakshmani, who had swooned in fright, and took her back to the palace.

Narada carried the news of Samba's imprisonment to Krishna. 'I tried to stop him, but failed, O lord,' he said. 'You must rescue Samba from the Kurus before they harm him.'

'I will not negotiate with that evil clan who refused to give my cousins, the Pandavas, their rightful share of the kingdom,' said Krishna. 'Samba must pay the price for persisting in folly, time and again.'

Balarama had a soft corner for the brash Samba and did not want him to suffer. 'I will lead the delegation to Hastinapura and persuade the Kurus to support the marriage,' he offered. 'I will take young Pradyumna with me in case they should prove obstinate.'

As Pradyumna prepared to leave, his young wife Rukmavati clung to him with teary eyes. What if the Kurus refused to release Samba and waged a battle instead? Everyone spoke about the might of the Kurus and the invincible maharathis who fought on their side. She knew her husband had fought and won against the dreaded Kaalasura, but here he was venturing forth with just a small retinue against a mighty force. Pradyumna consoled her and promised to return safely to her side.

When Balarama reached the gates of the Kuru capital with Pradyumna and a few soldiers, Duryodhana barred his way and refused to listen to his pleas for peace.

'We cannot allow our daughter to marry into a lowly race of cowherds and thieves,' he said. 'Krishna stole butter and clothes from the gopis, while his son tried to abduct an innocent girl from her home. Samba had the gall to challenge us Kshatriyas in battle—of course he lost miserably.'

Karna joined Duryodhana in his taunts. 'Krishna is the source of all your troubles. He allies with the Pandavas and dreams of defeating us. Warn him that he will be defeated if he opposes us.'

Balarama, whose temper was always volatile, grew incensed. 'You dare call us lowly?' he roared. 'You dishonourable lot think you can mock my brother and the dharma he upholds. I did not come here to attack you, but I see that I must. I will destroy you and your arrogance.'

He turned to Pradyumna and said, 'Make these fools regret their words. Send them flying with your valour, my lion.'

The young fire-eater advanced like Yama, his weapons leaving a trail of broken bodies, dead horses and shattered chariots. His mace whirled like a dervish and took down nobles and soldiers alike. The flash of his sword was awe-inspiring, cutting off heads as easily as if they were the stalks of plants. His arrows blinded the Kuru troops and had them fleeing from the field.

The Kuru maharathis found that they could not hold their army together, for Pradyumna seemed to be everywhere at once.

Shalva, the veteran of a thousand battles, received a deep wound in his side and retreated from the battle. Bhurisrava challenged Pradyumna, weaving a web of magic around him with his arrows, but the latter attacked Bhurisrava's chariot to engage him in close combat. The Kuru warrior could not match his rival's strength and ran away.

Yajnaketu confronted Pradyumna. 'You have wounded my friends and I must take revenge,' he bellowed like an old bull elephant. 'Show me if you have the courage to wrestle with me.'

The two engaged in a violent flurry, but Yajnaketu soon surrendered in order to save his life.

'I will not kill a man who has laid down his arms,' said Pradyumna, turning to face the rest of his enemies. 'Which of you is next? Isn't there a single warrior among the Kurus who can give me a good fight?'

Duryodhana signalled to his commanders to attack the prince in a formation. They organized a phalanx and surrounded him. But he slashed and whirled and slipped through their ranks, his mocking laughter ringing out.

Finally, Karna told Duryodhana that they could not win the battle and were heading to an ignoble defeat. 'Let us pacify the young fool and the venerable Balarama by agreeing to Samba's marriage with Lakshmani,' he said.

Duryodhana had no choice but to agree. He blew his conch to signal a cessation of hostilities and advanced towards Balarama, flanked by Karna and the other maharathis. Pradyumna came to stand by his uncle like an unyielding rock.

'I wish to bring this ill-advised battle to a close,' said Duryodhana, folding his hands to Balarama. 'Please accept our princess Lakshmani as Samba's bride and cast aside your anger.'

Balarama's eyes smouldered, threatening to scorch Duryodhana and his men. 'You clamoured for war when I spoke of peace,' he roared. 'You flouted the rules of dharmic war by having six maharathis attack Samba. You tried the same tactics again, only to find that Pradyumna is equal to a hundred of you. You stand before us, quivering in fear. Why should I accept your plea for peace? We will not stop until we have killed every one of you.'

He bellowed at the Kuru army like a behemoth, magnifying his form until he touched the sky. He swung his plough from his shoulder, uprooting Hastinapura from its very foundations.

'I will drag your city to the Ganga and submerge it in the waters,' he declared. The citizens screamed in terror as the city collapsed around them. The Kuru chiefs watched aghast and prostrated themselves at his feet, pleading for mercy. But Balarama would not be appeased.

Pradyumna began chanting his praises, reminding him that he was the merciful Adisesha, the serpent who made his home in the cosmic ocean. 'Remember the great purpose for which you took birth alongside Vishnu. You are Balarama to his Krishna, just as you were Lakshmana to his Rama,' he said.

He saw that his words were calming Balarama's rage. 'Mighty uncle, killer of the demon Dhenuka!' Pradyumna continued. 'You hold all the planets on your thousand hoods and constantly chant the glories of Vishnu. You take the form of the three-eyed Shiva at the end of each kalpa in order to destroy the universe. Cool your anger now for it is not yet time to end the world.'

Though he was quick to anger, Balarama was also easily placated by the prayers of the righteous. He looked at Pradyumna with gentle eyes and reassumed his human form. He released the city from the plough's grip and raised a hand in blessing.

'I am pleased with you, nephew,' he said. 'Your courage is increasingly tempered with wisdom, like that of my beloved Krishna. I wish your brother Samba had just one-tenth of your judgement, so he would not need us to rescue him.'

Samba, who had been brought from his prison, stood listening with bowed head and a seething heart.

Why does this keep happening to me? he asked himself. *Instead of being hailed as a victor, I am forced to listen to praises of Pradyumna's heroism.*

Duryodhana escorted the princess from her palace to seek Balarama's blessings. 'I entrust my daughter to you, my lord. Bless the couple with a long and fruitful married life,' he said.

The Kuru prince's humility softened Balarama's heart. He blessed Lakshmani and the Kurus, and assured them that he was no longer their enemy.

'I beg you for a further boon,' said Duryodhana. 'Your expertise in mace-fighting is legendary. Allow me to enhance my skills by learning from the master of the art.'

'So be it,' said Balarama.

The Kurus performed the marriage of Samba with Lakshmani with great opulence. The bride left for her new home, accompanied by elephants and horses, chariots and maids bearing her rich gifts and ornaments.

The people of Dwaraka turned out with garlands and aartis to welcome the bridal party. The soldiers spoke highly of Pradyumna's exploits and soon poets began to compose panegyrics in his praise, to the great displeasure of Samba and his mother. Others paid tribute to the way Pradyumna had blossomed under the guidance of the elders of Dwaraka.

'Brahma has chosen the finest features of mankind to mould his form and his mind,' said Narada. 'His gait is majestic like that of Nandi, Shiva's bull. In battle, he is like Rudra, Shiva's fearsome form. In archery, he matches Bhishma, the invincible forebear of the Pandavas. In speed and strength, he rivals Garuda, the king of the skies. And in dharma, he is a worthy son of his father.'

Pradyumna was overwhelmed by the love of his people. He felt like a seedling transplanted from a parched land to a fragrant meadow, where the gentle rain and warm breeze constantly encouraged him to grow strong and tall. He wiped his mind free of his dark past and eagerly absorbed the wisdom that his father and the sages offered. He studied the laws of time that govern the lives of men and grew to understand the folly of leading a sinful life. He drew inspiration from the rousing tales of Vishnu's great avatars. He studied the four Vedas, and the four facets and ten divisions of the astras. Krishna was pleased with his son's progress, for he knew well that unfolding events would challenge his mettle in profound ways.

24

Vir Pradyumna

Whenever the Yadukula tilakas, the stars of the Yadu clan, Krishna and Balarama, were together, there was much merriment and music. The two brothers, one so dark and one so fair, along with their queens, were sporting in the magic lakes of Pindaraka. With them had come Arjuna and Pradyumna, and their loved ones.

Pradyumna and Rukmavati had been blessed with a son, Aniruddha, who had grown now into a radiant, lovable young boy. Krishna was charmed by his grandson and would often take him on his lap and feed him little balls of butter, while telling him about his own capers in Vrindavan when he stole butter and earned the wrath of the gopis. He taught him little prayers and narrated stories about the myriad stars and galaxies. Rukmini told her son proudly that though he himself was the god of love, Aniruddha would win even more hearts than he ever could. Vasudeva and Devaki saw in Aniruddha the little Krishna whom they had not been able to cherish as they had been cast in Kamsa's prison. The sound of cowrie shells was often heard in their palace as the grandsire spent his afternoons playing endless games of pachisi with the boy. The citizens of Dwaraka proclaimed fondly that Aniruddha was the most adorable child ever born.

The day passed in languorous happiness, as the couples swam in the waters and rested on the beautiful rafts shaped like peacocks, serpents and fish. Apsaras like Panchachuda, Kaveri and Mahendree danced and sang for them. Their attendants laid out platters of sweetmeats and jugs of wine.

Pradyumna enjoyed the sylvan surroundings with Mayavati and Rukmavati, while the devoted pair of Balarama and his wife Revati rested by the lake. Looking at the couple, Narada compared them to the chakravaka birds that symbolize fidelity until death. Aniruddha, a bright and active boy, was eager to hear the story of these magical birds.

'Many years ago, the chakravaka birds were cooing loudly to each other to express their love,' said Narada. 'But the sages meditating in the forest were disturbed by their warbling, and cursed them to be separated from each other every day after sundown. Since then, the poor birds spend their nights calling out piteously to their mates and have grown to represent the ultimate in fidelity.'

'Devarishi, how does my grandfather Krishna assure his wives of his love when he has so many of them?' asked Aniruddha.

'Krishna is the ideal purusha, for he devotes himself to each of his wives, making her believe he is hers alone. I saw him once on one shore of the lake, playing in the water with his queen, and then on the other shore too, caressing another of his wives. He shared a goblet of wine with one while he threaded fragrant flowers through the tresses of another. I heard him woo one wife by saying that he disliked cloudy days that prevented him from fully appreciating her charms. Then he whispered to another that he wished for thunder and rain, as it would force her to seek refuge in his embrace. Each of these women is blessed to be wooed by the supreme lord!'

But the idyll was interrupted when the demon Nikumbha snatched away the princess of the island, Bhanumati. Nikumbha had won a boon from Shiva that he would be born thrice and would be indestructible, unless he confronted Shiva, Vishnu or the righteous of heart. He had already lost one life when he was born as Andhaka. Shiva had annihilated him with his trident for lusting after Parvati.

It appeared that the foolish demon had not learned his lesson and had succumbed to lust again in his second life. He had used his occult powers to slip past Bhanumati's guards, waited until she was alone in the palace gardens and carried her away.

Pradyumna heard Bhanumati's frantic cries for help and chased the demon along with Arjuna. They overtook Nikumbha near the gates of Vajrapur, one of the six asura cities, and challenged him to a fight. The demon held the princess captive in one arm and multiplied their forms. Arjuna and Pradyumna did not know which Nikumbha to attack, nor could they use their full strength, for they feared that they might injure the true princess.

Nikumbha's diabolical laughter mocked them from every direction. 'Run away if you want to stay alive, fools,' he roared.

The demon's powers were formidable, earned by his thousand-year-long penance to Shiva. A prolonged battle raged, but the two warriors were unable to defeat Nikumbha even with their combined skills. They managed to wound him with their glistering arrows infused with powerful mantras, but the demon escaped by turning invisible.

They searched for him far and wide, but were unable to find him. 'Use the mahamaya that you learned from me, my lord,'

Mayavati's voice whispered in his mind, for she was never far from him in spirit.

Pradyumna then invoked his occult skills and saw the demon and Bhanumati hiding in a forest in the guise of wood pigeons. Realizing that they had been spotted, the demon took off again with the princess, leading them on a chase around the earth.

Nikumbha finally arrived at the fringes of Gokarna, a mountain on the Malabar coast that was sacred to Shiva.

'No one can cross this mountain without the permission of the three-eyed god,' said Pradyumna. 'Allow me to tell you the story of this sacred place as obeisance to Shiva.'

Arjuna knew the story well, but was happy to hear it again while they waited to see whether the haughty demon would bow to Shiva.

'Ravana was on his way to Lanka with a linga given to him by Shiva himself,' said Pradyumna. 'Shiva had told him that he must not place the idol on the ground until he reached his final destination. So when he needed to stop for his evening prayers, Ravana entrusted the linga to a young cowherd, telling him not to put it down. "Make sure you return before the sun sets, for I must leave then to take my cows home," the boy said. Ravana went to the river to perform his ablutions. The sun set all too soon and the boy placed the image on the ground and vanished. Ravana hurried back in alarm and tried to lift the linga, but it would not budge. The cowherd appeared before him again and revealed himself to be Shiva's son Ganesha in disguise. Ravana realized that Shiva had never intended for him to take the idol home and left in anger. Ganesha named this linga Mahabaleshwar, the all-powerful, as even Ravana could not move it. Mahabaleshwar will now help us stop the demon.'

The two warriors prayed to Shiva, and watched and waited as Nikumbha, drunk with power, tried to fly past the mountain without offering prayers. Shiva did not let him pass and the demon crashed headlong to the earth. He shook himself from his daze and fled to Shatpura, another of the cities that Brahma had granted to the asuras.

Shatpura was a magical city, lit by its own splendour so it did not require the light of the sun or the moon. It was here that Nikumbha took refuge, placing the princess under guard. The pursuers reached the gates behind him and waited for dawn, when the arrogant asura charged out with his horde. Arjuna tried to kill him with a barrage from his divine bow Gandiva, but these arrows were blunted by the power of Shiva's boon to Nikumbha. As Arjuna stood dumbfounded, the demon stunned him with a blow to his head.

Nikumbha attacked Pradyumna next, but the young warrior was indomitable, retaliating with a fierceness that sent the demon army flying. 'Why do you flee, fools?' Nikumbha shouted. 'What will your women say when they see you fleeing like cowards instead of fighting to the death?'

Shamed by his words, the demons renewed their fight with double the vigour. Seeing that he could not defeat Pradyumna with his axe and bludgeon, Nikumbha summoned his occult forces. He chanted spells over a fire into which he tossed his soldiers as sacrifice.

A fiery demon, with flames rising from her head, sprang to life and multiplied into six fierce forms. These forms advanced in a snarling group, baring fangs that were three yojanas long. Pradyumna raised his hands over his head in prayer as he invoked the Mohiniastra, which annihilates all illusions and sorcery. The false demons disintegrated in a firestorm.

However, Nikumbha cunningly used the distraction to strike the warrior from behind with his mace.

Pradyumna fell unconscious. Arjuna, who had recovered from his blow and rejoined the battle, carried him to safety.

Arjuna then invoked Indra who came down on Airavataa to sprinkle holy Ganga water on the warrior and revive him.

Pradyumna tore into the battlefield again and flew at the demon with his own mace. Wounded by his frenzied blows, Nikumbha collapsed on the ground.

'The demon is dead!' exulted Arjuna.

But Krishna's son realized it was a ruse—the demon had become invisible once again and escaped. He traced Nikumbha with the help of his mahamaya. Nikumbha created a thousand replicas of himself, and of Pradyumna and Arjuna, and used the confusion to carry away the real Arjuna.

Pradyumna fought the illusory Nikumbhas, but they kept multiplying faster than he could cut them down. At his wits' end, he surrendered himself to Vishnu and invoked him: 'I bow to thee, Achyuta, Kesava, Krishna, Madhusudhana. You are the only truth. You are the only refuge. Bless me with your infinite mercy.'

The great Protector sent his incandescent Sudarshana chakra to Pradyumna. The weapon flamed with divine energy. The young warrior worshipped it and directed it at the demon. The fiery discus blazed towards Nikumbha, slicing his head with one fell stroke, then vanishing into the ether to return to Vaikunta.

As the demon fell dead, Arjuna, who had been in his grasp, plunged from the skies towards earth. Pradyumna flew through the air, caught him in his powerful arms and brought him down to safety.

Pradyumna then freed the princess from the harem in the asura citadel where she had been cowering, numb with terror, expecting the demon to ravage her upon his return.

The three returned to Bhanumati's kingdom to a grand welcome. Krishna, Balarama and the king showered praises on Pradyumna.

Meanwhile, Narada helped the princess understand why she had undergone this torture.

'Do you remember, Bhanumati, the day you met Durvasa in your father's court?' he asked. 'You were young and brash then, and failed to offer the sage due respect, laughing instead at his rough garb and matted hair. This incensed Durvasa—whose name describes his character, one who is difficult to live with—and he cursed that you would be abducted by a demon. The sage is unable to control his temper, which is the result of the way he was born. You have heard the story of how Shiva destroyed Tripura, the three mystic cities of the asuras, with one magical arrow. The arrow burned the cities and returned to Shiva, falling in his lap as a child. This child, a product of Shiva's rage, took earthly form as Durvasa.'

Narada then advised the king to get his daughter married to Sahadeva, the youngest of the Pandavas. 'He is a renowned warrior and is highly skilled in interpreting the stars and what they foretell,' he said.

The king bowed to the trikaala jnani and said that he would solemnize the wedding in Dwaraka with the blessing of the lord.

Later, Narada shared his wisdom with Pradyumna, whom he had taken under his wing. 'These events showed the world yet again that no one can escape the consequences of their errors,' he said. 'Nikumbha's lust for Parvati when he was born as Andhaka brought him death by Shiva's trident. Vishnu's chakra punished him for wrongly coveting Bhanumati. One more birth remains—one more opportunity for him to realize that desire can never be satisfied and leads inevitably to doom. But has Nikumbha learned his lesson?'

25

The Parijata

As earth is home to many sinful beings, strife always follows harmony, just as night follows day. The next conflict in Dwaraka arose over an ethereal flower born of the parijata tree, which had risen from the churning of the cosmic ocean. The tree with its golden bark and iridescent leaves had the power to grant eternal youth and beauty, and evoke memories of previous lives.

The parijata was the favourite of Indra's queen Sachi, and occupied pride of place in her garden in Amaravati.

Narada brought one of its delicate orange and white flowers as an offering to his beloved Krishna, who in turn gave it to Rukmini. When spies bore this information to Satyabhama, another of Krishna's queens, her jealousy flamed out of control.

Narada's soul was harrowed by a vision that indicated that his offering of the parijata boded ill for the Yadus. 'The signs are not clear, but I fear that death threatens a loved one,' he warned Rukmini.

At once Rukmini began to pray to the lord of Vaikunta, seeking his blessing to protect her family.

Meanwhile, Satyabhama flung her fine clothes and jewellery away and donned the robes of an ascetic. She shut herself up in her chamber in anger and refused all food, saying that she would give up her life, as her lord had chosen another queen over her.

Krishna addressed her with soft words. 'Satyabhama, the embodiment of true lustre!' he said, as he sought to take her into his arms. 'Your eyes are like the petals of a lotus. Your face is flawless like a radiant gem. You are so beautiful, even when you are not dressed in rich clothes and ornaments. You are my favourite queen, more beautiful than Rukmini or Jambavati. How can you doubt that I love you the most, and that you are more precious to me than life?'

'Prove it to me then, my lord. Bring me the tree itself from heaven,' she commanded.

'It will be yours before long, I promise,' he said.

Krishna sent Narada as his emissary to Indra to ask him to part with the parijata tree. But Indra refused. 'The tree belongs in heaven in the garden of the king. Why should I give it up for a mere mortal so he can bestow it upon his wife? Ask him to fight me and take it if he can,' he said.

'I cannot ignore his challenge,' said Krishna, when Narada conveyed the message.

'Give me your Garuda and I will claim the tree in your name,' said Pradyumna.

Krishna gave his blessing and Pradyumna made preparations to leave on his mission. Rukmavati was afraid that the celestial prowess of the devas would overwhelm the mortal powers of her husband. 'Our lord fights ceaselessly against the fiercest of asuras and the most powerful devas. I fear that he will lose his life in one of these battles and leave us bereft,' she murmured to Mayavati.

Mayavati reassured her, reminding her that Pradyumna was the Mighty One, whose valour and vigour were unmatched in the three worlds. She also offered a word of counsel to her husband. 'Remember, Indra helped you many times in your war against Kaalasura, my lord,' she said. 'Try to win the parijata from him by using soft words rather than weapons, for if he uses his vajra, all will be lost.'

As Pradyumna gazed at his wives, he was overwhelmed by a sense of his good fortune in having them in his life. One had been ready to brave the fire to come to him, and would match him, stride for stride as he surmounted the hurdles of destiny. And the other, so gentle and nurturing, inspired him to achieve what no man had until now.

Pradyumna soared to Amaravati on Garuda's back. Before long, Indra barred their way with his thunderbolt, his celestial army with their dreadful weapons behind him.

'Flee from us, mortal,' said Indra. 'Did you really think you could fight the god of war? Do not forget you used my chariot and charioteer to win your battle against Kaalasura. Remember too that I descended to earth on my Airavataa and revived you when you were in a deathly swoon.'

'You are my saviour, god of thunder,' said Pradyumna. 'Obeying you is not only my duty, but also my privilege. But I am here to execute Krishna's desire and that of his queen. I will not back away, though I know well that my life is at stake. Permit me to carry out my mission.'

'I cannot allow that, for I have sworn to protect heaven and everything here. Decide what you will do now. Will you run away or fight?' sneered Indra.

Pradyumna answered by uprooting the parijata tree and preparing to take it to Dwaraka. Indra and the devas roared in anger and attacked him with their combined fury. They advanced on their fearsome war chariots like mountains on fire. Their ornaments dazzled Pradyumna like planets in the night sky. The beating of drums, the neighing of horses and the blowing of bugles brought Brahma to the scene. He watched the battle from his chariot of pearl and gold, attended by the sages.

Pradyumna cut down the missiles hurled at him and wounded Airavataa with his arrows. The elephant retaliated by attacking Pradyumna with his powerful tusks. Garuda shrieked as he entered the fray, clawing the deities with his talons and tearing Varuna's noose to shreds.

Pradyumna shattered Yama's mace and drove away Kubera's yakshas. He hurled a deadly mace at Agni who fled from the field. His fourteen-edged arrows chased the maruts, violent storm deities with iron teeth, who roared like lions. The gandharvas deserted the battleground. Pradyumna scattered the vasus, the nature gods, through the three realms, with occult weapons that howled as they hurtled forward.

The terrible war echoed on earth as well. The seven seas became turbulent and mountains shattered of their own accord. Tempests and volcanoes erupted, and darkness vanquished light.

Indra's son Jayanta tried to snatch the parijata back from Pradyumna, shooting a powerful astra that would burn through his enemy's armour and kill him. Pradyumna evaded the weapon, rising into the sky to taunt his enemy.

'So this is the extent of your powers, Jayanta,' he scoffed. 'Be warned that my own prowess is not so limited. Run and hide before you are killed!' He let loose a lightning attack from the sky.

Garuda landed on the back of Jayanta's elephant with terrible power, forcing it to collapse. Unable to confront Pradyumna's weapons or to fight without his mount, Jayanta fled.

Seeing the rout, the devas scattered from the field, leaving Indra alone to face the young hero.

No god or asura can fight like him, thought Indra. *Maybe it is wiser to accept defeat and give up the tree as a tribute.* But a greater fear rose in his mind and subdued this impulse.

'I cannot let you take away the parijata,' he said to Pradyumna. 'If I do, you will be back tomorrow to demand my throne and my position as the king of the devas. It is better to kill you now with my vajra, which no one can survive. Brace yourself, braggart, for the blow of death.'

As Indra raised the vajra, Brahma appeared before him to stay his hand. 'Do not act foolishly, Indra,' he said. 'Pradyumna is not an asura to be killed, nor does he seek to seize your position. He is here on a mission from Krishna to whom you owe this throne. Have you forgotten the innumerable times Janaradhana has come to *your* aid, though you remind Pradyumna of your assistance?'

Brahma told the assembled warriors about an earlier time when he had granted the asura Vritra a boon. 'I told Vritra that he could not be killed by any weapon that existed then, whether metal, wood or other common materials. Vritra used this boon to seize the earth and Indra's throne. Indra fled for his life and sought refuge with Vishnu, who told him that the only way to kill the demon was to fashion an uncommon weapon, one created from the bones of Dadhichi, a sage with incomparable power. Dadhichi agreed to sacrifice his life to save the gods. Indra fashioned his vajra from the sage's spine and used it to kill Vritra.'

Brahma turned angry eyes on Indra. 'How dare you use the weapon you received through Vishnu's grace against his own son?'

Indra refused to consider Brahma's words. 'I will kill this youth who challenges my might!' he said, raising his vajra again.

Pradyumna's head bent in worship. 'I bow to the thunderbolt against which there is no defence,' he said. 'I am honoured to die in order to keep my word to my divine father and mother.'

The devas looked on in panic. What could they do to stop this horror? They realized with a pang that the time to intervene was long past. Things were no longer in their control. They could not prevent the death of the warrior.

The sun dimmed, a ferocious wind toppled the chariots, and all living beings sought shelter from the Pralaya that was to be unleashed.

And then, he appeared—the Blue God, the Jagadananda Karaka—the source of all joy in the universe. In his hand was the fierce Sudarshana chakra, ready to be deployed.

'Has your obsession with your throne blinded you to dharma, Indra?' he roared. 'Will you strike down a mortal youth because he single-handedly routed your heavenly army? He fought with honour, but you commit sacrilege. He is righteous, and willing to sacrifice everything to fulfil the promise he made to my queen and me. Direct your vajra at me if you must, and let dharma decide the winner.'

Indra was beyond all reason. 'You are a cowherd come to challenge the king of the heavens!' he screamed. 'You have gone too far, Krishna.'

He unleashed the vajra, which burned everything in its way like the fires of dissolution. The three realms quivered. The Blue God raised his hand and the vajra froze in the air. Indra was shocked to see his weapon neutralized. His face contorted in panic, and he turned and ran, afraid that the chakra would strike him and shear off his head.

Brahma appealed to Sage Kashyapa and his wife Aditi to intervene and save Indra from his folly. Aditi, the devas' mother, summoned Indra to her presence and counselled him.

'You have forgotten that Vishnu saved you earlier, when the asura Mahabali deposed you and proclaimed himself Trilokadipati,' she said. 'I prayed to Vishnu and he blessed me by coming into my womb and staying there for a thousand years until he was incarnated as the dwarf Vamana, armed with his conch, chakra, club and lotus. Vamana vanquished Mahabali and restored you to your throne.'

'Alas, my own mother declaims in support of the tyrant who wields the chakra,' Indra interjected.

'I speak thus to open your eyes to the extent of your folly. You taunt Krishna as a cowherd when you know well that he is Vishnu, who has taken birth as a mortal to vanquish evil.'

'Have you chosen then to sacrifice me rather than displease your more powerful son?' Indra roared.

Krishna, who had followed Indra into their mother's presence, intervened now. 'Do not confront our mother in this arrogant manner, Indra,' he warned. 'Those who disrespect a mother's love never prosper.'

Krishna turned to Aditi and bowed to her. 'My obeisance to you, revered mother,' he said. 'I seek your blessings.'

'My blessings are always with you, my son,' said Aditi. 'I fear for Indra's life if you should wield your discus against him. Spare him, I beseech you, as a token of your regard for me.'

'Your wish is my command, respected mother,' said Krishna. 'I promise that I will not use my chakra against my brother.'

Krishna then turned to address Indra. 'Your flight from the battlefield is a dishonour to the throne you occupy,' he said. 'I would rather allow you to retain the parijata than witness your cowardice.'

Indra was shamed by Krishna's magnanimity and realized that there was no threat to his throne. 'I have been blind,' he confessed. 'Pradyumna won the battle and also the right to take the tree to Dwaraka, where it will flourish in your grace. Forgive me, great one.'

He joined his hands in prayer. Apsaras and gandharvas sang praises of the lotus-eyed lord and his valiant son. Pradyumna placed the parijata on Garuda's back and flew to Dwaraka, while Krishna followed in his aerial chariot.

The victorious son blew his conch as he entered the city and went in procession with the cheering crowds to Satyabhama's garden where the priests consecrated the tree.

Satyabhama listened with sparkling eyes as her lord narrated the tale of the battle in the heavens. She blessed Pradyumna and offered him a reward for fighting the devas on her behalf.

'You need merely think of me and I will come to you at once to render any aid you require,' she said. The warrior bowed to her.

The citizens of Dwaraka were overjoyed that the parijata was now in their city, for the tree showered blessings on all those who prayed to it. The old became virile, the blind regained their sight and the sick were healed.

'Pradyumna grows more invincible with every battle,' the people said in praise of their brave son. 'He is a worthy successor to his father in his humility and his wisdom.'

While an outpouring of love surrounded the prince, a bitter kernel of hate festered in two hearts, threatening to grow to gigantic proportions in the days to come.

26

Nandi to the Rescue

'Why did Krishna send Pradyumna and not Samba to seize the parijata tree from the devas?' Jambavati ranted. 'My son has proved himself in battle so many times.'

She was irked further that Pradyumna's son Aniruddha too was emerging as a promising warrior, under the tutelage of his father and the great Arjuna.

Samba was plagued by the fear that his brother would supplant him as the successor to the throne. He had been the favourite for many years and had taken it for granted that he would succeed his father. Things had changed, however, and he attributed it to the scheming of the upstart and his mother.

'Is my father planning to crown Pradyumna?' Samba asked Narada, knowing that the devarishi could see into the future. He hated having to seek his advice, but matters had reached a critical state.

'Due to Yayati's curse, Dwaraka has no king, as you well know, Samba,' replied Narada. 'Only chieftains like your father.'

'Who doesn't know that?' asked Samba, trying to control his temper. 'I asked you if my father wishes Pradyumna to take his place.'

'I do not presume to know his mind, Samba. But I will remind you of the vision I saw when Pradyumna and you were born, and advise you to follow dharma. More importantly, you must surrender your will to the great Vishnu who sleeps on the serpent Adisesha.'

The fool couches his words in riddles so I will not understand, thought Samba. *But I will prove to my father that I am a greater warrior than my brother. I just need to find the right opportunity.*

A chance presented itself soon enough, as Kali Yuga loomed large and chaos had become the order of the day.

Pradyumna received the first warning in his sleep. The demon Nikumbha appeared in his dream, bristling with hatred. 'I have returned, Pradyumna, larger than before and more powerful. You can try to defeat me, but you will not succeed this time. I have sworn to avenge myself by killing you and sending you to naraka.'

The prince woke with a start and sent his men out to look for the demon. The news was not long in coming.

The righteous king Brahmadatta had been performing an Aswamedha sacrifice on the banks of the River Avarta for over a year in honour of Krishna. Nikumbha, taking his third and most brutal form, had arrived from his citadel in Shatpura to disrupt the sacrifice. He slavered over the offerings on display and lusted for the king's beautiful daughters.

'Hand over your riches and your daughters to me if you want to live!' he demanded.

'My offerings are for Vishnu as enjoined by the Vedas,' said Brahmadatta. 'How can I give them to a demon? As for my daughters, they will choose their husbands from the princes who will be in attendance at their swayamvara.'

'I was not seeking your permission, king. Stand by and watch as I carry your daughters and your wealth away.'

The monster seized the princesses and the offerings and vanished before the king's troops could be summoned. The soldiers chased after them, but could not keep up with the demon who could turn invisible and fly at will.

The king choked with fear and prayed to the Dark One for succour.

'Go now, my son, to aid the king,' Krishna said to his trusted Pradyumna. The prince used his sorcery to trace the princesses and whisked them away from the asura, creating lookalikes with his maya to take their place.

'I will kill the demon, father,' clamoured Samba. 'Let me go with the Yadu army to put an end to him forever.'

'Do so, son. But Pradyumna will lead the army, as his acumen and skills make him a natural commander,' said Krishna. Samba could do nothing but obey the lord's command.

Meanwhile, Narada saw an opportunity to humble the arrogant princes who had come to attend the swayamvara—the Kurus and the Chedis. He decided to use the asura as his instrument.

'Foolish asura,' he said to Nikumbha. 'You have been deceived by Krishna's son who has rescued the princesses and left you with mere illusions. The Yadus plan to marry Brahmadatta's daughters and approach now with a huge army. You must be cunning if you wish to stop them. Use the other princes who have come for the swayamvara. Bribe them with lavish gifts and seek their help in fighting Krishna's forces.'

'I am not afraid of the Yadus who strut like peacocks though they have no feathers to boast of,' said the demon. 'But I have taken the last of my invincible forms and must ensure that I do not lose now.'

He wooed the Kuru and Chedi princes with jewels, gold and slaves, and sought their help against their common enemy, Krishna.

The Pandavas were also present at the swayamvara, but refused to fight against the Blue God and advised the other princes against angering him. But the Kurus and Chedis were eager to fight. Their combined armies flooded the battlefield, fully armed and mounted on elephants, horses and chariots.

When Pradyumna saw this huge force arrayed against them, he mapped out an elaborate strategy. 'I will command from the skies, with Indra's son Jayanta fighting by my side,' he said. 'Aniruddha will protect the Yadu army from the rear. You, Samba, will lead our troops on the ground. I am grateful to Pravara, the powerful Brahmin warrior blessed with Brahma's boon of invincibility, who has come to help us in our fight.'

Bugles and drums shattered the silence of the morning to signal the commencement of the battle. The two forces clashed like two tidal waves slamming into each other. The Yadus suffered a serious reversal almost at once as Nikumbha's occult forces swamped their senses with sorcery. The demons paralysed Samba, Kritavarma and Sanatkumara, and carried them away. Samba awoke from the spell to find himself in a dungeon, taken out of action before he could strike even a single blow.

'We have lost already,' wailed the Yadus, lamenting the disappearance of their leaders.

'Fear not, I am here still,' said Pradyumna, soaring down to earth to lead them. 'The Yadus will not fail; I swear in the name of my father.'

He infused new hope in his men by using mahamaya to dispel the sorcery. Then he sprang to the attack. He flung out his arms and a blue fire darted from his fingertips. The fire catapulted the demons into the skies where Jayanta and

Pravara cut them down. He inflicted terrible hallucinations on the asuras, causing them to tear out their own flesh in chunks. They writhed in agony, twisting their bodies, contorting their faces and frothing at the mouth.

Pradyumna tried to isolate Nikumbha by convincing the other princes to leave the field. 'Why do you fight alongside the asura?' he asked Duryodhana, Karna and Drupada. 'You know that Nikumbha can never win. Why do you risk humiliation and imprisonment?'

'It is not we who risk our lives,' replied the arrogant Duryodhana. 'Your uncle Balarama tricked me into giving my daughter Lakshmani in marriage to Samba. Where is the valiant groom now? Wallowing in the darkness of a dungeon, unable to stand against us!'

'Samba is a coward like all the Yadus,' Karna joined in. 'They can only win by using trickery.'

'We Kshatriyas would rather not fight against your ragged band of cowherds. I will give you a last chance to save your life,' said Duryodhana. 'Run away and hide from the fury of our combined forces.'

'The greater a man's arrogance, the bigger his fall,' said Pradyumna. 'Our army fights in the name of Krishna, and no army on earth can match his forces.'

Angered by his words, Karna and Drupada let loose weapons that spewed fire over a hundred legions. The twanging of their bows sounded like the crashing waves of the Pralaya as it swallowed the world. The demons howled in delight at the attack and flew forward on their hideous vaahanas to tear out the throats of the enemy. They twisted off heads and disembowelled their foes.

And then came the breaking point. A terrible hissing filled the air as two enormous serpents, with a thousand heads each, sprang up before them, belching fire. The Yadu warriors ran away screaming, their courage failing them. Only a few stalwarts remained on the field with Pradyumna.

We are lost, he thought. *I am guilty of sacrificing my men in my arrogance, after accusing Duryodhana of the same crime. Now our only recourse is to kill as many of them as possible before they kill us.*

Then he heard his father's voice in his ear. 'It is Shiva's boon that endows Nikumbha with deathly powers. Only Shiva's grace will enable you to overcome him.'

At once, Pradyumna sent up a fervent prayer to the supreme lord of men and beasts. He sought the blessings of the Tryambaka, the one with three eyes, the source of creation, sustenance and dissolution.

All of a sudden the earth trembled and a mighty figure bounded towards Pradyumna who still stood with his head bowed in worship. The warrior looked up and saw Nandi, Shiva's divine bull who accompanies him in his cosmic dance, and embodies the lord's strength and devotion to dharma. He was massive, like a golden hill, and adorned with glittering ornaments. He was three-eyed like his lord and had four arms, in which he carried Shiva's own weapons, a trident, an axe, a golden staff and a deer that represented control over the restless mind.

'I thank Shiva for sending his majestic commander,' cried out Pradyumna, bowing to the celestial visitor.

'I have brought you a gift from my lord,' said Nandi. 'A noose that pulses with the power of Shiva's trishul. Use it to bind the princes who have sold their souls for gold.'

Pradyumna cast the noose at the enemy princes. It leaped forward with the deafening sound of a thousand thunderstorms and captured them in its coils, transporting them to the dungeons that were guarded by Aniruddha.

Nandi turned his fury on the demons with a roar that swept them from the field like leaves tossed by a whirlwind.

He transformed himself into a colossal bull and pawed the ground with his mighty hooves. He tore up mountains with his horns and cast them on his enemies. His tail stretched to a hundred yojanas and whipped the enemy into mounds of flesh. Blood flowed like a river and the clamour of dying and maimed warriors echoed across hills and vales.

But as soon as Nandi killed the demons, Nikumbha restored them to life, invoking Shiva's boon. The battle stretched on like an endless nightmare. Finally, Nandi said to Pradyumna, 'Invoke Shiva and pray for the sword that accompanies his fierce form of Bhairava.'

Once more Pradyumna surrendered to Shiva, who bestowed his sword upon him.

'Take me on in single combat if you have the courage,' Pradyumna challenged Nikumbha. He would spare his men more death and dismemberment by taking on the demon himself. 'Find out if you are truly as brave as you claim to be.'

'Do not try to frighten me with your posturing, fool,' laughed the asura as he unsheathed his own sword. 'You will die an agonizing death at my hands, and I promise to prolong your suffering.'

Pradyumna's soldiers watched in terror as the asura's mammoth figure towered over their prince. Their leader, however, was undeterred and used his superior skill and speed to inflict severe wounds on the asura. Nikumbha grunted in anger and pain and rushed at his opponent, aiming a fatal blow. The soldiers gasped, fearing that this was the end.

'Use your enemy's weakness to defeat him,' his grandsire Vasudeva had advised him, and Pradyumna used the asura's arrogance against him. He let the asura get close to him and then sidestepped, slashing swiftly with Bhairava's sword so that the force of the blow pierced the demon's heart.

Nikumbha fell down, lifeless. The Yadus were struck dumb for a few moments and then broke out in a clamour of celebration.

Pradyumna hurried to the demon's occult cave where Samba and the other Yadus were being held, and set them free. He directed Aniruddha to release the Kuru and Chedi princes from his custody. They left, shamefaced, for their own kingdoms, their greed having led them to a terrible humiliation.

King Brahmadatta was overjoyed at the death of the asura. He completed the Aswamedha sacrifice in peace and made his offerings to Krishna. The princesses chose their grooms in the swayamvara and the Yadus returned to their city. Samba slunk in alone, miserable and disappointed that his quest for fame had ended in imprisonment.

27

A Wedding and a Funeral

When the noise of battle died down and Dwaraka returned to its tranquil ways, Rukmini spoke of something that was close to her heart. 'We have faced many wars as well as disharmony in our family,' she said to her lord and Pradyumna. 'Perhaps we should plan a celebration that will erase the dark events from our minds.'

'When have I stood in the way of your wishes, my queen?' asked Krishna with a smile. 'What is your desire?'

'The wedding of our grandson Aniruddha,' she replied. The young lad was doubly precious to her for in him she saw the son she had lost to Kaalasura during his growing years. 'There is only one girl who is suitable for him. My brother Rukmi's granddaughter Rochana, who is as lovely as an apsara.' She turned to her son for his response.

Pradyumna nodded his consent. 'Your wish is my command, mother,' he said. 'I know you have my son's well-being at heart. Rukmavati will be pleased too as the girl is from her own family.'

'I give you my blessing,' said Krishna.

A retinue of Yadus soon travelled to Bhojakata, Rukmi's capital, bearing the marriage proposal along with gifts of gold and silk, jewels and horses. Rukmi received the guests with respect. His defeat at Krishna's hands still rankled, but he was not ready to take on the mighty Pradyumna or insult his sister by turning down her request. He agreed to the proposal and consulted his priests to set an auspicious date for the marriage.

Krishna led the wedding party to Bhojakata. However, knowing the hatred that Rukmi nursed against him, he warned Pradyumna to be prepared for any calamity.

'Rukmi consents only because he knows Aniruddha is capable of abducting Rochana like I seized Rukmini,' he said. 'You must be constantly vigilant, as Rukmi has never been honourable.'

The royal family left Dwaraka on caparisoned elephants and chariots drawn by magnificent white steeds, their retinue bearing gems and gold, incense and sweetmeats. Krishna was accompanied by Aniruddha, Rukmini, Balarama, Pradyumna, Samba and other family members, as well as the royal priests.

Rukmi welcomed them with soft words and fragrant offerings. His ministers provided them with luxurious mansions for their stay. All the houses in Bhojakata were festooned with flags and flowers. Mango leaves and areca nut palms decorated the doorways. The people gazed in awe at the gallant Aniruddha, his face and form as flawless as a lotus with a thousand petals.

Decked in resplendent silks, her body anointed with sandal paste, a sparkling gem set in her navel, armlets and necklaces adding lustre to her beauty, the radiant Rochana awaited her prince. Her teeth were like jasmine buds; her lips red as cherries. Her waist was slim as a reed and she moved with the grace of a swan floating on the surface of a pool.

The prince gazed at her and forgot to look away. She smiled, blushed and dropped her eyes, captivated by the passion and power he radiated. When Rochana came to stand by Aniruddha's side, the gathering gasped in awe, remarking that they looked like Vishnu and Lakshmi in Vaikunta.

The young couple completed the holy rituals before the sacred fire. The elders and sages blessed them with long life and happiness. The guests and the commoners of Vidharba feasted on the royal fare. The celebration on the streets continued for a full week.

However, the troublemakers in the kingdom were unhappy with the adulation being showered on the visitors. The Kalinga king Dantavakra, whose name meant 'crooked teeth', had a crooked mind too and provoked Rukmi by reminding him of his disgrace at Rukmini's swayamvara.

'How can you welcome the man who cut off your hair and beard when you tried to stop him from abducting your sister?' Dantavakra asked. 'He stripped you naked and used your clothes to tie you to the chariot's wheel for all the world to see. The stain on your reputation still remains, unwashed and unwashable.'

Rukmi's eyes reddened. The old humiliation flashed through his mind and his hatred flamed anew.

'What do you expect me to do when we are celebrating my granddaughter's marriage to his grandson?' he growled.

'Get back at Krishna by challenging his brother to a game of dice. Balarama loves to gamble, but is not an expert at the game. Ply him with wine and you will soon own all that he possesses.'

Rukmi's eyes lit up at the thought that he could win by guile what he could not win on the battlefield. After the sumptuous wedding feast, he set out the choicest wines before Balarama and invited him to taste them. Krishna's brother, clad in rich silk and wearing garlands of jasmine and sandalwood, was happy to indulge himself. As he quaffed the wine, Rukmi poured more into the goblet, ensuring that it was always full. Balarama was soon flushed with drink, and his raucous laughter grew louder as the day wore on.

'We should indulge ourselves in a game of dice, my brother,' said Rukmi. 'It is not often that we meet to enjoy this sport.'

'Yes, let us play,' said Balarama.

Rukmi brought out the board that he had kept ready. The two sides sat behind the players to watch the encounter. Dantavakra sat next to Rukmi, whispering advice, while Pradyumna and Samba sat beside their uncle, ready to help at a moment's notice.

The game began for a stake of a thousand gold pieces. Rukmi laughed loudly when the dice favoured him and he won the first game. 'Let's raise the stake to 10,000 gold pieces,' he said, challenging Balarama.

Balarama nodded. Rukmi won this game too. Dantavakra made a rude gesture and displayed his crooked teeth in a sneer.

Samba's face turned red and he staggered to his feet. 'What are you laughing at, fool?' he called out.

'It is only a game of dice, Samba,' said Pradyumna, forcing his brother down. 'Remember, we are here to celebrate Aniruddha's marriage.'

'How about a stake of 1,00,000 gold coins?' asked Rukmi, excited at his first win against Krishna's clan.

'Are you sure you want to continue, uncle?' asked Pradyumna in his uncle's ear. 'Shouldn't we return to our palace? It has been a long, tiring day.'

'Afraid, are you? The Yadus always run from a challenge!' taunted Rukmi. 'The great Balarama is afraid to play a game of dice.'

Pradyumna realized that his father's warning had been justified. Clearly, Rukmi and his friends had set a nefarious plan in motion, and he had to do his best to avert it.

'Gambling is not a noble sport, but the herald of doom,' he said, for he had learned dharma at the feet of the Dark One. 'It brought down Yudhistira himself and led him to stake his brothers and his wife. It is the gateway to hell—Dvaaram sughorum narakasya jihmam.'

'Aha, an ascetic in our midst,' mocked Dantavakra. 'What are you doing in a palace when you should be begging on the streets?'

Pradyumna felt the blood rush to his head. Balarama placed a hand on his nephew's arm and said, 'Relax and let me play. I cannot allow these lowly men to call us names.'

Rukmi flashed his eyes in triumph at Dantavakra as they began the next game. He would win this time against the hated Yadus, who had shamed him and driven him from his capital.

Pradyumna sat back in deference to his uncle's words, though he feared that the day would not end well. Samba sat with his hand on his sword, ready to spill blood if need be, his senses inflamed by the wine and the jealousy that ate at his heart. Once more, Pradyumna and his son had relegated him to the sidelines. He would enjoy marring Aniruddha's wedding celebrations with a violent tussle.

The game favoured first one side and then the other. Fate stood watching, waiting for the opportune moment. Balarama came close to losing his 100,000 coins, but then a change in fortunes brought him victory. He shouted out in joy. Samba slapped his thighs and glared at the opponents.

Rukmi was taken aback, but was unwilling to concede victory. His deceitful mind took over. 'You are mistaken,' he pronounced. 'I am the winner—ask my friends.'

Dantavakra jumped in to support him. His friends raised their voices in agreement. 'Rukmi is the winner. All of us saw it,' they said.

'Balarama's brain is muddled by too much wine,' scoffed Rukmi. His friends called out further insults.

'They are cheats who have never won anything honestly,' said Dantavakra.

Samba drew his sword in anger, and Pradyumna struggled to restrain him.

Balarama's voice cut through the noise. 'I wager one crore golden coins. Play me if you dare,' he shouted, pouring the contents of his goblet down his throat.

Silence fell, as no one could imagine a prize of this magnitude.

I must win this at all costs, thought Rukmi. *I will do whatever it takes.*

All eyes were fixed on the dice as it began to roll.

Rukmi cast an eight, and Balarama matched it with an eight of his own.

The dice rolled again. Now Rukmi scored a nine.

Then came the fateful roll. Balarama cast the dice—a winning eleven. He had done it!

'I win,' roared Balarama, rising to his feet in jubilation. But Dantavakra scooped up the dice in the blink of an eye.

'It was only a seven,' he shouted. 'Rukmi has won one crore gold coins!'

The Yadus protested vociferously and called their rivals cheats. Rukmi's friends stood up too and squared up to them. A shouting match began and, soon after, the wrangling became physical. Rough blows were exchanged.

Then a voice boomed from the sky. 'Rukmi makes a false claim. The winner is Balarama,' it proclaimed.

The Yadus cheered and heckled their rivals. But Rukmi and his clan of deceivers would not listen.

'I do not care if the gods themselves come to your support,' said Rukmi. 'There can be no doubt that I am the winner. You cowherds will never understand royal diversions like dice and archery. Go back to your cattle, for that is the only pastime you are fit for! You cannot defeat the king who was blessed with Shiva's divine bow.'

Destiny laughed as Rukmi hurtled towards his doom, having forgotten Shiva's injunction when he granted the boon. 'My bow will remain with you only as long as you do not confront Vishnu,' Shiva had said. Rukmi had now taken on Balarama, a manifestation of Vishnu and Adisesha.

Dantavakra moved forward to challenge Balarama, baring his teeth like a bear. Balarama lost his temper at his insolence. He could not be patient any longer just because he was a guest at Rukmi's palace, especially when his hosts had been so disrespectful.

'Come to me, Sunanda,' Balarama cried out, and his invincible mace flew to his hand. He rose in fury and brought his mace down on Rukmi's head, killing him instantly. Dantavakra turned to flee, but Balarama seized him by his hair and knocked out his teeth. His anger was unabated, and he lashed out at the other kings, smashing their arms and legs with powerful blows, filling the hall with bloodied limbs. They screamed in pain while Balarama roared in rage. Pradyumna tried his best, but could not restrain his uncle.

Samba too gave vent to his own bitterness, plunging into the enemy ranks to hack them with his sword.

Krishna and Rukmini rushed in upon hearing the sounds of battle. They stood speechless at the carnage before them. Rukmini saw her brother's body with its head smashed in and staggered back in shock. Her anger surpassed her grief, and she screamed at the combatants.

'Who dared to attack my brother in this fashion? Whose club was it that split his head open so that he would die like an animal?'

Her voice penetrated the fog surrounding Balarama and he stopped in mid-stride. He whirled around to face her. 'I did what I had to do,' he said, his face livid with rage. 'Rukmi lied and cheated and hurled unbearable insults at our clan. I could take it no more.'

'It was *you*? Did you save my brother from my lord at my swayamvara so that you could kill him yourself in this barbaric manner? You seem to forget that this is not a battleground, and we are not here to wage war. We are here to celebrate the marriage of our grandchildren.' Agonized sobs wrenched her body and she broke down.

Rukmi's men limped away as she spoke, carrying away their dead and wounded. Krishna stood silent, unwilling to take sides in a fight between his wife and his brother. It would take a long time for tempers to cool down.

He looked at the alcove where Shiva's bow had rested on a bed of velvet. The bow had disappeared, returning to Shiva when Rukmi attacked Balarama.

Krishna feared that war would break out over these deaths and more lives would be lost. 'We should not linger here any more,' he said to Pradyumna. 'Let us return to Dwaraka.'

They returned to their mansions in silence while their men prepared for the journey.

Rukmini wept until she could weep no more. She was heartbroken that the wedding festivities had ended with the funeral of her beloved brother.

Narada appeared before them, as he did whenever destiny took a momentous turn. His rich repertoire of fables about kings and gods, sages and curses, karma and dharma would help them view recent events with a clearer eye. It would help them understand the larger patterns of life and death.

'Many a kingdom has been lost in a game of dice,' he said. 'This game is the herald of the Kali Yuga, causing strife within families and encouraging sin. Duryodhana is in fact the embodiment of Kali, while his uncle Shakuni embodies Dwapara, the age preceding Kali.'

'We know that Kali Yuga is a time of unspeakable evil,' said Pradyumna.

'Yes. The world is plunged into torment, joy is lost and unimaginable diseases stalk the earth. Under the influence of Kali, priests forget the meaning of the Vedas. Devotees cease their prayers and vratas. Righteous people are humiliated and the virtuous flee to the jungles to escape from the thieves and murderers in power. Children are born deformed. Fine clothes are regarded as sufficient to indicate dharma. After 10,000 years of Kali, the sacred rivers return to heaven, and so does the tulsi plant, unable to bear the sinful atmosphere any longer.'

'A prospect too dreadful to contemplate. How long does this yuga last, Devarishi, and how can we escape from the demon?'

'Kali Yuga will last for twelve hundred celestial years, or 4,32,000 human years. The only way to escape Kali's influence is to avoid gambling, liquor and loose women. These bring sorrow, disease and degradation in their wake. You must also avoid the sinners who frequent these places, for they are lost to lust, greed and desire.'

'Why did Yudhistira, the son of dharma, indulge in this game? Was it his karma that compelled him?' asked Pradyumna.

'He knew it was wrong. Yet he said, "If Duryodhana challenges me, I will accept it." Then, when he lost everything, he blamed his fate. "Like lightning blinds the eyes, fate blinds clear thinking," Yudhistira said. He returned to Hastinapura to gamble a second time, saying, "The old king commands me to play and I will obey, though I know it will lead to my doom."'

'So it was not fate that compelled him to gamble; it was his own addiction to the game.'

'Yes. Everyone is free to decide how they will act. It is only the results of their actions that are fated.'

Narada took a drink to wet his throat and continued speaking. 'Yudhistira was not the only king who met with a dire fate because he gambled,' he said.

'Nala, the king of Nishadha, was eager to attend the swayamvara of Damayanti, the princess of Vidharba who was considered the most beautiful woman in the world. Devas like Indra, Agni, Varuna and Yama vied for her hand, and wooed her with a display of their wealth. But Damayanti had her heart set on marrying Nala, of whose exploits she had learned from a divine swan.

'When they discovered her intention, the devas threatened her with their powers and tried to change her mind, but Damayanti was unswerving in her desire to marry the virtuous Nala. The gods grew angry and disguised themselves as Nala in an attempt to confuse her. However, the strength of her piety helped her distinguish the true Nala from the others and she placed her garland around his neck.

'The devas recognized that the princess was no ordinary mortal. They accepted her decision and conferred gifts on her bridegroom.

'"I grant Nala the power to travel anywhere in the world with just a thought," said Indra.

'"I bestow on him the power to command fire," said Agni.

'"My boon will allow him to control the seas," said Varuna.

'"My gift is a divine skill in preparing food," said Yama.

'As the young couple bowed to the devas, a sudden wind gusted through the hall, and nocturnal animals were heard howling though it was still day. Moments later, the Kali demon entered the hall with his brother Dwapara.

'"I have come to carry away the princess of whose beauty the whole world speaks," Kali proclaimed. Then he saw the garlands around the necks of the bridal couple and realized that the swayamvara was over. He stormed up and down angrily, ranting, "So, the girl chooses a mere mortal, spurning all the devas. This is an insult to all of us. We cannot let her get away with this. I will kill the man she has chosen and take her with me."

'"We have blessed them already and will not allow you to attack them," Indra cautioned him. "Damayanti has chosen a virtuous man, who is equal to any deva. If you curse them, be warned that the curse will recoil upon you. Accept her decision with grace and be gone."

'The devas returned to the heavens after delivering their warning, and Nala set off to his kingdom with his new wife.

'Meanwhile, Kali tossed his bludgeon from hand to hand as he plotted Nala's downfall. "I will possess Nala and deprive him of his kingdom and his bride," he said to his brother.

'He followed Nala for twelve long years, waiting for the opportune moment to attack him.

'And then, one day, Nala gave him the opportunity by not washing his feet before beginning his prayers. Kali struck with the malevolence that had been building within him for years.

'He sought the help of Nala's brother Pushkara and tempted him with the prospect of seizing Nala's kingdom.

'"Challenge your brother to a game of dice," he said, "and I will take care of the rest."

'Nala's downfall began the moment he accepted his brother's challenge. Kali entered the dice and ensured that Nala lost everything—his possessions and his kingdom.

'"You have lost everything, brother. Why don't you stake your wife Damayanti as well?" Pushkara taunted, casting lustful eyes on Damayanti.

'"I may be a fool, but I will never stoop to such depths," said Nala, turning away from the temptation that had brought about his ruin. "I will discard my rich clothes and ornaments and retreat to the forest to perform penance for my sins. As for you, my long-suffering wife, I advise you to seek sanctuary in your father's kingdom, for the harsh forest is no place for a princess."

'"Where you go, I will follow," said Damayanti, and accompanied her husband when he walked away from his kingdom, renouncing everything. Nala's guilt grew when he saw how she suffered, though she did not utter a word of complaint. He slipped quietly away when she was asleep, so she would be compelled to seek shelter with her father. Wrapped in his own guilt, he failed to consider how dangerous it would be for her to make her way alone through the forest.

'Nala travelled deeper into the forest where he saw Karkotaka, the serpent king of the netherworld, struggling to escape a raging fire. He saved the serpent by using Agni's boon, which gave him power over the flames. But once free, the snake bit him.

'"Is this the way you repay me for saving your life?" asked Nala, as the poison burned through his veins and distorted his body.

'"Yes, it is," said Karkotaka. "Your twisted body will help you escape the notice of your enemies. My poison will torture the Kali demon who has taken possession of your body and force him to release you. Here is a magic robe that will restore you to your natural form once you are rid of the demon."

'Eventually, Kali was forced to leave Nala's body for he was unable to bear the vicious poison. Nala won back his kingdom

using the expertise in dice that he had acquired when he served
King Rituparna of Ayodhya, and was reunited with the faithful
Damayanti.'

Narada fell silent, and his listeners returned from the world he
had conjured up with his words to the palace in Bhojakata.

'Why did Nala not kill Kali when he was weakened by
Karkotaka's poison?' asked Pradyumna. 'The world would have
been eternally grateful to him for saving it from the demon.'

'That task is not so easily accomplished,' said Narada.
'Kali came to life when the ocean of milk was churned and the
halahala poison emerged. Shiva swallowed most of the poison,
but the small portion that remained became the body of Kali
and of vicious creatures like snakes and wolves. Every time Kali
faces death, he leaves behind his human form and his spirit
escapes to another world. Here, he awaits the birth of the next
kalpa when he permeates all life with evil and gradually takes
over the world.'

'A fearsome, invincible enemy,' murmured Pradyumna.

'Only a mahapurusha who is as pure as he is valorous can
hope to confront Kali,' said Narada.

The royal attendants came in to tell Krishna that
arrangements for their return had been completed. They set
out with Aniruddha leading them in his fine chariot, his bride
Rochana by his side. The mood was sombre, as the tragic turn
of events had destroyed the joy of the wedding.

What does the future hold for the clan, they could not help but
wonder.

28

The Flying City

'Why do some men persist in evil though they are warned again and again?' Pradyumna asked his great father, when he found him alone one day after they returned to Dwaraka.

'Men are motivated by three gunas or qualities,' Krishna explained. 'Sattva or goodness prompts right action. Tamas is the darkness of inertia and must be shunned. The third quality is rajas or passion, which is the foundation of all wrong action. This is what motivates evil men like the Kurus, leading them to their ruin.'

'Duryodhana failed miserably when he supported the asura Nikumbha against our army. Now he opposes you and dharma by depriving the Pandavas of an equal share of their kingdom. Does he not realize that he can never win this fight?'

'The nature of evil is such that it can never be suppressed for long. Men like him always choose evil, thereby accumulating a heavy burden of karma. This karma causes them to be born again and again, sinking deeper into the darkness of envy and anger. Men like Duryodhana are like defective pots made by a potter. Some break on the wheel, while some crack after they are removed from it. Some fall apart when they are fired in a kiln, while others shatter when they are being used.'

'I stand firmly on the side of the righteous Pandavas, whose sons Abhimanyu and Ghatotkacha are my closest friends,' said Pradyumna.

After the battle with Nikumbha, the Pandava princes had returned to their capital Indraprastha, built on the barren land which Duryodhana had given them, and the Kurus retired to their own capital Hastinapura, to brood over their defeat.

Their anger was fuelled further when Yudhistira invited them to attend a Rajasuya yagna in Indraprastha. The successful completion of the yagna would mean that Yudhistira would be recognized as an emperor. The thought of their cousin Yudhistira being crowned the king of kings was intolerable. Their envy flared higher when they saw the fabulous court hall constructed for the Pandavas by Mayaa, the chief architect of the netherworld. The Mayaa Sabha, as it was called, was lit by the soft glow of rare gems and crystals, and had pools reflecting the marble ceiling so artfully that they looked like floors. Fooled by the artistry behind these pools, Duryodhana fell into one. His ignominy was witnessed by the Pandava queen Draupadi who laughed at him, filling him with a fierce thirst for revenge.

After watching the crowning of Yudhistira, Duryodhana and his clan returned to Hastinapura, their minds corroded with envy.

'Despite all our efforts, the Pandavas achieve one victory after another. Yudhistira is now the emperor of the world when he is not half as brave as I am,' fumed Duryodhana. 'I hate him and his harlot wife who sleeps with all five brothers. I startle awake at night, hearing her mocking laughter when I fell into the pool.'

His evil uncle Shakuni tried to console him. 'As long as Arjuna, Bhima and Krishna fight by his side we cannot defeat him on the battlefield. But we can exploit his weakness for a game of dice. You know that I can control the dice and make them roll whatever number I choose. I will trounce him and make him lose everything he owns.'

Their laughter grew louder in the days that followed. Yudhistira fell into their trap and came to play, only to lose everything—his kingdom and his wealth; himself and his brothers and, finally, his fiery queen Draupadi.

Unfortunately for the Pandavas, Krishna was not with them when they received the invitation to gamble, or he would have prevented them from accepting it. He had been honoured at the completion of the yagna by Yudhistira and had stayed on with them. But a messenger had arrived from Dwaraka bringing the news that the Yadus had been attacked by Shalva, and he had rushed back to his city.

Shalva was a master of the dark forces and an ardent devotee of Shiva. Half human and half beast, clad in black silk clothes, Shalva struck terror with his mere appearance. He had acquired fearsome powers by performing dire penances to the three-eyed god. He stood in the middle of a towering fire and consumed only its ashes. He plunged neck-deep into icy streams and chanted Shiva's names. He balanced his entire body on one toe and sang the lord's praises. Still, Shiva refused to bless him. Finally, he began to sever his limbs one by one and feed them to the fire.

Shiva appeared then to stop his dire sacrifice. 'What is it you seek, Shalva?' he asked.

'Bless me with a vimaana, a flying disc that will be invisible and invincible,' said Shalva. 'It must obey my very thought and be capable of travelling to any realm. It must serve as a moving arsenal, with weapons mightier than any that exist in the world today. It must have the power to defeat gods, demons, humans, gandharvas, nagas and rakshasas.'

'So will it be,' said Shiva, granting Shalva the boon.

Shalva then employed Mayaa to create his Saubha, his flying city that could move at speeds that made it invisible. It soared like a comet, equally at ease on land, air and water. Sometimes it appeared as a ship on the sea and the next moment it floated over a hill or streaked across land like a chariot. It was a kingdom in itself, larger than any on earth. At times, it split into numerous discs, like luminous fireflies in the night sky, except that these were home to death. The aerial city moved so swiftly that it seemed the skies were studded with a hundred suns, moons and stars. The world was lit up by its splendid lights so that night became day. When it was finally completed, the vimaana was more wondrous than imagination could conjure.

Flying around in the Saubha, Shalva hurled rockets, battleaxes, three-bladed javelins, flame-throwers, and other missiles at his foes, spinning away like a whirlwind before the enemy could retaliate.

Shalva had formed an evil triumvirate with Jarasandha and Sishupala, and was incensed when they were killed by the Pandavas and Krishna.

When Jarasandha had refused to accept the Pandavas' supremacy, Bhima challenged him to a wrestling match. Despite repeated attempts, Bhima was unable to kill the king, for though he tore his body apart, the asura's body kept knitting itself together again. Krishna then indicated to the Pandava prince that he should tear Jarasandha's body in two and throw the pieces in opposite directions. When he did this, the king could not return to life, as the pieces could not merge into one. Sishupala had been forgiven for his crimes one hundred times, in accordance with a promise that Krishna had made to

Sishupala's mother. But when the Chedi king persisted in his sins and abused Krishna at Yudhistira's yagna, the Blue God sheared off his head with his Sudarshana chakra.

'I must avenge the death of my friends,' said Shalva. 'I will burn down Krishna's city while he is still gloating in Indraprastha over the successful crowning of Yudhistira.'

Shalva descended on Dwaraka in his Saubha, along with a vast ocean of soldiers. His first view of the city from up in the sky was more breathtaking than he cared to admit. It seemed as if the brilliance of the city, created by Visvakarma, the builder of Indra's capital, surpassed even the magic of his celestial chariot.

Visvakarma had given equal thought to Dwaraka's defence as to its beauty. Its walls were huge and well fortified and constructed in concentric circles. The outer walls were built on boulders reclaimed from the sea. The gates were high and wide enough to allow battle elephants to pass through, and embedded with sharp, stout iron spikes to keep the elephants of an invading army from breaking them down. Warriors stood guard on the turrets built on top of the walls, armed with cannons, cannonballs and huge vats of oil that they could set on fire. There were small openings in the wall through which archers could shoot at advancing armies. Thousands of war chariots protected the city. There were deep trenches and moats that could not be easily breached. Mines were buried underground, ready to be set off if the enemy were to break through the city's defences. Krishna and his advisers had also devised an elaborate scheme to prevent spies or enemy troops from sneaking into the city. The citizens carried seals embossed with a carving of a three-headed animal, representing the bull, unicorn and goat. They had to show this seal in order to enter or exit the city. The guards apprehended those who tried to enter through subterfuge, interrogated them and then jailed them.

'A city whose walls have never been breached at any time in its history,' muttered Shalva as he floated over it in his vimaana. 'I will bring you to your knees.'

His angry eyes took in the soaring palaces, the magnificent temples, and the well-designed roads and quadrangles. He saw the happy citizens going about their duties without realizing that death stalked them from the skies.

Rage choked his throat and he began to bombard the city's towers and mansions with huge tree trunks, boulders, thunderbolts and venomous snakes. He let loose a huge tornado that whirled through the city, blinding its people and rendering them helpless.

The citizens ran pell-mell, struck for the first time in their lives with the fear of death. Their children, their cattle, their possessions—how could they protect everything from this unseen attacker? Who was the frightful monster in the sky?

Even as they panicked and tried to gather their wits, the next wave of death battered them in the form of bludgeons, spikes and balls of flame. The weapons sliced off heads and limbs, gouged flesh, killing thousands.

Pradyumna erupted into the quadrangle when he heard the howling of the weapons and the wailing of his people. He sent up a swift prayer to his father, who was yet to return from Indraprastha, and took up command.

Dwaraka's brave generals rode out of the city with their legions to fight Shalva's huge land army. Each of these warriors was a maharathi, capable of killing thousands with his weapons. The unexpected onslaught had numbed them for a moment and proved deadly to their clan.

The valiant forces of dharma clashed with the cruel multitudes of adharma. The demon Kshemavriddhi attacked Samba with arrows that exploded in the midst of his retinue, instantly reducing them to ashes. Samba countered with fifty arrows for each of the enemy's arrows, covering the demon's body entirely with them. The demon began to bleed from hundreds of wounds but stood unmoved. Samba advanced on him and bludgeoned him with all manner of weapons, forcing him to flee from the vicious attack.

Vegavat, an asura with only one eye that was the size of a chariot wheel, hurled his mace at Aniruddha. The Yadu scion sidestepped the blow and wielded his mace with such fury that the demon fell dead.

Shalva's savage general Vivindhya took on Pradyumna, sending forth a flood of arrows that drove his enemy back, unable to withstand the ferocity. Pradyumna countered with Indra's Aindraastra that rained a hundred thousand arrows on the enemy soldiers, destroying them like flies. Vivindhya collapsed under this attack and was trampled to death by his own troops.

The Yadu warriors held their own against the asuras, wielding their weapons with the ferocity of Bhima and the skill of Arjuna. Shalva saw his forces being routed despite their greater numbers, and rushed towards Pradyumna, knowing that he was the force holding the opposition together. If he could slay him, he would win the battle.

'Fight me if you can, coward,' he taunted from the skies, his voice echoing from all the directions. His fearsome chariot bombarded weapons from the skies, striking dread in the hearts of the Yadu soldiers and sapping them of their courage.

Shalva conjured up many abominations that went against all known laws of nature and god. Monsters with many heads and demons with none terrified the soldiers with their grisly forms. Hideous dragons with the heads of wolves roared as they smashed the soldiers with their spiked tails. Lions belched fire and demon children with serpents crawling out of their eyes howled at them.

However, Pradyumna stood defiant against them all. 'Come to me, Yadus, and fight in the name of Krishna!' he roared. His strong voice filled his men once again with the fervour of the Blue God, whose power surpassed that of all demonic forces. They saw Pradyumna standing proud and unafraid, his arrows flying true and straight, like snakes that kill with a single strike.

'Shalva, prepare to meet your death!' he screamed. 'We will destroy you with the power of Vishnu.'

Pradyumna flew at the evil demon on his winged chariot, which bore the banner of the makara. Shalva brought his vimaana to the ground in order to engage Pradyumna in a duel. The air twanged with the sound of drawstrings, flying sabres and axes, lustrous spears and discs that hurtled between the mighty warriors. It seemed that neither could win, as both were invincible.

Suddenly, the war took a turn for the worse for the Yadus, guided by the guile and treachery of the demons who obeyed none of the rules of battle. Shalva's commander-in-chief Dyuman attacked Pradyumna from behind while he was engaged in his duel with Shalva, knocking him senseless.

Shalva was overjoyed and roared in triumph. 'Pradyumna is dead! Pradyumna is dead! Surrender to us now, worms!' His voice struck terror in the minds of the Yadus.

Aniruddha collapsed in grief. Pradyumna was dead. The battle was lost. Now the enemy would break down their walls and ride in triumph through Dwaraka's proud avenues. They would slaughter the men and children and ravage the women. They would plunder and loot, burn and pillage. The sounds of mourning would envelop the city like a shroud for the dead.

29

The Rage of God

Pradyumna's men did not realize that he was not dead, but had merely swooned from Dyuman's treacherous attack. The Yadu warrior was spirited away from the battlefield by his charioteer Kaunteya, son of Daruka, Krishna's charioteer. Kaunteya ministered to him until Pradyumna came back to his senses a short while later.

As soon as he opened his eyes, Pradyumna looked around and seized his weapons. Then he realized that he was no longer on the battlefield and collapsed in shame. He glared at his charioteer.

'All is lost!' he exclaimed. 'You may have saved my life by removing me from the battlefield. But you have exposed me to the world and to my men as a coward who flees from his enemies. How could you do this, Kaunteya? How can I ever forgive you for this shame?'

'I merely did what I had to do when I saw that you were wounded,' replied Kaunteya. 'It was my duty to protect you until you recovered from Dyuman's dastardly blow. Your father and your men will thank me for saving you. And no one who saw you fight today could ever call you a coward.'

'My heart breaks when I think of the fate of the men whom I abandoned. Drive me back at once so that I can discover what has transpired in my absence.'

The battle was still raging when Pradyumna returned, though his men were in low spirits. He headed straight for Dyuman. 'Face me now, monster, and fight honourably!' he cried out.

Dyuman reeled in shock upon seeing that Krishna's son was alive and well. Before he could respond, a volley of eight arrows flew at him from Pradyumna's bow. Four arrows took out Dyuman's horses. One killed his charioteer, one shattered his bow and the seventh shredded his flag. The last arrow severed the demon's head from his torso. Blood gushed out from the asura's neck and his colossal body crashed on to the ground.

'Come and get me, Shalva!' Pradyumna roared again. 'Fight fairly if you dare. And stop your attack on the unarmed citizens of my city.'

Shalva charged towards him, first attacking Kaunteya for having saved Pradyumna. The charioteer collapsed, wounded grievously. Pradyumna could not fight without someone guiding the chariot. He had no choice but to turn back from the confrontation, giving the enemy another chance to call him a coward. As he reached for the reins of the horses, Pradyumna saw the wounded Kaunteya vanish from sight, and a warrior princess take his place. He gasped when he saw Mayavati, clad in armour, taking up the reins of the chariot to help her lord win the battle. She turned to smile at him and then forged ahead, taking them closer to Shalva's celestial craft.

Nothing could stop Pradyumna now. He shattered Shalva's occult powers with arrows that were as deadly as those from Arjuna's Gandiva. Their duel raged fiercely as they fought from their chariots, on the ground and in the air. Pradyumna's swordplay spun a web of death around the asura that brought to mind Sahadeva's lightning sallies. His blows with his mace echoed the ferocity of his rakshasa cousin Ghatotkacha.

Shalva reeled back, unable to take on this Pralaya in human form.

Pradyumna strung his bow with the Naagaastra. 'Die now, demon!' he roared. Mayavati held the chariot steady, facing the asura.

And then he heard the voice call out to him: 'Stop now, in the name of Brahma!'

Pradyumna paused with the Naagaastra pulsing in his hand, ready to put an end to the savage Shalva.

Narada appeared before Pradyumna and said, 'Dauntless hero, you have defeated the demon in full view of the world. Now you have the power to slay him with your astra. But I beg you to stay your hand, as Brahma has ordained that only Krishna should slay Shalva. Do not prove Brahma's words false.'

Pradyumna's body shook as he exercised his will to control his mind. He did not want to stop when he was on the verge of avenging the deaths of his people. But he could not disrespect the gods and disobey their command.

He finally detached the Naagaastra from his bow and returned it to his quiver, letting Shalva escape.

'The devas recognize today that you are not just a great warrior. You have displayed the discipline of a tapasvin and the humility to respect your elders,' said Narada. He clasped Pradyumna to his chest in a rare gesture of affection.

As Pradyumna turned to the battlefield again, he saw that Shalva had renewed his vicious assault. Warriors on both sides dropped like flies; the horror raged unabated, as if it would end only when there was no one left alive on either side.

Where was his father? How long could his people bear this torture? It was not right that more of his soldiers should die while he waited for Krishna. His heart plummeted under the weight of his responsibility.

Then out of the red sky emerged a radiant vision—a chariot that surged ahead as if on wings, cutting through the fighting hordes. On top of the chariot blazed the flag of Garuda.

The Yadus let out a roar as they realized that Krishna had returned from the Pandava capital. 'Victory is ours!' they shouted. 'Who can win against the Blue God?'

Shalva bellowed a challenge on seeing his hated enemy. He welcomed him with an Agneyaastra, Agni's weapon that flashed across the sky, raining flames. The fire incinerated everything in its path, but Krishna cut it to pieces with his arrows. Shalva hurled his bludgeon, causing the Saranga bow to fall from Krishna's hand. He then shot a flurry of arrows that obscured the Dark One, his charioteer Daruka and his glorious steeds Saibya and Sugriva.

Daruka groaned in pain, trying hard to stay conscious despite the arrows piercing every part of his flesh.

'Accept defeat, knave. Let the world see how unworthy you are,' shouted Shalva, certain that he had won. 'You took my friend Sishupala unawares and killed him. You helped Bhima kill Jarasandha, who was like a brother to me. Now you have met your equal who will send you screaming to naraka.'

Krishna lifted up his conch, Panchajanya, whose name signifies control over the five elements. He blew on the conch to announce that the real war had begun.

Pradyumna flew to his side on his chariot, with his sarathy Mayavati. They bowed in obeisance to Krishna and prepared to fight by his side. Krishna stayed them with an upraised hand.

'You betray your foolishness with every word,' Krishna said to Shalva. 'Great warriors act. They do not boast. You totter on the edge of Yama's world, but are unable to see your own doom. You have seen your allies suffer the consequences of their arrogance, and yet you persist in evil. You abuse Shiva's trust and the boons he granted you. This is your last chance to redeem yourself, Shalva. I urge you to take it.'

'The false god entreats me. Soon, you will beg me to spare your life and that of your loved ones. Prepare yourself, wastrel!' Shalva's weapons splintered the air, setting it on fire as they hurtled towards his foe.

Krishna took up his own weapons and unleashed iridescent astras on the enemy. Shalva roared in mockery and used his magic powers to evade them. He disappeared from sight, leaving behind a black pall of smoke that blinded his enemies.

As Krishna looked around for him, a weak old man came weeping to him, bringing harrowing news. 'Shalva is now within our city walls,' he stuttered in fear. 'He battered your poor father Vasudeva with his club and carried him away in his Saubha.'

Krishna froze. *My father may be dead,* he thought. *But how could this happen when Balarama and my sons stand guard over our city?*

As he stopped to gather his senses, day turned to night and then back to day. The weather became cold and turned hot again. A fierce wind howled like a banshee and was followed by a hailstorm.

A ripple of fear spread through the Yadus as they looked up at the sky. Krishna saw Shalva above him, laughing like the devil, clutching Vasudeva in one giant arm.

'Look upon your father for the last time,' he called out. 'I brought him here so you can watch him die.'

He dangled Vasudeva by his hair and in one stroke, hewed his neck with his sword. An anguished wail erupted from a thousand throats. Shalva held the severed head in his hand and laughed louder still as Vasudeva's limp body fell to the ground with a crash.

Krishna rushed to the headless torso and bent over it with tears pouring from his eyes. He tried to lift it up in his arms, but the body vanished without a trace. He looked around in a daze and saw that the frail messenger from Dwaraka was missing too.

He realized that the whole scene had been an illusion created by Shalva. The demon watched his torment from his vimaana that now stood on the battlefield.

'See how easy it is to fool a god,' he mocked. 'So much grief over the seeming death of a servant! Was not your father Vasudeva once Kamsa's slave?'

'Vasudeva is safe,' shouted Krishna to his men. 'I will make the sorcerer pay for his cruel sport.' His eyes flashed in rage, as though he too would sport a third eye like Shiva's. Even the men who fought on his side retreated from him, unable to bear the blaze of fury that emanated from him.

Krishna flew towards Shalva's vimaana and attacked it with his mace Kaumodaki. The mace roared as it consumed the Saubha with its intense energy, its cosmic power reflected in the implacable face of the avatar. Warriors on both sides watched in fear and awe.

Shalva jumped to the ground as the vimaana burned to ashes. He ran towards Krishna, hurling axes and thunderbolts at him.

Krishna took up his Sudarshana chakra to destroy the evil that had taken an immense toll on mankind. The chakra glittered on his finger, gathering into itself the powers of dharma.

The winds stilled, the waves froze, and the world was in thrall. The weapon waited, poised on his finger—blinding the world with its incandescence.

Krishna thrust his finger forward and the chakra soared towards the demon. Shalva's head with its enormous kundalas and his war helmet went flying, and his body fell to the ground.

The last of the evil triumvirate had fallen. Shalva had met his death as it had been ordained—by the hand of Vishnu.

Krishna blew his conch in triumph, and the Yadus exploded in thunderous cheers. He made his way through the throng, with Pradyumna and Aniruddha taking pride of place beside him on his chariot. Together, they rushed to Vasudeva's palace to seek his blessings.

Later, when the crowds had left, and the night grew silent, Pradyumna had a question for his father. 'I have never seen you so enraged, father. Was it the seeming death of grandsire Vasudeva that provoked you?'

The lord replied with a smile, his face calm again. 'I have taken a mortal body that is subject to its laws, but I am beyond the qualities of man. I experience the feelings that are natural to men, but I transcend both dying and undying beings. My anger was fuelled by the evil that I see so deeply entrenched in some beings. I offer them refuge and redemption, but they spurn me. They persist in their folly, abandoning themselves to lust, anger and violence. They force me to wield the Sudarshana, whose energy is the fire of dissolution at the end of the kalpa. And it is the pure fire of the Sudarshana that will illuminate you too on your path to your destiny.'

Pradyumna bowed his head and chanted a hymn in praise of the eternal chakra:

Sudarshana mahaajvaala koti surya samaprabhaa

Agnyaana andhasyame deva Vishnor maargam pradarsaya

O Sudarshana, the great flame as brilliant as a hundred thousand suns! Lead me from the darkness of ignorance to the path of Vishnu.

30

The Princess of Sonitapura

Sonitapura. The city of gold. The majestic capital of Banasura was located on the banks of the Brahmaputra, and surrounded by beautiful valleys and the snow-capped Himalayas. It was steeped in wealth that rivalled even that of Kubera, the treasurer of the gods. Its gilded walls challenged the skies and its mansions sparkled like gems.

Banasura was the grandson of the pious Prahlada, an ardent devotee of Vishnu. When Prahlada's evil father Hiranyakasipu tormented his son for praying to the lord, Vishnu himself had erupted from a pillar as the half man, half lion Narasimha, and slain the demon.

Prahlada's son Mahabali had a hundred sons, of whom Bana was the first. Bana hated Vishnu as he believed the god had cheated his father out of his kingdom. Mahabali was a righteous and charitable king, with unmatched skills as a warrior. He steadily expanded his realm to include the underworld and the heavens too, driving Indra from his throne. Indra's mother Aditi prayed to Vishnu to come to Indra's aid, and the lord took birth as her son Vamana. The diminutive boy avatar set forth to Mahabali's kingdom and asked the king to grant him three paces of land.

Mahabali looked at Vamana's small feet with derision. 'I have never turned down anyone's request for alms and will certainly not refuse you this paltry boon,' he said.

'Do not rush into this, king. I fear this is a trick,' protested his guru Shukra. But Mahabali went ahead and granted the boon, his arrogance blinding him to sound advice.

Vamana smiled, and then grew bigger and bigger, taking on a giant form that stunned the king and his courtiers.

'You have made a terrible mistake,' cried Shukra. 'The boy is Vishnu himself.'

Mahabali fell at Vishnu's feet, chanting his praise. He raised tearful eyes to worship the lord's visvaroopa, a breathtaking form embodying the world and all its elements. He was awestruck by the vision, and his ego crumbled. 'I see in you the mountains, the earth, the skies, the rivers and the oceans,' he whispered. 'I see Mahalakshmi and all the gods nestled in your chest, the clouds in your hair, the Vedas in your words, day and night on your forehead and death in your shadow.'

With one mighty step Vishnu covered the heavens. With the second, he measured all the earth.

'Now where shall I place my third step?' he thundered. 'You must keep your promise or face eternity in the netherworld.'

The chastened king offered his head to the lord as the ultimate offering.

As soon as Vishnu's foot touched him, Bali's sins fell away and his soul shone pure and radiant.

'Your piety pleases me,' the lord said. 'I hereby grant you a place among the immortals—Hanuman, Bhargavarama, Vibhishana, Ashwathama, Veda Vyasa and Kripa.'

However, this supreme honour did not placate Mahabali's son Bana. 'The vile Vamana seized my father's life and kingdoms falsely,' he said. 'I will reclaim my father's realms and his fame. I will take my revenge on Vishnu, however long it may take. I shall seek Shiva's help, for he is equal to Vishnu in power.'

And so Bana began a harrowing penance. First, he set aside food and sleep. Then he controlled the number of breaths he took every day. Next, he meditated on one leg for thousands of years, with his hands joined above his head in prayer. Slowly, the forest wrapped its thorny tentacles around him, and insects and snakes crawled all over him. Still, he prayed, adamant in his purpose.

The fierce heat of his tapasya rose to devaloka and frightened Indra.

'Grant him his boon, Shiva,' he prayed. 'Otherwise, we will all be burned.'

Shiva rewarded Bana for his devotion with a shower of gold that fell continuously for three days, gilding his city, its mansions and its gardens, and giving it the name Sonitapura. He made Bana the overlord of all the riches in the world, as well as the lord of the precious gems under the surface of the earth.

'What do you desire, Bana?' he then asked his devotee.

'I wish to be immortal—invincible against gods, demons, humans and animals,' said Bana. 'I wish to possess the power to destroy Vishnu.'

'All creatures that are born must die,' said Shiva. 'I cannot grant you immortality. As for your hatred of Vishnu, do not court death by seeking to fight him. No one can defeat the lord of Vaikunta and his radiant chakra.'

Bana would not relent and returned to his tapas, hanging himself upside down from a tree over a terrible fire, breathing only the smoke for the next thousand years.

Indra and the devas rushed to Shiva again, begging him to stop Bana before the flames rose to scorch them.

Shiva appeared before Bana once more to ask him what he desired.

He will not grant immortality, thought Bana. *How then can I protect myself from Vishnu?*

'Mighty Shiva, bless me with success. Let me become a son to you, like Karthikeya and Ganesha,' he prayed. 'I request you to come to my defence whenever I need you, to protect me against my enemies.'

'So be it,' said Shiva, who was Ashutosha, one who is easily pleased. 'I grant you a further boon. A thousand powerful arms with which you can conquer the world. I bestow upon you a banner of fire and a peacock vehicle like that of my son Karthikeya. But I must warn you again—do not confront Vishnu for even I cannot protect you from him.'

'I promise,' said Bana, overjoyed by his good fortune. He missed no opportunity to express his gratitude to his protector. Whenever Shiva danced his tandava of creation and dissolution, Bana played the drums for him with his thousand arms. Shiva blessed him with a daughter, who was named Usha. Parvati raised her in Kailasa, and bestowed upon the child all her skills and wisdom.

Over time Banasura grew arrogant and cruel, basking in the protection of Shiva and his ganas. The devas, including Indra, trembled in his presence and went into hiding. Thereafter, Bana began a reign of terror, abusing the boons he had won through piety. Finding that there was no one ready to fight with him, he decided to confront his sworn enemy, the avatar of the god he hated.

'I will see if this Krishna has the courage to stand against me,' he proclaimed, setting off for Dwaraka with his deadly phalanx.

In Kailasa, Karthikeya said, 'He has disregarded the promise he made you, father. Shouldn't we stop him before he reaches Dwaraka?'

'He has chosen his path,' answered Shiva. 'We must let his karma take its course.'

Bana reached the gates of the Yadu capital and called out a challenge. 'Come out if you dare, cowherd.'

Out strode Balarama, his plough over his shoulder, his eyes shooting fire. 'You abuse Shiva's trust and have forgotten the promise you made him,' he said. 'Your arrogance blinds you to your folly.'

'I promised not to confront Vishnu, not a cowherd who cowers from me in fear. Where is he now, and where are your soldiers?'

'I do not need him or my army to defeat you. My plough will decimate you and all your men.'

'So why are you still talking? Let us fight and find out.'

Balarama soon rendered Bana unconscious with his powerful blows. As he lifted his plough to finish him off, Shiva appeared before him.

'You are not the one destined to kill him, Balarama,' he said. 'Control your anger and stay your hand.'

The warrior bowed to Shiva and retreated to his city. Shiva disappeared.

Bana opened his eyes and staggered to his feet, eager to continue the fight. He saw Balarama walking away and shouted out to him. 'Why are you running away, coward? Stand and fight.'

Balarama's face twisted in anger, but he continued on his way.

'He walks away in obedience to Shiva's command,' said Bana's commander. 'He could have easily killed you if Shiva had not intervened.'

'Who asked Shiva to help? How dare he interfere? I will attack Kailasa and defeat him and his people, showing the world once and for all that Bana is greater than even Shiva.'

Bana stormed to Kailasa, but Karthikeya blocked him with his golden lance before he could enter the sacred city.

'You dare take on the three-eyed god who granted you your powers?' he challenged the asura.

'Do you think I am afraid of him? I am now more powerful than he is and will subdue him.'

Bana's intemperate language angered Karthikeya, but the son of Shiva restricted himself to defending Kailasa and did not take the offensive.

'Are you afraid, Karthikeya? Is that why you do not attack me?' taunted Bana. 'You must be worried that your father will come running if I call, and do not wish to fight him.'

He let loose a flurry of blows, forcing Karthikeya to decide whether to attack or accept defeat. He knew what he had to do.

He knelt before the demon and bowed his head. 'I surrender to you, Bana,' he said. 'I do not wish my father to fight for someone like you.'

'Coward! Surrender your flag to me as a mark of your subjugation and that of all the devas.'

Karthikeya relinquished his peacock flag, his eyes turning red as he struggled to accept the humiliation.

Bana roared to the skies, thumping his chest in victory. 'I am the master of the gods,' he proclaimed. 'Indra will now serve as my slave. His queen will grace my antapura. Vayu will carry me on his back and Surya will stop the seasons at my bidding. There is no one who can withstand me. Where are you, Shiva? Are you hiding from me too?'

A flash of lightning blinded him, and the next instant Shiva stood before him. His face was stern, and his matted locks bristled with anger. 'Your pride will be your downfall,

Bana. How can you say you have conquered the world when you cannot conquer your own mind? Be warned that you are rushing to your doom with your actions.'

'And still you refuse to fight with me,' taunted Bana. 'Who then will be brave enough to send me to my doom?'

'You are fated to die at the hands of a yug purush who has taken birth in this age in order to save the world. He is an enlightened soul who is of this time and yet of all time. He acts in accordance with the rules of this universe, transcending its limitations at the same time. His actions, thoughts and perceptions are not constrained by his earthly form, but are animated by his divine purpose.'

'Do not speak in riddles in the hope of frightening me,' spat Bana. 'I have defeated the devas and the demons, and your threats cannot scare me. Where is your yug purush now? Let him come. My weapons have rusted and my shoulders throb in vain, for I have no opponent against whom I can test my mettle. Not even you and your sons dare take me on.'

Shiva's third eye throbbed, but he knew he could not destroy the asura, contravening his own boon. 'Watch for the day when the peacock banner falls to the ground,' he said. 'That will be the sign that heralds your doom.' He paused. 'And as you consider yourself too powerful to need my help, I will return with my family to Kailasa.'

'I grant you permission to leave,' said Bana, sneering. 'But remember, you are sworn to protect me and must return when I summon you. Unless of course, the great Ishwara does not honour his promises . . .'

The ganas quaked at his arrogant words to the Jagadisa, the master of the universe. Shiva merely smiled as he turned away.

Bana exulted to his minister Kumbhanda. 'Do you see how Shiva flees when I speak of battle? Not even Vishnu will dare oppose the emperor with a thousand arms and the support of Rudra.'

'Do not tempt fate, my liege,' said Kumbhanda. 'Pay heed to Shiva's warning.'

'Get away from me, old man, before I burn you as a traitor,' growled Bana. He vented his anger on the soldier who was following him, carrying his royal staff, and cut off his head before storming into his antapura to seek solace in the embrace of his concubines.

Evil omens shook the three realms. A shrieking tornado shattered the rooftops of Sonitapura. The temple tree worshipped by Bana's daughter Usha fell to the earth with a crash.

But Bana was drinking and making merry with his dancers. They soothed his fears with silken praises and staged parodies mocking the devas.

One of the soldiers guarding Bana's gates came running in, wailing. 'The peacock banner has fallen, mighty king,' he said. 'I fear that evil is upon us.'

The dancers stopped their revelry and began to scream too.

'Silence, fools!' shouted Bana. 'What disaster can bring me down when I am invincible? Be glad that I am full of wine and do not wish to put an end to your sorry lives.'

Bana's wives rushed in and began to plead with him. 'Pray to Shiva and ask him to return so he can protect you, my lord,' they said.

'I laugh at your stupidity and refuse to be cowed down by your fears,' he replied. 'Instead, I will begin preparations to stage a grand swayamvara for my daughter Usha.'

Narada, who had been listening to the clamour, decided to make his appearance.

'My respects to you, Bana,' he said.

'Aha, the old man scurries in as soon as he hears of a swayamvara,' taunted Bana. 'Don't you remember the humiliation of your monkey face when you tried to win the hand of Vishnu's wife? This time, you will lose your head, not just your self-importance.'

'I forget nothing,' said Narada. 'My arrogance caused my fall, just as yours now leads you to your death, Bana.'

'What death?' asked Bana. 'How can I die when Yama has deserted his domain in fear of my prowess? It is I who determine life and death now.'

'Listen to me. You still have time to repent. Surrender at the lotus feet of Vishnu, the Anantasayana, who reclines on the serpent. He will give you refuge.'

'Oh, the god who killed my father Mahabali by deceit? Tell your Vishnu to make recompense by fighting with me now in an honourable way. We will see who wins.'

'I have done what I came to do. Death will come to you through the warrior destined to win your daughter's hand.'

'The Trilokadipati fears nothing, not even destiny. I will overcome my fate by ensuring that Usha meets no men henceforth. There will be no swayamvara. She will stay unmarried, confined to a fortress guarded by women. I laugh at the stratagems of your gods that are doomed to fail.'

He bayed like a wolf, challenging the heavens.

31

Through the Flames

A legion of Banasura's men built Agnigarh, the fortress of fire, atop a hillock. A perpetual fire surrounded the citadel through the blessings of Jvalamukhi, the fiery form of Parvati, worshipped wherever subterranean fire erupted from the earth.

It was in this fortress, to which no man had access, that Bana's daughter Usha was confined. An ethereal beauty, she was in reality the apsara Tilotamma who had been cursed by Sage Durvasa to be born on earth.

Usha prayed to Parvati, who loved her and watched over her like a mother, and sought her help in escaping her prison.

'You will soon meet the man who will set you free,' promised the goddess.

With Parvati's blessings, Usha soon caught a glimpse of this warrior, but only in a dream. The dream was so vivid that she felt herself swept away on a tide of passion for the handsome youth whom she had never met. She blushed; she moaned in his arms. Then she woke up to discover that it had all been a dream.

'Oh my love, why have you left me?' she whispered to her unknown lover, unable to bear their parting.

Her friend Chitralekha, the daughter of Bana's minister Kumbhanda, soon uncovered her secret passion. 'Who is this man?' she asked. But Usha did not know.

'I will draw a portrait based on your recollection of his face and appearance,' said Chitralekha. 'Once we discover his identity, we can find a way for you to meet him.'

Usha closed her eyes in ecstasy as she saw him with her mind's eye. 'His skin is dark and his eyes are like lotus petals,' she said. 'His chest is powerful and his lips wear a bewitching smile. His neck is slender like a conch and his hair falls in a riot of curls. His arms are like the branches of the kalpavriksha, and upon his head rests a crown. My prince is more dashing than Kama himself.'

Chitralekha, who was blessed with the vision of a yogini, drew portraits of Indra, Surya and Agni, who were famed for their good looks. But Usha shook her head at each one, saying that her prince was more godly in appearance than the devas. Handsome gandharvas, vidyadharas and yakshas came to life through Chitralekha's artistry, but Usha rejected all of them. The other images her friend drew—of kings and princes of the richest kingdoms on earth—suffered the same fate.

Next, Chitralekha sketched the Kurus and the Pandavas, the magnificent Karna, Duryodhana, Yudhistira and Arjuna. Usha became distraught for the man of her dreams was not among them.

Her companion then drew a picture of Balarama. At once Usha's eyes sparkled and she exclaimed, 'Yes, he is like him, only darker.'

Chitralekha sketched the portraits of Krishna and Pradyumna, the other scions of the Yadu clan.

'Yes, yes,' said Usha. 'But much younger.'

Aniruddha sprang to majestic life through Chitralekha's art, and Usha blushed and nodded. 'This is him,' she exclaimed. 'Tell me who he is. Tell me everything you know about him.'

Chitralekha was happy to identify him as Aniruddha, son of Pradyumna and grandson of Krishna.

Usha clasped the portrait to her heart and pleaded with Chitralekha to help her meet him. 'Find your way to him with your mystic powers and tell him of my love,' she said. 'Beg him to raze the wall of fire that imprisons me and take me with him.'

'You ask me to do something that is not within my powers, Usha,' said Chitralekha. 'Aniruddha lives in Dwaraka which is protected by countless war chariots and warriors. Even if I bypass them by becoming invisible, I cannot deceive Krishna's Sudarshana chakra which protects the city whenever Krishna resides there.'

'I will die if I cannot meet him. Please find some way to bring us together,' Usha begged, clinging to her in agitation. 'Now that I know who he is, I will not rest until I am united with him. I can barely breathe when I am awake and when I try to sleep dreams keep me tossing and turning in a fever.'

'You must pray to Parvati,' said Chitralekha. 'Didn't she promise that you will be rescued by your prince? You know her blessings can never fail.'

'I will pray ceaselessly at her altar,' declared Usha. 'I will forsake food and water. I will die if she does not bring me my lord.'

The cosmic messenger Narada entered her palace in his mysterious way, unseen by her guards. The princess begged him to be her messenger and speak to the prince.

'Events unfold according to a divine plan,' he said. 'But you will face many hurdles if you persist in your love.'

In Dwaraka, Aniruddha too had a dream, in which he saw himself in bed in an unknown palace. In his arms was a celestial beauty whom he had never met before, and his heart pounded with desire. He spent every waking moment after that wondering who she was and how he could make her his own.

Narada came to him and discovered that he was as lovelorn as the princess. 'The woman in your dreams is Usha, the princess of Sonitapura and the daughter of Banasura, the king with a thousand arms,' he said.

The passionate prince sprang up in a frenzy. 'I will go to her kingdom and win her hand,' he exclaimed. 'If the asura stands in my way, I will cut off his thousand arms and throw him in the dungeons.'

'The task is not so easy, Aniruddha,' Narada replied. 'Shiva has promised Bana that he will come to his defence if he is summoned. And the princess is confined to a fortress of fire which can be entered only with the blessing of Jvalamukhi.'

'I bow to your wisdom, Devarishi,' said Aniruddha. 'Help me in my quest.'

Narada counselled him on winning the blessings of Jvalamukhi, and Aniruddha hastened to her shrine. Her sanctum was guarded by a retinue of sixty-four fierce yoginis who refused him access. Undeterred, he began a fervent prayer at the entrance to the temple, closing his body and mind to everything except the goddess.

But Jvalamukhi was not so easily pleased.

'I cannot wait any longer,' said the impetuous prince. 'I will enter the flames that surround your shrine if you will not grant me your boon.'

There was silence still as the goddess continued to test his faith.

He chanted 'Om Durgaye Namaha' for the last time, and jumped into the raging fire. Back in her palace, his mother

Rukmavati's heart stopped for a moment as she sensed that her son was in peril. Pradyumna shivered as he felt a strange fear cross his mind.

But Krishna smiled, for he knew that this was merely the leela of Jvalamukhi.

The flames licked Aniruddha's body, but they did not sear his flesh. They were transformed instead into a garland of crimson hibiscus that fell around his neck. A divine fragrance wafted through the air and he heard the music of a thousand cymbals and lutes. Durga appeared before him in her gentle form, smiling on the young tapasvin.

Aniruddha prostrated himself before her and found that he had lost the power to speak. But she was the divine Shakti and knew everything that was in the hearts of her devotees.

'I know what you seek, son of Pradyumna,' she said. 'I grant you the hand of the fair Usha who is lost in love for you. I give you the power to fly through the air to reach her fortress and walk through the fire. Prepare yourself to play your part as an instrument of our grace.'

The vision faded. Aniruddha found that he could move and speak again. He made his way back to his palace in a state of bliss. He determined to hurry to his princess and whisk her away from the fortress, and vanquish the thousand-armed asura in battle if he dared oppose him.

Armed with his powerful weapons, Aniruddha set off for Sonitapura, flying through the skies, passing over hills and dales, sparkling rivers and uncharted kingdoms. He followed the path of the stately Brahmaputra that cascaded down Himalayan slopes and through narrow gorges, emerging to flow like a majestic sea along the plains.

Guided by the blessings of Jvalamukhi, he finally arrived at Agnigarh. He chanted the names of the goddess, and the flames parted to allow him to enter Usha's palace. The guards, all women, were caught in the coils of a charmed sleep. He passed through gilded corridors to enter the inner chamber. The amethysts and emeralds embedded in the walls lit the room with their gentle glow. He saw the princess tossing sleeplessly in a bed that was lined with the finest swansdown.

He moved on soft feet to stand by her bedside, and looked down at her radiant face and smooth limbs glistening under fine silks. Her beauty surpassed that of all the lovely women he had seen in Dwaraka.

As he devoured her form and face, Usha sensed his presence and looked up at him. The scream that had bubbled up to her lips when she realized a stranger stood over her died, for she knew at once that he was the man she had been waiting for. Their gazes mingled with a fierce passion, as if they could make love with their eyes alone. She sprang up in her bed, with an inviting yet bashful look on her face.

Not a word was spoken as the two came together like a river rushing to embrace the sea. Destiny smiled as the blessed couple united in a gandharva vivaaha, a marriage sanctified not by rituals and elders but by the coming together of two souls.

Usha showed her adoration by anointing him with sandal paste and incense, and garlanding him with fragrant flowers. He in turn adorned her with the glittering ornaments he wore, crafted by Visvakarma himself for the grandson of the avatar.

The two young lovers spent days and nights together in a haze of passion, protected by Chitralekha who kept the guards out of Usha's antapura. She threw a circle of magic around them so that no sight or sound betrayed the presence of the intruder.

But the guards soon began to whisper their unease and carried word to the king that something mysterious was going on in his daughter's palace.

'We are kept out of her chambers, lord,' they said. 'We are anxious as we do not know what transpires within. But we swear that we have been vigilant and not allowed anyone, living or dead, to enter her chambers.'

'How dare you make such allegations about my daughter?' Bana shouted. 'How can you even suggest that she would betray me?'

Once they left, however, Bana felt a growing unease and decided to visit the fortress himself to see if all was well. He arrived at Agnigarh with his band of fierce warriors. Leaving them outside, he passed through the ring of fire by chanting an ancient mantra. He strode through the outer chambers to reach the antapura and flung open its doors at a time when Chitralekha had relaxed her vigil.

What he saw inside was beyond his worst fears. His daughter was in the embrace of a young man whose powerful shoulders indicated that he was a warrior.

Bana let out a roar that made the lovers spring apart and face him. The king did not recognize the man's face, but realized from its radiance that this was not a foe to be taken lightly. His mind was roiled by agitated questions.

Was Narada's prophecy coming true? Was this the one who would cause his death?

'Father!' exclaimed Usha in panic.

Bana's attention was focused on her companion. 'How did you get past Parvati's circle of fire?' he demanded. 'Who are you?'

Aniruddha folded his hands together in a gesture of respect. 'Our union has won the favour of the Devi,' he said. 'I am Aniruddha, son of Pradyumna and the grandson of Krishna. We seek your blessings.'

'My daughter become part of the clan who are my sworn enemies? Never!' shouted the asura.

'I beg you to reconsider. Regard this union as a way to end our enmity and pave the way to peace.'

'Your intrusion will result not in peace, but in the decimation of your clan. Let go of my daughter's hand. Usha, tell me what magic this deceiver used to bewitch you.'

'No magic, except that of love,' she replied. 'I saw him in my dream and prayed to Parvati to help me unite with him.'

'Your mind is not in your control. Listen to your father and renounce him. Or I will treat you too as my enemy and kill you.'

'Not as long as I am alive,' said Aniruddha. 'Usha is my wife now. She is the daughter-in-law of the valiant Yadus. I will not let you lay a finger on her.'

He pulled out his sword and faced the asura with a challenge in his eyes.

Usha stepped between them, trying to stop a war between her father and her beloved. 'Father, if you cannot accept peace between our clans, allow me at least to leave your kingdom with my husband.'

'You would choose this deceitful Yadu over the father who raised you all these years? How can you oppose me in this way?'

'I do not oppose you, father. I am merely saying that your arrogance cannot vanquish love. If you love me as you say you do, how can you stand in the way of my happiness?'

'You forget to whom you are speaking. If it had been anyone else, they would have lost their head by now. I will sacrifice even my life for you, but I cannot sacrifice my self-respect or that of my clan. I will not let you marry the grandson of a man who cannot even count the number of wives he has.'

Aniruddha roared in anger. 'Fight me then, asura. But I will not stand by and allow you to insult my family.'

Bana pushed Usha aside and advanced towards Aniruddha. 'The gates of Yamaloka are yawning wide for you, young man.'

'I stood silent so long as I did not wish to fight my wife's father. But if swords are to do the talking, so be it. Let us see who enters Yamaloka, you or I.'

'Let us kill him, king,' pleaded Usha's guards as they ran towards the intruder with their swords unsheathed.

Aniruddha pushed Usha to the corner behind him and twirled around on lightning feet, bringing down the guards with his fierce sword. The initial attackers fell, but more poured in. Their combined onslaught sent his sword flying from his grasp, and he ripped out the heavy door behind him to use as his weapon. He flung it on the attackers, smashing them to the ground, sending the others fleeing like jackals before a lone lion.

Bana realized that he would have to kill the intruder himself and sprang to the attack with his mace and sword. Aniruddha held his ground. The walls of the palace came down as the two opponents exchanged terrible blows. Jvalamukhi retracted her circle of fire.

'Have you lost your mind, stripling?' asked Bana as they paused for breath. 'Don't you know you are fighting with the emperor blessed by Shiva himself? Run away now before I twist off your rash head.'

'It is you who are ignorant of my courage and lineage,' shot back the youth. 'I hail from the Vrishni clan. My father Pradyumna killed the evil Kaalasura who claimed to be the Trilokadipati just as you do now. Accept me as your daughter's husband and escape defeat.'

'A groom from a family of cowherds? You infuriate me with your impudence,' said Bana. 'Even if I accept that Krishna is Vishnu himself, I have sworn to fight him for he killed my father Mahabali. I have been waiting to destroy your whole clan and will hunt you down even if you hide in Vaikunta.'

Bana put his giant bow to his shoulder and sent forth a barrage of deadly arrows. Aniruddha countered with his own fusillade, keeping the asura at bay. Bana hurled weapons that spurted flames and cornered the young warrior.

'I have you now,' he shouted. 'You will not escape this fire.'

But the young lion invoked the astra of the rain god that quenched the flames with a flood.

The demon raised his spiked bludgeon and rushed to strike him over the head. Aniruddha wrenched it from his hand and dealt a fierce blow that rocked him with its force.

'Surrender to me!' he shouted. 'I do not wish to kill Usha's father.'

'Do you see the peacock banner that flies on my flag post? I wrenched it from Karthikeya, the commander of the deva army. Why would I surrender to a mortal youth?'

'That flag is not a sign of your power. It is a sign that your doom is near.'

As they circled each other, Bana's commander whispered to his king, 'Use your sorcery, my king, or you will not win.'

Bana at once made himself invisible and took to the skies. He rained down scythes, scimitars and discs of fire on his enemy. Aniruddha looked around in confusion, unable to trace the attacker. As he stood defenceless, Bana shot his Naagaastra at him. Thousands of snakes engulfed Aniruddha, binding him in their coils and rendering him immobile.

'I will kill you now, wretch,' said Bana, descending to earth like a mountain and roaring in triumph. 'Then I will track down the cowherd and kill him too.'

Aniruddha struggled within his serpent bonds, but could not break the asura's sorcery. As Bana raised his sword to hack off his head, Kumbhanda intervened.

'Stay your hand awhile, king,' he said. 'Listen to your minister who has sworn to protect you with his wisdom. The young sprig claims he is from the house of Yadus. We must verify his antecedents and learn of his intentions in seducing the princess. Maybe he has been sent by the Yadus as part of a strategy to defeat us in war.'

Bana lowered his sword hand and listened as Kumbhanda continued. 'Your daughter has married him by gandharva rites. Consider also if you wish to have the blood of her husband on your hands.'

'How does one more life matter when I have killed so many?' scoffed Bana. 'I will kill him, then wed Usha to someone of my choice. What gives me pause is the fear that he may be part of a larger plan. I will torture him until he reveals the plot and then lure the so-called god into my clutches.'

Bana ordered his men to cast Aniruddha into the dungeons in Agnigarh and imprison Usha as well. The silence that descended on the ruins was broken only by the sobs of the princess who refused to leave the place where she had enjoyed such bliss.

'Who in the whole wide world can save us now?' she wailed.

32

Shiva Confronts Vishnu

Dwaraka was in turmoil. The disappearance of Aniruddha without a word to anyone and his prolonged absence made his loved ones anxious about his whereabouts and his safety. His wife Rochana took to her bed in distress. His mother Rukmavati was inconsolable; she imagined that something terrible had happened.

'Maybe an asura snatched Aniruddha like his father was taken by Kaalasura,' she wailed.

The agitated Yadu warriors flocked to her palace, brandishing their weapons. 'A fox can never capture a full-grown lion, O queen. How can anyone pass through our ranks to kidnap him? How can you doubt your son's valour and ours?' they asked.

'If not an asura, maybe it was Indra who seized him to avenge the loss of the parijata,' said Rukmavati.

'It is more likely that our son is lost in the charms of a beautiful girl, my queen. There is no reason to fear for his safety,' said Pradyumna, who had just entered the palace. He turned to his men and told them, 'Go look for him in the mansions of Dwaraka, instead of exhibiting your bravado here.'

However, the men soon returned to say that no one had seen Aniruddha.

The first twinges of unease struck the father's heart. His son was still young and brash. Perhaps one of their enemies had lured him outside the protected walls of their city in order to capture him. Aniruddha was skilled in the use of the astras, but had not yet learned the art of mahamaya that was essential to tackle occult weapons.

The fear of Narada's prophecy about the extinction of their race was ever-present in Pradyumna's mind. Was his son the price he had to pay for the burden of karma he had brought from his past life?

Even as his thoughts focused on the devarishi, Narada arrived at the scene of gloom, sensing that his presence was required.

'I bring you a message of hope,' he said. 'Aniruddha has been snatched by neither deva nor demon. He ventured out on his own to marry the princess of Sonitapura, whom he saw in a dream. Princess Usha is the daughter of Banasura of the thousand arms.'

'If this is true, why has he not returned to Dwaraka?' asked Rukmavati, relieved that her son was safe.

Narada looked silently at her, wondering how to break the news of Aniruddha's capture to his anxious mother.

'Do not torment us, Devarishi,' she said. 'Please tell us what you know.'

'The asura king is not happy about their marriage and has imprisoned your son.'

'Did my young lion not fight the asura? Was he so easily captured?' asked Pradyumna.

'He fought like Karthikeya, the commander of the deva army,' said Narada. 'He brought down the walls of the fortress with his fury and almost killed Bana. But he was subdued by the asura's sorcery.'

Rukmavati began to pray to the gods to deliver her son safely back from the kingdom of the thousand-armed Bana.

'So my fears have proved right,' said Pradyumna. 'We must set forth at once to kill the asura and retrieve our prince and his bride.'

His soldiers clamoured, ready to wage battle, but fell silent when they saw Krishna come into their midst.

Samba, who had come to gloat when he heard that Aniruddha was missing, now stepped forward to voice his opinion. 'So, our men must again risk their lives in a fight with a formidable asura. And for what? To rescue the son of Kama who is just as lustful and reckless as his father.'

The soldiers gasped, but only Narada countered him. 'You speak unwisely, Samba,' he said. 'Don't you remember it was Pradyumna, whom you dismiss as lustful and reckless, who rescued you from the Kurus when you forced your way into Lakshmani's swayamvara? Lakshmani did not welcome your advances, but in this case, Usha prayed fervently to the gods to allow her to marry Aniruddha.'

Samba grew angry at his words, but decided to stay silent when he saw the hostile faces of the assembled men. Why should he worry if these fools rushed to their death? He decided to retire to his mother's palace, where he was sure to find support.

Pradyumna turned to his father for guidance.

'The task is more complex than you think, my son,' said Krishna. 'You have killed many asuras and defeated Indra. But Bana is not like the others. You cannot win this battle by courage alone; conciliation will be key as well. Bana is protected by Shiva and his ganas. You must convince Shiva that the asura is beyond redemption and needs to be humbled. The god of gods must stand aside and allow karma to run its course. This is not a task you can accomplish by yourself. I will fly with you on Garuda to Sonitapura, while our troops follow by land.'

Pradyumna nodded, realizing that there was much more that he needed to learn from his father.

Garuda made his appearance as soon as the lord thought of him. 'Give me permission and I will shatter the asura's city with a flutter of my wings,' he said. 'The foolish Bana courts death by imprisoning your grandson.'

'All the realms sing your praise, Garuda,' Krishna said, smiling at his mighty mount. 'You stole the nectar of immortality from the gods and gave it to the serpents in order to free your mother from their custody. And you brought back the nectar by a ruse, preventing the snakes from acquiring eternal life. There is nothing that you cannot accomplish. But we will go with you to Bana's city to rescue Aniruddha and his bride.'

'There can be no greater honour than to carry you on my back,' said Garuda. 'I bow to you, lord of the Vedas, and master of past, present and future.'

Krishna lovingly put his own garland, embedded with the Kausthuba, the divine gem that emerged from the ocean of milk, around Garuda's neck. He ascended his back with Pradyumna and sounded the Panchajanya. The gods appeared in the skies to bless the expedition.

'Victory to you and your son,' they proclaimed.

Garuda soared into the skies and made the mountains shake with the flapping of his gigantic wings. Pradyumna saw below them the massive Sumeru mountain where Bana had lit five sacrificial fires to protect him from the attack he knew was coming. The flames leaped to the sky, and Pradyumna realized that they could not cross them without quenching them.

Garuda created for himself a thousand massive beaks with which he drained the sea and poured it over the fire. At that the fires took hideous forms and wielded awful weapons to fight off the intruders. Their leader Angira, born of Brahma, the creator of fire, and the others flung fiery tridents that threatened to reduce Garuda to ashes. Garuda swooped and soared amidst the clouds to escape them.

The fires then hurled flaming scimitars, bolts of lightning and hurricanes to blast Garuda out of the sky, but Pradyumna destroyed these with his own astras. Angira let loose his deadly maya, making the flames invisible in order to lure Garuda and his precious burden into their clutches.

Sensing that sorcery was at play, Pradyumna released the Bhaskaraastra, Surya's weapon that dispels all illusions. The evil fires stood revealed in their fiendish forms.

As Krishna strung his bow to assist his son, Pradyumna stopped him. 'Let me tackle these demons while you rest, father,' he said respectfully. 'They are not worthy of your intervention.'

Krishna nodded in agreement and watched his son's ploys with pride, pleased that Pradyumna could hold his own against his enemies.

Pradyumna decided to fight fire with fire and used the Agneyaastra to burn up Angira and the others with its white-hot intensity.

Their path now unhindered, Garuda soared onwards, arriving at the walls of the citadel of Sonitapura shortly. As they descended to the ground, Krishna sounded the call to battle.

Hearing the mighty conch and seeing the avatar at their gates, Bana's demons were petrified. 'How can we win against

Vishnu?' they gasped. 'Narada prophesied our doom when the peacock banner fell.'

Their fearful whispers enraged Bana, but he knew that he had to win their support in order to win the war.

'Who says that he is the lord of Vaikunta?' he bellowed. 'This is another ploy employed by the cowherds to frighten us. The Yadus always employ deceit, and never show any shame or self-respect. They sent a young man to bewitch my daughter and seize my kingdom. They disrespect Shiva through whose boon she was born. Tomorrow they will send others to snatch your daughters. What will you do then? What do you choose now—surrender or war?'

His angry troops began to roar, 'War, war, war!'

The asuras opened the gates of their city and poured out in vast numbers. They were vicious and ready to wage their kutayuddha, unrighteous war—based on the laws of the jungle.

Krishna and his men, however, waged dharmayuddha— warfare based on neeti and shaurya, ethical principles and valour. They would fight only with the soldiers and not harm women, children, the elderly or those who were unarmed. They would not burn the enemy's land or fell trees, for they respected the earth and her blessings. They observed kshatradharma, the law of kings and warriors.

The asuras were armed with many strange and fearsome weapons. The bindipala that they carried, a huge club with a sinister bent end, ripped out the entrails of their enemies. The nalika, a big musket drawn on a cart, belched death on thousands. The masundi, a heavy cudgel with eight killing sides, could tear through the strongest armour, rendering it useless.

Krishna countered the fierce assault by whirling and slashing with his mace Kaumodaki and his bow Saranga, while Garuda shredded the demons with his beak and talons. Pradyumna fought ably beside the Blue God and his mount, using his skill with mace and bow to kill demons by their hundreds. Then he hurled Varuna's noose to choke the demons, a thousand at a time, until their eyeballs exploded from their sockets.

The Yadu army joined them by land, on elephants, horses and chariots, fighting off the enemy and advancing inexorably towards the city gates. The demons surged towards them, their blood-curdling howls splintering the skies.

The colossal Shiva-Jvara emerged from Sonitapura, petrifying the Yadu soldiers with his terrifying form. He had three legs, three heads, six arms, nine eyes and a voice that echoed like thunder over the surrounding mountains. Shiva-Jvara was Shiva's death weapon, destroying enemies with a ferocious heat that was twelve times the intensity of the heat from the sun. The earth blazed as he advanced. The heat burned eyeballs, seared the soldiers with every breath they took and scorched their insides.

The monster enveloped Pradyumna in its blaze, and the warrior collapsed with a moan. Krishna hurried to embrace him, reviving him with his cooling touch.

'Fight with me if you dare,' Krishna shouted to Shiva-Jvara, who began to assault him with weapons of incendiary heat. The Blue God stood unfazed and countered with blows to Shiva-Jvara's chest that brought him down like a giant tree. However, the fever had entered Krishna's body too and attacked him from within, weakening his limbs. He had to invoke a counter weapon to neutralize the enemy.

Krishna, therefore, called upon Narayana-Jvara, the weapon of chilling cold, who proceeded to freeze the breath in the lungs of the enemies, making them drop like leaves caught in a hurricane. The paralysing cold reduced Shiva-Jvara to the point of death, and he fell at the lotus feet of the lord, seeking sanctuary.

'I will spare your life,' said Krishna, showing him his infinite mercy.

The demons who were still alive began to run for their lives.

'Stop, you cowards,' screamed Bana, who had hurried on to the field upon hearing news of the rout of his army. 'I will invoke the great Ishwara to come to our aid. Follow me into battle, for victory is ours.'

He raised his arms to the skies and summoned the three-eyed god. 'Come to my aid, Shiva, and keep your promise.'

Shiva prepared to leave from Kailasa after a final word to Parvati, Karthikeya and Nandi. 'I have given Bana my boon of protection. However, this does not constrain you to fight on his side,' he said.

'I go where you go,' said Karthikeya.

'So do I. How can I bear to be separated from you?' asked Nandi.

Parvati hesitated.

'Speak your mind,' said Shiva. 'You know that you are free to make your choice.'

'Forgive me, but I cannot fight against my brother Vishnu, who is now on earth as Krishna,' she said. 'Nor can I oppose Usha's marriage to Aniruddha when I blessed their union and helped them unite with each other.'

'Do not fear, Devi, all will be well,' said Shiva, who departed for Sonitapura on the back of his mount Nandi. Karthikeya rode to the battlefield in his aerial chariot.

'I knew you would come,' laughed Bana, when he saw the divine army. 'You had no choice, did you? But where is your wife? Did she choose her brother over you?'

'Your confidence may be your strength, Bana,' replied Shiva. 'But when it turns to arrogance, it becomes your weakness. You have chosen to ignore my warning not to fight with Vishnu and have thus brought death upon yourself.'

'I do not consider this cowherd to be Vishnu. And even if he were, I regard this as an opportunity to avenge my father's death at his hands.'

'Surrender your ego to him, Bana, and he will offer you refuge. If, on the other hand, you set yourself up against him, your death is certain.'

'That is why I summoned you to help me. Aren't your powers equal to his? Then why should I fear him?'

'I am here because I promised to protect you, not because I support your stance. Understand that no army on earth can defeat Krishna. He is a purna avatar, a complete incarnation of heavenly power and glory.'

'So are you. How can he defeat you?' asked Bana.

'Vishnu and I are one and the same. You cannot use me to defeat him.'

'You made a promise and you must live up to it, whatever it entails.'

'Get ready to meet your fate then,' said Shiva.

He advanced on the enemy with Nandi and Karthikeya, like a forest fire that devours everything in its path. Behind him followed the ganas, with the heads of fierce tigers, lions, horses and goats. Shiva was Bhootanatha, the lord of the underworld, and all its dire citizens came with him too. Bhootas, pretas, pramathas, guhyakas, dakinis, pishachas, kusmandas, vetalas and the dreaded brahma rakshasas . . .

Krishna bowed to the god and Shiva nodded in return.

'This war is between the Yadus and Bana. You must not intervene in this, Shiva,' said Krishna.

'You forget that I have promised Bana my protection. I must fight,' replied Shiva.

'I do not wish to attack you, but I will if I must. What is your final decision?'

Shiva raised his trident high, and sprouted eight arms and four faces that pointed in the four directions.

Krishna nodded. 'War it is, then.' He ordered his men to take up battle positions.

'Fight me if you dare,' thundered Shiva, who was an army in himself, endowed with cosmic fire. In his four right hands he held the trident, the thunderbolt, the axe Khatvanga and a sword of radiant fire. In his left hands he wielded the divine bow Pinaka, an arrow, a noose and a goad.

Krishna loomed over him in fury and shot a hundred thousand arrows from his Saranga, aiming them at the bhootas and rakshasas. They dissipated under the attack like the morning mist in the fierce rays of the sun. The three-eyed god took revenge by aiming his blazing arrows at Krishna himself. Blinding fireballs lit up the skies and the netherworld.

'How can the world survive a conflict between these mighty gods, O father?' Narada asked Brahma.

'Their bond goes deeper than anything you can imagine,' said Brahma. 'And it does not change with time or circumstance. Shiva has to stand by his boon, whatever the consequences. And Vishnu has to oppose him in order to restore the cosmic balance. You must have faith that dharma will eventually emerge victorious.'

Shiva hurled a shakti a hundred yojanas long at Krishna, but the weapon transformed itself into a string of blue lotuses and garlanded the Dark One's neck. He then released his Pasupataastra, which he could summon with his mind, his eye, his bow or his words. The devastating weapon threatened to destroy not just the enemy but the entire world. The Blue God countered with the Narayanaastra, from which there could be no escape, except through total surrender. Millions of chakras, arrows, maces, spears, fireballs and bludgeons poured out from its blinding centre, spreading death like a volcano spewing molten lava. Anyone in its path was instantly destroyed, and the weapon flared brighter with the added energy.

The two weapons came together, causing a cataclysmic explosion. Mountains sank into the ground; earthquakes shattered the earth. The seas dried up and an inferno sprang up in all eight directions. Lakes turned red with blood and the sun and moon appeared side by side in the sky, circled by ruddy rings of light. All the air was sucked out of the universe, and living things swooned in near-death. The stench of burning flesh permeated the realms.

The devas descended to earth to placate the two fierce gods, but neither would cease. 'This is a war of dharma. Retreat is not a possibility,' said Krishna. 'Whoever stands against us is our enemy and we must fight. There is no place for weakness or doubt.'

Hearing this, Shiva shook his shoulders, making the weapons in the hands of the Yadus vanish. Krishna at once armed his men with bludgeons that emitted fiery sparks. Shiva thrust out his chest and uttered a hoonkara, a long *huuum* sound, and the soldiers went careering through the air.

Krishna shot an arrow into the sky, and a whirlwind descended on the field and obscured everyone's vision. He stood facing Shiva in its midst so he could talk to him without being observed.

'Why are you fighting for adharma?' asked Krishna. 'You gave Bana wealth, power and a wonderful daughter whose marriage to Aniruddha was blessed by Parvati. But Bana opposes the marriage and abuses your boons.'

'I have always been equipoised, favouring neither the devas nor the asuras,' said Shiva. 'Bana performed a fierce tapasya and I granted him my boons as a reward for his devotion.'

'You have been just, but Bana abuses your trust and plunges deeper into evil. If you help him now, you will be taking the side of evil and injustice. How will the world value dharma when they see the great Shiva supporting a sinner and fighting against me? Petty minds that see us will perceive us as enemies and not as two parts of a whole. They will not understand that neither of us can exist without the other.'

But Shiva was adamant that he had to honour his word at all costs.

'You are the fury that propels the universe and gives it its energy, while I am the balance that restores harmony and order. In this, we are the same, yet quite different,' said Krishna. 'Let us put an end to this unseemly war.'

'You have your duty to perform and I have mine. Let us carry out our tasks, whatever the price may be,' said Shiva, returning to the battlefield.

He hurled his trident at Krishna in order to put an end to the battle. The trishul was the weapon of Rudra, the Invincible One with a thousand heads, a thousand eyes and a thousand quivers.

The demons rejoiced, confident that their tormentor would die. The trident flashed fires in a hundred wild colours as it hurtled forward. Thousands of conches, drums and bugles blasted an infernal accompaniment, even though no hands or lips touched them.

Krishna was equally determined to win this battle for dharma. He countered with the radiant Sudarshana chakra that embodied all his energy. He followed like a blue fire in the path cleared by the chakra's crimson dance of death.

Krishna roared and roared, his voice thundering over the sounds of the dying and the wounded, until the world hushed. The two weapons clashed and exploded in a blinding fury.

The heat of the battle eclipsed the sun and total darkness fell over the field. Shiva hurled terrible weapons at Krishna who retaliated with his fierce mace that cast Shiva down in a swoon. Bana raced up on his chariot and took up Shiva with him.

Meanwhile, Pradyumna was waging a relentless battle with Bana's legions, hoping to decimate them by the time his father ended his war with Shiva. The fury of the attacks brought Mother Earth shuddering to Brahma, pleading for his intervention. 'The heat of this combat will burn me up along with all living beings,' she said. 'I can bear this no longer, Brahmadeva. I entreat you to stop it now.'

Brahma hurried to Shiva, who had emerged from his swoon, and reasoned with him. 'This fight has gone on too long and will end the world before its time,' he said. 'Why do you fight Krishna so ferociously when you yourself have stated that you are both one and the same? You ordained Bana's downfall, saying that it would happen as soon as his banner toppled. You warned him that the yug purush would mete out just punishment for his sins. Why then do you stand in the way of fate?'

Shiva listened as Brahma continued to speak. 'I once had a dream in which I saw you with a blue skin, carrying the conch, the chakra and the mace, and riding on Garuda,' said Brahma. 'I then saw Vishnu on your bull, wearing a tiger skin and wielding your trishul. What does the dream mean, Ishwara?'

Shiva replied in a calm voice, returning to his usual equanimity. 'Vishnu and I are the same, merely taking on different forms and colours, like water moulding itself in a vessel. We create the elements and rule over the universe together, regulating time and life. We manifest as the two-eyed or the three-eyed, fair in form or dark, dressed in silks or tiger skin, the beloved of Lakshmi or Parvati, the protector or the destroyer.'

Brahma listened with reverence as Shiva expounded the principle of Hari-Hara, the transcendent unity of Vishnu and Shiva.

He knew that Shiva would not return to fight by Bana's side.

>———————

In another corner of the battlefield, Shiva's son had taken over the command of the army in his father's absence. Karthikeya was born of six fiery sparks emitted by Shiva's third eye, and was a fearsome god with six faces and twelve hands. He had freed the devas from the torturous reign of Tarakasura after shattering the Krauncha mountain which had barred his way. He was not just a warrior but was renowned for his wisdom, having expounded on Om, the pranava mantra or the primal mantra of creation, to Shiva himself.

Shiva had created eleven Rudras from his mind and bestowed them on Karthikeya as his weapons when he sent him to fight Tarakasura. They were Mahadeva, Hara, Rudra, Sankara, Nelalohita, Essana, Vijaya, Bhima, Devadeva, Bavothbhava and Kapaaleesa. Karthikeya carried their powers with him in the form of the spear, flag, sword, mace, arrow, goad, bell, lotus, bow, noose and axe. In his twelfth hand, he carried the lance that had the power to destroy the pancha boothas—the five elements of earth, water, fire, air and sky—and erase all evil. Karthikeya confronted Pradyumna with all his might. 'You have challenged the son of the Destroyer,' he said. 'You will now pay the price for your folly.'

He let loose a volley of arrows that flew like thoughts from his mind.

Fully aware of his enemy's boundless powers, Pradyumna fought undeterred, intercepting each of Karthikeya's arrows with two of his own. When Shiva's son aimed the Brahmaastra at him, he retaliated with his own Brahmaastra. When he released a violent hurricane with his Vayvayaastra, he stopped it with a Parvataastra—a mountain that stopped it in its tracks. He opposed his Agneyaastra with torrents of rain from the Varunaastra.

'You are but a child,' scoffed Pradyumna. 'I will let you escape to your mother, leaving the war to your elders.'

Blinded by fury, Karthikeya decided to put an end to it with his golden lance, imbued with the shakti of his mother Parvati. The lance scorched through the air towards its target, spewing flames.

The world watched in terror. Devas and demons alike knew that Pradyumna would be annihilated in the blink of an eye.

The seas stilled and the planets of good fortune orbited backwards. The ghastly wail of the spirits of the dead echoed in the sudden stillness.

Had Pradyumna survived battles with asuras and devas, only to die in Sonitapura?

33

The Chakra and the Demon

And then, Krishna intervened. He flew on Garuda to interpose himself between his son and the golden lance, staying the radiant weapon with an upraised hand. The lance quivered in mid-air for a moment and then dropped to the ground at his feet. The incensed Blue God took up his Sudarshana chakra to slice off Karthikeya's head.

Immediately, a huge figure rose before him, dark and mountainous, with red eyes, wearing wild elephants as earrings and the skins of animals as garments. Her mouth was fanged and her talons were like scimitars. She sat astride a fierce lion, which tossed its mane and roared like a thousand thunders, waking up the nagas in patala.

'You must fight with me first if you want to kill my son,' said Kotavi, who was the eighth part of Parvati, come from Kailasa to protect her son from certain death.

Krishna's anger was tempered when he saw that his sister stood before him; he could not harm her. Instead, he addressed her in affectionate tones: 'Remember your promise to help unite Usha with Aniruddha, Devi. As Jvalamukhi, you blessed him so he could walk through the flames and win her hand. You know too that the time has come for Bana to pay for his arrogance in challenging both Shiva and me. Go in peace with your son, and allow me to complete my mission.'

The wrathful Kotavi transformed into the gentle Parvati, and she left the battlefield along with Karthikeya.

Bana was distraught to see the Devi and her valorous son leave, for now he would have to face his enemies himself. He sounded his war bugles in defiance and raced to confront Krishna.

'I offer you a final chance to retreat,' he said to the Blue God.

'I offer you peace if you surrender and let us take Aniruddha and his bride to Dwaraka,' replied Krishna. 'I do not wish to kill someone born in the clan of my great devotee Prahlada.'

'A mortal seeking the surrender of the Trilokadipati?' bellowed Bana. 'Have you come here to die, after bidding farewell to your many wives?'

'Rash words and raised voices do not win battles. You have finally met someone who is not afraid, someone who is destined to kill you.'

'Then why did it take you so long to come face-to-face with me, coward? asked Bana.

'I can fell you in an instant, but as you have challenged me to a fight, let us fight,' said Krishna, taking up his bow.

Bana unleashed weapons that he had seized from Indra, Agni and Surya. He stood resolute like Yama in a new avatar, wielding several hundred bows in his thousand arms, along with maces and swords. But his rival's Saranga twanged lustily and its unerring arrows brought down the weapons in the twinkling of an eye.

The asura invoked the Brahmaastra, from which hundreds of weapons erupted. Darkness shrouded the battlefield as the sun was obscured by the fusillade. The asuras cheered. But Krishna used his Shakti, embodying Indra's power of lightning, to dissipate the darkness.

The Blue God unleashed a flood of silver arrows that smashed Bana's chariot, and killed his charioteer and his horses. The asura was flung from his seat and Krishna's final arrow pierced his heart. He fell down in a deathly swoon. At once, Bana's peacock, given to him by Shiva, began to attack the foe with its sharp talons, only to be killed by a fierce blow from Garuda's wings. Shiva's bull Nandi charged up to Bana and took him up on his back to carry on the battle. Bana recovered and shot the Brahmashira, a weapon that was four times as powerful as the Brahmaastra, drawing its power from Brahma's four heads. Only another Brahmashira could take this on, and Krishna hurled his own to neutralize Bana's. The two weapons collided in the air, spreading waves of death.

He destroys my fiercest weapons, and batters my body and my mind, thought Bana. *And yet, his smile never leaves his face. How much longer can I withstand his attack?*

'This combat has gone on too long,' Krishna proclaimed. 'It's time to put an end to your arrogance.' He raised the Sudarshana chakra on his finger, ready to cast it on the asura. The weapon flamed with a blinding incandescence.

'Protect Bana from the chakra or he will perish,' Shiva entreated Parvati. She returned to the battlefield and stood between the two opponents.

'Bana's end is near, Parvati. You know I cannot allow him to escape this time,' said Krishna.

'His fate may be ordained, but I request you to stay your hand, brother,' said Parvati in a sweet, clear voice. 'Shiva has accepted him as his son which makes him dear to me as well. I cannot bear to see him die.'

Shiva appeared and praised the Blue God to reduce his anger and remind him of his radiant self in Vaikunta. 'The sky is your navel, Krishna, and the fire is your face. Water is your life force and the clouds your hair. Heaven is your head, the earth your foot, the moon your mind and the sun your eyes. I am your soul, Indra your arms and Brahma your intelligence. You are the Para Brahman, the Supreme God. Remember that Bana is the great-grandson of your devotee Prahlada and show him mercy.' Krishna returned to his serene self, the ever-merciful Vishnu with his beatific smile, reclining on Adisesha in the abode of bliss. He nodded in respect to Shiva and Parvati, who were as precious to him as his two eyes.

'I will spare his life,' he said. 'Your boon to him will be honoured, as well as mine to Prahlada—that I will not kill any of his descendants.'

Krishna appeared to Bana in his form of Vishnu, with four arms carrying his conch, mace, lotus and chakra. Bana's eyes were dazzled and he wondered for a moment if his rage was blinding him to reality. Then he shook his head, casting away his doubts as marks of cowardice. 'You show me false visions to confuse my mind,' he shouted. 'But nothing you say or do can stop me.' He took up his mace again to strike the lord.

The fiery chakra could be stopped no more. It shrieked towards the asura and chopped off all but two of his arms, and then whirred above Bana's head, ready to execute the final blow.

The touch of the incandescent chakra scorched the asura's arrogance and forced him to face the truth. His mammoth army had been decimated; his thousand arms had been reduced to two. He was helpless and alone, with the rutilant chakra hovering over him, threatening to consume him. He had one last hope: submit himself to the mercy of the supreme lord of the universe.

Bana fell headlong at Vishnu's feet. 'What have I done?' he sobbed. 'How did I not recognize that I was opposing the one who is Kesava, Krishna and Madhusudhana? I ignored your warning, and slighted the counsel of Shiva and Parvati who protected me as if I were their son. How do I atone for my blunder? Dare I hope that you will look upon this sinner with compassion?'

'Rise to your feet, Bana,' said the lord. 'Your soul is immortal now and free from fear. Pay obeisance to Shiva and Parvati who saved you from my anger.'

Bana prayed for Shiva's forgiveness. The kind-hearted god healed his wounds, gave him a new form and elevated him as one of his attendants, with the name Mahakala. Bana's minister Kumbhanda pleaded for mercy and was crowned the ruler of Sonitapura.

Parvati brought Usha to Krishna so he could bless her and her marriage to Aniruddha.

Pradyumna went to the dungeon to release his son who was being held immobile by the snakes' poisonous breath and glittering coils. He freed him with the power of Garuda, whose fierce screech swept the serpents away.

Aniruddha rejoiced at the reunion with his people and with the princess for whom he had risked his all. The formal wedding of the young couple soon took place with the blessings of the gods.

The bridal party returned to Dwaraka to a jubilant welcome. Giant arches of victory sprang up along the way. Conches and drums set up a cheerful beat. The priests and the common people came to the city gates to greet the victors.

34

The Enemy Within

All of Dwaraka was agog as the returning soldiers narrated the tale of the defeat of the asura with the thousand arms. The people sang the praises of Krishna who took on Shiva, and of Pradyumna who fought the mighty Karthikeya. They told and retold the stories of Aniruddha entering the fortress of fire, the fight with Shiva-Jvara and the chakra cutting off Bana's arms. They marvelled at the beauty of the princess who had come to their citadel as Aniruddha's bride.

'How fortunate we are to live in Dwaraka with our lord and his son Pradyumna!' they exclaimed.

Two souls, however, remained mired in hate, realizing that they had faded into oblivion when compared to Rukmini and her son.

'I had hoped that the upstart and his son would be killed and things would return to the way they were before,' said Samba to his mother. 'Everyone now speaks of Pradyumna as the heir to the throne. Even the gods have forgotten that I built the grand Sambaditya temple on the shores of the sea.

I will stop making offerings to them if they continue to favour the pretender.'

'We do not need anyone to support us, my son,' said Jambavati. 'We can deal with Pradyumna ourselves. Does he have four arms, three eyes or divine armour to protect him? We should not have let him live this long.'

'I must make him suffer for trying to take what is mine,' said Samba. 'Maybe I should pretend to accept him and then vanquish him when he least expects it, turning his joy into agony.'

'Greetings to you, Samba, and to the queen!' said a voice.

They turned to see Narada standing before them. The devarishi disregarded their angry expressions to offer his counsel.

'I see that excessive anger troubles your minds,' he said. 'I spoke to you earlier about your animosity towards Pradyumna. He is not fortune's favourite as you seem to think. His childhood was ill-fated and spent in the midst of demons, without knowledge of his real parents or his identity as Kama. He battled alone against the terrible Kaalasura and fought his way to gain acceptance in Dwaraka. Don't you think he deserves your compassion rather than your hatred?'

'Our hearts overflow with pity for him,' scoffed Samba. 'Didn't he plot with his mother to make Rukmavati choose him instead of me? Now he fools the people into thinking he is their saviour.'

'He saved you too when you were imprisoned in the Kuru dungeons.'

Samba's eyes flashed angrily. 'Did I ask him for his help? I could have freed myself from that prison and brought Lakshmani with me. You forget that it was Balarama's threat to submerge their city in the Ganga that frightened them into releasing me. But the upstart pretends to be the one who rescued me.'

'Why do you harbour such hatred towards Pradyumna when he has always shown you the highest respect?'

'How can we respect someone who married his own foster mother, a woman who is older than he is?' asked Jambavati. 'Though you call yourself a devarishi, you do not condemn his marriage to Mayavati, which is against all Vedic rules.'

'This marriage of Kama with Rati was ordained by Shiva and Parvati. Krishna too has sanctified their marriage. Why do you censure what the mighty gods themselves have blessed?' asked Narada.

'Mayavati is a sorceress who taught him the occult arts,' said Jambavati. 'She lived for years as the wife of an asura and now expects to sit on equal terms with us. How can we allow this?'

'Mayavati is a model for all women—she brought her husband to life again through her tapasya,' said Narada. 'Do not speak ill of her, for Krishna does not allow anyone to insult women. He has even declared himself the enemy of the Kurus who tried to strip Draupadi in the royal court. You tempt fate by cursing the virtuous.'

'If Krishna is so honourable, he should have given me the parijata tree, as I am his foremost queen.'

'Do not stray on to the thorny path of envy, O queen,' said the devarishi. 'Duryodhana inherited his envy from his parents and that has caused all his misfortunes. His mother Gandhari was envious of Kunti when the latter gave birth to Yudhistira. She beat her womb in frustration, resulting in the birth of her hundred evil sons. Her husband Dhritarashtra was envious of his brother Pandu, who preceded him on the throne, and encouraged his son to treat his cousins with great cruelty. Duryodhana carries on this legacy, depriving the Pandavas of their rightful share of the kingdom. His doom may be inevitable, but you still have the power to save your son.'

'Why do you always chastise us, Devarishi?' she raged. 'Why don't you advise Rukmini and her son instead?'

'Let me tell you of another queen who was felled by envy,' said Narada, trying to avert the doom that he himself had predicted. 'Kaikeyi insisted that King Dasaratha anoint her son the ruler and banish Rama, the son of Kausalya, to the forest. Rama obeyed her command and left the kingdom, but his grief-stricken father died of a broken heart. Kaikeyi's son Bharata refused to ascend the throne or to call her "mother" again. She died alone, a bitter outcast, hated by everyone.'

Jambavati turned her back on Narada, refusing to listen.

'You have heard this tale many times, I know,' he continued, 'but I repeat it now so you can learn from her fate. You can never win a kingdom through adharma. The Bhagavata Purana says that there is a hell called Dandasuka just for people who sting others with their envy. They are devoured again and again by seven hooded serpents and suffer endless agony. Why will you not listen to me, O queen?'

'Why are you still speaking?' shouted Samba. 'Pradyumna is my enemy and nothing you say will convince me otherwise. Be on your way before I forget you are an ascetic and raise my arm against you.'

'Your greatest enemy is within you, Samba,' said Narada. 'Your anger creates foes where there are none. You must first master yourself before you can aspire to rule a kingdom, or you will lead your people to ruin.'

'You have said enough,' said Jambavati in a strident voice. 'I will not tolerate your speaking thus to my son.'

Narada bowed and turned away. There was nothing more he could do.

35

Kama Shastra

Samba's resentment festered within him and overflowed in bitter words whenever he saw Pradyumna. His obsession grew by the day, distorting his vision and distracting him from his responsibilities. His friends, warped souls who delighted in fomenting strife, egged him on. The courtiers contributed unwittingly to his envy by speaking of Pradyumna as the crown prince, a fitting heir to Krishna's wisdom and valour. They repeated endlessly the story of the lost child who had returned to the bosom of his family.

One day, after a dance that was staged in honour of the newly-weds, Aniruddha and Usha, Samba waited for the elders to leave before taunting Pradyumna.

'Brother, your son has proved to be your worthy successor. He married Rukmi's granddaughter, setting off a terrible carnage that resulted in Rukmi's death. Soon after this, he went away without a word to anyone to look for a new bride—a girl he saw in a dream. His bravado landed him in prison from which he had to be rescued by our men, many of whom died.'

Pradyumna and Mayavati were dumbstruck on hearing the barrage of hate. But Samba was not done yet.

'But one can't blame your son for his sins, for he has inherited his nature from you,' he continued. 'After all, you are Kama, the embodiment of animal lust. You claimed that your mother is Rati, just so you could marry her. You talk of a great love that transcends ages and then marry Rukmavati before the year has ended. No woman is safe from you, for you are still the lustful prince from the asura court.'

Pradyumna was accustomed to being insulted by Samba, but he could not bear the hatred directed against his son. He felt that Samba should look upon Aniruddha with affection, just as he himself regarded Samba's children.

'Aniruddha's marriage took place according to a divine plan, as our father told us. How can you question it?' he asked.

Mayavati moved quietly to stand beside Pradyumna, offering her support.

Samba carried on his tirade, undeterred. 'I wish I could speak like you, brother, giving my selfish desires the gloss of virtue. You say that I cannot question my father, as he is god. Then why is this god so unjust, promoting one son at the expense of another? He has not granted me my position as crown prince, even though I have slaved for him these many years.'

'One should not worship god as a means to wealth and power,' said Pradyumna, 'but as our means to redemption. Why do you speak ill of the one whom the three realms recognize as the living god? Why do you resent him when he adores you?' He laid a hand on his brother's arm to calm him down.

Samba shook off his hand. 'He adores me? Is that why he cursed me with leprosy when his queens threw themselves at me?'

Mayavati could not stand by in silence any longer. 'Don't you love your brother, Samba?' she asked. 'Has he ever treated you badly?'

'This *brother* of mine came like a beggar with nothing but the clothes on his back and his whore whom he called his wife,' Samba spat. 'Now he wants everything—my throne, my father, the affection of my people. And you want me to love him?' He pushed his brother away with a blow to his shoulder. 'Stop the deceit, Pradyumna, and reveal yourself as you truly are—an evil master conniver. Or I will rip your mask off myself. Fight openly with me, for I am confident of my own strength. Do not dream that I will bow before you or anyone else.'

He turned to Mayavati, who had dared question him. 'You say you are the faithful wife who prayed for many years to be united with her lord. Why then did you serve the asura in his bed with your lips and your body? When you found out that he was destined to die, you switched your loyalties to a new lover. And now you dream of ruling Dwaraka with him.'

Pradyumna's hand reached for the hilt of his sword. He wanted to cut Samba's tongue out for the insults he spewed, but Mayavati clasped his arm and restrained him.

'You have chosen the wrong brother, Mayavati,' said Samba. 'However, all is not lost. You can be my mistress when I am king. I will happily share my bed with you, and please you better than he ever can.' He reached for her hand.

She recoiled from him, saying, 'I would rather bed a snake than share your chamber, Samba. Nothing can protect you from facing a foul death.'

'Though you are my brother, I will kill you if you ever talk to her like this again,' said Pradyumna. 'Stay away from me if you want to live.'

Samba strode off, his black heart burning. His vanity was wounded, his anger overflowed. He would kill Pradyumna and make the harlot his own.

Pradyumna was in turn angry and distraught as he pondered Samba's vitriol. He sought the counsel of Rukmini, the wise mother of the universe.

'Maybe what Samba says is true,' he said. 'Krishna says that lust and anger are born of darkness and are barriers to moksha. I am the embodiment of kama, desire that is never satisfied. It is my sinful nature that has caused my birth as a destructive force, first as Kartaviryarjuna and now as Pradyumna. Wasn't this the vision that Narada saw at my birth?'

Rukmini laid a calming hand on his shoulder. 'It is true that the devarishi said that one of you would be the destroyer, but the Supreme Lord Krishna said that the other could save humankind. Why do you believe that you are destined to destroy the world? You know that our redemption lies in our own hands.'

'Do not dismiss kama as darkness or sin, my love,' said Mayavati. 'Without desire, there can be no life. Shiva knew this even when he opened his third eye to burn you. That is why he did not destroy you completely, but made you ananga, formless. Kama is of the mind too, not just of the body. It includes the pleasure we take in the finer aspects of life—food, ornaments, music and dance. Krishna denounces only the lust that is contrary to dharma and the laws of society.'

'You speak wisely,' Rukmini said to her daughter-in-law and then turned to reassure her son. 'Desire was the first emotion to be created by Brahma. It is the basis of all love and compassion. It is so vital to life that Brahma facilitated love by creating shrubs and trees, flowers and ponds, rippling cascades and singing birds and bees that buzzed around the blooms. He provided you with five arrows to evoke the moods of desire—attraction, arousal, confusion, enchantment and ecstasy.'

'Your arrows are so potent that they provoked Brahma himself to lust for his daughter,' said Mayavati. 'They filled Indra with desire for Sage Gautama's wife and made Surya transform himself into a stallion to follow his wife Sanjana, who had taken the form of a mare, to earth.'

Pradyumna's mood brightened as Mayavati continued to speak. 'Your arrows created such a storm of passion in Shiva that he plunged into the Kalindi river to cool himself. The waters turned black with his heat and dried up. Still, his ardour raged and he wandered through the forest of Daruvana, attracting the wives of the rishis who began to follow him. The sages cursed him and he in turn cursed you. Understand, therefore, that kama wields immense power—a power that even the gods cannot withstand.'

Rati chanted the names of her beloved. 'You spring from the heart and are therefore called Bhavaja and Manoja. As the son of Krishna, you are Karshni. As the son of Lakshmi, you are Srinandana. You are also Abhirupa, the beautiful; Dipaka, the inflamer; Mara, the destroyer; Mayi, the deluder; Ragavrinta, the stalk of passion. Men worship you as Rupastra, the weapon of beauty; Vama, the handsome; Pushpadhanus, the one with the bow of flowers; and Makaraketu, carrying the banner of the sea dragon.'

Rukmini's eyes looked into the future as she spoke to her son. 'Your name will shine as long as there is life. And kama will be regarded as one of the ultimate goals of life, along with dharma, artha and moksha.'

36

Kurus or Pandavas?

After losing his kingdom to Shakuni in the game of dice, Yudhistira was forced into exile for thirteen years, along with his brothers and wife. When they returned after passing twelve long years in the forest and one year in hiding, Duryodhana refused to keep his word and restore their share of the kingdom. War seemed inevitable.

'A war between the two kings will involve all the Kshatriyas and cause a bloodbath more devastating than the world has ever seen,' said Krishna. 'I will do all I can to stop it. And if I fail, I will have the satisfaction of knowing I did everything I could.'

Krishna travelled to the Kuru capital to persuade Duryodhana to return the Pandava capital of Indraprastha to its rightful owners, but the Kuru prince laughed at him.

'Give them at least five villages, one for each of the Pandavas,' Krishna said next.

'I will give them nothing, not even enough land to cover the point of a needle,' scoffed Duryodhana. 'Tell them to fight and take what they can.'

Krishna appealed to Duryodhana's father. 'Wise Dhritarashtra,' he said, 'you know well that war entails terrible losses. Your sons will be killed and your race obliterated. Do not let Duryodhana bring disaster upon the world. Dark omens at the time of your son's birth indicated that he is a monster who is better killed. Stop him now. Lock him away in the dungeons. Then make peace with the Pandavas.'

The father hung his head. 'Alas, Krishna, I cannot control my son,' he said. 'I should have tried to curb him earlier, but those days are long gone.'

Duryodhana's mother Gandhari pleaded with her son to stop the war. But he stormed out without deigning to reply.

He came up instead with a foul plan that shocked the elders. 'Let us imprison Krishna in our dungeons,' he said. 'Without him, the Pandavas will never be able to defeat us.'

'How can you imprison Lord Vishnu?' screamed his father. 'You might as well try to capture the wind and the sun in a cage.'

Krishna laughed at the foolish Duryodhana and assumed his visvaroopa, his cosmic form embodying the entire universe, dazzling their minds and eyes. Even Dhritarashtra's blind eyes could see Vishnu's ultimate reality, from which emanated the legions of heaven and earth, the elements, the three realms and all living things. Duryodhana fell face down on the ground and tried to shut his eyes and ears, but he could not escape the searing vision. Still, his diseased mind refused to accept the avatar.

The light faded and Krishna returned to his earthly form. He realized that there was nothing more he could do. What he had feared would come to pass. He left the court, his face furrowed with grief.

The Kuru elders cursed Duryodhana. 'Your downfall is certain, for no one can stand against Krishna and win. But as you have issued the challenge, prevent his fighting for the Pandavas by meeting him first and seeking his help in the war.'

The reluctant Duryodhana went to meet the Dark One. The Pandava Arjuna came too, with the same hope.

'As both of you seek my help,' said Krishna, 'I give you a choice. My army, the Narayani Sena, will fight on one side, while I myself will support the other side, though I will not wield a weapon. Make your choice first, Arjuna.'

'I choose you,' said Arjuna, 'for I cannot imagine fighting against you.'

Duryodhana chortled. What was the point in having Krishna on his side if the Blue God would not fight for them? He would rather have the powerful Vrishni army on his side.

Messengers flew to the allies of both the kings to gather their support. The Pandavas formed seven divisions of soldiers with the help of the kings of Kasi, Kekaya, Mathura, Magadha, Chedi and Pandya. The Kurus had a much larger force of eleven divisions supported by the kings of Matsya, Anga, Kekaya, Mahishmati, Avanti, Gandhara and many others. The armies of dharma and adharma took their positions on either side of the plains of Kurukshetra, poised for battle.

Pradyumna was dismayed to realize that war was drawing closer by the day. 'Why do you not prevent this ghastly conflict between brothers, father?' he asked. 'Is it impossible even for Sarvabhauma, the one who is everything?'

'You know the efforts I made to enforce peace, my son,' said Krishna. 'I gave the Kurus many chances to redeem themselves. However, some things even I must accept as inevitable, for I too am governed by the nature of man and the universe. Men choose their own path in life and sometimes their actions result in problems that even god cannot solve. When conflict becomes inevitable, I ensure that dharma wins, whatever the cost.'

The Yadus were equally perturbed by the developments. They felt torn in two as both the contenders were their kin. Their lord supported one side while his sena fought on the other. Balarama was in great distress at the course of events and came to meet the Pandavas, along with Pradyumna, Samba, Akrura, Uddhava and other leaders of Dwaraka.

Balarama was his usual resplendent self in his blue silks and garland of golden flowers, but his face betrayed his anguish. Krishna and the Pandavas greeted him with reverence.

'I am disturbed by your insistence on war,' Balarama said to the Pandavas. 'Many thousands will be slaughtered, leaving behind grieving widows and children. Blood will flow like water and the clan of Kshatriyas will be wiped off the face of the earth. I do not understand why Krishna supports you when the Kurus are also entitled to his affection. But there's little I can do when I know that he always chooses Arjuna over the others.'

His brother smiled, for he knew Balarama favoured Duryodhana, his pupil in mace fighting, though Bhima was his student too. The Pandavas and their allies listened uneasily as Balarama made his preference clear. Did this mean that he would fight against their army?

'Krishna will ensure that Arjuna wins the war at all costs,' Balarama continued. 'I do not agree with him, but I cannot oppose him in war. I cannot play a part in the destruction of two families that are close to my heart.' His eyes filled with tears. 'Therefore I plan to leave on a pilgrimage to distant parts of the land so that I do not have to witness the carnage.'

Krishna was tearful too as he embraced his brother. However, he knew that the war had to continue to its inevitable conclusion.

Samba was surprised by the turn of events. His desire was to oppose the Pandavas whom his father favoured. In fact, he often suspected that Krishna cared more for Arjuna and Abhimanyu than for himself.

I would like to fight against Arjuna and my father, he thought. *But then I'd be on the losing side, for even Balarama says that the Pandavas will win.*

As he watched the tragedy unfold, Pradyumna pondered on the twisted relationship between brothers that made them enemies. How could he question the Kurukshetra war being fought between cousins, when he knew that his own brother Samba hated him and would readily kill him?

If he stayed close to his brother, open hostilities would break out between them too. Two war elephants could not live together in the same stable without one killing the other.

Pradyumna made up his mind. 'I agree with my uncle's stance,' he said. 'I too cannot fight against my father or against the Narayani Sena. I will stay away from Kurukshetra and travel to other lands where I may be required,' he said.

His father nodded his acceptance.

Samba listened in dismay. He had thought that Pradyumna would choose to fight for his friends, the Pandavas. He could then have said that he would fight for the Kurus, just so that he would have a chance to kill his brother. Death and defeat did not matter when weighed against his hatred for Pradyumna. Now what was he to do?

Krishna was looking at him, waiting to hear his decision. Samba wanted to get away from all these people whom he loathed.

'I too will stay away from the war,' he snarled. 'What else can I do but follow the example of my valiant brother?' He curled his lip and stormed away.

Pradyumna embraced his father and the Yadus and turned to leave. How many of them would he see alive at the end of the war?

37

Suchimukhi

In another corner of the universe, the mighty asura Vajranabha was performing severe penances on Mount Sumeru to propitiate Brahma. The golden Sumeru was 84,000 yojanas tall and was the sacred centre of a gigantic complex of seas and mountains. A huge ocean formed a moat around the square base of Sumeru, and seven mountains and seven seas in turn encircled it. Beyond these was the outer sea, on which the continents formed small islands.

Sumeru was rich in treasures, celestial fruits and flowers. Surya and the other planets orbited the sacred mountain in worship, for it was Brahma's abode. Below Brahmapuri were the eight golden cities of the deities of the eight directions: Indra, Agni, Yama, Nirrti, Varuna, Vayu, Kubera and Isana.

Vajranabha travelled here with his mystic powers and prayed to the four-headed god, who finally appeared before him to ask him what he desired. 'Bless me with strength that is superior to that of even the devas,' he said. 'Let my city be unrivalled in beauty in all the realms. Let it be so secure that no one, not even the wind, can enter without my permission.'

'So be it,' said Brahma, and blessed him.

The city of Vajrapur rose swiftly, surrounded by beautiful gardens and blessed with all the wealth known to man. It was in the midst of a huge lake; its walls were strong, its gates wide and its people secure in their invincible fortress. Their life was free of care, and every day was a carnival of music and dance. There was no need to work and earn money, for they were richer than Kubera.

The asura's prowess and arrogance grew unchecked, and one day he strode to Indra's sabha and challenged him. Indra and the devas were his stepbrothers, for they were the sons of Sage Kashyapa through his wife Aditi, while Vajranabha and the asuras were born to the sage's other wife Diti. The enmity between the two families was bitter and of long standing.

'Your time to rule the heavens has come to an end,' said Vajranabha to Indra. 'Surrender to me and become my slave. Or fight me, if you dare, and see if you can hold on to your throne.'

Indra knew he would lose against Vajranabha, as Brahma's boon had made the asura invincible. He decided to try to delay the inevitable. 'I must consult my guru and the devas,' he said. 'Our father Kashyapa is conducting an Aswamedha yagna for Vasudeva. We should wait until it is over and he is free to guide us.' The asura warned Indra that he would not wait forever and returned to his city.

The finest performers from all the lands entertained the guests at the yagna, foremost among whom was an actor named Bhadra. His scintillating shows so pleased the sages that they asked him to choose any boon he desired.

'Bless me with the power to travel through the air to any place in the universe,' he said. 'Grant me immunity from dangers, the power to take any form I choose and to please everyone.'

'So be it,' said the sages.

Indra left the yagna in order to meet Krishna and seek his help in defeating Vajranabha.

'We must kill the asura before he kills you,' said Krishna. 'Our biggest obstacle is that no one can enter Vajrapur without Vajranabha's permission. We must find a way to penetrate his city, and we can do this with the help of Pradyumna. There is no warrior on earth equal to him in prowess and acumen. He himself wishes to travel to a far corner of the earth to avoid the carnage that will soon begin in Kurukshetra.'

'We can make the asura believe that he is Bhadra so that he will welcome him into Vajrapur,' said Indra. 'My stepbrother has an overwhelming love for performers of every kind.'

Indra sought the help of the hansa, the shimmering swan with the power to discriminate between good and evil, between the eternal and the evanescent.

'Divine Suchimukhi, speaker of sweet words,' he said to the swan queen. 'There is no kingdom where you are not welcome and no border which you cannot cross. I seek your help in sending a message to Vajranabha's lovely daughter Prabhavati.'

'What can I do to please the king of the heavens?' asked the talking swan.

'I want you to tell the princess about the exploits of the heroic Pradyumna and ensure that she falls in love with him. You must awaken love in his heart for the asura's daughter, so that he too desires to meet her. He will enter the citadel in the guise of the actor Bhadra who travels around the world in many forms. Once Kama is inside, what can possibly stop him from winning Prabhavati's heart?'

Suchimukhi flew to Vajrapur and landed gracefully in the asura's garden. 'I have come from devaloka in order to see the city that surpasses Indra's capital in splendour,' she said. 'I can see now that Vajrapur is indeed unrivalled.'

The asura was flattered by her praise and invited her to live in the royal pools, where she soon became his daughter Prabhavati's favourite companion. The princess was red-lipped, fair-skinned and excelled in music and dance. Soon she began to spend all her waking moments with Suchimukhi, listening to tales of distant lands and heroic people.

The swan came to love the princess and advised her on choosing the ideal groom. 'You must choose only the finest among mortals and devas,' said Suchimukhi. 'And I know just the one for you. His name is Pradyumna, Kama born on earth as the son of Krishna. The prince is wiser than the devas and mightier than the asuras. He is skilled in battle like Arjuna and learned in the scriptures like Yudhistira. His looks inspire passionate love in the hearts of all maidens. His face is radiant like the moon, his skin fair and his stride majestic.'

'Tell me more, sweet bird,' said the besotted princess.

'The world praises his valour in killing the demon Kaalasura who kidnapped him as a child. He defeated the demons Shalva and Banasura. He overcame the devas under Indra and brought the parijata tree to earth. He is the best of men, destined for great things. His people love him, the sages praise him and his rivals fear him. There is no one more suited to be your husband.'

As Suchimukhi stayed with the princess, telling her more about the prince's exploits, Prabhavati melted in desire.

'I have heard of the great Krishna whom the world worships as Vishnu's avatar,' she said. 'Now you tell me his son rivals him in courage and form. I yearn to meet Pradyumna, though his clan is an enemy of the asuras. Sweet Suchimukhi, be my messenger and ask him to come to me and claim my hand.'

The bird was delighted that her task had become so easy. 'I will carry your love to the prince,' she said, 'and tell him of your beauty and charm. But before that, I must speak to your father.'

The swan told the king about Bhadra, the actor with magical powers, and the king at once expressed his eagerness to watch a performance.

Suchimukhi then informed Krishna and Indra that everything was in place. 'Pradyumna and his men will enter Vajrapur in the guise of Bhadra and his troupe,' she said. 'Prabhavati is already in love with Pradyumna, and the prince will destroy the asura when he comes between him and the princess.'

The swan spoke winningly of the princess to Pradyumna, arousing passion in his heart. When he expressed his desire to win the hand of the princess, Indra came to him, asking him to stop the asura who threatened the universe.

'I am fortunate to serve the gods and happy that this task will take me away from the war,' said Pradyumna. He attired himself in the colourful robes of an actor and prepared for his journey to Vajrapur. With him would travel a band of Yadus, also dressed as stage performers.

Pradyumna was relieved to be away for a time from his brother whose enmity he could no longer ignore. But he soon discovered that this was not to be. Samba was livid when he found out that his brother had been chosen to head an expedition to kill the asura and win his daughter's hand.

'The more my brother is praised, the more I hate him. I can forgive my people for their folly in choosing him over me, but my own father?' he ranted.

Krishna began, 'Pradyumna wished to go far away so he would not have to take part in the war—'

'Did you forget that I am not fighting either?' Samba interrupted rudely. 'I too wish to visit this fabulous kingdom and marry the princess who is said to be the loveliest on earth.' He paced back and forth, his mind seething. Then he said, 'I will go too. No one can stop me. And I will win the hand of the princess.'

But in his heart lurked a darker plan. *I will be away from Dwaraka and all the courtiers who fawn over Pradyumna,* he thought. *I will never get a better opportunity than this to kill him. And I can blame it on the asura. Watch your back, brother. You are likely to be stabbed before long.*

38

Prince in Hiding

Pradyumna and his men entered Vajrapur to a riotous welcome. The people of the city, who spent their days in luxury and peace, were always eager for new forms of entertainment. They followed the performers to the palace, playing lively music on their trumpets and drums. Vajranabha garlanded them and asked his men to take them to the stage they would be using.

Soon the city echoed with the troupe's repertoire of rousing dialogue and lively music as they performed dramatic scenes from the Ramayana. Pradyumna was Rama, while Samba played Ravana. This was not the role Samba would have chosen, but he could not match his brother's talent in devising elaborate spectacles or in playing the hero on stage. Pleased with the performance, the king presented them with a bag of gold coins and garlanded Pradyumna with a necklace that he was wearing around his own neck. Seeing this, Samba's resentment deepened, and he began plotting his brother's downfall with the vilest of the asuras.

The next day, Pradyumna and his men staged a play depicting the descent of River Ganga to earth, interspersed with dances by actors who took on the roles of apsaras.

The more Prabhavati saw of Pradyumna, the deeper she fell in love. His poise, his smile, his magnificence—all surpassed her wildest dreams. He too found himself looking for her charming face in the audience, sneaking glances at her when he should have been concentrating on his performance.

Alas, they were unable to speak to each other for she was surrounded by guards at all times. They sent passionate messages to each other through Suchimukhi, who finally brought the princess some welcome news.

'The prince will meet you tonight in your antapura,' said the swan.

On hearing this, Prabhavati showered the bird with kisses. Soon, however, she fell silent.

'What if he doesn't like me?' she asked eventually, her face growing pale with anxiety. 'What if my guards capture him and take him to my father?'

The next moment she flushed pink with desire and clasped the bird round its neck. 'I cannot wait any longer to hear his sweet words,' she whispered. 'Why does time move so slowly today?'

Finally, Suchimukhi came to tell her that the prince had evaded the guards and entered her palace. 'He can take any form he wishes to, princess. He hides now in the form of a bee in the rose garland you just wore around your neck.'

The princess trembled as she took off her garland with gentle hands. A bee flew out from the flowers and transformed itself into a magnificent man. Her eyes met his and then dropped again. He took her hand in his and looked at her with his heart in his eyes. Her body thrilled with love.

'Do not be shy,' he said, 'for you have nothing to fear from me. I am a slave to your charms and desire nothing more than to be united with you.'

She could say nothing. She glanced at him and blushed. He drank in her beauty, curbing the intense longing to clasp her in his arms. He would do nothing without her consent. She had to be wooed with soft words and tender promises.

The moon was full, the breeze was scented, and Kama was struck by his own arrow.

'I have travelled from a distant land to make you my own,' he whispered. 'I will stay here for as long as it takes to win your heart. I know that the asura clan is our enemy and we will face fierce opposition. But nothing matters if you love me too for where there is love, there is no room for fear.'

Slowly she looked up at him with adoring eyes. He spoke gently to her, coaxing her to trust him. And when dawn lightened the sky, she told him that she would have no one else as her husband.

'I am overwhelmed,' he said, clasping her in his arms. 'Let us be married first by the rites of gandharva vivaaha.' They touched the glowing jewel on his ring as a symbol of the holy fire, and he spoke the sacred words that sanctified their union.

'I must leave now before your guards discover my presence,' he said. 'I can hardly bear to be parted from you, but I will be back as soon as the evening's performance is done.'

He gave her one long kiss and left the way he came, in the form of a buzzing bee.

The day limped by, until it was finally night again. Pradyumna strode into her chambers and seized her in his arms. She welcomed him with a gasp and a moan. He enveloped them in a magical haze so that the guards would not discover the stranger in their midst. The night flew by in kisses and caresses, as if it were merely an hour long. They parted in the morning and waited restlessly for nightfall again.

The world seemed to be created anew each time they met, and they were its first lovers.

The bridal pair spent as much time as they could in each other's company. The fierce warrior became once again the exuberant Vama reliving his youth. He played his flute and composed verses to the arch of her eyebrow, the flare of her hips, the cruelty of her eyes and the sheen of her skin. She painted portraits of his handsome face and form, and titillated him with sensuous songs. He braided her hair with fragrant jasmine buds and drew sunbursts on her skin with mehndi. She teased him with riddles. He gifted her the rare gems he wore.

Meanwhile, the actors and their plays had grown in popularity. Gunavati and Chandravati, the daughters of Vajranabha's brother, fell in love with Pradyumna's brothers Samba and Gada, who were so much more handsome than the asuras. They too got married in secret.

The swan conveyed the news of the marriages to Indra, who was waiting for Kashyapa's yagna to be completed.

When the yagna ended, Vajranabha hurried to seek his father's help in overthrowing Indra. But the sage was not pleased with his request. 'Be happy with your own kingdom, my son,' he said. 'Indra is pious and better suited to be the king of the devas. Fighting with him and the other gods will only bring you defeat.'

The asura turned away in anger. Why should he be afraid when Brahma's boon granted him protection? He would defeat Indra and show his father that he was not inferior to the gods. He decided to bring his legions together for the battle, unaware that danger lurked within his kingdom.

Meanwhile, Prabhavati and her cousins conceived and gave birth to rosy-cheeked sons in short order, as was natural among the asura kind. The secret could no longer be kept hidden.

The guards went to Vajranabha, quaking in fear, to tell him that the sanctity of the antapura and the royal maidens had been compromised. They had seen the newborn infants and knew from the nobility of their features that the fathers were not asuras. They must be members of the troupe of actors.

Vajranabha was livid when he found out that he had been fooled. 'Surround my daughter's palace and arrest the intruders,' he ordered his men.

Prabhavati and her cousins were terrified at the turn of events and feared for their husbands' lives. 'How will you escape the mighty army of asuras that is already assembled for battle?' asked Prabhavati. 'My father is vicious and will not spare your lives or even those of our children.'

Pradyumna looked deep into her tearful eyes. 'Have faith in me,' he said. 'I was ready to bow to your father if he would accept our love. Now that he has declared war, I must fight to protect you and our loved ones. Do not doubt that we will win, even though the odds are against us.'

Prabhavati was shattered, for at the end of the conflict, either her husband or her father would be dead.

Pradyumna looked at her anxious face and offered another solution. 'If you are afraid, I can use my mahamaya to transport you, your cousins and our children to a safe place, until the war is decided,' he said, giving her an option to escape.

She thought deeply for a moment and then looked up at him with a steady gaze. 'You offer us an escape route, though you will not take it yourself, my lord,' she said. 'I know that as a warrior, you will not shy away from battle. You would rather choose to live just one day in valour than a hundred years in fear, for then your fame lives on for all time. But remember that I too made my choice when I agreed to wed you by gandharva rites. Permit me to stand by you now as a warrior's wife, whatever the consequences may be.'

Pradyumna drew her into his arms and held her close, elated that she had proved herself his true mate. He was fortunate to have had this life with her and their son, though it might well prove to be short-lived. He turned his eyes to his son, who was crawling around their legs. He had been able to spend more time with Ajaya than he had with Aniruddha, for his time in Dwaraka had been taken up in learning statecraft and keeping their enemies at bay. He was astonished by the way Ajaya had grown in quick spurts, in the way of asura children. The boy had begun to crawl very soon after he was born. Maybe he would begin to walk the next day, when his father lay with glazed eyes on the battlefield.

Pradyumna lifted up his son, who was now sitting and playing with his toys, and held him close, kissing his cheek, absorbing his sweet smell and feeling his warm breath on his face. He closed his eyes for a moment and sent a prayer to his father to keep the little one safe. Then he kissed Ajaya on his forehead and set him down on the ground so he could leave for battle. But his son clutched at his hands, pulled himself erect and took a wobbly step forward even as his parents watched in surprise.

'Thank you, my son, for letting me see you standing on your own feet,' said Pradyumna, his eyes welling with tears. 'I have a gift for you on this great day.' He gestured to the lady-in-waiting, who quickly brought him a small dagger, its hilt embedded with rubies.

'My Ajaya, my invincible one,' said Pradyumna, placing the dagger in his son's hands. 'I entrust the care of your mother to you while I am away,' he said.

Ajaya stared solemnly back at him. He had yet to say his first word, but his intelligence shone through his eyes.

Prabhavati reached out to support her son's arms so he would not drop the dagger. She then took it from him, placed it in its scabbard and hung it over her son's shoulders. Ajaya staggered for a moment and then planted his legs sturdily to balance himself.

Pradyumna looked fondly at the child once more and turned away, feeling as if his heart would break. Prabhavati gazed into his eyes as she murmured a prayer and applied a red tilak on his forehead. Then she brought him his jewelled sword and handed it over in ceremonious fashion.

'Glory to Pradyumna, who brought the parijata to earth. Mighty slayer of Kaalasura, powerful son of Krishna—may Shiva go with you,' she said.

'Take on the asuras on land,' Pradyumna said to the Yadus as they prepared for battle. 'I will attack them from the skies.'

Suchimukhi hastened to convey news of the impending battle to Indra and Krishna. 'I will send my son Jayanta to their aid,' said Indra. 'I will also send them my chariot and my battle elephant, the five-headed Airavataa. But I fear that my brother, armed with Brahma's boon, will be too powerful for your son.'

'My dharma lies in Kurukshetra,' said Krishna. 'It is where I will fulfil the purpose for which I was born as a mortal. Pradyumna must face the trial in Vajrapur armed with his own strengths, for this battle will determine his role in the future of the world.'

The small band of Yadus joined Pradyumna when he marched from the palace to face Vajranabha, who immediately let loose his occult skills to confound them. An evil cloud of smoke blinded them and made them fight one another. The asuras advanced, shrieking at them. Pradyumna fought back with the Mohiniastra to shatter the effects of sorcery. Then he multiplied his own form into thousands and attacked the asura warriors with a volley of arrows.

Jayanta joined him in the skies and rained death on the enemy, shattering limbs, cutting off heads and causing a flood of gore. Airavataa tore into the bodies of the foes with his immense tusks and roared as he smashed them to a pulp with his giant limbs. Those who survived began to flee from the battlefield, convinced that this was their last day on earth. However, greater numbers poured in to take their place, inundating the small force that Pradyumna commanded.

'My Yadu army is too far away to help. Have I come so far only to die in an alien land?' Pradyumna despaired. He lifted his thoughts to his brother in Vaikunta and sent out a plea for his intervention.

Suddenly, a violent gale lifted the asuras off the earth as a huge form took over the skies, blocking the sun. 'We are doomed,' cried the demons as the bird tore them apart with its huge beak and fierce talons. The divine Garuda had come to assist Pradyumna and to serve as his mount. Pradyumna bowed his head in reverence and soared on to the giant bird's back to engage Vajranabha in a battle to the death. They fought with swords and maces, bludgeons and thunderbolts, clashing like beasts of prey, neither succeeding in slaying the other. Pradyumna took advantage of a moment's distraction and dealt a massive blow to the asura's chest with his cudgel, making him collapse, vomiting a torrent of blood.

The asura's chariot carried him away to safety, but he soon returned to fight Pradyumna.

'Prepare to die, mortal,' shouted Vajranabha, uprooting a mountain and hurling it at his foe. It struck Pradyumna like

a thunderbolt and he fell unconscious. Garuda quickly carried
him to safety and revived him.

'The asura's spirit is unquenchable and his prowess greater
than any enemy I have encountered,' said Pradyumna. 'Despite
your help and Indra's, I fear that this is a war that I cannot win.'

He looked around at the few men who still stood by his
side, wearied and bloodied. He wondered if he would ever
see his wives in Dwaraka, his son or his father again. His eyes
closed in anguish.

39

The Lake of Snakes

The tall figure strode confidently into Prabhavati's palace, his face and body as handsome as that of the Yadus. Behind him came his bodyguard, taller and fiercer than his master, armed with a sword.

'Where are you, my sister?' called out the visitor, casting his eyes around.

Prabhavati entered the chamber, looking at the stranger with fearful eyes. Who was this who called her sister, and how had he managed to cross the circle of protection around her and her son?

'Have you forgotten your brother Mahendra who loves you more than life itself?' he asked, smiling gently at her. She stared open-mouthed, unable to believe that this soft-spoken, smooth-faced man could be the fearsome Mahendradamana.

'What . . . how . . . ?' she stuttered, her hands fluttering helplessly.

'Thankfully, I have a friend in your new family who helped me enter your palace, and I took on this form to fool your human guards. Moreover, I thought my disguise would please you too, for I am told that you now favour humans and have married one of them.' Prabhavati gasped, but he continued smoothly. 'You did not invite me to your wedding, sister, but I am here nevertheless to give you my blessings.'

Prabhavati trembled, wondering if Mahendra was playing one of his cruel games. He had told her often that she could only marry someone who could defeat him in battle. He was probably toying with her before he went out to fight alongside their father and kill Pradyumna.

Mahendra moved forward and placed a gentle arm on hers. 'Trust me, sister. I come here to offer my support to you and your husband. My father's time is past, and I will make him accept your marriage, by force if necessary.'

She stood paralysed, unable to believe that her asura brother could be so completely transformed.

Mahendra bowed his head and looked contrite. 'I have given you much cause to distrust me, sister, but I want to assure you now that I have grown tired of my old ways. I come to greet you and bless your son, a symbol of the new life that I hope to share with you. But I will return the way I came if you do not desire to make peace with me.'

He cast an imploring look at her and turned to go.

Prabhavati was in a quandary. She wanted to believe Mahendra; he was her brother after all and must have some fond feelings for her. Maybe he was honestly trying to make amends for his past behaviour. What if she spurned him now and lost him forever?

She put out her hand to stop him, and eager words tumbled from her lips. 'Wait, brother. I am sorry to have been so unwelcoming. It is true that I kept my marriage to Pradyumna a secret, as I feared you would be displeased. But I am now eager to accept your hand of friendship.

I assure you that my husband is valorous and deserving of the highest respect. I regret that our father has decided to fight against him, not realizing that he will lose his life if he fights Krishna's son.'

Mahendra stood listening in silence, waiting to hear her final decision.

'I request you to wait while I bring your nephew to you for your blessing,' said Prabhavati, turning to go inside her antapura. She returned in a few moments, leading her toddler son by the hand, while her cousins followed behind. The child looked up at his uncle with a curious eye.

'Bow to your uncle, Ajaya, and seek his blessing,' said Prabhavati. Her son toddled forward.

'Do not lose hope, Pradyumna,' Garuda said to the dejected warrior. 'Remember that it is not easy to defeat an asura who is protected by Brahma's boon. Take advantage of the asura's weakness that springs from his arrogance. Vajranabha sought Brahma's protection only from the gods, but not from mortals whom he regarded as too weak to pose any threat. So gird yourself once more for battle and show him what a man can do. Imbue yourself with the powers of Vishnu in his Narasimha avatar, wherein he donned the body of a man and the face and claws of a lion.'

Pradyumna concentrated his body and mind as he began to chant the Sri Narasimha mahamantra:

Ugram viram Maha Vishnum jvalantam sarvato mukham
Nrisimham bhishanam bhadram mrityur mrityum namamyaham

O angry and valiant form of Mahavishnu! Your fire permeates the world. O Narasimha, you are everywhere. You embody the death of death and I surrender myself to you.

The fierce dharmic fire of Narasimha suffused his body and mind. Pradyumna charged on to the battlefield like the god who carries weapons in his sixteen arms. His ferocious dance swallowed the demons and Vajranabha before the asura could even comprehend the enormity of the threat. The asura's body was pierced by a thousand arrows and his head hewn off by the warrior's sword. 'The enemy of the devas is dead,' exulted Indra. Rose petals rained from the sky on the victorious Yadus, and apsaras danced amidst the clouds. A thousand rishis and vidyadharas cried, 'Jaya to Pradyumna!'

Indra descended on the battlefield to shower Pradyumna with priceless gifts: the calf of his elephant Airavataa, the foal of his horse Ucchaishrava and a chariot made by Brahma, to help Pradyumna travel between Dwaraka and Vajrapur whenever he wished.

The warrior returned to his city on Garuda, and was greeted with drums of joy. Jayanta followed him on Airavataa. Gada accompanied them on Indra's chariot drawn by seven magnificent steeds.

Pradyumna bowed in respect to the divine visitors as they returned to the heavens. He could not wait to clasp his wife and son again in his arms.

One of Prabhavati's maids came hurrying with the good news. She bowed to Prabhavati and the visitors. 'The mighty Pradyumna has killed Vajranabha and decimated his troops. The warrior comes now in triumph to share his joy with you and his son,' she announced.

Warring emotions chased across Prabhavati's face as she tried to grasp what this victory meant for her and Ajaya. Regret, that her hitherto invincible father had gone to his death, that too at the hands of the man she had chosen as her groom, was quickly followed by relief that Pradyumna had not only survived the battle, but also emerged victorious against overwhelming odds. And finally came the realization that she no longer need live in fear, but could walk openly on the broad avenues of Vajrapur with her husband and son.

Then she remembered her brother standing before her and turned in fear to see how he had taken the news of their father's death.

Mahendra was smiling at the little boy and placing a hand in blessing on his head. 'I can hardly wait to meet your brave husband, my sister,' he said. 'Come with me, and we will all go to greet him on his victory.'

He lifted Ajaya in his arms and Prabhavati followed, unable to believe that her troubles were now over. Mahendra placed his nephew in his chariot and helped his sister get in.

'To the Lake of Snakes!' he ordered his charioteer, who instantly whipped the horses into flight.

'You promised to take us to Pradyumna, you monster!' screamed Prabhavati, trying to reach for the reins to stop the chariot. Mahendra, now restored to his usual asura form, dealt her a heavy blow and pushed her to the floor of the chariot where she lay moaning.

'Get down, you devil,' he told Ajaya, who had climbed up on the seat, his hand flying to the dagger at his waist. He held them down with one huge arm as the chariot hurtled forward.

'How easy it was to fool you, sister,' he gloated. 'Did you think I would so easily forgive you for defying us and marrying a cowherd's son? Alas, I did not expect him to vanquish our father, the invincible Vajranabha. But I will make the fool pay for his crimes. He will watch and wail as I torture and kill you and his son before his eyes, and then I will send him too to naraka.'

Prabhavati cried helplessly as the chariot flew onwards to Mahendra's kingdom. Why had she trusted her brother when he had never shown any signs of goodness? How could she have endangered her son's life? She had failed in the one responsibility that Pradyumna had entrusted to her before leaving for the battle.

Prabhavati's cousins heard her screaming and ran into the courtyard to save her. But the asura's chariot was already some distance away. The few guards that were still there ran around in confusion, lacking a leader to tell them what to do. The women began shouting for help, alarming Pradyumna, who could hear their cries as he approached in his chariot from the opposite direction. He spurred his horses on, realizing that some tragedy had befallen them.

'Prabhavati and Ajaya are in danger!' shouted Chandravati, as he approached. 'Our brother Mahendra has seized them. The guards tell us that Samba brought Mahendra into the palace.'

Pradyumna looked in the direction that she was pointing to, and saw the chariot disappearing in the distance. His face paled. He shouted to his charioteer to follow the kidnapper.

'Who is this demon of whom I have never heard?' shouted Pradyumna to the charioteer Ansuman, over the sound of the galloping horses.

'No one wishes to speak or even think of Mahendradamana,' said Ansuman, 'for he is more vicious than his father. Many tribes, including my own, fled from the regions he now controls, unable to bear his torture. My ancestors used to lead a peaceful life, grazing our cattle, until Mahendra incited his brother Viradha to stop the flow of the River Vagmati to the ocean. Viradha took the form of a giant turtle and blocked the waters. Our land was flooded and we lost our homes and grazing lands. The monsters killed our children for their sport, forcing us to flee.'

'Prabhavati risked the wrath of so many of her kin when she married me,' murmured Pradyumna. 'I must save her and my son, whatever the cost to myself.'

'Mahendra and Viradha are not your only enemies here,' said Ansuman. 'We are fast approaching Lake Naghrada, home to fearsome snakes that swallow our cattle whole when they venture near the lake to drink water. The snake king Karkotaka allies his dark powers with those of the asuras and wields control over the very elements, ravaging these lands with drought and plague.'

Pradyumna cast his eyes on the parched land, the huge cracks running across a clear sign that it had been many years since the last rains. Then he narrowed his eyes again to judge the distance between their chariot and the one hurtling ahead. Ansuman had considerably shortened the gap with the help of his horses that galloped like the wind.

'This is no ordinary snake, my lord. Our elders tell us that Karkotaka lives under the waters of the lake where he hoards his great wealth. His palace is decorated with gold and diamonds, sapphires and rubies. He sits on a giant throne, under three umbrellas of white diamonds. And lovely naginis sing and . . .'

'Stop prating and spur the horses on,' shouted Pradyumna, his heart pounding with fear for his wife and child when he saw the asura's chariot stop by the shores of a huge lake, perhaps the one that Ansuman spoke of.

A giant lotus glittered in the middle of the waters, with its thousand golden petals, diamond pistils, ruby anthers and stalk of lapis lazuli.

'The lotus that fell from Vishnu's hand,' said Ansuman, as he brought the chariot up behind Mahendra's. Pradyumna jumped out even before the horses had come to a complete halt.

Where were Prabhavati and Ajaya?

'Do not come nearer,' shouted Mahendra as he emerged from his chariot, hauling out his prisoners. The asura was mountainous, with a hideous face and tawny eyes.

'Let your sister and her son go,' said Pradyumna, hoping to remove his wife and son to safety before he engaged with the asura. 'You know they are innocent of any wrongdoing.'

'She is the cause of my father's death and must pay the price!' Mahendra bellowed. 'And you will watch as I kill her and her evil spawn.'

'If you will not heed my request, then I must command you as the new king of this land,' said Pradyumna. 'Free them at once or face the consequences.'

Mahendra let out a roar of laughter that echoed from the surrounding hills. There was an ominous silence when the sound faded. The birds had stopped wheeling in the sky, and even the cattle stopped their lowing. Ansuman tore away to hide behind the trees. 'The new king!' jeered the asura. 'You will not live much longer to boast of your conquests. I will make an example of you so that no one will ever defy me again.'

'You do not know to whom you are speaking, Mahendra,' said his foe. 'I am Pradyumna, the son of Krishna, the god of gods. The slayer of Kaalasura, Nikumbha, Banasura and Vajranabha.'

'You are nothing more than a braggart,' scoffed Mahendra. 'Watch now and see how real warriors act.'

Mahendra raised Ajaya high in the air and flung him into the lake of snakes. A huge black snake reared its ghastly head over the waters and began following Ajaya as he tried to swim to the shores.

'My son!' screamed Pradyumna, raising his arm to invoke an astra to kill the snake, but no astra appeared in answer to his call.

Pradyumna's face turned ashen and he called to his winged friend. 'Mighty Garuda, come to my aid!'

No golden wings broke the air to herald the arrival of the enemy of serpents.

'Your powers are useless in my kingdom,' laughed Mahendra. 'Watch and wail, son of Krishna, as the snake swallows your son.' He laughed as Prabhavati began to run towards the lake, screaming her son's name. 'Bring me my axe,' he shouted to his charioteer, as he took a swift step forward to seize her and pinion her with one iron arm.

Pradyumna saw his wife being crushed in the asura's hold and took a hasty step towards her, only to whirl around as he heard a terrible hiss behind him. He watched in horror as the enormous snake closed in on his son, opening its giant jaws to engulf Ajaya.

He had to choose between wife and son, for he could not save both. There was no time to lose.

Pradyumna ran to the edge of the lake and hurled himself into the waters, hoping that he would be close enough to his son to rescue him. The dank waters swallowed him and he flailed his arms to rise to the surface, emerging just as the snake closed its jaws around Ajaya.

'No!' screamed Pradyumna, slashing furiously with his sword at the snake's mouth.

The snake's mouth fell open and Pradyumna quickly stuck his sword between its jaws to immobilize them. He saw his son swirling deeper into the snake's insides and shouted to him to hold on to the jaws. The snake lashed its tail and set up giant waves as it tried to free its mouth and attack the enemy. Its furious threshing and hissing sent out a cloud of poison that slammed Pradyumna in the face, and made Ajaya gasp and slip further inside. Pradyumna reached for his son, but Ajaya had slipped too deep for him to reach him.

'Use your dagger, your dagger!' he shouted to his son, seeing the child's pale face looking up at him in desperation. Ajaya's small hand closed around the jewelled hilt and he pulled it from his belt.

'Thrust it into the snake's throat and use it to pull yourself up,' roared Pradyumna, holding on to the snake's jaw desperately despite the noxious fumes that assailed him. Ajaya thrust the dagger into the snake's throat, but it bounced back, as the flesh was too thick to be pierced by his feeble blow.

'Harder, harder, you can do it!' screamed Pradyumna, terrified that his son's breath would fail before he could break free. Once he fell inside the monster, there would be no escape. He would be digested slowly by the venom, his organs consumed bit by bit in a horrible death.

Ajaya struck once more at the snake's throat, this time managing to hack into its gelatinous throat. The action let loose a slimy, horrific sludge that engulfed him in a searing flood. His eyes burned unbearably, and he screamed in agony, almost losing his hold.

'Don't let go, son! Now climb up towards my voice.'

Ajaya heard his father's voice and pulled himself upwards, his eyes closed against the poison. Pradyumna willed him on with the force of his own mind, peering into the creature's maw, fearing that the sickly green substance that was gradually bubbling upwards would submerge his son. Ajaya screamed as a huge worm wriggled through the sludge and wound itself round his body. The putrid smell overwhelmed his senses. He forced open his eyes for a last look at his father. His heart surged with a new hope as he saw his father hanging on to the snake's jaws, reaching out a frantic arm to him. He was close, so close. Ajaya leaped upwards with his last breath and grasped the arm. Pradyumna heaved with all his strength, fighting the clammy hold of the snake on its prey. Ajaya broke free with a scream, and his father raised him above his head and hurled him with a mighty effort to land among the bushes on the shore.

Run, Ajaya. Flee to safety in Ansuman's chariot, he shouted silently, as he felt himself falling . . . falling to his doom. The fierce wrench that had freed Ajaya had also dislodged the sword that had forced the snake's jaws apart. Pradyumna had now fallen into its mouth, and was sliding deeper into its noxious insides that were ridged and pitted like giant craters. He grabbed at the slippery sides, but the reptile undulated its body to send him tumbling further through its coils. He tried to draw out the dagger that hung at his waist, determined to fight his way out, but his body no longer obeyed.

The venom that seared through his tissues and muscles had paralysed his limbs. The fumes attacked his skin, and flooded his mouth and nose. He gasped, unable to breathe, as the poison overwhelmed him. His eyes were inflamed and his vision grew murky. The eerie green sludge submerged him, and gobs of half-digested flesh clung to him like a shroud of death. He fought to retain his senses.

I must escape. Prabhavati . . . Ajaya . . . I must save them.

His breath was fading. His eyes closed and he saw again the images of his past life. His last glimpse of Ajaya's face . . . his fight with Vajranabha . . . Prabhavati struggling in Mahendra's hold . . . his gandharva vivaaha with her . . . his departure from Dwaraka . . . his parents . . . Aniruddha's marriage to Usha . . . Krishna confronting Shiva . . . Karthikeya hurling his lance . . . Shalva hewing off Vasudeva's head . . . Nikumbha attacking them with phantom lions . . . Indra fighting him for the parijata . . . Krishna saving him from the vajra . . . fighting the Kurus to rescue Samba . . . Ghatotkacha and Abhimanyu telling him of their pranks . . . Aniruddha fighting by his side . . . Rukmavati's swayamvara . . . Mayavati swearing eternal love . . . the battle with Kaalasura . . . Bhargava telling him he must fight . . .

And then . . . he went further back in time to another life, when he was burning in the fire of Shiva's eye, his soul was leaving his body. The end of all hope. His every breath was a gasp of agony.

Then he heard her voice . . . his divine consort, Rati. Trying to hold on to him with her fierce love. Pleading with him again, as before. 'Do not die. Do not leave me. How can I live without you?' Her voice praying to the Trimurti. 'O Brahma, father of the universe, protect your son. O Vishnu, you who lie on the divine serpent, save him. Shiva, O three-eyed Supreme, do not allow him to die.'

He focused his dying breath on her voice, knowing that she was his last hope. Rati was now Mayavati and she was within him . . . exhorting him to fight . . . to return to life . . . to save his loved ones.

Pradyumna prayed with her. He felt a surge of energy and shot out his hand in one final move. His fingers closed around his dagger. He grasped it and thrust mightily into the snake's thick tissues. He hacked and slashed and sawed at the leathery flesh, shredding it to ribbons. The snake doubled up in agony, and tightened its coils in a frantic attempt to kill the enemy.

Pradyumna's body was smothered in the putrid remains of the snake's innards. He fought to keep his eyes open and strike one more blow, and then another. His dagger tore through the final layer of the snake's hide and he pushed through with one frantic shove, using his whole body as a weapon. He emerged from within the snake, covered in gore and noxious flesh, and fell into the water. The snake's body crumpled and sank to the bottom of the lake. Pradyumna submerged himself to clear the gore and then began swimming desperately for the nearest shore, forcing his exhausted limbs to move by sheer will alone.

Shivering, he pulled himself on to the rocks that fringed the lake, and raised his head to look around. An eerie darkness shrouded the landscape. There was not a soul in sight. The asura had most certainly killed Prabhavati and Ajaya.

Pradyumna collapsed on the ground, broken in spirit and body.

40

The Snare

'Your son is dead, Prabhavati, swallowed by the snake. And your husband has jumped to his death,' Mahendra taunted his sister, dragging her to a rock and readying her for the final blow.

She sobbed piteously, for she was well aware of the powers of Karkotaka and the dangers of the poisonous lake. She had seen Ajaya and Pradyumna disappear in the murky waters. How could she live after they were gone? If her brother did not kill her, she would have to look for another way to embrace death.

'You weep now, but did not stop to consider the consequences of your lust,' Mahendra continued. 'Now you must pay for your crimes. I had intended to torture you until you begged for a merciful death. Alas, my father's throne calls out to me, and I must hasten to proclaim myself king. But before I go my way, sister, I must kill you.'

Prabhavati closed her eyes and prayed to be united with her husband and son in another world.

Mahendra raised his axe and swung it in a downward arc to deliver the killing blow. But his arm was stopped mid-stroke by a powerful hand that clasped it in a fierce grip. His eyes opened wide in shock and he tried to free himself from the crippling hold, but with little effect. The unseen attacker began to force the asura's arm relentlessly backwards, though Mahendra struggled. The axe moved closer and closer and finally dug into his chest, deeper and deeper, splitting it in two. The asura's eyes lifted to the attacker's face in wonderment as his dying body slipped to the ground.

He beheld a handsome, resolute face and a powerful body reminiscent of the gods. Mahendra's mouth fell open in surprise and then, slowly, his eyes glazed over in death.

Prabhavati waited in agony for the blow that never came. Instead, a gentle hand helped her from the ground. Her body shook as she turned to see what new torture her brother had devised for her. It was not her brother's face she saw, however, but that of someone she loved more than life itself. She wondered if she was in heaven for it was her son who held her upright, gently wiping away her tears. This Ajaya was a man, who had grown into the fullness of his powers. She saw in his demeanour the majesty of her beloved Pradyumna, grandsire Krishna and the divine Kama. Surely, this was heaven.

It was only when her gaze fell on the dead asura at their feet that Prabhavati understood that she was alive. Her son had attained his full glory, in time to save her from her brother's axe. She reached out to touch Ajaya's face, her eyes lighting up with love.

Suddenly she realized that Pradyumna was missing.

Where was he? Where was her lord? She looked around with tearful eyes, the question quivering in the air.

'Rest now, my mother,' said Ajaya, speaking for the first time in his life. 'I will find father.'

Pradyumna awoke from his tortured sleep to hear a soft voice pleading for his attention. He opened his eyes and saw an ethereal figure standing over him.

'I am River Vagmati, come to offer my respect to the dauntless Pradyumna!' said the goddess. 'I beg you, O lord, to kill Viradha who has taken the form of a giant turtle and blocks the flow of my water, preventing me from joining my sister Ganga.'

'I do not deserve to be called dauntless just because I emerged alive from the snake's jaws,' said Pradyumna, his head bowed in sorrow. 'Even my sword has left me and rests now at the bottom of the lake.'

'I will restore your sword to you, warrior,' said Vagmati. 'I request you to use its power to restore nature's balance.'

As Pradyumna huddled on the ground, weakened in body and mind, Vagmati conjured up his sword from the waters. It floated towards him, twirling in the air, its blade glinting in the light. He staggered to his feet and grasped it by the hilt. He bowed his head in gratitude to Vagmati and fought to emerge from his stupor. But his grief sapped his strength and weakened his spirit.

His wife and son would never have left him if they were still alive. They must have been slaughtered by the demon. He would first repay Vagmati's kindness by freeing her waters and then look for Mahendra so that he could avenge their deaths.

He summoned up his inner strength and pulled himself erect. Time enough to mourn once his task was done. As he looked towards the distant turtle hill, he saw two figures advancing towards him—a young man, supporting a woman on his arm. He narrowed his eyes and looked again. The woman . . . it was Prabhavati! He turned his gaze back to the face of the youngster, a wild hope springing in his breast.

It was Ajaya, his son. He raised his eyes to the heavens, in thanksgiving for his son's growth into a man at this propitious time. Then he raced forward on unsteady legs to clasp the two in his arms. Prabhavati was overwhelmed at the sudden turn in their fortunes, and tears flowed unchecked down her cheeks.

'You are alive, my lord,' she murmured. 'You are alive!'

'Yes,' said Pradyumna, whose eyes were brimming over as well. 'I thought that I had lost you both to Mahendra. Where is he? We must be prepared for his next assault.'

'Our son has dispatched him to naraka, my lord,' said Prabhavati. 'He saved me from my brother's axe and turned it on him.'

'So my son has killed the hateful demon,' said Pradyumna, looking at his son's magnificent form with pride. 'Now I must perform my final duty before leaving these shores. I must free Devi Vagmati from the clutches of Viradha.'

He prayed to Krishna and raised his sword to the sky. Now that Ajaya had killed Mahendra, Pradyumna's powers had been restored and the sword blazed with divine energy once again. He flew to the top of the hill that embodied Viradha's spirit and slashed a gorge through it.

The demon died with a terrible shriek, and Vagmati was finally free to flow to the ocean. She cascaded down the gorge, with many ripples and swirls, dancing her way to her sister Ganga from whom she had been separated for so long.

Pradyumna flew three times around the lake to pay his obeisance to the celestial flower that glinted in the middle of the waters. As he bowed in reverence, the lotus vanished and in its place rose a sacred hill, the swayambu or self-created, to be worshipped by all humankind as the embodiment of Vishnu, the Protector.

At once, the mighty king of snakes, Karkotaka appeared before Pradyumna. The snake had a human face and hands, and the body of a serpent. Above his face five snakeheads spewed flames from fanged mouths.

Pradyumna drew his sword to end the creature's life, but Karkotaka folded his hands and addressed him in a reverent voice.

'The lotus has changed into a swayambu as per the prophecy,' he said. 'The son of Krishna is here to free me from my evil karma. Forgive my sins and that of my guardian snake that attacked you and your son. I claim kinship with you, son of Krishna, as I am the brother of Adisesha, now born on earth as Balarama. I beg you to save my species from the consequences of your fury.'

Karkotaka pointed to the lake, which was rapidly emptying through the gorge, sending the snakes flying down the hillsides along with the water, to be smashed against the rocks.

'Permit the few snakes that still survive to live in a small portion of the waters. In return, I swear not to harm your people hereafter,' said Karkotaka.

'You brought them drought and plague, causing hunger and death. Why should I show you mercy?' asked Pradyumna.

'I will make ample recompense by showering rain on the parched earth, allowing the plants and trees to blossom and bear fruit. When your people and your herds feast on these crops, they will be cured of all their sickness.'

As he spoke, rain clouds showered their bounty on the land. Fruits, flowers and grains appeared instantly; drought and disease disappeared. The people came out in droves, wondering at the marvellous transformation.

Still, Pradyumna was undecided on forgiving Karkotaka. The snake began to plead in earnest. 'Even in darkness there is hope of light,' he said. 'The wise always give sinners a chance to redeem themselves. Nala freed himself from the Kali demon with my help and I now promise to aid you too should you have need for me.'

Pradyumna remembered that Krishna had always told him of the need to temper courage with wisdom. He had to follow his precepts.

'I will permit you to live with your subjects in the smaller lake that remains,' he said. 'It will henceforth be known as Lake Taudaha.'

The snake king bowed and returned to his underwater home. Pradyumna divided the rich lands left exposed by the draining of the water among the gopalas, the Vishnu worshippers who herded cows, and among the mahishapalas, the Shiva worshippers who herded buffaloes.

He asked the people of Vajrapur to build a temple to the gods of Vaikunta—Narayana and Adisesha, with sculptures of serpents hanging from the roof to offer worship. He declared that the kingdom be divided between his sons and those of Jayanta, Samba and Gada. 'Samba's sons should not pay for their father's betrayal,' he said. Jayanta would act as steward until the time that the grandsons of Krishna were able to take up their responsibilities.

Now Pradyumna could delay no longer. It was time he returned to face whatever horrors awaited him at the end of the war.

'I must return to Dwaraka and find out what transpired at Kurukshetra,' he said to his wife. 'The Pandavas would have won the war no doubt, with my father's support and the heroism of Abhimanyu and Ghatotkacha. But the Narayani Sena that fought against them would have suffered grievous losses, and I must offer my people comfort. Take care of our son. I will return to Vajrapur soon.'

Pradyumna made his way back to Dwaraka on the elephant given by Indra, along with Gada. The scenes that he saw as he neared their city were of bleak despair. His people told him that their entire sena had been annihilated, leaving behind desolate parents, wives and children.

Narada came to him when he entered the royal court in order to prepare him for what he was about to see. 'Duryodhana and his brothers, Drona, Karna, Bhishma and the other kings who fought with the Kurus have all been killed,' he said. 'The Pandavas have won the war, but paid a great price. Just a handful of those who fought survived.'

He laid a comforting hand on Pradyumna as he continued. 'Toughen your heart, prince, to hear what I must reveal. Among the dead was your friend and companion Abhimanyu—slain by a grisly display of adharma.'

'Abhimanyu dead?' Pradyumna was shocked. 'The hope of the Pandavas, the son of Arjuna, the nephew of Krishna—how can he die? Tell me you misspoke, Devarishi.' Then he saw Narada's look of compassion and wailed as if his heart would break.

'When I left for Vajrapur, he embraced me and said that I would return to hear rousing tales of his bravery. I had defeated some asuras no doubt, but he would be taking on the greatest maharathis on earth. He was so thirsty for life . . . Was it because he knew he was not long for this world? How can I live another day when I know I will never see his brilliant smile again?'

'He fought with the strength of a thousand soldiers,' Narada said softly. 'He died a great warrior, whose fame will live forever. His death on the thirteenth day of the war turned the tide and spurred the Pandavas to destroy the Kurus.'

'What is the merit of victory when it comes at such a cost?' asked Pradyumna, collapsing into a seat. 'How did my father and the Pandavas allow this to happen?'

'Let me narrate the events that unfolded that fateful day, when the Kurus fought under Drona's command,' said Narada. 'Abhimanyu was indomitable, destroying a whole akshauhini of the Kuru army, consisting of 21,870 chariots, 21,870 elephants,

65,610 horses and 1,09,350 infantry. He killed the sons of Duryodhana and Shalya, and Karna's younger brother. He forced Karna to flee the battlefield and struck Drona down, making him swoon.'

'A lion among men . . .' Pradyumna said in awe. 'Then how was he killed?'

'Drona recovered and warned his commanders that if they did not kill the young warrior, he would destroy their entire army. His men were afraid and said that no one could withstand Abhimanyu, not even the Trimurti. Drona then decided to use deceit to kill Arjuna's son and stave off death and dishonour.'

'And the hyenas set forth to trap the lion.'

'Drona deployed his men in the chakravyuha, the spinning wheel of death, with Duryodhana at the centre and ring upon ring of Kshatriyas surrounding him. None of the Pandavas could break into it nor could they kill the enemy soldiers who were constantly moving in a circle. The Kurus mowed down the Pandava army by the thousands until Yudhistira feared that they would lose the battle that day.'

'But Arjuna and Krishna know the secret of the maze.'

'Yes, they were the only ones other than you to have learned its intricacies. However, you were far away in Vajrapur and they had been lured away by the Samsaptakas, who had sworn to kill Arjuna or die fighting him, and had issued a challenge that he could not refuse.'

'Did Yudhistira decide to sacrifice the sixteen-year-old son of his brother? He knew that Abhimanyu could enter the formation, but could not make his way out. Bhima, Nakula, Sahadeva, Satyaki, Dhristadyumna—did they all stand by as my brave Abhimanyu went to his death?'

'Yudhistira had no choice. He told Abhimanyu, "We will follow close behind you with our fiercest warriors. All you need to do is to break into the heart of the vyuha."

Abhimanyu was delighted at the opportunity to display his courage. "I will make my father and Krishna proud," he said, and rode towards the monster wheel. His charioteer warned him of a trap, but he would not let fear dictate his actions. He forged on, tumbling into the snare that Drona had set up to kill him.'

'Do not tell me any more, I cannot bear it,' wept Pradyumna, but the story had to be told.

'The Pandavas followed at his heels, but were stopped by Jayadratha, the Sindhu king who had been waiting to take revenge against them for an earlier humiliation. He was armed with Shiva's boon that allowed him to hold off the four Pandavas in the absence of Arjuna and Krishna. As he kept them out, the vyuha sealed itself around Abhimanyu. The young warrior was caught alone in the midst of the dastardly Kurus.

'Abhimanyu realized that his uncles could not help him, yet he fought on, killing everyone who stood in his way. "You cannot kill him face-to-face," said Drona, inciting Karna to cut his bowstring from behind. Then Drona killed his horses, Kripacharya killed his charioteer, and Kritavarma smashed his chariot. "Is this your dharma? Are you cowards or maharathis?" Abhimanyu spat at them. He leaped down from his broken chariot and fought them off with his sword and shield. Drona smashed his sword and Karna broke his shield. Abhimanyu picked up his chariot wheel and stood unbowed, his body streaked in crimson. "Follow Kshatriya dharma and fight with me one-on-one," he challenged.

'He felled Ashwathama's horses with his mace and smashed the chariots of his foes. Then Duhshasana's son knocked him to the ground and crushed his head in before he could get up. The Kurus erupted in joy. Yudhistira heard them roar and knew that their prince had fallen. Drona's plan had succeeded.'

'How am I still alive after hearing this?' Pradyumna sobbed. 'I could have followed him into the vyuha and saved his life. But alas, I ran away.'

A few moments passed and then a new thought struck him. 'What happened to Ghatotkacha, the valiant son of Bhima? Did he not try to save his cousin?'

Narada replied, but did not answer his question. 'Bhima's son, being a rakshasa, was lord of the night,' he said. 'He scourged the enemy with sheets of fire, hurricanes, lightning and demonic maya. He killed the demons Jatasura and Alayudha, and forced Karna to retreat. He fought as if he were two armies in himself, one in the air and one on the ground. Duryodhana knew he had to stop Ghatotkacha or lose the war.' The rishi seemed unable to continue.

'And then?' Pradyumna whispered, fear choking his throat.

'Karna used the Shakti, the weapon Indra gave him, saying that he could use it only once.'

'So he used the weapon with which he had hoped to kill Arjuna on Ghatotkacha. Was this part of a divine plan to save Arjuna, whatever the cost? Did the Pandavas readily sacrifice the loving giant who had come to fight by their side out of his fondness for them?'

'Yudhistira was heartbroken,' said Narada. 'He reminded everyone of the many times his nephew had helped them, even carrying Draupadi through the jungle when she could walk no longer. When the Shakti scythed through his bones, Ghatotkacha still ensured that his body crashed like a mountain on to Duryodhana's soldiers, killing them by the thousands. The Pandava army went berserk with grief watching his final act of courage.'

'My heart is like a stone. I have no tears left to shed. My mind is animated by just one thought—to avenge the death of my friends.' Pradyumna struggled to gather his

thoughts. 'But no, that too is not possible, for you said that
Duryodhana and his brothers are all dead. I must speak to
my father at once and demand an answer for all that has
transpired. I thought he loved Abhimanyu and Ghatotkacha
as much as he loved me. Tomorrow, will he stand by and
watch me die too?'

There was compassion in Narada's eyes, for he knew what
the future had in store. He prepared Pradyumna for the task
by narrating the Bhagavad Gita, the song of god, bestowed on
Arjuna by Krishna.

41

A Vile Killing

'As the world trembles on the edge of Kali Yuga, the only certainty is faith in the lord,' said Narada to Pradyumna. 'Just by uttering the word "Gita" at the time of death, you can attain moksha. No sin can impinge on you if you recite it regularly. The lord himself resides wherever the Gita is read, heard, taught or studied.

'You will require many lifetimes to fathom the meaning of the lord's word. For the present, you must go to your father who has gone to Hastinapura to console Gandhari, the grieving Kuru queen. Submit yourself to his wisdom, for it is the only truth that can keep mankind alive.'

Pradyumna entered Vidura's mansion in Hastinapura, which was where his father always stayed when he visited the Kuru capital. When he finally stood in his father's presence, he saw on Krishna's face a depth of anguish that he had never seen before. He ran to fall at his feet. His father helped him up and clasped him in his arms.

Krishna was touched with pity for his son who was clearly wrestling with a loss that had rocked the foundations of his universe.

He let his son weep and waited for him to recover his composure. Finally Pradyumna spoke, a heavy sense of guilt burdening his mind.

'I knew the secret of the chakravyuha, not just to enter but to exit it as well,' he said. 'I could have stayed behind and fought alongside the Pandavas, thereby preventing Abhimanyu's death. Or I could have taught him the complete skill myself. But I chose to go away and enjoy myself in Prabhavati's arms, while the fledgling fought alone in a den of vipers. How can I ever forgive myself? Devarishi Narada said that Abhimanyu had been married only a month when he died, and that his wife Uttara is with child. How can I ever look upon her face? What can I say to console my aunt Subhadra? I blame myself as much as I blame the cowards who struck him down.' His torment poured out in a flood of words.

Krishna remained silent, letting him talk. 'Why did this have to happen, father?' he asked next. 'You must have known what would happen and could have stopped it. You could have insisted that I stay and fight along with the Pandavas. Or you could have stood by Abhimanyu's side. Now, I carry a weight of guilt that threatens to break me in two.'

'His death was not something you could have prevented, my son,' said Krishna. 'Everything happens as a result of actions performed over several life journeys taken by a soul. Even gods are subject to karma, which is why the virtuous Rama went into exile and spent years separated from his wife. The loftiest souls suffer due to their destiny, and sinful souls enjoy success, at least for a while. The upright Bhishma had to fight on the side of adharma. Karna had to fight for Duryodhana as the Kuru king was the only one who supported him when the world mocked Karna as a charioteer's son.'

Pradyumna quietened down and sat at the lord's feet. He had to pay attention to the words of the Purushottama, the highest of all beings, or he would be lost.

'I will tell you why Abhimanyu died so young. For that I must take you back many years to a time when the Dwapara Yuga was at its peak,' said Krishna. 'The forces of wickedness had multiplied, burdening the earth and tormenting men of virtue. The devas approached me in Vaikunta and entreated me to take birth on earth to uphold dharma. I asked them to be born on earth too and provide me their support in the battle against evil.

'I grew up in the arms of Yashoda, while the sons of Yama, Vayu and Indra were born as Yudhistira, Bhima and Arjuna. Nakula and Sahadeva were born from the Asvini twins, the physicians of the gods. Karna was Surya's son. Draupadi and her brother Dhristadyumna were Agni's children. Devaguru Brihaspati and one of the Rudras took human form as Drona and his son Ashwathama. Dhritarashtra was a gandharva king, while Shakuni and Duryodhana were forms of the Dwapara and Kali yugas, born to foment war.'

Pradyumna's eyes widened as he tried to fathom the grand plan of the gods. 'You have not mentioned Abhimanyu's name, father. Was he a deva too?'

'He is Varchas, the son of Chandra, the moon god. Chandra sought a boon that Varchas be born as Arjuna's son and become the saviour of the Pandavas. He wanted his son to return to him in sixteen years, after completing his task. I granted him these boons, which is the reason why Abhimanyu died so young. Abhimanyu's son, when he is born, will be the only Pandava offspring to survive the battle at Kurukshetra.'

'How can that be?' asked Pradyumna. 'Draupadi herself has five handsome young sons.'

'Alas! Drona's son Ashwathama killed them all when they were asleep in a tent, after the war ended.'

Pradyumna's heart sank and a red mist obscured his vision. He remembered the innocent faces of Draupadi's sons and shuddered as he imagined them covered in blood. He pictured Draupadi beating her breast and tearing out her hair in agony.

'May Drona's son roast in naraka for this abomination,' he roared. 'I will slash him open and garland myself with his organs if he has not been killed by the Pandavas. How could all this happen despite your presence?'

'The Pandavas and I were resting under some trees by the riverside. I had a premonition of evil, but dismissed it, as all the Pandavas were safe before my eyes. No one could have imagined that Ashwathama would stoop to such depravity.'

'They say Draupadi was born of fire . . . but how many trials can she bear?'

'She was maddened with grief and swore that she would die where her children lay, if the killer was not brought to justice. Bhima chased the evil son of Drona. I followed with Arjuna, as I knew Ashwathama had the Brahmashira and would not hesitate to use it. Bhima would not have been able to survive its fury. We caught up with them just in time to see Ashwathama invoking the weapon. Arjuna countered it with his own Brahmashira. The two weapons roared forward, threatening to consume the sea, burn up the mountains and incinerate the world.'

'And then?'

'Narada and Sage Vyasa, in whose ashram Ashwathama had taken refuge, employed the combined shakti of their tapasya and stopped the weapons before they could collide. "Withdraw the weapons before they devour the universe," said Vyasa.

Arjuna obeyed him at once, but Ashwathama had the blood of the innocent on his hands and could not recall his weapon. "Give the Pandavas the jewel you wear on your forehead as recompense for your sin and turn the astra away from the Pandavas," said Vyasa. Ashwathama's hatred was so powerful that he decided to wipe out the Pandava race. He directed the astra at the wombs of the Pandava wives and their sons' wives, rendering them barren. The astra flashed into Uttara's womb and killed Abhimanyu's son, the last of the clan.'

A cry of horror broke from Pradyumna's lips. 'Abhimanyu's son . . .? But what about your boon to Chandra? Has it been proved false?'

'No,' said his father. 'I brought Uttara's child back to life with my powers. Through him, the race will be kept alive.'

Pradyumna felt a desperate hope stir in his heart. 'If you brought Uttara's child back to life, why not Draupadi's sons too? Their deaths are more offensive to dharma than even Abhimanyu's, for he was a warrior and knew he could die on the battlefield. Is this not possible for you, Jagannatha, lord of the universe?'

'The answer again lies in their past karma,' said Krishna. 'Draupadi's sons, the Upapandavas, were born on earth because they had been cursed. Sage Vishvamitra wanted to test King Harischandra of Ayodhya, whose honesty was unparalleled in the world. He tricked him into losing everything—his kingdom, his wealth and even the clothes he wore. He made him sell his wife and son, claiming that he was owed some dues. The five guardian deities of Ayodhya condemned Vishvamitra, whereupon the sage cursed them to be born as mortals. When the deities begged for forgiveness, he told them they could return to devaloka after a short spell on earth. These deities were born as the sons of Draupadi and returned to heaven once their karma was complete.'

'So they have returned to heaven. But what about those left behind on earth? How can all this help them overcome the grief that tears them apart?'

'I understand your feelings. I know too that your grief is too raw to speak about someone very dear to you. You want to ask me if I sacrificed Ghatotkacha in order to save my beloved Arjuna.'

'Yes, I do,' nodded Pradyumna. 'Why did Ghatotkacha have to die, unless it was to deflect Indra's Shakti from Arjuna? How could you rejoice when victory came at such a price?'

'I would do anything to save Arjuna, for he is the Nara to my Narayana. Without him, honour would be defeated and the purpose of my incarnation would be lost. However, the gods did not use Ghatotkacha as a pawn in a cruel game, my son. He was your loving companion, but he lived a rakshasa life, killing sages, defiling yagnas and destroying dharma. He had to pay for his sins. But now he has returned to his lofty position as a yaksha, a guardian spirit of the treasures of the earth.'

Krishna continued. 'Those who perished in Kurukshetra have been freed from the cycle of life and death, regardless of their sins,' he said. 'Kuru, an ancestor of the Pandavas, performed a fierce tapasya there in order to establish the eight-fold virtues. He used his golden chariot to make a plough, and yoked Shiva's bull and Yama's buffalo to it. When Indra did not answer his prayers, he cut off his own limbs to use as seed, and prepared to sever his own head as a final offering. Indra then granted him a boon that those who died in that dharmakshetra would reach heaven, and that it would be called Kurukshetra, after Kuru.'

Krishna's words quietened Pradyumna's grief and opened his inner eye.

'Everyone and everything that is born must die once the karma for that life is completed,' said the lord. 'When the war was over, I asked Arjuna to step down from our chariot. I stepped down too, and Hanuman flew from my banner. At once, the horses and chariot erupted in flames, because the purpose for their creation had been fulfilled. They had continued to exist only because I needed them. This is true for you and for me as well. I too will depart once my task has been completed.'

Pradyumna was dismayed at the thought of losing the father he had found so late in his life. Krishna looked at him with firmness tinged with compassion. 'You still have a lot to learn, Pradyumna, and a long way to travel. Do not lose heart. Continue to perform your duty. Come with me now to support me in a difficult task that is more distressing than anything I have faced.'

42
Torment

When the Pandavas returned to Hastinapura after fourteen long years of exile, it was as victors. But the victory was bitter, for the city was desolate, with young and old mourning the death of their men. The wailing reached a crescendo when the people saw Yudhistira and his brothers, and hurled threats and curses at them. The brothers walked on, knowing there was worse to come when they met the blind king and his wife who had lost all hundred of their sons.

Krishna knew that the king's anger towards Bhima, who had killed his sons, would result in dire consequences. So when King Dhritarashtra held out his arms to embrace Bhima, Krishna placed within them a metal statue of the Pandava that Duryodhana had had forged in order to test his strength. The king embraced the statue with such force that it shattered. Dhritarashtra drew back, horrified that he had killed his nephew, only to be reassured by the Blue God.

His wife Gandhari's eyes fell on Yudhistira's toes and her fierce anger scorched them. But the old couple soon recovered from their rage and expressed remorse. They knew that the Pandavas had been forced to fight for the kingdom that Duryodhana had usurped.

The procession of mourners set off to perform the funeral rites at Kurukshetra, with the Pandavas accompanying Gandhari and the Kuru widows.

As they approached the battlefield, they saw unimaginable horrors stretching out before them. There were bodies without heads, heads without bodies, chests and heads smashed open and rivers of blood. Foxes, vultures and hyenas were feeding on the flesh, while rakshasas and pishachas hovered in the air. The terrible scene, permeated with the stench of death, stupefied the women who had come looking for their brothers, husbands and sons. They collapsed as if they too had joined the dead. Voices rose from souls in torment.

Gandhari, the cursed mother of a hundred sons, came to the barren ground where the rotting bodies of her sons and grandsons were strewn. They had been so brave and handsome, with broad chests and noble features. Now their limbs were scattered on the field for wolves to prey upon. Gandhari's favourite son Duryodhana lay on the ground, his thigh broken by Bhima's mace, his body destroyed and his eyes gazing blindly at a cruel fate. His golden armour and his lofty crown had been unable to save him.

Evening bled into night. The mourners retired to their tents to wait for the dawn when they could perform the last rites, feeding the bodies to the ravenous pyres. Then they would offer obsequies on the shores of the Ganga.

'Rest with us, dear mother,' said the women to Gandhari.

'Come with us, queen,' said her counsellors.

'Leave me alone with my sons and my pain,' she raged, and they retreated.

There she spent the night, turning her blindfolded eyes on
the vultures that stole near the bodies of her sons, waving her
stick to drive them away. 'Who will mourn you, Duryodhana?
Who will call you righteous, Vikarna?' she moaned. 'They
say Abhimanyu is brave and narrate his tale to their sons and
daughters. They call Draupadi's sons valiant for fighting like
lions before they were slaughtered at night by Ashwathama.
But who will mourn my sons or hold you up to adulation? You
shamed our ancestors by disrobing Draupadi in the open sabha.
You refused to give even five villages to your cousins, after they
spent fourteen years in exile. You were traitorous, you were
ignoble . . . but you are still my sons. How can I not mourn you?'

She sobbed as if her heart would break. And then her voice
rose again, breaking the silence of the dead. 'Who is to blame
for my sons' actions? Is it the king who could not rule because
he was blind? Is it my own conceit that I blindfolded myself
and refused to see the path my sons travelled? If we were at
fault, then so was their grandfather Vyasa. He did not realize
that the Pandavas were not his blood, that the true heirs to the
kingdom were my sons, sinners though they were . . .

'Isn't my pain as great as Draupadi's? Bhima's mace
shattered Duryodhana's thighs in a blow that broke every rule
of fair combat. The son of Pandu tore open Duhshasana's chest
and drank his blood.

'Is this your idea of dharma, Krishna? Is this what you
preached to your favourite Pandava?'

Krishna flinched, for he could hear every question, even
though he was still some distance from her. Pradyumna was
silent, his heart breaking as he pondered on the slaughter let
loose in the name of war. A travelling bard with his lute came
upon them and raised his voice in a lyric of despair.

'The noble Gandhari, the daughter of the king of Gandhar,
fainted in a daze near the bodies of her sons,' said the storyteller.

'And then she slept, a tortured sleep, until a terrible hunger rose from within her, a hunger the likes of which she had never known before. Her insides were aflame; all she could think of was food. She called out weakly, asking if there was anyone within earshot. A lone vulture hovering above her screeched in fear for it had thought that she too was dead.

'Then she smelled something divine that stoked the hunger within her. It was the sweet fragrance of a mango. She raised herself towards it, reaching out with desperate hands. She could not touch the fruit so she climbed upon a large stone. Then she placed another stone over the first one and then another, until she could pluck the fruit and bite into it. The fruit exploded in her mouth. The juice ran down her tear-stained cheeks. She devoured it until she had nothing left except its core.

'Her hunger left her and her conscience returned. "Why am I eating when my sons lie dead on the field?" she thought in disgust. "I am a rakshasi who still feels hunger at this cruel moment."

'She recoiled as she climbed down from the stones, holding them for support. But they were not stones. They were soft, pliant—like bodies. They were her sons' bodies. Alas! She had climbed on her dead sons to reach the fruit to feed her ravening hunger.'

The Blue God and his son stood listening to the ghastly tale that echoed across the lands and the seas. The bard continued on his journey and silence descended once more.

When they finally arrived at Kurukshetra, Krishna and Pradyumna came upon Gandhari who was weeping as if she would never stop. Krishna wept too as he shared her torment. Her blindfolded eyes sensed his presence. She lifted her ravaged face and spoke in a fierce voice.

'Is it you, Krishna, come to gloat over my pain?' she asked. 'You enfolded me in your maya and made me suffer a pain even greater than the loss of my sons. People call you divine and worship you as Vishnu. But this is who you really are—a fierce, cruel, heartless god. If you were merciful, why did you not prevent this terrible killing? Your mother Devaki lost seven children at birth so that you could be born. But to what purpose? So you can stand over me as I mourn the loss of a hundred sons?'

Her white hair was dishevelled and her body was bent and trembling. She lifted a hand and pointed at him. Her voice rose in a wail that rent the heavens. The devas trembled as they felt a harrowing threat looming.

43

Cursed

Krishna stood without speaking, knowing that nothing he could say would justify his actions to the grieving mother.

'Could you not save even one of my sons to perform the ceremonies when we die?' she ranted. 'Not even my righteous son Vikarna is alive, even though he was the only one in the court who tried to stop Draupadi's disrobing. He advised his brothers not to gamble or disrespect women. He supported Draupadi when she said that Yudhistira could not stake her in the game after he had lost himself. His was the lone voice that pleaded, "Let her go," when elders like Bhishma, Drona and Dhritarashtra were silent. What did he do to deserve this fate?'

Krishna let her speak, knowing that fate had them in its clutches.

'Did not Bhima himself mourn the loss of Vikarna? He knew that it was Vikarna's duty to fight by Duryodhana's side. Even the simple Bhima realized that war is a curse upon men when innocents are sacrificed. But you, who are the Paramatma, the

Supreme Soul—you did not stop the massacre. You betrayed my faith in you.'

By now, several others had gathered to witness the encounter between two indomitable minds. Wounded warriors, their wives, the Pandava and the Kuru widows came to listen. Gods, devas and sages in the heavens paid homage to the woman with the power to question the lord.

'I worshipped the ascetic Shiva, forsaking the pleasures of the world in order to serve my husband,' she said. 'I upheld dharma and stood firm when Duryodhana came to me before the final battle. I did not bless him with victory but said instead, "Yato dharma stato jayah." Where there is dharma there is victory. But I knew even as I spoke that it should be "Yato Krishna stato jayah". Where there is *Krishna* there is victory.

'I knew you would support Arjuna and his brothers, though my sons needed you more. The Pandavas needed you to win their kingdom, but my sons needed you to deliver them from adharma! Why did you choose Kunti's sons, Krishna? Why did you fail my sons and their wives? You are God himself, not a mere mortal. *You have no right to fail!*' Her voice rose in a shriek. Then she broke down again.

'You came to Hastinapura as a messenger of peace and pleaded against war. You showed your visvaroopa to persuade my son. But you had already promised Draupadi before you came that the Kurus would pay with their blood. You assured her that she would wash her hair in Duhshasana's blood before she tied it once more.

'Krishna! You had decided that my sons would die on the battlefield, but enacted a drama of mediation, then made sure it would fail. The war was of your own making and now you too must face the consequences.'

Sambhavami yuge yuge. Krishna takes birth, millennium after millennium, to protect the righteous and to destroy the wicked. And as he alters the cosmic balance, he too must surrender to karma.

He smiled, for he knew what she was about to say.

Gandhari saw his smile with the subtle vision that Vyasa had bestowed on her. It had an incendiary effect on her, like ghee poured on the sacrificial fire.

'Why do you smile, Krishna? Do you mock the anguish of hundreds of thousands of innocents? Listen then and repent.' Her voice rose higher. 'If my prayers to Vishnu have been true . . . if my devotion to my husband has been true . . . *you* will pay the price for the death of my sons. Every wail and every shriek that rises up from the women here curses you.'

Krishna bowed his head and let the thunder wash over him. His suffering as a man had begun.

'Your men too will lie dead like ours,' she proclaimed. 'They will not die honourably in war, but covered in shame after a drunken brawl. This war was fought for eighteen days. I give you twice the number of years to live and watch the sins of your people. They will become a burden on earth and so powerful that they can only be killed by their own kin.

'You will watch helplessly as your children, your grandchildren and your entire clan slay one another. Only then will you die—all alone, great god. You will die like a beast at the hands of a common hunter. Your women will wail like our widows today and wicked men will ravish them.

'The seas will devour the glorious city of Dwaraka. People will forget your name, and your glorious Gitopadesha will be lost to humankind.

'May the world perish. May the world perish!'

End of Book I

Glossary

Antapura—inner chambers
Artha—wealth
Aswamedha yagna—horse sacrifice
Avidya—ignorance
Bhootas—fierce, evil spirits
Brahma rakshasas—fierce terrestrial demons
Dakinis—malevolent or vengeful female spirits
Gandharva—male nature spirits with great musical skills
Guhyakas—nature spirits who are attendants of Kubera
Kusmandas—evil beings
Mahamaya—benign cosmic power of illusion
Odhni—upper garment worn by women
Naginis—snake women
Patala—netherworld
Pishachas—spirits that eat raw flesh
Pramathas—macabre, all-powerful spirits
Pretas—spirits of those who died an unnatural death
Samhaara—killing
Tapasya—deep meditation and asceticism
Trilokadipati—master of the three worlds

Vaahana—vehicle
Vetalas—vampires
Vidya—knowledge
Vidyadharas—celestial dancers
Yakshas—guardian spirits of the treasures of the earth
Yojana—Vedic measure of distance equalling eight kilometres

Acknowledgements

Huge thanks to Srinath, whose inspired ideas added depth and drama to the book; Sriya, who helped me stay the course with her unflagging support; and Kumaran, whose wonderful insights helped me shape the book into what it is now. My deep gratitude to Vaishali Mathur, the finest editor any author could hope for; Shatarupa Ghoshal for her meticulous eye for detail; Jay Thakur and Pia Alize Hazarika for the beautiful cover; and to the dynamic team at Penguin Random House for the time and care they spent on the book. Thank you all!

'*You* will pay the price for the death of my sons. . . The seas will devour the glorious city of Dwaraka. People will forget your name, and your glorious Gitopadesha will be lost to humankind.

'May the world perish. May the world perish!'

Darkness gathers over the world as the Kali demon descends on earth to inflict unspeakable wickedness and suffering. Can Pradyumna, the son of Krishna, stave off the cataclysm?

First, he must appease Gandhari who demands that he bring her son back from Yamaloka. To do this, Pradyumna needs the blessings of Shiva. But will he dare to confront the god who had burned him to cinders earlier? As he struggles to find a way across the seething river of naraka, destiny closes in and his brother Samba brings down a new curse on the Yadus. Krishna returns to Vishnuloka, leaving his son to face his enemies alone.

Doom seems certain. The Kali demon, aided by Alakshmi, the evil twin of Lakshmi, challenges Pradyumna to a battle that is lost before it has even begun. For this demon can never be killed . . .

But there is one potent weapon still. The secret surrounding Pradyumna's origin. Will this help him fight off the inevitable? Or will mankind suffer for thousands of years as it waits for Vishnu's Kalki avatar? And how many times can Kalki be born to destroy the rampant evil of the Kali Yuga?

Gods and goddesses, Vishnu's chakra and Shiva's trident, journeys to Yamaloka and Vaikunta, demons and snakes . . . all these populate the pages of this exhilarating thriller, as our hero takes on his own karma and that of the world.